To *Know* You

SHANNON ETHRIDGE
and KATHRYN MACKEL

NASHVILLE DALLAS MEXICO CITY RIO DE JANEIRO

Published in Nashville, Tennessee, by Thomas Nelson. Thomas Nelson is a registered trademark of Thomas Nelson, Inc.

Author is represented by the literary agency of Alive Communications, Inc., 7680 Goddard Street, Suite 200, Colorado Springs, CO 80920. www.alivecommunications.com.

Thomas Nelson, Inc., titles may be purchased in bulk for educational, business, fund-raising, or sales promotional use. For information, please e-mail SpecialMarkets@ThomasNelson.com.

Publisher's note: This novel is a work of fiction. Names, characters, places, and incidents are either products of the author's imagination or used fictitiously. All characters are fictional, and any similarity to people, living or dead, is purely coincidental.

Library of Congress Cataloging-in-Publication Data

Ethridge, Shannon.
To know you / by Shannon Ethridge and Kathryn Mackel.
pages cm
ISBN 978-1-4016-8866-0 (trade paper)
1. Sick children--Fiction. 2. Domestic fiction. I. Mackel, Kathryn, 1950- II. Title.
PS3605.T48T6 2013
813'.6--dc23

2013015674

Printed in the United States of America

13 14 15 16 17 RRD 6 5 4 3 2 1

Advance Acclaim for *To Know You*

"Even though I'm known for writing nonfiction, fiction is what I love to read—and Shannon has created a storyline with more twists and turns than a mountain road. But more important than the twists is the way this story explores love and sacrifice and the effects of our decisions. This book will grab you and not let go. Anyone who reads Shannon's nonfiction books knows she hooks you with her narrative, and now she's put that skill to great use in her first novel!"

—Shaunti Feldhahn, best-selling author of *For Women Only* and *The Veritas Conflict*

"Can you ever truly escape your past? Shannon Ethridge weaves a gripping story of a respected Christian woman who has to dig up the past she thought buried in order to save her son's life. And amazingly, sometimes even the things we hoped we could forget end up being the things God uses to bring real wholeness to our lives. A no-holds-barred realistic portrayal of a messy life that finds peace when we confront our pasts, not try to ignore them."

—Sheila Wray Gregoire, author of *The Good Girl's Guide to Great Sex*

"*To Know You* is one of the best emotional roller coasters I have been on! Who knew it was possible to interweave so many powerful sexual, emotional, and relational themes into one story and so seamlessly? This novel is what other Christian fiction needs to be: refreshingly honest, grace-inducing, and the opposite of 'preachy.' A work well done!"

—Michelle N. Onuorah, author and screenwriter

"In *To Know You*, Shannon Ethridge does a brilliant job of turning the truths she is known for teaching into a dynamic, page-turning narrative that will touch your heart and stir your soul. She takes the reader on a very real journey of temptation and redemption along with the characters, crafting a story you do not want to miss."

—Leigh Congdon, freelance writer

"I literally read *To Know You* in one night. I couldn't put it down. Everything about the characters is so real. There is no sugar-coating their struggles and temptations, and it made the entire book very relatable. But most of all, I loved the story of how the redeeming power of God's grace transformed them one by one. Such a great example of God's unconditional love! The world needs more books like *To Know You*!"

—Amber P.

"*To Know You* offered an exhilarating escape each time I picked it up, and I felt so spiritually uplifted each time I put it down. I recommend this book to anyone looking for a riveting yet wholesome story that gets your heart racing and your blood boiling at the same time!"

—Michele A.

"I picked up the pre-released version of *To Know You* while on vacation. The first chapter totally hooked me and I couldn't stop. I did not expect to identify so closely with some of the characters, and more particularly with some of the characters' personal struggles. It helped me realize that I am *not alone*, and that no temptation seizes us but what is common to man (and woman!). I'm so grateful for gripping stories like this, and the power they have to transform the heart and mind—especially *my* heart and mind."

—Gretchen E.

To *Know* You

Shannon: To my sister Donna, in anticipation of getting to know you more when we meet again in heaven.

Kathryn: To Jeanne Dignan, who blesses me, even now.

one

Dallas

Saturday, 9:15 a.m.

Don't ask, Julia Whittaker wanted to scream.

But the words were sawdust in her mouth. Matt would ask because it was his nature to take in information, cradle it, and rebirth it so the world made sense.

"How—

Moments away from being irrevocable.

—long?"

If Julia couldn't bear the asking, how could she ever bear the answer?

"The transplant committee moved Dillon up. He's near the top of the list," Dr. Ann Rosado said. She was a pediatric gastroenterologist at Cedar Springs Medical Center, specializing in liver diseases. The Whittakers had known her all of Dillon's life.

"Just near? Not at?" Matt was rubbing his stubbled head as if he could massage this fact into something closer to his liking. They hadn't been home in two days. His gray slacks were wrinkled at the knees, and his oxford shirt was stained with salad dressing. He had shoveled food into his mouth to set the example for her. *You have to eat,* he'd said.

Yeah, Mom, Dillon had said. *You have to eat.* He had made an attempt on her behalf, picking apart a muffin and smearing scrambled eggs on his plate.

Black coffee and Red Bull were all Julia had patience with. The acid in her stomach was a welcome relief from that sinking sensation of time slipping away.

Of Dillon slipping away.

She dug her fingernails into her palms and stared at the pictures of children on Annie's wall. Some were pink-cheeked with health, others had sallow skin and shadowed eyes—the autumnal shades of liver disease.

Thirteen years ago Julia had studied the pictures, looking for a sign of hope. *"Are these the survivors?"*

"I don't differentiate," Annie had said. *"They are all my patients."*

"But which ones are still a—" Julia hadn't been able to finish the question. The cruelty that children could be born blighted and die without a future was unbearable.

"They all live in my heart," Annie had said. *"They all live in God's heart because He doesn't differentiate either."*

Where was God's heart today, after thirteen years of dealing with this? Certainly not in that void between *how* and *long.*

She curled her fingertips into the arm of the sofa and counted the lights on Annie's Christmas tree. There were no "Wait Until Christmas" tags on the presents because some children—like Dillon—could not wait until the twenty-fifth.

Julia had bought her son's gift a month ago, the expensive Arriflex 235, which would allow him to shoot video underwater. She and Matt nixed the notion of a motorcycle rig that would allow him to shoot high-speed chases.

When I'm sixteen I'll get my own motorcycle, Dillon had said, even as his blood pressure climbed and the toxins backed up in his liver like a clogged sewage pipe. Sixteen was more than three long years away and, even if she dared to let Matt ask *how long*, three years weren't possible.

Not without a transplant.

"Dillon's beaten the odds since he was born," Dr. Annie said. "We'll find him that liver."

"Of course," Matt said, his blue eyes distant. Computing the odds, Julia knew, because she had asked him once when they prayed together, *Where do you go when you disappear?*

Where the numbers add up, he had said.

She had prayed everywhere. Prayers in a dark closet. Prayers on a mountain top. Prayers in Matt's car. Prayers in his arms. Prayers in Jerusalem. Prayers in the bathroom.

Don't lose hope, Matt always said.

Imagine all that Dillon has before him, Matt had said shortly after Dillon was diagnosed with biliary atresia. Infancy became toddlerhood. *Look, the Kasai procedure is holding, and now he's made it to kindergarten. Cheer, Julia, because he's in Little League and wow, can you believe our son won the sixth-grade spelling bee? Listen to his voice squeak into manhood and whatever you do, sweetheart, pretend you're impressed by that fuzz on his lip.*

Imagine what we have before us, Matt would say. *College and a lovely daughter-in-law and bouncing grandchildren and a long life of blessings. Look how our son is beating the odds.*

Until three weeks ago—when he wasn't.

Dr. Annie talked on, her soft voice no veil for the ugly words coming out of her mouth. *Hepatic encephalopathy. Coagulopathy. Ascites. Cerebral edema.*

Matt's fingers tightened on Julia's. He exhaled, his mouth forming a soft O.

"No," she said. "Don't."

"How—"

"Please. Don't—"

"—long?"

Julia jumped up, pulse thundering, hands pressed to her ears to block out Annie's response.

"Not long."

She staggered to the door, willing God to stop the sun in the sky like he had for Joshua. But from the moment her son had been cast in her womb with a doomed liver, she knew she had no say in the matter.

From somewhere in the gloom, Matt called her name and Dr. Annie said, "I know this is hard."

Maybe the sun did stand still outside Dr. Annie's office. Maybe on the other side of this door Dillon was strong and thriving, playing sports and chasing girls and tripping over his feet and being brilliant in one moment and utterly ridiculous in the next. She needed to go to her son and promise he had all the time in the world.

Julia yanked at the door but it didn't open. So she punched it. And punched it again and still the door wouldn't open.

"Julia, stop," Matt called out of the distant haze. "Stop it."

She couldn't stop, just kept punching the door.

Because she couldn't punch God.

Saturday, 4:32 p.m.

Julia opened her eyes to the harsh glow of hospital lighting.

A nurse appeared out of nowhere, said *the surgery was a success*, and wanted to know *how do you feel, Mrs. Whittaker?*

Like cat vomit, Julia would have said, if the cat didn't have her tongue.

Dr. Annie had pulled every favor in her considerable book to get Julia scheduled for surgery within hours after breaking her hand.

"Where's my husband?" Julia said. The words came out *where's my hubcap*?

"I'm here." Matt kissed her forehead. "How're you doing?"

"Hurts."

"That's what happens when you shatter three fingers." Matt brushed her hair back. "What were you thinking?"

"I wasn't thinking anything. I just couldn't get the door open."

"That's because it pulls inward. You were pushing it out."

"I had to get out—"

"I know, I know. Just relax," Matt said. "The nurse said she'd bring you some painkillers."

"No. We don't have time. We have to find Dillon a liver." Julia pawed at her left hand, trying to rip out the IV. No go—her right hand was engulfed in a mummy-wrapped splint the size of a loaf of bread. Her fingers were captive, reconstructed with tiny pins and plates and swathed in gauze. Only the tip of her thumb extruded from the bandage.

Julia tried to curl her hurt hand into a fist. Pain spiked through her wrist and she cried out. The nurse scurried in. "Keep calm," she said. "Your pulse is racing." She took Julia's blood pressure, fiddled with the monitor, and glared at her with an admonition to *just relax*.

Matt laced his fingers gently around the IV site on the back of her wrist. His face was stubbly, his eyelids heavy. At least she had had a few hours of anesthetized slumber. How long had it been since he'd slept?

"It's okay. It's okay." He said it over and over so it became one word—*sokay, sokay, sokay*.

"I am so sorry, Mattie. I really messed up."

"Nothing that a few plates and screws didn't fix."

"It's late. Wait—Beth was supposed to get tested today," Julia said. Beth Latham was their office manager and dear friend.

Matt made that *hmm* sound high in his palate, an indicator that things were bad but he wouldn't let it get to him.

"What?" Julia said.

"There's good news and bad news that's really good news."

Julia groaned. "Just tell me."

"Beth was a match."

"Really?"

"She can't do it. She wants to badly. But she can't. Not for eight months at least."

Her heart sank. "She's pregnant? I thought she and Bruce had stopped trying."

"They had. She was having the physical, mentioned nausea, and they ran the test."

"That's wonderful news, Matt." Julia's voice came back hollow. They were all hanging on by fingernails. They needed to find a liver—immediately.

A terrible twist of fate had made both her and Matt ineligible as living donors. Her A-positive blood type with Matt's B positive could have combined to AB positive in their son, the blood type that can receive all comers. But they both carried recessive genes—like hidden sins—into their pairing and gave birth to a type-O, Rh-negative baby.

Were he healthy, Dillon's blood type would make him a universal donor. How ironic that he would have been sought after by the Red Cross to give blood every two months once he turned eighteen.

He could share with anyone but only receive O-negative blood and could only survive a transplant from a type-O donor. The fact that he was in the majority blood type made the process trickier because he had to compete with everyone on the waiting list.

Though giving up a lobe of one's liver had some peril and an extended recovery time, friends and family had volunteered to be tested. Six—counting Beth, their office manager and dear friend—had the right blood type.

All six were ineligible.

Her assistant, Patricia, was ruled out due to her chronic asthma. Matt's brother, Todd, had too many tattoos from his wild days, including two from his mission time in India. Their accountant, Charlie, had a history of melanoma. Pastor Rich had chronic malaria from time spent in Africa. Dillon's debate coach, Isaac, had undiagnosed hepatitis A. Her design assistant, Trevor, had active Lyme disease. By the time he finished the rigorous course of treatment, it might be too late for Dillon.

Without a live donor identified, the last option was grim and unpredictable.

Someone would have to die from a crushing head wound, and that someone would need to have an organ card in his wallet or have a merciful next-of-kin who could see through their grief long enough to say *yes, let's redeem our loved one's death.*

"I'm sorry," Julia said.

Matt laughed. "You pack a mean punch. I'm going to be a lot nicer to you from now on." He squeezed next to her on the hospital bed and draped her injured hand over his shoulder so she could snuggle into his chest. Even though it was December, he smelled like summer.

"You know what we have to do," he said.

"I can't."

"Dillon's got two sisters."

"They don't know any of this. They don't know each other, they don't know me."

"They are the only hope Dillon has."

Julia dug the fingers of her good hand into his shirt. "I don't even know where they are."

"I do," Matt said. "I know where they are."

Saturday, 6:18 p.m.

When Dillon was eight years old, he'd asked for a grown-up Bible. *Hallelujah*, Matt and Julia whispered in delight. *We've got the next Billy Graham.*

Wrong.

Her son was the Spielberg of Scripture. Since graduating from *Wally McDoogle* to the wall of Jericho, he had devoured and then dramatized the Bible from creation to the Apocalypse. Matt joked that the lesson was that when you give your kid a Bible, you hide the video camera.

"He's reading Samuel," Julia said when he was nine. *"Adultery, madness, murder—"*

"The stuff movies are made of," Matt said.

For all those years, the Kasai reconstruction of his bile duct held strong, draining bile from his liver into his intestine. Allowing him to grow and even to thrive. Those were good years, but deep in Julia's gut, she knew the Kasai was the wall of Jericho that would someday come tumbling down.

Tonight Dillon looked like an under-ripe tomato with his round cheeks and yellowed skin. Propped up on pillows and tucked under a blanket, he was surrounded by electronics. Heart monitor, IV, blood-pressure cuff, bed controls, landline phone, and call button—all belonging to the hospital. His laptop, tablet, and smart phone were never out of reach of his blazing thumbs.

He glanced up from his game and said, "Mom! Wait 'til you see." He waved the remote and turned on the television. Julia's image was frozen in high-definition. Her hand was a bloody mess, her fingers twisted in a strange and terrible way.

"How did you do that?" she said, half in wonder and half in horror.

Dillon turned his iPad so she could see it. On-screen, Tanita—the patient in the next room—waved at her. The teens on this floor all linked up—chatting, playing games, and flirting in cyberspace.

"Tanita was heading down to Ultrasound this morning," Dillon said. "She had her tablet with her because you know how boring the wait can be. And then she caught you in the hall, looking like Dr. Annie had put your hand into a meat grinder. So what happened? Did you punch someone or what?"

"I . . . no, I didn't punch anyone. I just got it caught in the door and . . ." And what? Lying had to be okay if it was to spare your son's feelings. "I was holding the edge of the door, talking to Dad and Dr. Annie, and my foot caught on something and my whole weight just slammed against the door while my hand was still in it."

Dillon narrowed his eyes at her. His eyebrows were becoming bushy and a wisp of a moustache formed over his upper lip. She'd ask Matt to buy him an electric razor with a trimmer. *Oh dear God, please let him need it, please God, please God—*

"Mom! I asked you a question."

"I'm sorry, hon. What did you say?"

"I said Tanita heard pounding. Like someone was bashing something. She thought there was a fight or something in Dr. Annie's office. That's what made her flick on the video."

"I don't know what she heard, Dil. Maybe someone's working on something upstairs."

"If you say so."

"You probably should close out that picture. It's pretty gross."

"It is very gross. Exceptionally gross, masterpiece-level gross. I think I'll use it in my next film." Dillon leaned back into the pillows. This simple exchange had exhausted him. He smiled as he stared at her image on the screen, his lush imagination already planning a whole story around the battered fingers on her hand.

All the time not recognizing that his death sentence was on her face for the whole world to see.

Saturday, 10:16 p.m.

Julia often thought she should have wrangled cattle for a living. Or maybe she should have become an eighth-grade teacher. As strong as steers were and as nasty as hormone-soaked thirteen-year-olds could be, they could not compete with brides who could afford a million-dollar wedding.

Fickle. Panicked. Arrogant. Terrified. Inspired. Loving and kind and crazy and mean, all in the same breath.

God was good to give the gifts He had, but Julia sometimes wondered if she absolutely had to be blessed with this particular talent. Her company, Myrrh, specialized in high-end, sophisticated events, usually weddings. She was the face of the business, the artist with the singular eye and inspired vision.

Matt was the spine, the man who watched the money and tamed the madness. He did his own wrangling, mostly with caterers, designers, florists, and musicians. Myrrh might be expensive, but they did not allow clients to be soaked for every penny.

They succeeded because they could not be hired. Their selectivity about whom they would serve had given them the edge of exclusivity. Prospective brides and grooms underwent a grueling interview process with Matt. If they were at all unstable or uncertain, they never made it to Julia. Once she met with them, if she could conjure an amazing vision for the nuptial week, Myrrh would book the event. Otherwise, she sent them elsewhere.

Her favorite wedding was the first one she had ever done. She hadn't even met Matt, just put together a free event for her dear friend Jeanne Potts. It was a sunrise wedding on the coast of Maine. The bride wore an ivory silk princess dress and a single Bethlehem rose in her sun-streaked hair. After the ceremony, the guests ate fresh blueberry muffins and cheered as the bride and her love kayaked away.

Myrrh was a curse when it forced Julia to be away from family and home; a blessing when she watched love walk down the aisle or sail across the bay and knew she had crafted a vision of what heaven will be for those who save the date.

I have come into my garden, my sister, my bride;
I have gathered my myrrh with my spice.

Her business attire consisted of expensive silk blouses and tailored slacks. She needed to give a bride confidence in her taste, and she did that with incredible accessories. Hand-painted scarves from Kenya, bulky silver jewelry, quirky handbags. But she made sure the bride would always be the star of the show.

Now she ripped blouses out of her closet like a crazed bride at a fire sale.

Her beautiful tops with the fitted sleeves and fine cuffs would not fit over the club on her right hand. She could go sleeveless, if her jackets fit over the cast. The nurse had instructed her about swelling and taking antibiotics and to *be sure to report if her fingertips turned blue.*

No one had warned her that it would be impossible to get her good clothes on.

Nothing would fit except tank tops she wore for gardening and the gym. "I can't wear this stuff," she said to Matt. "I need to make them like me."

"They'll like you." Matt put her toiletries into the suitcase.

"Are you kidding? I drop out of nowhere and say, 'Hi, I'm your biological mother and I need a lobe of your liver.' They're just girls, Matt."

"They're grown women now, honey."

Twenty-four and twenty-two years old—but in her mind, Julia saw her daughters as infants. Born seventeen months apart of different fathers, they didn't know they had a biological half-brother. They didn't know they had each other, and they didn't know her.

Adoption had been the right thing to do. The loving thing to do. The *only* thing she could have done and survived.

Destiny Connors—the eldest—was just a plane ride away in Los Angeles. Matt said that the adoptive parents kept her name. An impulsive choice because Julia had been only twenty and thought maybe the name would bring her child the strength Julia didn't have.

"I'll have one shot to make a good first impression, and oh—my hair! I can't work the curling iron and brush with one hand."

"So stop at a salon on your way to . . . um . . ." He coughed to hide the catch in his throat.

It could not have been easy to hear about Julia McCord, the girl who had gotten pregnant by two different men and bore two babies out of wedlock. She and Matt had buried that past so many years ago, had lived in the present every day of their marriage, because that's what Jesus said to do and that's what Dillon needed.

Matt tapped at his phone.

"What're you doing?" Julia asked.

"Patricia texted Camille and asked her to open her store. She'll run by there for us and pack up what you need. Wait." He paused as the text came in. "She says to bring your shawls. The black one and the camel one. Wait . . . wait . . . okay, get that big scarf you sometimes wear on your shoulders." Matt grinned. "Can you believe I'm dispensing fashion advice?"

Matt owned eight pairs of charcoal slacks for work and a pair of Dockers khakis he wore on Fridays. His one concession to style was pairing muted ties with snowy white shirts. Simplicity could be stunning, something Julia tried to impress on her brides.

Matt slipped his phone into his pocket. "We'll stop at Camille's and get you dressed on the way to the airport."

"When?"

He glanced at his watch. "We still have three hours or so. The jet just came in from Toronto." They shared a private jet with two other business owners from their church.

"I can't wait."

"We have to. They have to check mechanicals, refuel. It's going to be awhile."

Matt drew her into his arms. He breathed steadily, his eyes closed. After twenty years of marriage, she knew what he prayed.

God, please don't let Julia drive herself crazy in Los Angeles.

Please give her wisdom, strength, graciousness.

Please heal her hand.

Please save our son.

Please afflict me in his place.

Thy kingdom come . . . Thy will be done.

Julia pressed her lips to his—gently—to taste his goodness, his steadfastness. Matt kissed her back and suddenly, she was famished for him.

"Julia, your arm . . . ," he murmured.

Though she was insufficient in so many ways, somehow Julia

knew she was—and had always been—what Matthew Whittaker needed.

"We'll work around it," she said.

On the way to the airport, Julia and Matt met friends for prayer. Pastor Rich, her assistant, Patricia, and her brother-in-law, Todd, encircled them. Hedging them in. *Where can I go from Your presence?* Julia prayed silently. *If I go up to the heavens—You have got to be there or I'll lose my mind.*

You created my inmost being; You knit me together in my mother's womb.

And that was where Julia always stumbled, because God knit Dillon together in her womb and *look what's happening now, please, Father, please.*

Count your blessings, Matt would say.

Blessings. Indeed, she had blessings.

Friends.

So many friends who loved her. Church family. Her college roommate and dear friend, Jeanne. Her colleagues, Trevor and Patricia. Parents of children they had met, first in the pediatric wing, now in the transplant wing. Joys and devastations were never far from open arms. Some of her brides and grooms had become like family.

Julia had two enemies. First and always was herself. Try as she might, pray as she would, follow as she must—there was that old Julia McCord trying to bust out. Like an ingrown toenail, something no longer alive but able to hobble her just the same.

And the second enemy: biliary atresia.

When a baby was born, you counted fingers and toes. You didn't poke their belly to see if their liver was filling up with garbage. *Your baby boy is ten pounds and lively, and that jaundice is natural,* they'd said.

Until the baby couldn't gain weight even though he was a hearty eater. Until his stools were like clay because what God designed the body to be rid of was being trapped in the abdomen that Matt loved to tickle. In that belly was a perfectly good liver, going bad because the bile ducts just wouldn't work.

Julia wanted to punch God until she remembered she had no choice but to love Him. She'd once had a choice, when Jesus came calling. She could have said no. Long before she knew Matt, long before they became one and Dillon became theirs, Julia McCord suffered from her own spiritual biliary atresia.

She was lost in bitterness and bile, and she could not get clean until Jesus said He would do it for her. And she had felt that untangling, that draining of toxins, that constant and loving presence of life, and she knew then as she knew now that she was held. That was why she could be furious with God—for a moment—and fall into His arms for an eternity.

Julia had friends, she had enemies. And she had love. Matt, steady and unpretentious, was the ballast to her sails, the canvas to her art. Not perfect, which made her love him more. Dillon, whose heart beat with hers for nine months, now a funny-voiced, shaggy-haired young teen. And who could ever deny the love shown by Dr. Ann Rosado, with her chaotic hair and summer-sky eyes?

Count your blessings. Friends. Family. Love.

And now—now what?

Two daughters whom Julia had loved enough to walk away from. They would be appalled, offended, disgusted by what she was about to ask of them.

Love compelled Julia to take this journey. Could grace compel them to join her?

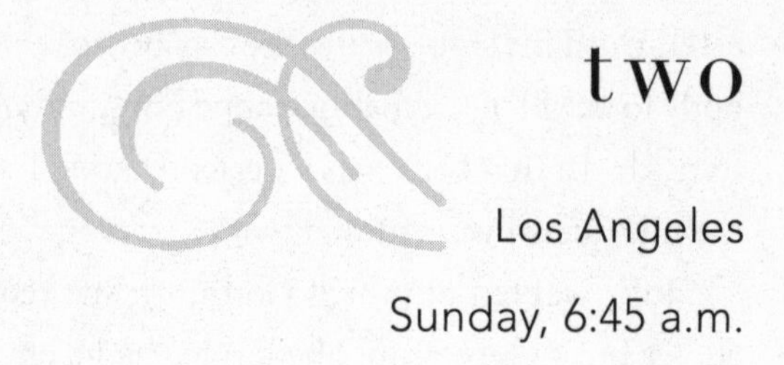

two

Los Angeles

Sunday, 6:45 a.m.

Jesus told Luke Aviles to stop sleeping with Destiny Connors.

She was not cool with that. Not cool at all. Which was why she tossed Luke's belongings off the deck, one piece at a time. Her bungalow was perched high in a canyon in the Hollywood Hills. Forty rickety steps led up from the driveway to the front door—a climb Destiny hated, even though the view was spectacular. At night she could stare down at the lights of the city while listening to the coyotes howl.

She liked that sense of the wild.

Luke had shared that same sense with her until he got this "Jesus says" attitude. Maybe sending him back to his grungy apartment would shake some sense into him.

Black jeans, up and over the railing.

Orange and lime-green running shoes. Gone.

Brown leather belt with silver falcon buckle. Adios, baby.

"Why are you doing this?" Luke scurried around the driveway, retrieving his garbage, playing the innocent party because that was his gig now. Innocent and so full of forgiveness—for the director who left Luke on the virtual cutting-room floor because he was hotter than the lead; or for the fool in line at Starbucks, some poser producer ripping someone's eyeballs out on his cell phone just to show he could; or the homeless fellow on their corner with the limp and one crazy eye who assaulted Destiny's MINI Coop with Windex every time the red light timed her out.

Luke prowled like a hungry lion on the hunt for more unworthy souls to wrap those strong arms around. Care and concern for all who needed it.

Except Destiny—the woman who knew how to love him without measure. It was about six hours ago now that he said, "*We can't have sex anymore, Dez. Not until I figure this out.*"

Which was the Christian version of *It's not you, it's me.*

She had skidded into silence, then detonated a white fury. After that played out, she wept simply because she didn't know what else to do. When the sky lightened to ash, he volunteered to make a bagel run. While he was gone, she decided to make her own run, backpedaling to the old Destiny Connors who turtled her tears so fiercely that no one could divine them from her hard ground.

By the time Luke got back with her extra-large hazelnut, light on the cream, and sesame-seed bagel, she had padlocked the gate at the bottom of the stairs. Unless he wanted to scale thirty feet of canyon wall, he was effectively barred from her bungalow.

She didn't want him back, not as long as he reeked of sainthood and celibacy. So she hauled another armful of his stuff from the bedroom out to the deck.

Memory foam pillow. The smell of his shampoo on the pillowcase made her eyes water. Up, over, and bye-bye.

Baltimore Ravens hooded sweatshirt, smelling like honey. He had worn it last month to help that pal who had a beehive on the roof of those high-rise condos in Santa Monica. Good riddance to that shirt and that disgustingly sweet sense of wonder Luke brought home with a jar of honey. *Amazing, Dez. Just awesome how God put it all together.*

Did he see what his God was now ripping apart?

"Hey! What are you doing?" Down below, Luke stood in cold shadow. Sunrise was a mystery in this part of the canyon; sunset a spectacular sight.

"What do you care?" she yelled and stomped back into the house. His fiddle perched on the window seat, his wetsuit hung in the front closet, his backgammon board sat on the breakfast bar. Luke had vined his way into every corner of her life.

And she had welcomed him. She should have known better.

She went to the hamper, dragged out his Orioles T-shirt and assorted socks. When she got back to the deck, Luke had folded his clothes and stacked them neatly on the gate.

He expected her to wilt again and let him in.

Not happening. Dirty laundry—over the railing and going, going, gone.

"Destiny, aren't you being a bit melodramatic?"

"If you won't listen to me, maybe this melodrama will get through that holy haze you're in."

"I'll listen to you. Just let me up so we can talk."

"I'm sick of you talking."

"Okay then. I'll shut up and you can talk."

"Not happening." His tenderness scared her. Why this—and why now? Of all people who *didn't* need saving, he was the best.

"You've lost your mind, babe."

"Really? I'm not the one talking in tongues and hearing voices." Back inside, then out with as many clothes as she could carry.

The Malibu Jazz Fest T-shirt. She and Luke had lain in the grass and let the music drift around them, their fingers touching—

because that's all they needed—as the music and stars soaked into their skin.

She whipped the shirt high into the wind, watched it flutter down like a piece of paper.

Early morning, birds going nuts, sky still a sad shade of pink. Normally she'd already be at work, even though it was a Sunday. The call sheet would be pinned to her board with photo stills, the first of her actors stumbling into the trailer, bleary-eyed with a fruit smoothie in one hand and coffee in the other. Yesterday they had wrapped. She wasn't contracted to do another for three weeks or so.

Her mother wanted her to come home to Nashville for a few days. Her father wanted her to come to DC, spend some time among the power brokers. He knew she hated politics. She did love drama, though, and Dad's job provided plenty of that. Maybe next time.

All she wanted to do today was rip Luke Aviles off her heart like a Band-Aid. Then she'd sleep until her next gig.

Dr. Phil would call that depression. Destiny called it making a decision and learning to live with it. Question was, could she learn to live without Luke?

He looked like he always did, with long, blond hair and a coppery beard. A plain navy T-shirt showed his muscled arms and the tattoo she had designed. A phoenix—rising out of the ashes.

They had done that together a couple years back. Given up the coke, the partying, the late nights and rancid mornings, and settled in. Now he was thirty feet below her, hands outstretched, staring up at her with those blueberry eyes. How she loved his eyes.

How she hated this misty compassion he wore like a halo.

What had happened to the heat, the passion? It had been twenty-three days since they'd made love. When she called him on it last night, he said it didn't seem right anymore. How anything so completely natural could be twisted into something dirty and shameful was beyond her.

Then again, her own mother had made a business of pointing out the spiritual dust bunnies under every soul. So Destiny got it—all too well—and had moved far away from it. She had shed the trappings of religiosity like a snakeskin.

"It's a cult," she said. "Just admit it, Luke. You've been seduced."

Luke laughed. "We sit in folding chairs and sing with guitars and a keyboard. We pray easy, just like you and I are talking here. No frills, no pressure. Come along this morning and see."

"No way." Destiny leaned over the railing so she could look square at him. "I did my stint in the house of corrections."

"Dez, it's not like that."

"Two services on Sunday, Wednesday prayer meeting, my mother signing me up for every youth activity she could find. Church softball, church quilting, church theater, church basket weaving. It was all the same story—Jesus loves us and look how happy we are, so don't you want to be just like us? Join us and all your problems will be solved because Jesus works in all things." Her voice escalated to the edge of shrieking.

So what. She didn't care who heard her. Maybe if she was loud enough, it would penetrate Luke's sanctity-soaked brain.

She grabbed his precious flannel shirts and dumped them.

Cord slacks, obligatory navy blazer, his one tie. Up and over.

Black leather jacket, brown leather vest, even leather pants—he was not a vain man except for the leather. Gone, gone, gone.

His RIDE T-shirt.

Destiny clutched it to her chest. They had worn the red shirts when they biked in the convoy through Death Valley, a fundraiser for one of their mates who had suffered brain trauma in Afghanistan. She had her own Harley, but that day she had ridden with him, arms tight around his waist because they had seen what a bomb had done to Nicky, seen how he couldn't recognize his wife.

Seen what it was like when you were torn from the one who loved you and left to wander in some desert.

"No one's making me join anything," Luke said. "It's just a welcoming place, and it's nice to have something like that in a town like this."

He had admitted to restlessness, had sworn that he loved her completely and this new urge to search out a greater purpose had nothing to do with her.

"You think I don't know how it is?" Destiny waved the T-shirt like a banner. "They draw you in with the handshakes and hugs, and everyone's got those clear eyes and gentle smiles. And they ask *How was your week?* and *What is Jesus doing in your life?* and *How can I walk alongside you?* and then they feed you muffins and coffee and potluck suppers and never let you go."

Luke held up his hands. "Slow down there, girl. How is it a bad thing when people want to share each other's thorns and roses?"

Destiny threw his clarifying shampoo like a missile. The bottle splat on the driveway. White and creamy, the shampoo ran like spilled milk *but no crying*, she thought. No crying over spilled milk and no spilling tears into the water running under the bridge.

"Babe," Luke said. "Please." He picked at his beard, a nervous gesture she could soothe with a touch. He needed to trim it now that his pirate gig was done. "I'm not trying to be like anyone, not trying to do anything except . . . be better at things. I want to be better for you, Dez. So let me in. Please."

No. If she unlocked that gate, he would take her in his arms and she would be as lost as he was. Destiny could not allow that. She had to hold on to the anger so she could seal her resolve.

"They told you," she said, swallowing tears. "They told you it's sinful to fornicate outside of marriage. And you—the most wonderful of fornicators—took the bait."

"No one told me that."

"Jesus told you that. That's what you said. No sex." Destiny grabbed his favorite pair of boots, flung them at him. Though he was big as a bear, Luke was nimble as a cat and ducked with ease.

"He—or I guess it's the Holy Spirit talking—said if I loved you, I'd honor your spirit instead of using your body."

"Love means withholding love?"

"Love means placing your needs above my own." His voice echoed off the hillside. Getting loud now. Good. She was finally getting through.

"So cliché, Luke. What's next? *You had me at hello?*"

"I want to do right by you."

"What if I tell you *I* need you?" Destiny's voice caught in her throat on the truth of it. She needed to feel the pulse in his neck and smell the tang on his skin from his lemon soap. To feel his chest rise as he breathed. She knew every breath he took. The deep sighs when he was tired, the measured panting of a heavy workout, the steady, deep breathing when he held her close.

His size and strength had never scared her. Controlled chaos, his stunt-buddies called him. Perfectly choreographed until it was time to do the impossible.

Destiny dug her fingernails into the railing. "Just go."

"I love you with everything in me, Dez. Which is why I need to just back off for a little while. So I can hear clearly."

"Tell me," she said. "Tell me what you're hearing."

"I'm hearing . . ." He kicked at a pile of clothes. "I'm hearing that every time I love you with my body, I'm leading you into sin."

"You want to hear clearly?"

"Destiny . . ."

"Hear this. Get out."

"What?"

"I said get out." She clutched at the denim jacket that she had bought him last Christmas and hand painted herself, a smirking raven in gold and purple that drew delighted stares whenever he wore it. *There's irony for you. Wear the jacket that you got for Jesus's birthday out the door.*

"I'll take a ride, come back in a couple of hours."

"Go, Luke. Please. Just go. That's what Jesus says and for once, I agree with the dude. So just go."

"Destiny."

She turned her back to him, staring into the hard sand and brush of the canyon wall that framed the side of her bungalow. This was a fire trap. Anyone who lived perched up high knew a hard wind and bright spark could take their home at any time.

Nothing really lasted. You can paint a pretty picture over your life, veneer it with good intention and solid commitment. There was no way to hold joy. You hold too tightly and you strangle it lifeless. When something begins to rot, it's best just to be rid of it. Even when it hurts.

Luke knew it too. Which was why he fired up his Harley, gave her one last look over his shoulder, and rode away.

Destiny stood for a long moment, listening until the sound of his bike faded into the morning.

It wasn't until she wiped away the last of her tears that she saw the dark-haired woman standing in the driveway. She had a strange cast on her hand and an even stranger look on her face.

"What?" Destiny snapped. "What do you want?"

"Well, well." The woman smiled. "I see you've inherited my temper."

Sunday, 7:15 a.m.

Everyone lies.

Prepare for that reality and you won't be caught with your wits in the wind. So it wasn't the woman's claim to be her birth mother that convinced Destiny.

It was her eyes.

Long lashes framed eyes so dark brown that they photographed as black if not properly lit. So round that Julia Whittaker—and Destiny—appeared to be perpetually surprised. They also shared the same arched cheekbones. Where the woman used a faint blush for youthfulness, Destiny preferred shadow.

The right makeup could tell any story you wanted.

Julia's skin was firm; despite her obvious exhaustion, the age lines were imperceptible. Some good genetic news—birth mommy shows up and she's a beauty. Yippee.

If Destiny had inherited Julia Whittaker's height, she might have modeled. That had been her plan. Get paid for her exotic looks, make enough money to sculpt and paint. Her father had balked at any vocation that *empty*. After high school, her parents dropped her off at Wheaton College in Illinois with three suitcases of clothes and a mini-fridge. *For milk and juice*, Mom said. Nothing stronger than 2 percent.

A day later Destiny hitchhiked her way to Los Angeles with a knapsack and a sketchpad. She left behind the three suitcases and the mini-fridge, filled with Budweiser.

By the time she had finished her apprenticeship as a makeup artist and conceptualist, she realized models were just blank canvases on which people like her hung their art.

Isn't that what she was to Julia Whittaker?

The woman must have spent these twenty-four years imagining

what her daughter looked like, what she had grown into. Judging by her fine wool slacks, silk shell, and cashmere wrap, she was likely very disappointed.

How many times had Mom—Melanie Connors—nagged Destiny about some test she had failed or some chore she'd left undone and she had sneered, "*My real mother wouldn't be such a hag.*"

She was about fifteen when Mom finally snapped. "*Your real mother isn't here, is she? She never wanted to be here—never wanted to know you. She made that abundantly clear.*" And then she had blanched and said over and over, "*I'm so sorry*" and "*We love you so much*" and "*Your birth mother blessed us beyond measure.*"

Destiny had wept for an hour, cried off and on for a week. Mom had been there the whole time, blotting her tears, fielding her curses, and making her ice-cream sundaes with homemade fudge sauce. Were she here right now, Mom would be gracious and welcoming but—because *everyone lies*—she'd want to rip off Julia Whittaker's face.

"I know this is a shock." The woman glanced around the driveway, pretending to ignore Luke's scattered jockey shorts. Destiny had come down the stairs but wasn't inclined to unlock the gate. Not yet. "I would have called before I came. But time is of the essence, and I didn't know if you'd take my call. Because there had been no indication that you . . ."

Her deep breath seemed a plea for mercy, the space for Destiny to rush in with *I've always wanted to meet you* or *I can't believe you're here at last.*

In this moment, mercy was as far as east from west. "You are the one who said no contact. I had no say in any of it." Destiny hated herself for memorizing Julia's farewell note, for tracing the letters with her own hand as if she could somehow glean understanding from the swirls and swoops of the ornate handwriting.

Her hand always ached because she was left-handed and couldn't follow the path her mother left behind.

"I couldn't bear the thought of . . . of seeing pictures of you on your birthday and at Christmas. Or making a yearly visit and then . . . then having to leave you again."

Destiny folded her arms over her chest. She resented the way the woman stared at her, as if repossessing something she had once owned. "So why are you here now?"

"That's complicated."

"Isn't it always?"

"Could I take you to coffee or breakfast? So we can get to know each other a little?"

"Not unless you answer my question."

"I—" Julia swayed.

"Hey!" Destiny reached over the gate and took hold of her shoulders to steady her. "Are you all right?"

"I'm sorry. I've been up for three days straight now."

"What happened?"

"I shattered my fingers. Made a real mess."

"How did you do that?"

"I punched a door because it wouldn't open."

"What?"

"I punched a door because—"

"Why?"

"I was mad at God."

"So you punched a door?"

"I'm afraid so." Julia smiled easily now, without a drop of sheepishness.

Everyone lies, but sometimes the truth leaks out.

"In that case," she said, "I'm starved. Let's go eat."

Destiny hopped on her Harley, motioned for Julia to follow in her rented Camry. Even though Sunday morning meant quiet streets, she kept her speed down. Driving in LA was hard enough for out-of-towners; it had to be a beast to steer with that mummified right hand.

They settled in at a bagel shop a couple blocks off Sunset where they could sit outside. It was warm for December, pushing seventy degrees. Julia ordered a coffee and whole-wheat toast. Destiny got baked ham and Gouda on a poppy-seed bagel. She was tempted to add a dark ale to her order to see how Julia would react, but decided against it. She might need her wits about her. Something was up for this woman to drop out of nowhere on a Sunday morning.

If Julia wanted a relationship, she would have called, friended her, made some sort of tentative contact. Was she working a scam? She didn't dress like someone who needed money, and though Destiny was self-sufficient, she wasn't rolling in the green. Maybe she had lost her job or was going through a divorce and this *let's-meet-the-daughter* thing was a whim.

Destiny took two bites of her sandwich, washed it down with black coffee. "So. Why?"

Julia's hand shook as she dumped sugar into her coffee. She tried to put the top back on the Styrofoam cup, almost spilled it.

"Here," Destiny said. "Let me do that for you."

"Thanks." She sipped the coffee, didn't even look at the toast.

"So—that *why* is still out there, Julia."

"Maybe we could get to know each other a little first?"

Just get to it, Destiny wanted to snap. But the woman's haunted eyes made her say, "Sure. Go for it."

Julia gave her the basics. She was forty-four years old. Her maiden name was McCord. She lived in Dallas; she was from Oklahoma and had shed the accent when she attended college in Boston. She and her husband owned an event planning business named Myrrh.

Destiny had heard of Myrrh. They specialized in elite weddings, like the one they'd recently done for the daughter of the former president. One of the actors in her last shoot had attended, said it was a real work of art.

"I was twenty years old when you were born."

"Do you have my birth certificate? I should be asking for some official something or other."

"Sure." Julia dug it out of her bag, handed it to Destiny.

Now *her* hands shook. *Stop*, she told herself. It's only paper.

Destiny Jeanne Bryant. Female. Born to Julia Elizabeth McCord in Boston on December third at 3:30 a.m. No one could say she wasn't consistent. She had been a night owl all her life, had driven Mom and Dad bonkers.

Father, Thomas Nathan Bryant. Age twenty-five. Occupation, attorney. Place of birth, Dorchester, Massachusetts. Destiny had always pictured her father as Harrison Ford or Liam Neeson. Wouldn't that have been a hoot?

She ran her fingers over her father's name, felt the wear in the paper. "Does he know you're here?"

"We haven't spoken in . . . a while."

Destiny glanced up. "How long?"

"Twenty-four years." Julia picked at the wrapping on her hand. It looked like a removable cast, wrapped in an Ace bandage. Gauze poked out from the fingertips, stained with blood.

"Tell me about him."

"Tom was incredibly attractive and devastatingly smart. I can't imagine that has really changed. You have his smile."

"How would you know? I haven't smiled yet."

"I know. Trust me. He had the same wide mouth you do, same perfect teeth even though he'd never had braces."

"I never did either." Ever-cautionary, Mom wanted her to get them anyway, couldn't believe that her wild daughter wouldn't find some way to screw up her own teeth. Destiny said that was stupid and she'd bite off the orthodontist's fingers if he came near her.

For once, Dad took her side. *You don't get what you don't need*, he'd said.

Destiny took a bite of sandwich, chewed slowly before she finally swallowed. "What else? About my father, I mean."

"He was driven. So driven. I imagine he's a big success now, at least in his public life. His private life—I don't even go there."

Ah, there's the bitterness. Destiny felt better now. "He knew about me, right?"

She smiled. "Tom used to lay his hand on my stomach and call you *jackrabbit* because you kicked so hard."

"That's ironic given that he rabbited on you." She watched Julia, waiting for a cringe that never came. "Am I correct?"

"When the time came for you to be born . . . he was working fourteen hours a day, trying to study for the bar exam. He felt it was a terrible time to be starting a family. He had worked so hard—"

"Not hard enough to wear a condom, apparently."

"Mistakes happen."

"So I'm a mistake?"

"No." Julia reached across the table to take Destiny's hand.

Destiny jerked hers away and hid them in her lap.

"We wanted you, wanted a big family. We had sunny plans about getting married and having a family after his career took off and I finished college. And then—we thought we were careful."

"You sound like a dumb teenager."

"I *was* a dumb teenager. Nineteen years old, first time away from home. I thought the pill was foolproof—until I missed my first period, and then my second. I was a sophomore in college, Tom working his first job. It was the wrong time for me to do what was right for you."

First Luke, now her birth mother. Jesus said to give you up for your own good. Nice, real loving.

Destiny took a long gulp of her coffee, let it settle before saying, "So the sperm donor got cold feet, huh?"

"The whole notion of becoming a father was a mountain that he tried to climb and kept rolling back down. We had bought a bassinet—couldn't fit a crib into the studio apartment we were supposed to move into. I tried to put it together but my back hurt so much and I'd drop a screw and then couldn't pick it up. He promised he'd do it the next night. The days turned into weeks and he still hadn't done it, and by then I was as big as a hot-air balloon. I was days away, maybe less, from you being born, and Tom hadn't been to the warehouse store like he promised to get the diapers and wipes. He missed my baby shower. I was freaked out, thought he'd been hit by a drunk driver or something. I finally tracked him down at work.

"'Jules, you know I'm a prisoner here,' he'd said. 'Can't breathe unless I can bill it out.' Work wasn't what he meant. *I* was the prison, you and I were the bars about to trap him."

Destiny swore loudly enough for the people at the next table to look up from their croissants.

Julia laughed. "Yeah, that's what I thought too. My friends and I lugged all the presents up three floors of stairs to find it empty and cold. He gave the excuse that his mother's house was closer to work and he needed to crash. 'Tomorrow,' he'd said. 'I'll clear my desk and tomorrow I'll come home.'

"I believed him. *You* knew better—you were so quiet for two days that I finally went to the doctor to make sure you still had a heartbeat.

"The day after you were born, he signed a surrender of parental rights. I let my mother arrange a private adoption. This friend of hers knew the Connors were desperate for a baby. And they were good people. Right? Your parents are good people?"

"Yes," Destiny said. "That's what everyone says. Good people."

Julia stretched her hand across the table, staring with teary eyes. "Please know a big chunk of my heart is still shredded from that morning I had to say good-bye. But if I had kept you . . . Tom was gone and I was alone and I had nothing to give you."

"Yeah. Okay. I get it." She nodded at Julia's left hand. "So you're married now."

"Eighteen years to Matthew Whittaker. Let me show you." She fumbled as she tried to get her phone out of her purse with her left hand.

Tough to navigate life with your nondominant hand. Like navigating life without Luke? No. She was not going there. She was vulnerable enough at this table, with this stranger, without stirring him into the mix.

Julia finally slid the phone across the table. "There's Matt."

He looked as crisp as fresh lettuce in his buttoned-down shirt and dark slacks. The camera caught something in his eyes, a humorous intelligence.

"And the kid?" As if Destiny had to ask. He had *the* eyes. Hungry eyes, like the boy was looking beyond the camera for what came next.

"Dillon," Julia said. "He's twelve in the picture. He'll be fourteen next month."

It had never occurred to her that she might have a biological sibling. The very notion seemed a betrayal to her younger sister, Sophie, the biological daughter of her adoptive parents.

Nature or nurture—was she closer in essence to this woman with the round eyes and the cast on her hand? Or the parents and sister she had spent her life with?

This kid in the picture—skinny and floppy-eared—was her brother. Looked like a total geek and probably read the same comic books she had, watched the same superhero movies, maybe sketched in the same left-handed way.

Destiny zoomed in on the picture so she could study him closer. A knot formed in her stomach. "He's sick."

"Not in that picture."

"Yes, he is. His skin tone doesn't match yours or his father's, and there's a small pouch under his right eye." She knew faces, having spent her early career hiding hangovers, bruises, and the ravages of drug use.

Something was wrong with this kid, something terrible that prompted Julia Whittaker to seek out her daughter after two decades of ignoring her.

"My kidney," Destiny whispered.

"Excuse me?"

"That's what you're here for. You need me to donate a kidney." Destiny jumped to her feet because she needed to throw up, but she didn't dare move because she'd spill her guts right here and now, and wasn't that exactly what Julia Whittaker wanted?

"I don't want your kidney."

"Bone marrow, then."

The woman shook her head, would not look her in the eye.

"You want something from me. You don't show up out of nowhere and shove this picture of my—you don't shove your son in my face if you don't want something."

"I'm sorry." Julia dabbed at her eyes with a napkin.

Destiny's head spun and she had to sit. "So what part of me do you want?"

Julia worked her left hand against her cast as if she were compelled to lock her fingers together. "Dillon is a great kid. He's a really good student and so creative, makes his own films. He loves coming up with special effects, like getting into the kitchen and creating dried blood out of mashed figs and strawberry jelly. And he's got about twenty friends who volunteer as extras for his battle scenes. Quite a few have made a career of dying unspeakably."

"Still waiting." Destiny cleared her throat to disguise the tremble in her voice.

"Dillon has had liver disease since he was born."

"Oh."

"Most infants with biliary atresia need a transplant in the first few months to survive. Dillon had a special surgery called the Kasai procedure that bypasses the bile duct and connects the small intestine to the underside of the liver. Sometimes it lasts for a lifetime, most often not. He's been one of the blessed kids who's held on to it into his teens. A few weeks ago something happened. A virus, an injury, we don't know. His liver was never what it should be. You saw it in the picture from a couple years ago. Suddenly, the slow creep became an avalanche and we were all caught short. No one we know is compatible or, if they are, they've been disqualified. Not me, not Matt, not his uncle, none of our friends."

Destiny could barely find the breath to speak. "So you want my liver?"

"The liver is the miracle organ. If someone donates part of theirs, it grows back within a year and there's no real risk except . . . well, whatever comes with having surgery."

"So that's why you're here? For a piece of my liver?"

"I never wanted to find you on such . . . extreme terms. I am so sorry, Destiny. I have not forgotten you. Not ever. I pass by someone on the street with dark hair and these eyes and I wonder . . . could she be my baby?" Julia gasped for breath around the tears. "And every day I thank God for Matt and for Dillon and for Destiny and for Hope. And I'm so sorry that I have to come to you now. Like this."

"Sorry? That's all you have to say? You're sorry. Nice. Real nice." Destiny pushed her chair back. "I assume you can find your way back to wherever you came from. Just stay away from me."

"Don't go. Please."

Destiny strapped on her helmet. "Don't touch me. Don't call me. Forget you know my name or where I live. I mean it."

"Wait. Please." Julia pressed the birth certificate into Destiny's hand. "My number's on the back. I know it's a lot to process. I'll stay in town for the day. Please just think—"

Destiny shoved the birth certificate in her pocket, kick-started her bike, and roared away.

Sunday Afternoon

So much for the good life.

Destiny had arranged everything perfectly. A job she loved and excelled at. Hobbies she enjoyed. Charities she supported. Her family happily intact and three thousand miles away.

A man who soothed her soul and roused her body.

She couldn't stand looking at the empty rooms of her bungalow. So she stayed on her bike, no destination in mind, just putting miles between her and Luke Aviles and Julia Whittaker. Maybe she'd catch the PCH and ride up the coast for a day or two. Wash off the smog of the city, let the salty air of the Pacific cleanse her of any illusion that life could be good.

Illusion? Delusion was more like it.

Most adopted kids dreamed of being royal changelings whose father and mother would show up and say, *We've won the battle so now it's safe for you to come home and be celebrated and loved and live happily ever after.*

Not Destiny Connors.

She had imagined her biological mother as an artist slashing canvases with startling color and dark undertones. Not conforming to instruction. Rebelling against conventional form. A woman brutally offended by what passes for contemporary art.

Destiny had seen some horrors with high praise and high price tags in the galleries. A Big Mac cast in acrylic. A self-portrait pierced with safety pins and paper clips. A fool spitting beet-colored mucous into a cup and calling it performance art.

Her real mother would rebel against the critics and the patrons. Her real mother would find solace in a cold attic with amazing light and would live for art and spend her passion on—certainly not on a lawyer.

She had imagined her father as a quiet man, maybe a writer who was on the verge of a great novel when he was struck down with a raging cancer. His story untold, his child still unborn, he had left the world clutched in the arms of his artist-lover.

She pushed her bike hard coming around the corner. Some plastic-faced, blossom-lipped woman glared at the roar.

Destiny saw herself coming into the world in a roar of pain and triumph, her mother holding her all night until the time came to send her to a home with heat and light and yes—loving arms.

For years afterward, her birth mother would paint the intersection of beauty and pain and see her child's face in every shadow.

If the universe were good and just, her real mother would not design celebrity weddings. What a holy waste. Julia Whittaker clearly had the artist's eye. So why squander it on silly brides and on marriages that barely lasted past the reception?

A Mercedes skidded to a stop at a yellow light. Traffic building into the typical LA stop-and-go-like-mad. Straight streets, hurried drivers, constant lights.

Someday, Luke said, *we'll move to the mountains and soar.*

That's probably what Julia's mother thought when she sent her to Boston, that her little girl would soar. If Julia McCord had been only twenty when Destiny was born, Julia's mother was probably under fifty at the time. That wasn't too old to take in a baby. Women in the film industry got pregnant—with lots of hormonal assist—in their late forties.

Was a child born out of wedlock that abhorrent to Julia's mother that she searched around until she found an adoptive couple in Tennessee?

Destiny loved Melanie and Will Connors. She loved her little sister, Sophie. It wasn't their fault that she couldn't live with them. It had taken them a couple years since the college fiasco, but they finally accepted that their eldest daughter danced to a different fiddler.

Cutting left on LaBrea now, she let the bike simmer. A dark-haired woman sat on the stoop of an apartment building, watching two little boys dig in the dirt. She said something and the bigger of the two laughed.

Sunday is family day, Mom always said.

Now Destiny had a different family.

Dillon. Julia. Thomas Bryant. Likely her biological dad had his own family, so there would be more siblings. Cousins and uncles and aunts.

Maybe among all of them was someone who saw life like Destiny did.

Someone who did not fear bold colors and sharp angles and spaces that were hard to fill. She thought Luke had been that gift. So why had Jesus put a claim on what she truly needed?

Was this God's idea of a joke, bringing this woman to Los Angeles? First Luke rips out her heart and now her mother wanted to rip out her liver. She wanted to tell God what she thought of this.

Since they weren't on speaking terms, maybe she'd tell Luke instead.

Christians loved the sound of their own voices.

Destiny had been standing outside the storefront church on Pico Boulevard for over an hour, listening to the rock praise, the fervent choruses. Luke worshipped at this place with a couple of his fellow stuntmen. *A diverse congregation,* he had said, *with some musicians, a host of out-of-work actors who were really just waiters, a bank executive, a kid who pitched in the Dodgers' minor league system.*

This congregation had the usual misfits that gathered in the City of Angels, waiting for their dreams to descend from on high. And by the sounds of it, they were still waiting for the Spirit to descend on them. Praise chorus after praise chorus, upbeat and catchy, lots of rhythm and bass, and with enough repetition to cement the words into a singer's brain.

Memorize Bible verses and you'll have security in tribulation, Mom used to say.

A crutch for someone who could already walk just fine, thank you. That's how Destiny saw it. She had walked ten miles away from that college, hitchhiked to Los Angeles, and took a job waiting tables and washing dishes. Within six months she had her own apartment, an apprenticeship with a well-known makeup artist, and lots of extra cash from her custom tattoo designs. From there, it was a short jump into conceptual design, creating the monsters and mirages that blockbuster movies thrive on.

A good life, Luke. So how could he choose this instead?

Destiny could pull Luke out of the service. No, she couldn't. What if *she* had been today's prayer concern? People would turn and look with that knowing gaze. *The prodigal is here. We prayed and God answered.*

Growing up, she had been a frequent resident of many prayer lists. Was she such a bad seed, she had to be prayed into line? Sure, she smoked a little weed, cut a little school, and that pregnancy scare had been a close enough call that she'd had to confide in Mom. That made her normal. Not an object to be fussed over in hushed prayer and knowing glances.

Luke was easy to spot through the plate glass. With his broad shoulders, he was taller than almost everyone in the group. Blond hair now in braids, he sang his silly heart out. If he had thrown her backside into the street, she would have clawed her way up the side of the hill, wrapped her arms around him, and held him so tightly he'd have to take her back.

Luke hadn't even tried.

Destiny started her bike up and headed home to the Hollywood Hills. When she got to her street, she proceeded slowly in case Julia Whittaker lay in wait.

The road was quiet except for the birds, chirping in delight. Luke's clothing was still scattered in the driveway. His boots were gone. Stolen, most likely. Why should she care?

Caring gets you nothing except a bad headache.

She scooped up the clothes. She'd wash them before boxing them up. Her legs ached as she climbed the forty steps. Waiting up all night to toss Luke out on the street had sapped her strength. Julia was just a sprinkle of salt in her open wound, as faded now as the names on that birth certificate.

Destiny shoved the clothes into the washing machine, added fabric softener to ease the guilt. She went to the kitchen, juiced carrots and strawberries, mixed in some honey and protein powder. She gulped it down, took a deep breath, and found her mother on Skype.

Sunday afternoon in Tennessee.

Working, Destiny thought. Always working, except for Saturday when she took what she called her sabbath rest. That meant attending Sophie's gymnastic meets, having dinner out with Dad, going to church Sunday morning. He would fly back to DC, Sophie would hang with her youth group, and Mom would get on the computer.

"Hey. My baby girl." Melanie Connors smiled warmly. She was a small woman with shy eyes. "How are things?"

"My birth mother appeared in my driveway this morning."

"What?"

Destiny held up the birth certificate, trying to steady her hands so the image would be legible. "Infant daughter of Julia McCord and Thomas Bryant. Born in Boston. Is this right?"

"I can't confirm that," Melanie said. "It was a closed adoption."

"Come on, Mom. Tell me Daddy didn't have them checked out." Will Connors was the chief of staff to a United States senator. With resources and access, nothing slipped by him.

Her mother rubbed her temples. "What did she want?"

If Destiny told her, Mom would be on the first plane to the coast, standing at the gate to Destiny's house with a baseball bat. She was, indeed, a woman with shy eyes—and a spine of steel.

"Destiny." Melanie's face was close to the screen now. "Tell me what she wanted."

She wanted her son to live. Did Julia really pray for Destiny every day when she prayed for the sick boy? For Dillon?

"She was just passing through and decided she wanted to see what I looked like. I must not have impressed her because she didn't stay long."

"Are you okay?"

"Why wouldn't I be?"

"Do you want me to come out there? Sophie and I can come out tonight."

Her mother homeschooled her younger sister so they could go anywhere, anytime. Melanie had tried to homeschool Destiny, but she wouldn't have it, was probably the only kid in history to run away *to* school.

"Stay put, please. This is no big deal. She's a stranger and going to remain a stranger. We had a nice chat and she's gone."

"Gone where?"

"To wherever. Vancouver or something. You can google her—she runs Myrrh. You know, those artful celebrity weddings. I have no plans to extend the relationship. It was just a go-see and good-bye."

Everyone lies. So often to protect someone they love.

"Are you okay?" her mother asked.

"Asked and answered."

"Destiny, please . . ."

"I'm sorry. Okay, so I'm a little freaked. But really, I'm fine. I just wanted to check in with you and make sure someone wasn't running a scam."

Her mother bit at her thumbnail. "I should come out there."

"I'm fine. Stay and get the house ready for Christmas."

"You're still coming, right?"

"Of course." Sophie needed her to make the occasional visit, to assure her that the family was fine. The Connors family together under one roof was a rare enough sight. Given Destiny's aversion to home cooking and Dad's . . . whatever. Who knew why he stayed in Washington and Melanie in Nashville? They were kind to each other when they were together, so it wasn't really her business.

"And Luke?" Melanie said. "He's coming too. Right?"

"Mom, I've got to go. Got a shoot tonight. Need to make beautiful people more beautiful."

"Is Luke there? I'd love to say hi."

Destiny held her smile, felt the strain behind her ears. Her parents were fond of Luke but hated their living arrangements, so this rift would be no disappointment. "No, he's working. Why?"

"I wanted to ask him to keep an eye on you."

"He will. Now I have to go."

"I love you and I'll pray for you."

"Love you too."

Destiny gave her a wide smile, the one she had inherited from Thomas Bryant. *She wants a piece of my liver, Mom.* "Tell Dad and Sophie I said dittos on them."

"You sure?"

"Sure that I love them?"

She wants me to save the kid she picked, Mom. The kid she chose instead of me.

"Sure you don't want me to come out there, work this through?"

"Nothing to it. Now say bye-bye, Mom."

Melanie blew a kiss at the screen. Destiny pretended to catch it and pin it to her cheek. Then she shut her laptop.

Mom praying for her every day. Luke would be impressed.

What was it that Julia said? *Every day I wake up and say a prayer of thanks for*—For Matt. For Dillon. For Destiny.

For hope. Or was it—for Hope?

Destiny found Julia's cell number. When Julia answered, Destiny said, "Who is Hope?"

"Ah. Hope. *Hmm.*"

"*Hmm* what?"

"Hope—her name is Chloe now—is seventeen months younger than you."

"You and Tom got back together?"

"No. She . . ." Julia exhaled. "There was a different guy."

Why, you little tramp. "Where does Chloe live?"

"North Carolina."

"Are you going to ask her for a liver too?"

"Not the whole thing, Destiny. Just a lobe."

"Are you?"

"I wouldn't be doing this if we had other options."

"I'm sorry," Destiny said.

"I'm sorry too. I know this is a terrible thing to do to you, and to Hope. If you could just think about it."

"I will think about it. On one condition."

"Anything," Julia said. "Name it."

"Take me with you. Take me to meet my sister."

three

North Carolina

Sunday, 11:14 p.m.

Chloe and Jack Deschene had a schedule, and he made sure they stuck to it.

"It's the only way we can get things done," he would say. *"The curse of the overachievers."*

She would smile that he saw overachievement as a blessing and not a curse.

They had vigorous majors, Jack in economics and finance, and Chloe in premed. Their schedule decreed law school for him, medical school for her. He'd go for the doctorate while she did medical school, and he'd do his fellowship in applied economics while she did her residency.

By the time they were thirty, she would be a pediatrician and he would be assisting third-world nations in protecting their economies from corruption. By the time they were thirty-two, Jack and Chloe would have one house, two careers, and the first of two children.

"Will we have time to catch an occasional movie or go out to eat?" Chloe asked.

"Absolutely," he said. "We'll go to the theatre, volunteer at church, walk the dog—"

"We don't have a dog," Chloe said, tickling his chest. He was sensitive in the oddest places. "I bet you've got one picked out."

Jack laughed. "Everyone knows golden retrievers make the best family dog. The shedding is an issue, however, so we may have to go Labrador. The only downside there is that they tend to be hyper."

"And we're not hyper?"

"Maybe a tad." He nibbled her ear. She loved him and his schedules, and believed him when he promised they'd even break routine once in a while.

So she submitted to the schedule because if she didn't, she would get lost in her machines and miss all the obligatory premed courses and the daily workout and the family devotions she and Jack shared while the pasta cooked for supper.

The schedule decreed bedtime by 11:00 p.m., no exceptions, because the demand on their minds and bodies were so heavy. She started her nightly routine at twenty minutes before the hour, brushing hair and teeth, plastering body lotion on her legs and arms and sometimes—rarely now—her husband would do that for her and they'd fall into a gentle lovemaking.

Because if another moment of Chloe's life was scheduled, she'd scream.

That would wake up Jack, wake up her mother who believed nothing bad could happen to her little girl, wake up all Chloe's professors who said she had such promise. What good is a promise when you don't get to unleash it?

She'd found another way of letting go.

Into bed at eleven tonight, like every night. She felt Jack's muscles unwind without touching him and listened as his breathing simmered into the gentlest of *whuffs*.

He was asleep and it was time for her to come awake. Awake and so off-schedule.

Chloe trudged into the bathroom, waited to see if Jack stirred. She made a moderate show of washing her hands. If he turned in the bed that meant it was too early.

He stayed in his dreams, curled on his side, with his hands clenched under his chin.

She crept down the hall, stopped in the office to grab her computer, then scooted into the kitchen. They lived in a four-thousand-square-foot townhouse their parents had bought them. They lived in a gated community with twenty-four-hour security because Mother insisted.

Chloe sat at the island, her screen tilted so if Jack got up, he would think she was designing an experimental protocol.

Studying was his passion, and hers too. Not book work or design-of-experiment meetings. Whenever possible, she built things. There was something satisfying in understanding how something worked from the inside out. Though Jack said she should probably stop fussing with wires and pumps, she didn't want to.

Her father had built powerful jet engines and sleek passenger planes. Chloe had inherited that passion—perhaps through osmosis since it couldn't be genetic. She sometimes ached to get hands-on with life instead of seeing it filtered through textbooks and lab equipment and Jack's plan.

That passion leaked into unexpected places, like a magma flow trapped under stone, needing to find a vent. Perhaps she'd been venting a little too often this semester. It had been a tough one. Jack had been consumed with writing his thesis while she struggled with scheduling her volunteer work, laboratory research, and med school interviews. They went to church on Wednesday night for Bible study and Sunday for worship, because that's what the schedule said.

Chloe had her own schedule, one she enjoyed with a glass—or

two—of white wine. She stashed it behind the gallon of olive oil and the oversized bottle of balsamic vinegar Jack had insisted on buying at the warehouse store because *it was a good deal and we can make our own salad dressing.*

Opening her computer, Chloe typed in the URL. She knew enough not to keep it as a favorite even though Jack was a measured gentleman who would never snoop.

www.talkatnight.com

Like opening a door. Opening a door and looking at the world outside her walls.

She typed in her username: *Hands_On.* She had meant it innocently because she loved protocols where she got to build an experiment with her hands. It quickly had been perceived as profane—something that absolutely disgusted her. She blocked everyone but the few who showed some soul and intelligence in their night talking.

Tonight she sought out one special user, found him in his virtual garden that bloomed as a background in her screen as soon as he accepted her invitation to chat.

WAVERUNNER: You're late. Tough day?

She appreciated that he didn't type in shorthand; that implied he also logged on from a laptop and was facile enough to keep up conversing like adults and not stupid kids.

HANDS _ ON: Only 2 minutes. You missed me?
WAVERUNNER: Maybe.
HANDS _ ON: Just maybe?
WAVERUNNER: You might be a tad more interesting than my crewmates. Just a tad.

WaveRunner was the tech officer for a large commercial fishing vessel that sailed off the Grand Banks. He and Chloe had stumbled into an online friendship when they connected in a chat forum about mechanical engineering. She liked his life; the notion of keeping a large boat on course in dangerous waters appealed to her dueling sense of order and risk.

WAVERUNNER: What did you do today?

She launched into a detailed discussion—not about the disease model that she labored over in her research, but about taking apart the sampling machine and clearing the pump. *WaveRunner* actually listened, thought about what she said, and replied with intelligence and encouragement.

When she finished, he gave her an account of how he climbed inside a steering console and was stuck there for hours while he traced a faulty circuit. The alarms hadn't rung to warn of a problem because a rat had chewed through a nest of cables. The backup to the backup hadn't been programmed correctly and never kicked in.

WAVERUNNER: I worked flat on my back into the evening until I got it all replaced.
HANDS _ ON: Are you ok?
WAVERUNNER: Yeah
HANDS _ ON: Really? You're not a gymnast, you know.
WAVERUNNER: OK, so maybe my neck is a little stiff. A lot stiff actually.

Chloe paused, like she always did in this moment. She had to be true to herself, didn't she? Before she could please Jack and Jesus and everyone else, she had to have this little amusement in her life. Or she'd go nuts.

Her fingers tingled as she typed.

HANDS _ ON: If I were there, I could rub out the knots.
WAVERUNNER: What an awesome thought. If you were here . . . I would show you the stars like you'd never seen them. Hold your hand, if that would be ok with you.

WaveRunner's hands would be calloused and strong, with clean nails and maybe a smudge of grease on the back on his right hand. As Father aged, his hands softened—he was a CEO who had forgotten how to build the jet engines that had made his family fabulously wealthy.

Someday, he used to say. *Someday I'll get my hands dirty again.*

Jack's hand was the first she'd ever held and his kiss the first she'd ever tasted. She liked his steadiness, his respect, his dreams, his schedule. But magma flowed beneath the surface, and that foundation trembled.

HANDS _ ON: I think that would be more than ok.
WAVERUNNER: It's icy out there tonight. I would have to be a gentleman, hold you close so you'd be warm. Share my coat.
HANDS _ ON: I wouldn't say no to that either.

What would she say no to? Chloe had never had the freedom to find out. In her mother's, and then Jack's, scheduling of her time and talents, they had programmed in goodness and steadfastness because there was no time for fervor or risk.

When they finally signed off, she climbed into bed and snaked her arms around Jack's chest. She roused him to a half sleep and tried to imagine making love under the stars.

Stars weren't on the schedule tonight.

Los Angeles
Sunday, 9:35 p.m.

Julia paced the private terminal and FaceTimed with Matt. "God forgive me," she said. "I don't think I like her very much."

"You must have made some connection. She agreed to come with you."

Matt slouched in an orange chair in the hospital's waiting room. His eyes were puffy and, as trim as he was, he seemed to have grown jowls overnight. Even with all the stress, he had managed to book her a suite at the Hilton in Durham. He knew she would need time and space to decompress once they got to North Carolina.

Bless him for his attention to detail. Except when it came to his own well-being. "I don't like the way you look," she said.

He gave her the closest thing to a leer she knew he could manage. "I love the way you look. From head to toe to—"

"Don't change the subject. Has anyone checked your blood pressure?"

"This isn't the time to be worrying about me," he said. "And yes, Dr. Annie took it because she thought I looked like a baked potato. It was 130 over 85."

"High."

"Normal for a guy my age."

"What was Dillon's last pressure?"

"Since two minutes ago when you asked me? Why don't I ask the IT guy to stream his numbers online for you?"

"Could you?" She meant it as a joke. The desperation was unplanned, a near constant.

"Julia!"

She paced to the windows and back to the check-in desk. "I can't bear being away, Matt."

"I know, Julia. I know."

She pressed her forehead to the screen, wishing God would open up time and space—just for a minute—so she could step into Dillon's hospital room and hug him until he yelled, *"Uck, Mom! Will you stop already?"*

The early morning flight from Dallas to Burbank had been a blur. She thanked God that the jet they rented was available this week. At least she hadn't had to battle through checking luggage and boarding.

"I don't know what to make of her," she said. "She's edged with attitude and wears rebellion like some women wear those Louboutins."

Matt raised his eyebrows. "Sounds like a snapshot of one Julia McCord."

"You got it." Julia laughed. "Not that I could tell her that. I suspect no one can tell her anything."

"You're worried about her not giving you a chance, not getting to know you. Remember that you need to know her too."

"I'm afraid I already do. That's what scares me." Yesterday Julia had seen Destiny's anger, a shade of her own. Destiny had been wild in the womb, Hope—no, she was Chloe now—Chloe had been quiet, as if not wanting to be noticed. It had been the second daughter—the second heartbreak—that opened the door to God.

From the moment Julia had said yes to Jesus, she had prayed for her daughters' adoptive parents. Now she knew their names and a bit of their history. Google gave up its secrets in seconds.

Melanie and William Connors. Both semipublic personas, well-regarded in their circles, active in their church. Destiny had a sister named Sophie, whose name appeared in regional gymnastic meets. Destiny had many film credits as crew and some precious ones in design.

Susan and John Middlebrooks. He had been owner and president of Middlebrooks Avionics until he died a decade ago. Mrs. Middlebrooks was active in charities and ministries. Chloe had received many academic honors, as did her husband. She had no siblings.

Perhaps she'd take kindly to meeting an older birth-sibling.

God couldn't have found better families for her babies. Stable, accomplished parents. And yet—

"If only . . . ," Julia said.

"What? Talk to me."

"If only we could have had more children."

"Sweetheart, don't start. We have the family God gave us."

How could she help but blame herself? Julia had waited too long after enduring all the drama around Dillon's birth. And when she was finally ready to bear Matt a second child, endometriosis made her uterus inhospitable.

"If only you had been their father."

Matt leaned in to his screen so his lips were just a whisper away. "God's will, not mine. You did right by them."

"Does she know that?" Julia wandered to the window overlooking the parking lot. Nothing stirred outside except a shiver of palm leaves. "Matt, what if she doesn't come?"

"She'll come."

"How do you know?"

"She left home two months after she graduated high school and apparently never looked back."

"Which proves she's independent."

"Or . . . she's looking for something."

"I just don't—" Julia's breath caught as a single headlight flashed in her peripheral vision. "She's here, gotta go."

"Wait, wait! Show me. All I've seen is the license photo."

Julia turned the phone to the parking lot. Hopefully Destiny wouldn't catch the camera action. "That's her, getting off the motorcycle. With the bright-red helmet."

"She's got an eye for color," Matt said.

Destiny took off her helmet, locked it into a box on the back of the bike. She shook out her rich, black hair and headed for the terminal.

"Wow," Matt said. "She looks a lot like you. And yet, nothing like you. That's weird."

"I have to go. Hug our boy for me."

"Tight as he'll let me."

As Destiny neared the door, she spotted Julia and gave her a nod. And then a frown.

"Matt?"

"Yeah?"

"God help me," Julia said, trying not to wilt under her daughter's gaze. "I don't think she likes me much either."

"I expected a puddle jumper," Destiny said as the security guard escorted them to the jet. "A Falcon 900 is a sweet ride."

"You're up on private planes?" Julia said.

Destiny laughed. "It's Los Angeles. I'm up on everything excessive and expensive."

Julia checked her watch. Even if they caught a tail wind, they'd arrive in North Carolina in the middle of the night. Matt had begged her to let him call, see if he could set up some sort of meeting for the following day. Julia had absolutely refused. That left too much room for the girl to decline.

If she lost Chloe, Destiny would back out of the trip.

A surprise visit would at least give Julia a chance to see her. Maybe Destiny's presence would be incentive for both girls to be patient and get to know each other.

If they knew Julia better, maybe they'd trust her enough to at least get tested. One step at a time—if only she didn't need to be quick-stepping this.

Their pilot appeared from the front of the plane. Sally Jeffries was a veteran of American Airlines and a member of the church where the Whittakers worshipped. Matt had asked specifically for her. Her presence on the trip would be a comfort.

Julia gave her a quick hug, then settled back in her seat. She ached to her marrow, absolutely had to get some sleep before meeting Chloe.

Sally had a bright smile for Destiny. "We restocked the fridge. Would you like something?"

"Champagne," Destiny said. "We're celebrating."

"Sally is our pilot," Julia said. "We do our own attending."

"Oops."

"Hey, I'm up," Sally said. "Can I grab you something, Julia?"

"I'm on pain meds," Julia said. "Water will be fine."

Destiny strapped into the recliner, raised the footrest. "Let's relax and you tell me about Thomas Bryant."

"There's not much more to tell," Julia said.

"It's my story," Destiny said, "and I'd appreciate hearing it."

Glancing out from the galley, Sally caught Julia's eye. Sally pressed her hands together and bowed her head. Julia launched into the tale of Julia McCord and Thomas Bryant.

four

Boston

25 Years Earlier, Winter

Julia McCord had come to Boston to make great art.

She'd imagined herself in studio classes, cutting stone, molding clay, and slinging paint. On the weekends, she'd kick back and argue with her fellow artists about whether taking graphic art or secondary education as a minor was a sellout or a smart decision for the future.

They'd ride bikes along the Charles, poke fun at the MIT nerds, and secretly envy the elites at Harvard. They'd stop in for a brew at Kenmore and maybe go to Fenway Park and pretend they were like the other tens of thousands of students who flooded the city every September.

They would be different because they had vision, and they had come to Boston to marry that vision to revelation and call it art.

They would go back to their dorms and hunker down with sketchpads and maybe some cheap wine and draw vivid dreams that most of the world wouldn't dare to consider.

What she hadn't expected was spending the second half of her freshman year at Massachusetts College of Art on her knees, chalking streets and sidewalks.

A news story in January had ripped at her in a way she hadn't imagined possible.

Something had gone terribly wrong or—as Julia now believed—miraculously right and a baby had survived a midterm abortion.

With one feeble leg kicking and a tiny chest struggling for air, the little boy died in a metal basin. Someone had deliberately brought the basin within view of the security cameras, retrieved the tape of what the physician called *the results of the procedure*, and tipped off the radio talk shows.

The story had legs until the mainstream press shut it down.

A matter of privacy between a woman and her doctor, the pro-choice people proclaimed, if it had actually happened at all. Who could trust these anti-abortion freaks and their lies? In men's cruel and manipulative attempts to regain control over women's bodies, they probably fabricated the whole thing.

A pro-life group stopped the disposal of the child's remains within minutes of his death. They had an injunction from a friendly judge that was issued months earlier, as if preparing for this rare event. Another perversion because why didn't the person who caught it all on camera offer the infant one or two precious puffs of air and perhaps a warm towel to swathe him as he died?

The state tagged him Baby Doe and stepped in to claim his remains. Caught in a political firestorm, they filed him away in a morgue locker. Julia would lie awake at night and think about his lonely fate.

The anger at his abandonment smoldered in her chest. What could she do? She wasn't political, wasn't connected, wasn't given to public speaking. The only thing she knew how to do was draw pictures.

The first night she took to the streets was in February. The razor edge of a Montreal Express shrouded the city in sub-zero temperatures. Her friends were pontificating in useless circles about their art. The lounge stank with self-importance.

In search of fresh air, she grabbed her backpack and wandered outside. She tried to think about her fabric art class. The cold air clung to her like shrink-wrap and she thought about Baby Doe, kept on ice in some dark compartment because two groups of people fought over his body like dogs over a scrap of carrion.

The chalk was in her backpack because when her group got wasted enough, they'd riff in color on the chalkboard in Metropolitan Hall. The janitor washed it every morning as if to proclaim that they were just some talented kids with nothing real to say.

The blue chalk with its dusky hue seemed right. A block from her dorm, Julia bent over the sidewalk, ripped off her mitten, and wrote FREE BABY DOE. She outlined the words in amethyst because of the way the veins on her hand had withered into blue and red threads within minutes.

The next day a low-pressure front rolled in and the sky pelted rain. The amethyst ran into the blue, the blue ran into the street, bleeding into a smear on the pavement and then—nothing.

Julia pressed her face to the window of her dorm room and said *show me what to do.*

25 Years Earlier, Easter Sunday

The police finally caught up to the artist the press called the Midnight Chalker on March 26 at 1:46 a.m.

Julia had chosen Christopher Columbus Park in the North End as her coming-out canvas.

Since she'd begun the tagging, she'd kept to quiet streets where she could have an hour of solitude or could hunker between parked cars when someone drove by. But Baby Doe's remains still belonged to Massachusetts instead of God, so she decided it was time to make the message more visible.

She had advanced from slogans to full images, sketching barren trees or broken cars or earth-quaked villages, spreading from the left corner of her stone canvas into whatever vision of wholeness she embraced in the icy dark.

And always, in what had become her trademark hues, the sorrowful blue and biting amethyst: FREE BABY DOE.

It was after midnight, Easter Sunday, when she got caught.

She labored over a field of wilted lilies when a man yanked her by the collar. She panicked and unleashed a stream of pepper spray. Ten minutes later she sat in a booking room, charged with assaulting a police officer.

When offered her one phone call, Julia had done what she thus far had avoided. She'd called the overnight desk at Fox25. Her only thought was for someone to film her drawing of Baby Doe rising out of the earth in the rosette of a lily before Public Works hosed it away.

The film aired on the 6:00 a.m. newscast.

Two hours later the local pro-life group sent a lawyer to the police station. She told him to pound sand.

At 9:00 a.m., her roommate, Jeanne Potts, charged into the holding room, her hair still wet from her shower. "You should have told me you were the Midnight Chalker," she said. "The whole Baby Doe thing has been eating at me too."

Julia hugged her. "I don't want to become a cause," she said. "I just want the baby at peace."

Jeanne called the son of a family friend who was about to graduate from Suffolk Law.

"He's smart and driven," she said as they waited for him to

arrive. "He says he can make this about freedom of speech and steer clear of the issues."

"So he's not into politics?"

"Nah," Pottsie said with a laugh. "He's basically into himself."

"That's probably what I need right now. What did you say his name was?"

"Tom. Thomas Bryant."

25 Years Earlier, May

Two miracles happened in May.

The state of Massachusetts transferred the remains of Baby Doe to the cloister of the Sisters of Still River. The good sisters promised Julia that he had been buried under a tree that rustled in the wind.

Thomas Bryant became more into Julia McCord than himself. They were completely incompatible, she of the ripped jeans and wild hair, and he of the white shirts and crimson suspenders. The miracle was that they were a perfect fit.

"He's glommed onto you like acrylic," Jeanne Potts said. "Do you know how many hearts—and bodies—this guy has left strewn in his path?"

Julia tapped her toes and tried not to grin. "A guy has to grow up sometime."

"Seriously. He's like a kite that flies high and nosedives when the wind changes. This is new for him. Just be careful."

Careful melted away like ice cream on hot pavement.

"Don't go back home this summer," Tom said the night she was packing to go home to Oklahoma.

Julia slipped her hands under his shirt so she could feel the muscles in his back. His skin was cool under her fingers, his scent a subtle musk. "Lucky me, I have a job at Safeway."

"You can make good money painting," he said.

Julia laughed. "I haven't found a Medici to be patron to my da Vinci."

Tom kissed her forehead. "I mean, *paint* paint. There's this guy at work who is going to New York to be an in-house attorney for one of our corporate clients. It was all"—he snapped his fingers—"just like that."

He touched his nose to hers, so close that she felt his lashes on her cheeks. His breath smelled like bubblegum. "Anyway, he's just bought this house in Nahant for a cool mil. A wreck of a mansion, right on the water. He was going to work weekends restoring it and then turn it around for resale next year. Now he's stuck with it, doesn't want to sell as is because it'll be a loss."

Julia leaned back so she could see his face. Tom's hair was very dark, almost black. His eyes were on the blue side of gray, could go from merry to gritty in a snap because there was never a neutral moment, not with this man.

"And he wants someone to paint his house?" she said.

"Inside and out. Plus wallboarding, crown molding, cosmetic changes. It's a good gig for me while I study for the bar exam. If I get a crew together, it's a better deal for him because he won't have to pay contractor fees. Think of it, baby. Summering at the shore, getting paid for it."

Thomas Bryant in July. Ocean breezes, hot sand, clear nights—what an absurdly perfect notion.

"And where do I live? On the Common, like the guys with their shopping carts and booze in a bag, hon?" She cringed at the *hon*;

she tried hard to wash the Oklahoma out of her speech, just like Tom tried to rinse South Boston out of his.

"You're living in the house. With me."

25 Years Earlier, Summer

Six of them lived in the house that summer: two of Tom's friends from Suffolk Law, Jeanne Potts, her brother Richie, Julia, and Tom. They hammered, painted, papered, sweated, and hung out.

Nahant was a self-contained village, surrounded by ocean and bay. North of Boston, take a turn through Lynn, known for the old jingle: *Lynn Lynn, the city of sin, you never come out the way you go in.* Drive through the sketchy downtown, take a right at the Atlantic Ocean, and pass over the causeway, a narrow stretch of highway and beach that connected Nahant to the rest of the world.

The scenic peninsula was kept pure for the townies with a resident-only parking ban. Boston was only a glance away to the southwest, but it could take an hour to get back there, especially with beach traffic and wending back through *you never go out the way you come in.*

Julia felt like a causeway, balancing the girl trying to walk in God's will and the woman desperate to pour herself into Thomas Bryant. *Everything in its season,* she told herself, and then forgot to listen.

The rambling stone-and-shingle house had been abandoned to what little wild there was in Nahant. Vines climbed the massive stone porch, shrouding it with thorns and briars. The gardens were choked with weeds and dead leaves.

Julia took on the grounds as a personal mission. She needed the fresh salt air and the sun on her shoulders. Oklahoma would have been the wiser option. Distance was all that could cool her off; that and scampering down the rocks and thrusting her head and shoulders into the cold Atlantic.

She would labor all morning in the gardens, only coming in for their lunch of baloney sandwiches and Diet Coke. Her arms were often scratched from clearing and pruning. Tom would take her aside and tenderly kiss each of her wounds as if he took them personally.

The house had six bedrooms. The guys roomed in one, Jeanne and Julia in another, while they rotated rooms for restoration. A committed Catholic, Jeanne Potts was Julia's anchor whenever she wavered. When Tom started talking about the future, the waver became a tilt.

"Someday I'll buy you a house like this," he said, helping her pull weeds from what used to be a glorious bed of peonies. The others had gone to Boston, tickets to a Sox afternoon game.

"And what would I do with a house like this? Besides clean it all the time."

"Fill it with kids."

"All by myself?"

"I'll help," he said with that devastating smile. "I've already picked out the names."

Julia poked his chest, left mud on his sweaty T-shirt. "That's a girlie thing to do."

"Joshua. Ben. Brogan. Michael. Good South Boston kids."

"No, no. You've got it wrong."

"I do, do I?"

She grinned, rubbed her dirty hand down the back of his shirt. "Devon will be a redhead like your sister. Kelsey will be quiet and studious and grow up to be a college professor. Sophie will have my eyes and be a drummer. And Savannah will be a people-person like you."

"Four females?"

"Sure. Why not?"

"Doesn't seem fair to me." He tapped her on the nose. "So let me plea bargain this and ask—why not have all of them?"

Julia sat back on her heels and made an exaggerated show of exhaustion. "Eight kids. I'd be too busy for anything else."

Tom wrapped his hand around the back of her head and pulled her in for a kiss. Off-balance, she rolled sideways into the grass. He rolled with her, sliding his arm around her waist. The smell of paint and perspiration intoxicated her.

"If we're going for eight someday"—his whisper was hot in her ear—"we'd better start practicing."

"I can't—"

"Shush. We both know where this is going."

"Tom. No." Julia knew she should pull away.

But everywhere she moved, Tom was there to meet her.

24 Years Earlier, Spring

Last summer seemed an eternity ago. The hurried pairings in hidden places. A bower under the overgrown rhododendron. A section of flat rock between slippery boulders. The long ride to New Hampshire, Tom making her wait until they crested Mount Eisenhower before he took her in his arms and lay her gently on a bed of moss.

They had protection, did their best to use it. Sometimes in the gaze of the full moon, wrapped in a sleeping bag to keep mosquitoes off, sometimes things got overlooked and what did it matter because they were *destined*, Tom said. Their fate was to live happily ever after with four girls and five boys; five because he said they needed enough for a basketball team and besides, the girls would rule anyway.

Julia would dig deeper into his arms and believe him.

Jeanne Potts figured it out before she did.

They were back at school, plunging into their studies like they had into the restoration of the Nahant house. The first semester had breezed by with challenging studio work. Tom was buried deep in his books, continuing with the Nahant restoration and studying for the bar.

One April evening Jeanne came out of the bathroom in shorts and a T-shirt, a towel wrapped around her head. "You do realize—you're late."

Julia looked up from her worktable. She sketched painstakingly in ink, each tiny stroke a struggle. "Is there someplace I was supposed to be?"

"You haven't used any of our supplies. Not for a while now."

"You count them or something, Pottsie?"

"Last semester I ran out every month because you'd finish the last of them and forget to replenish the box. And now . . . the past two months, nothing."

Annoyed, Julia tried to refocus on her drawing. "You want me to go out and get a box?"

"Yes." Jeanne squeezed her hand. "The kind with a pregnancy kit in it."

24 Years Earlier, Summer

"We'll figure this out," Tom said, and for a couple more months they didn't figure out anything because the hormones rolled in waves and Julia desired him more than ever. He went with the flow, seeking a refuge of mindless pleasure as he began his first real job for a Boston law firm. Julia and Jeanne spent another summer in Nahant, making drapes, cleaning windows, and staging the mansion for sale.

One rainy July day Jeanne asked, "Have you considered adoption?"

"This baby already has two parents." Julia ripped off a length of thread to sew the corner of the crimson silk drape. They had rented furniture with straight lines and neutral colors and were making the house pop with accessories, pillows, and drapes. She photographed each room as they completed it and designed the brochure. "We'll be getting married and I know you'll laugh when I say this—we plan to live happily ever after."

"Just remember," Jeanne said. "Tom's *ever after* is concrete one moment, sand the next. I know him, Jules. He's a runner."

"Not anymore, Pottsie. He's a keeper now."

"Whatever." Jeanne clumped up a ladder, positioned a length of drape so Julia could check the hem. "I'm here for you . . ."

The unspoken *when he leaves* fell heavy on the room. Julia knew to her toes that she and Tom were destined to be, and Jeanne would know that eventually. Maybe not until their third child or tenth anniversary, but she'd forget this shadowed moment and celebrate belatedly.

In August, Alicia McCord arrived in Boston. *To see the sights*, she had said. Her mother just wanted to snoop into what was keeping her daughter in the city for the second summer instead of coming home to Oklahoma.

"I have to tell her about the baby," Julia said to Tom. "She'll see the bump."

"We'll tell her we're going to marry next spring," he said. "Give you a chance to lose the baby weight and do it right."

"Are we?" Julia touched the worry line on his forehead. Tom worked night and day. *The bondage of a junior associate,* he told her. *It's okay because I'm their rising star.*

"Of course," he said. "Why wouldn't we?"

Alicia McCord was not delighted that she would become a grandmother sometime between Thanksgiving and Christmas.

"You came to Boston with such great promise, with a solid upbringing, good Christian values. And you've been lying to me this whole time?"

"I told you how I spent my summers." Julia heard the whine in her voice, felt like an eight-year-old. "And I told you about Tom."

"Clearly not everything."

"Some things are solely my business."

"You're my daughter. That makes it my business."

Julia rubbed her lower abdomen protectively. "And this is my daughter. So you'll need to trust me to do what's right."

Alicia dabbed her eyes with a tissue, came away with a mess of mascara. "Do you love this man?"

"With everything in me."

"And does he love you?"

"Of course he does. How can you ask that, Mom? I wouldn't have . . . fallen into this if he was just a fling."

"Then why aren't you getting married right now? I could help set something up in a local church—"

"Not yet. If I get married, I could lose my scholarship because of the change in financial status. And besides, I get free prenatal care because I'm a single mother."

"Single mother. Do you know how tragic those two words are?" Alicia shook her head. She had been a single mother for the past twelve years, since Julia's dad booked it to Idaho.

"Everything's a tragedy with you if it doesn't fit into your worldview."

"It's not my worldview. It's the gifts and responsibilities that God has set before us."

Julia took the tissue, carefully wiped the mascara from her

mother's cheeks. "I'll lose the baby weight and come back to Oklahoma next summer, get married there. Tom is all for that. We can start planning now."

"Child, oh my child." She framed Julia's face with her hands. "He won't marry you, you know."

"How can you say that? You don't know him." Julia tamped down the fury, held it between her heart and her baby because her mother didn't deserve the anger that she felt every time someone tried to tell her they knew Tom better than she did.

Her mom pulled her close, a tight grip on her shoulders until Julia relaxed and allowed herself to be hugged. "He's like a sparkler you light on the Fourth of July. Bright light, then quickly cold ash."

"You don't know him."

"Just consider giving the baby up for adoption. Please, sweetheart."

"What?" Julia jerked away. "No. How could you even suggest that?"

"I can help connect you with a Christian couple who can provide an excellent home for a baby. What can you give her or him, Julia? A tiny apartment and a man who works all the time, and then resents you because he has no life and you have no life. What happens when the baby becomes a millstone instead of a blessing?"

"Don't, please just . . . don't." She could barely breathe. "She will always be a blessing. I love her, Mom."

"Give her a chance, Julia. If you love her, give your baby a chance."

Julia felt a flutter under her navel, her daughter making her will known for the first time. She would never give this child up, never give Tom up, never give up the dreams that burned through her skin. The foolish teenager who had helped Baby Doe go free would be the devoted mother who would bind her daughter tightly to her for a lifetime.

And Tom would do the same.

24 Years Earlier, December

The week after Thanksgiving Jeanne helped her set up the apartment. She filled in for Tom, who'd said something about a sudden injunction or some urgent business that couldn't penetrate Julia's pregnancy haze.

It was good that Tom worked all the time; Julia looked like a buoy. She had needed the time apart to get her semester's work done early and to get about the business of nesting.

He'd won the fight with Social Services to get her welfare benefits. The state had claimed her scholarship was the equivalent of a salary and she wasn't eligible for any assistance. Tom had argued strenuously—pulling some South Boston strings—that her college fulfilled the welfare-to-work requirement and couldn't be held against her financial status. *If they started picking at a client's college financial aid*, he said, *the whole federal system would come tumbling down.*

He had found a studio apartment in Dorchester that the housing voucher would cover. Julia cringed at taking entitlements but told herself it was just until they got settled and the baby was born. Next August Tom would have his first-year review at the law firm, get a raise, and be able to afford a nice two-bedroom near the college.

The apartment smelled like fermented apple cider. The one window looked out on a convenience store and a bus stop. The bathroom was tight with a toilet, tub, no shower. Julia had to wash her hair with a bucket. Mismatched table and chairs would serve as her worktable and Tom's computer desk. He hadn't moved in yet; too busy with the firm and studying for the Massachusetts bar exam.

The work in Nahant had given her a notion of how to use space. Even so, they'd have to be creative with the baby furniture. Jeanne had filled in for Tom when he was too busy to shop the garage sales with her. Her back ached, her stomach was on fire with heartburn, her feet had swollen so much she had to wear sandals in the cold weather.

The baby kicked in lightning bursts. *Boom, boom*, like a boxer.

"That baby's going to kick her way out of you," Jeanne said. "Are you sure you don't need to lie down or something?"

"We have to get this changing table put together."

"What about day care?" Jeanne said. "Did you check out that place I told you about?"

Julia was breathless, trying to screw the frame together. "I'm taking next semester off, Pottsie."

"Jules, you said you'd be ready to go. The timing is perfect. Isn't it?"

Timing is everything. While she was growing into a mountain, Jeanne had bloomed. The shy girl from Quincy—who went to Mass every day, crafted incredible fabric, volunteered as a Big Sister—had somehow matured into a composed woman with thick, blond hair and long eyelashes.

Perhaps her beauty came from *not* knowing she was beautiful.

"I can't . . . I just can't see how I'd manage it," Julia said. "The baby needs someone around and Tom's never here and I don't see that changing any time soon."

"I'm sorry." Jeanne didn't spout reassurances like *he'll find the time* or *you'll be okay* or even, *I'll help you,* though Julia knew she would. "I pray for you every morning. You know that, right?"

"I know, I know." Julia hugged her tight, ashamed that her prayers—when she remembered them—were only for Destiny and Tom.

Something pinched her groin and suddenly soaked her legs. "What's happening?"

"Your water," Jeanne said. "Your water just broke."

The labor came a scant five minutes after, fevered and hard. They called everywhere but couldn't find Tom.

Jeanne took Julia to the hospital and held her hand as Julia groaned and shrieked, her body rebelling against gravity and common sense.

Destiny was born a red-faced, dark-eyed little girl who peeled the paint off the walls with her wails. "A nine-ten on the Apgar," the doctor proclaimed. "Couldn't be healthier. Or more ready to take on the world."

They slipped the baby into Julia's arms. She was too exhausted and in too much pain to hold her, so Jeanne rocked the baby for a while and then took her to the nursery. As she was leaving, she hugged Julia and said, "I left messages everywhere. He'll be here soon."

Alicia McCord arrived in the middle of the night, blabbering about layovers in Omaha and Cincinnati before finally arriving in Boston. Then she started her pitch: *the baby is beautiful* and *did you think about what we talked about last spring, about giving your daughter a good life* and *wherever is this child's father?*

Julia folded her arms, kept them tight even when the nurse brought the child to be fed. She would not hold her baby until Tom came and shared that moment with her. Her mother took the two nighttime feedings.

"He'll come," her mother said. "But he's not going to stay."

"You can't know that."

"Oh, honey, I'm afraid I do. The nurses are asking for her name," her mother said. "Devon, right?"

"Destiny."

"What? That's an odd name."

"She was meant to be my destiny, so Destiny she will be."

"It's such a . . . trendy name."

"She's my daughter. I get to name her. Now, please, I need to sleep." But sleep wouldn't come. Julia tossed and moaned softly until someone made her take a pill and she tumbled into colorless dreams.

Tom arrived the next morning, unshaven and bleary-eyed, smelling faintly of booze. "I was in New York," he said. "They sent me for a deposition. I told you I was going, left you the phone number."

You didn't, Julia wanted to say, but all she could muster was, "Oh."

And she realized in that moment that Tom was not the sparkler like Mom had said. *She* was. He set her ablaze and when her light had dimmed to a musky coal, he had turned elsewhere.

When he said, "Alicia and I had a long discussion this morning. About what's best for the baby and best for you," Julia knew that the case had been closed without her even registering a plea.

Julia asked for time alone with the baby. She held her, rocking back and forth, trying to drive out the agony of her body being torn open and then being torn away from her baby. *Oh, God, how could You let this happen to us?*

She kissed her daughter's cheeks and eyes and smelled her wispy hair, marveling that the child had finally stopped kicking and found peace.

Perhaps this newborn child has more wisdom than I do.

She signed the papers that Tom had already signed and surrendered her baby to a destiny different from the one she had planned.

five

North Carolina

Monday, 7:03 a.m.

Jack kissed Chloe's cheek as she straggled past him for the coffee. He was buttoned-down and bright-eyed, his blond hair like a halo. Last night she had danced like a six-inch stiletto; this morning she flapped like a moldy old sneaker.

Fifty more years of this, she told herself. *It's good. Good to be safe with a good man.*

"My turn to do the shopping." Jack poured coffee into his oversize thermos. He eschewed Starbucks for thriftiness, though they could afford designer brews or even a housekeeper to make their morning coffee. Two children with trust funds fall in love, marry, make a life. In the scheme of God's things, such fortune didn't seem fair to her husband. So at every possible corner, Jack cut expenses and Jack cut guilt.

"Chloe. Are you listening? Need anything from Costco?"

She waved her hand over her mug, trying to muster a physiological response from the coffee. School. Costco. Jack. Manna and quail—she was ungrateful. Her own ingratitude was just another trap she could not escape.

"The usual stuff, I guess," she managed. How many thousands of rolls of paper towels, bags of boneless chicken breasts, and jars of spaghetti sauce would make up fifty years?

Jack called their spare lifestyle *training in godliness*, apparently unaware of the irony of chewing on Costco dinner rolls while living in a million-dollar condominium. Was his lack of passion also training in godliness, or was there something so decaffeinated in Chloe's love that he doled out his desire like he shuffled those stupid coupons?

"Christmas is just a few weeks away. I suppose we need to start thinking about wrapping paper and the like," she said.

He touched the small of her back, tenderly possessive. "You still haven't told me what you'd like for Christmas."

"Jack. What I really want . . ." She clunked her mug on the counter and turned to face him. "I want a vacation."

"What?"

"We haven't been away since the honeymoon. Remember the honeymoon, darling?"

He put his arms around her and blended into her. A nice fit. Everyone said so. His eyes were blue like his father's, narrow like his mother's. He said she had doe eyes, as if that were a compliment and not a description of a girl running scared.

Her eyes were so dark brown that when people looked at her, Chloe was convinced they only saw their own reflection.

"I'm planning to polish the thesis over the winter break," he said. "You know that."

"Bring your laptop. It's a small world now. You can log in from anywhere, anytime. And do anything you want." Goose bumps ran up her neck because she had proof of that.

"I can't . . . sorry, love." He pressed his face to her neck. His skin smelled like Irish Spring soap. "The timing is off. Maybe we can plan something for graduation. Something amazing."

Chloe locked his arms around her waist. "We're never going to graduate, Jack. There will always be one degree or another to go after. I need a break now."

"We could drive south to Florida for a couple of days, I suppose. Though the crowds will be horrible with Christmas vacations and all. Maybe if we steer clear of Orlando—"

"Let's go to St. John's or Palm Island. You can study and I can lie in the water and tip my head back and let the sun enfold me. Doesn't that sound lovely?"

"Sounds poetic." He laughed, showing a dimple and perfect teeth. "You're not having a midlife crisis twenty-five years early, are you?"

"No. I just want to see something other than a lab or a classroom."

"Chloe, you could tell me if you needed something." He leaned back, studied her face as if he were solving a mystery. "You know that, right? Anything at all."

She needed out of the pressure cooker of their lives. Jack would never admit his conviction that a Deschene or a Middlebrooks should not have needs because they had been given so much. *Look to the needs of others*, he said. He believed that, lived that, all the while missing her desperate desires.

She needed him—or someone, *forgive me, God*—to love her slowly, deeply, without measuring that love like a coupon. She needed Jack to stop thinking of her as the girl who came to him as a virgin and to start searching for delight in the woman who was his wife.

Did he ever roil deep inside, ribs aching with something more than class schedules, lofty plans, and good stewardship? Or was she selfish and greedy and—*dear God*—what is so wrong with wanting to lie back in the sunshine and feel the breeze dance over her skin?

"Chloe." Jack cradled her face. "Is there something I need to know?"

She pressed against him so he couldn't see her eyes. "I just need a vacation."

"Okay. Let me think." His shoulders stiffened. Not from resistance, she knew. Just from the pain of possible rescheduling. "You do realize the resorts are probably booked solid."

"Then we could sail. I would love to sail for a few days." Sun glinting off the water. The gentle rocking of the boat. Sand flung into the wind becoming stars.

Endless stars. Endless skies.

Chloe spilled tears now, tears that Jack wiped away with his thumbs. "Are you all right, darling?" he said. "You can tell me if you're not."

"No. I mean, sure," she said. "I'm fine. Just tired."

"You're not pregnant, are you?"

"What?"

"You've been acting *hormoney* lately."

Chloe laughed. "Hormoney is not a word."

"It should be."

"So . . . what if I were?"

"Hormoney?"

"Pregnant."

Jack smiled, his eyes crinkling under his wireless-rimmed glasses. "We'd make it work."

"Make it work? That's how you see us?" She pushed away, went to the refrigerator for the half-and-half. They bought it by the quart; cheaper that way.

Jack sipped his coffee, studied her. "You are tired, aren't you?"

"Aren't you, Jack? We've been pounding out milestones since we got to Duke. One checked box after another. Chloe and Jack

Deschene—a well-constructed spreadsheet, a well-executed program. Bang bang, mission accomplished and on to the next goal."

He squinted and tipped his head to the side. He was a brilliant student but not given to intuitive thinking. "Is there something wrong with deciding what we want and then working our backsides off to get it?"

"What if we don't really know what we want?"

"Oh, Chloe." Jack hugged her, pressed his face to her neck. "Forgive me, darling. Forgive me if I'm not doing something right."

How could she tell him that he did everything right, and that was part of the problem?

Chloe nestled into her husband's shoulder and stayed there—silently—while the toast burned.

Monday, 7:31 a.m.

The intercom buzzed as they ate oatmeal with figs and walnuts. Chloe stood up. "What if Mother—"

"I'll get it." Jack motioned for her to stay seated. "It's probably Marj, locked out of her apartment again."

"Yeah, probably." Their neighbor was a genius linguist at Duke, sweet-tempered and so forgetful that they kept a set of keys for her at their apartment.

He snatched Marj's keys from the key tray. "Why would you think something's wrong with Susan?"

"No reason. I just . . . she's getting up there. She seems brittle."

"I'll make sure we see her more often, then." Jack pressed the intercom call button. "Yes? What is it?"

"Mrs. Deschene's mother is asking to come up."

"Okay. That will be fine. Thanks."

"I told you, Jack. She's never out this early. Something's wrong." Chloe was already on her feet, skimming the possibilities. Her cousins were all in their late thirties, almost a generation removed from her. Her mother's sister was a hardy eighty years old. No one had cancer or heart problems. Had someone been in an accident? Had Mother received some horrible diagnosis, like breast cancer or heart trouble?

Jack kissed her cheek, then headed for the foyer. "Nothing to worry about."

"Right," she said and followed him anyway.

He opened the door to an attractive woman wrapped in a smart charcoal gray scarf, probably in her early forties. A girl stood behind her wearing jeans, a pink hoodie, and motorcycle boots.

"Who are you?" Jack's tone was starched. "You have a lot of nerve, posing as my wife's mother. We don't know you."

The floor seemed to tilt under Chloe's feet. "She's not posing, Jack."

"What do you want?" he asked.

"Could I come in?" the woman said.

"Certainly not." Jack started to close the door.

The woman stuck her hand—encased in a cast—into the door. She yelped in pain but didn't move her hand, just kept saying, "Please, please let me explain."

"Chloe, call security," Jack said.

"No." Chloe could see herself in the woman's eyes. "Look, Jack, just look. She is my birth mother. And you . . ." She inched around his shoulder so she could get a better look at the girl. ". . . you must be my sister."

"Guilty as charged," the girl said with a grin. "Guilty as charged."

Monday, 8:04 a.m.

Jack roused their lawyer away from his breakfast to do a background check on this stranger who had barged into their lives.

"Inherited money is more curse than blessing," John Middlebrooks used to say. *"It takes years to know whom you can trust. And even then . . ."*

The *even then* was always followed by a cautionary tale, which was why Mother was thrilled when Chloe began dating Jack Deschene. Serious, intelligent, focused—a young man with his own family money and a heart for Jesus.

While they waited for Henry Metzler to arrive, Jack sat Julia down in the living room and offered her a cup of tea. The woman stared at Chloe so long that Jack whispered, "Can you give us some time alone? Maybe head over to school for a few hours."

"No." She glanced at Julia, and at Destiny Connors. "Why would I want to do that?"

My mother, my sister. How bizarre after all these years. How wonderful.

Jack stepped so close that she couldn't see the two women. "I need you to give me some time. Please."

Chloe stepped around him. "If you would excuse me . . . I have a couple things to attend to."

"Fabulous idea," Destiny said. "I'll come with you."

"I'd prefer you stayed here," Jack said.

Destiny ignored him, followed Chloe back into the foyer. Chloe liked that.

"Does your boyfriend always order you out of the room like that?" Destiny said.

"He's my husband."

"How's that? You're younger than me, right? Seventeen months. April birthday, right?"

"Yes."

"So you're, like, twenty-two? Legal age and all that."

"I don't drink," Chloe said too quickly. That bottle of white wine was hidden in the kitchen, twenty feet away.

"It's been an intense twenty-four hours," Destiny said. "So let's go out, get some coffee."

I can make coffee, Chloe almost said and then thought, *No.* She had already dipped a toe into the unknown when Jack had opened the door to two strange women. Why not take a full step?

Chloe slipped on a green cardigan. Grabbing her coat from the back hall, she tossed Destiny a jacket. Her sister was from Los Angeles and Julia Whittaker was from Dallas. That's all that Jack would let them say until he'd consulted Henry.

He's blind. It's clear as the sun in the sky that we're all related.

Jack must know that. He just didn't know why they were here today. And he was right—better to be safe than scammed. But a sister . . . she had always wanted a sister. The Middlebrookses' house was nearly a mansion and her footsteps had always sounded so empty.

"Chloe." Jack swung into the kitchen, phone in hand. "I think we should all stay put for a little while."

"We're only going for coffee." She flushed—how must this sound to Destiny?

"I'll bring her back in one piece," Destiny said. "And I'll buy the coffee."

Jack gave her a nod, turned back to Chloe. "Let's take a little while to sort things out before we . . . share too much. Please."

"Sure," Destiny said. "You're the boss, Jack."

They took the back stairs, went through the parking lot, and crossed the grass in silence. The complex's green space was more park than lawn, immaculately landscaped to create a barrier of privacy from the campus and the city.

The brisk air was invigorating. Normally she and Jack would be in their cars with the windows up and heaters going, he off to some stimulating seminar and she going to the lab to pretend she really wanted to be a doctor instead of an engineer.

It was soothing to see Christmas lights on the rhododendrons and to hear the rush-hour traffic beyond the barrier of fir trees.

It was exhilarating to hear her sister's footsteps clatter in time with her own.

Chloe had been singular for so long. The only child. The lonely girl, too smart to really click with a group. The only woman Jack had ever loved. It was exciting to be part of something else. Jack had sniffed out that eagerness almost immediately. That was clear from the muscle jumping in his cheek. The background check was a stalling tactic until he could figure out what to do.

Chloe had made her decision the second she left the condo with her sister.

"It's pretty here," Destiny said. "We saw the campus on the drive from the airport. All I know about Duke is basketball, Coach K and all that. Luke likes to— Anyway, I see the games in March."

"Luke?"

"Yesterday's news. So you—twenty-two and already married? That's radical."

"Yes."

"You can answer with more than one word," Destiny said. "I won't bite. And if I do, I don't leave teeth marks."

"I'm still kind of stunned," Chloe said. "I mean . . . I was heading out for school and *bang*! Here you are."

Destiny laughed. "I say *bang* all the time."

"I wonder . . ." They stopped at the crosswalk. Chloe pushed the walk button.

Destiny grabbed her arm, jaywalked her across the street. "You wonder what else we do the same? Like *The Parent Trap*."

"I've never seen it."

"Here's the pitch. Twins separated at birth by divorced parents meet at a summer camp, decide to switch places so they can get their folks back together. There's this one scene where they stand side-by-side at a mirror." Destiny stopped in front of a clothing store. Not open yet for the day, its windows were dark enough to offer a reflection of the cars passing on the street. "Like this."

"Too weird."

She tugged at Chloe. "That's the fun of it. Look."

Chloe saw an instant resemblance in the shape of the faces and the eyes. Night and day personality-wise, something anyone could see. Destiny was like something out of a quirky comedy, with her hip clothes and edgy makeup. Chloe was the stereotypical prep-school girl who could pass for twelve instead of twenty-two.

"She's taller than us," Destiny said.

"She's got to be pushing five ten. I always thought I was tall at five seven."

"Me too. Size two and trust me, I'm not bragging. I eat like an elephant, burn calories like a hummingbird."

"Lucky you. I have to pick and peck like a chicken to be this size," Chloe said. Her sister—what an amazing thought *sister* was—shared the same body type, thin to almost skinny.

"The women I work with would kill to have natural highlights like yours," Destiny said.

"What women? Are you a stylist?"

"I make monsters."

"What?"

"I do a lot of conceptual art for the studios. Sometimes get TV work when they're looking for some particularly freaky stuff. You?"

"I'm a professional student. Jack doesn't see either of us done with our various degrees until we're thirty."

"Jack . . ." Destiny curled her lips into a tight smile. "He seems nice. And really, really tight. Which I guess he should be, given the circumstances."

"He is nice and he is very careful." Why were *nice* and *careful* suddenly deficits? Why did just going out in the cold for a coffee with this girl feel like a betrayal? What would Mother think when she learned the birth mother had literally appeared out of nowhere?

She should have warned Jack not to tell her.

Destiny put her thumb under Chloe's chin, tipped her head up. "I think we have her chin."

"I guess." Chloe turned away. "Starbucks is on the next block." She loved their coffee, wished Jack understood that it's not a sin to do a little something for yourself.

"So, Mrs. Professional Student. What're you studying?"

"Premed. So . . . cell biology, genetics, that kind of thing."

"Holy baloney." Destiny smiled. "That will make our mummy proud."

Chloe turned and asked, "Why are you here? Really?"

"Me? I didn't have blood relatives until yesterday morning when Julia showed up at my house. When I found out I had a sister and she was coming to see you, I couldn't resist hitching a ride on her private jet."

"But why now? What does she want?"

"I promised not to say anything. She wants"—Destiny's face darkened—"she wants to explain it herself."

"Is it bad?"

"I honestly can't answer that." Destiny lowered her gaze. "I guess I was hoping we could figure that out together."

They settled into a Starbucks, Chloe with a black coffee and Destiny with a latté and a chocolate-chip muffin.

"So?" Destiny tapped her arm. "You. Jack. Story?"

"We are so boring, so conventional, I can say it in two sentences. You could say it was our destiny."

"Spare me the puns. Can you believe it? Who names their kid Destiny? Besides some teenage, single mom. So, back to you and Jack."

The hunger for each other had started at prep school, fueled by shadow kisses and passionate embraces. They had both pledged chastity, so Chloe or Jack would say *stop*, he more often than her. She was the weak one, unbuttoning his shirt and pressing her lips to his collarbone like a bird swooping in for prey. By the time they said their vows and finally made love, it felt anticlimactic—as if they had passed some perfect moment and not even realized it.

The work, she told herself. The work came before the passion. They carried heavy academic loads, dreamed of lofty futures. Act justly, love mercy, walk humbly. That had to be their passion now.

"He was my high-school romance. We hung on into college. We're both focused personalities and figured we'd better get married so we could concentrate on our studies."

"Focused personalities?" Destiny laughed. "Tell me about it. Your place looks like a showroom."

"It's easier to clean up a mess immediately than let it linger," Chloe said. "Ask Julia Whittaker about that."

Destiny stared at her. "Is that what you think we are to her? Lingering messes?"

"Given I've only known about you for half an hour, I have no way to pose a theorem. Want to give me a hint?"

"I can't. I promised."

"At least tell me about our father."

"Oh, this is rich." Destiny leaned over the table, her voice taking on a conspiratorial tone. "We have different fathers. Julia said your father is your story. I don't know anything about him. Not yet, at least."

"And your father?" Chloe said.

Destiny shrugged. "Same old, same old. Guy charms girl, guy beds girl, guy dumps girl."

"And Luke?"

"Who said anything about Luke?"

"You did," Chloe said. "Your face did."

"Nothing to tell. Not anymore." Destiny smiled. "So tell me how you ended up married already."

"Same old, same old," Chloe said.

Monday, 9:15 a.m.

People weren't dying fast enough. What a horrendous notion—that Julia had to pray for someone to die, and die soon—from head trauma. How God must despise her prayers.

What would happen if Chloe refused to sit down with her, get to know her? That would be all the excuse Destiny needed to hop a plane back to Los Angeles, and Julia would have lost two precious days that she should be spending with Dillon. How odd—how heartless—that there wasn't enough time or mercy or liver to go around.

Matt was in a rare fury. "You gave them our social security numbers? And our bank accounts? What's next—the 401(k)s?"

"I gave them that as well." Julia had returned to the Hilton and called her husband to ask that he help pray Destiny would be patient while all this financial and legal maneuvering took place. The background check would show how stable and reliable the Whittakers were.

Except neither she nor Matt felt very steady right now.

Dr. Annie had discharged Dillon from the hospital to wait for a liver. Matt had settled him in the family room with his electronics and multitude of medications that were palliative, not restorative. Their son was on the brink of catastrophic liver failure. If that happened, there would be no turning back.

"Julia. I asked you a question." Matt smiled wanly, his eyes unable to lie. As a man of measured action, this waiting ate at him. Jack Deschene clearly was a man of measured action as well. The two would probably get along fabulously.

Julia pressed her fingertips to the screen. "They won't let me talk with Chloe until they do a background check."

"They couldn't just get one of those generalized checks—the kind we have to do to teach Sunday school? Why do we have to lay bare our financials before them?"

"Honey. That takes at least two weeks. Does . . ." The thought *Does Dillon even have that long?* jammed in her throat. The screen flashed a soft blue as Matt pressed the phone to his chest. She could almost hear his heart pound.

If only they had a liver for Dillon today.

If only Chloe or Destiny were a match.

If only one of her daughters could show amazing grace.

If only, God. If only You would show mercy or at least show Your face. Are You afraid I'll punch You? Would that jar You into action to save my baby?

"It's okay, love." Matt's voice was low, soothing. "I gave them everything they asked for. And then some. It'll be okay."

"Nothing's okay. You know it and I know it. No one in their

right mind would even consider this. Chloe doesn't know, Destiny is pretending I never asked, and this Jack Deschene is so controlling, I want to shake him."

"What's your impression of Chloe?"

"She doesn't strike me as a girl who is used to making her own decisions."

"So we have to consider: are you wasting your time in North Carolina?"

Julia shrugged, groaned as she shifted her hand. The long-lasting numbing agent the surgeon had injected had begun to wear off. "What choice do I have? We have to play this out, if only for the opportunity for Destiny to get used to . . . to . . ."

"The weirdness of it all?"

She laughed. "You do realize that it's a miracle that she agreed to hop a plane with me? And given what . . . ah . . . *reserved* people the Deschenes are, it's a miracle that they let me in the door."

"There's our hope. Hold on to those two small miracles and wait for the big one."

And if it didn't come? Julia couldn't go back to the way she used to be, that hollowed-out shell. Losing Tom and giving up Destiny had seemed like the end of the world. Losing Chloe had been the end of herself.

After that adoption, God trickled back into her life like sunlight under the door. Julia pressed her face to the floor of her soul and let love creep over her until she was ready to love God again.

Now Jesus was like a receding tide with not enough ebb to pull her along. She pressed the phone to her cheek, closed her eyes. "Pray for me, Matt. Please."

"Heavenly Father, you promise in your Word that by your Son's stripes we will be healed. May our son become living proof of that promise."

Monday, 9:45 a.m.

This whole thing is like something out of the twilight zone.

Julia, the organ-grabbing bio-mom. Chloe, the convention-clinging new sister. Jack, the gargoyle snarling at the gate.

That's your problem, Mom used to say. *It's all a story for you, all an opportunity for embellishment and revision.*

And the Bible isn't? Destiny would throw back at her. *Tell that to the Amorites, Hittites, Perizzites, Canaanites, and all the -ites that Joshua wiped out. Dude, historical revisionism is the stuff contemporary righteousness rides on.*

Chloe had gone back to her place to await Jack's permission to meet with her birth mother. She had insisted it would be a decision they made together. Out of deference to their newfound sisterhood, Destiny had swallowed her snort and refused their lawyer's offer of a ride to the hotel. The hike to the Hilton was three miles of shops and restaurants, of brisk air and holiday lights.

The perfect way to clear her head.

The perfect place for the crazies to sneak in.

Like that urban myth of people who woke up in bathtubs filled with ice and discovered their kidneys had been cut out of their bodies. Destiny framed the scene in her mind. Start with a long shot of white, chipped tile. Slowly sweep to the open door. Beyond, a bed and bloody sheets. Keep moving to the sink, green mold on the faucets and blood stains on the porcelain.

Follow a trickle of mildew at midheight until a hand comes into view. Slumped at the wrist, the skin is stark white. Until the little finger flutters.

What a shock. What a cliché.

Destiny rubbed her back as if she could feel that crudely stitched slash of bloody tissue, that feeling of something vital missing. Her phone rang.

Luke. Right. Something vital missing.

This was his third call, following a couple of *where R U* texts that she had ignored.

She should let it go to voice mail like the others. Then again, if she answered, she could tell him to leave her alone. "What?"

"And good morning to you too." Luke's voice was annoyingly cheerful, that *praise the Lord* ready to leap out of his mouth and down her throat. "Where are you?"

"Not your business."

"Of course it's my business. I love you, Dez."

Destiny clenched her jaw so she wouldn't say the words, *you love me but you love Jesus more.* That would give him the opportunity to go all testimonial on her. She knew the legalities of being separated from God and the doctrine of Christ as the only way back. She disliked new Christians with their sunny eyes and doggy smiles, their tails wagging in expectation of blessing, their ignorant hearts not understanding that God is tough and cold and stays far away when you mess up.

How God must love the shrink-wrapped Chloe Deschene, hemmed in by a million-dollar condo and a husband who doesn't sweat. In her black tank top, J. Crew cranberry cardigan, and gray toothpick cords, Chloe could model for a catalog of good-living Christian girls.

Chloe, a.k.a. Hope McCord, came to the marriage bed as a virgin. She admitted it over coffee, seemed proud of that sad fact.

Luke came to the unwed bed as a tiger and slinked away as a neutered housecat or—as he claimed—a virgin in Christ.

"Babe, where are you?"

"Stop asking."

"Stop trying to hide."

"Don't make me block your number, Luke."

"Just because I'm concerned about you?"

"You and Jesus go save the world. I'll call you when I'm back."

"Just tell me wher—"

Destiny ended the call. Let him go play at righteousness. She had her own existential questions to work through. Now that Julia had brought her to meet Chloe, she had to consider being tested. She had promised that—too quickly, of course—but she didn't back down on promises.

What if she were compatible with Dillon? What if she were compatible and refused to let them take a part of her liver? She would be the worst person in the world.

What if she agreed to the surgery and then had one of those rare complications? If she died and Dillon lived, would Julia grieve? Or would her birth mother be happy that the lesser obligation—the one she had shipped off at birth—was six feet under?

Twilight zone thoughts.

Monday, 10:18 a.m.

Jack has people running everywhere.

He had sent Julia Whittaker to the Hilton to wait for their phone call. Henry Metzler volunteered to drive Destiny there, but she refused his help, said she would walk. She gave Jack a mock salute and left.

Jack steered Chloe to his office. She had her own because he said they shouldn't be distracted when they were trying to work. The four-bedroom, five-bath condo was a wedding gift from his parents and her mother.

Her husband had tried to refuse the gift. He wanted a stripped-down lifestyle, to live as if they had to hustle for every jar of spaghetti sauce. Mother would not relent. *If you're not moving into that darling guest house on the estate, please let me be assured you're safe. You're still so young.* The Deschenes backed her up by suggesting the condo.

Would she and her husband have been happier if they studied side-by-side instead of across four thousand square feet of silent home? Not that he was unhappy. Sometimes she wondered if any sort of unease had a place in Jack's life plan. Was there something organically wrong with her that she couldn't be content with the blessings that had been showered on her?

"Let me show you what we've learned so far." Jack handed the stack of paper to her with the same pride and satisfaction that he showered on his essays and reports.

Chloe scanned the printouts and then tossed them onto his desk. "This tells me nothing."

"It tells you she was arrested in college—"

"Twenty-five years ago."

Jack shuffled the papers back into order. "Are you going to let me finish?"

"I apologize. Go ahead."

"She was arrested once in college and that's it. For both her and Matthew Whittaker. Their financials are good, if somewhat variable. That's because of the business model. They take in huge fees, put out large expenses. They've got some significant medical expenses. We can't ascertain how these were incurred because of confidentiality."

"I know about HIPAA, Jack."

"Point being—these expenses seem significant, and something you need to think about before you have your conversation with Mrs. Whittaker."

"You're ignoring what's right before your eyes."

Jack tilted his head. "What?"

"The family resemblance, Jack. The eyes you say you love so much."

"I'm trying to protect you. Can't you even grant me that?" Jack put his hands on her waist, touched his forehead to hers. "Please, darling."

She kissed him, tasted coffee, and what she called his *everlasting* mint, the Altoids he popped because Jack Deschene was the total package, whether in wing tips or sneakers, pinstripes or denim.

She admired him because he always strode for something and always clothed that something with Christ. If only he understood that she had been cut from a different cloth, that meeting her birth mother and her sister was a miracle and not some nefarious scheme to defraud them of the family fortunes.

"Think, Chloe. She wouldn't have shown up out of nowhere if she didn't want something," he said. "And want it right now."

"We're so well protected, she'd need a can opener to pry something loose from us."

"I can't protect this, darling." He laid his hand over her heart. "Sometimes I think you're too tender for your own good."

"Tender? Or weak? That's what you think, isn't it? That I'm weak."

"Of course not. You're a capable woman, and certainly the most intelligent I've ever met."

She pressed against him. "I'm capable and smart and still something to be fenced in like a goat."

"Listen to yourself." Jack stepped back. "You hang out for an hour with the girl from Hollywood and now you're fit for a soap opera? Come on, darling."

"You know it's true. I can't live in Bubble Wrap, Jack."

"Is that what you think I am—Bubble Wrap?"

"Of course not. You're a loving hedge of protection, but how high does the hedge need to be?"

He pulled her to him, arms around her waist, unaware that his bear hug made her point perfectly. "I'm trying to do the best I can to provide exactly what you need."

"Then do it—provide exactly what I need—right now." She pushed him against the desk, untucking his shirt.

"What're you doing? They'll be here shortly."

She melted into him, imagining the wind over the waves, sun on her shoulders, the schedules and obligations sinking into the horizon. "Which is why this could be so much fun."

He warmed to her, his skin flushing. She ripped at his shirt, smiled at his gasp—until he pushed her away. "You popped off my button."

"That was the point, Jack."

"That is never the point."

"Can't you . . ." She swallowed, trying not to let a single tear escape. "Can you just relax with me and have fun?"

"We're not in a movie, Chloe. We have things we need to do. Duties."

Chloe pressed her lips to his ear. "Do I . . . displease you in some way?"

"Never."

"Sometimes I think that you don't want me."

He stroked her face. "I always want you. Don't you understand?"

"I don't, Jack. I don't know why you're so careful."

"I have to be." He cradled her face. "You do understand that there will always be forces trying to pull us apart?"

"And you do understand," Chloe said, "that we *both* need to be able to stand on our own two feet? That you can't be the only one making decisions? It is my decision whether or not to have a conversation with my birth mother. It can't be yours."

"I'm sorry. I haven't been thinking straight . . . we need to pray."

"Making love is supposed to be a form of prayer. Isn't it?"

"Of course. Everything in its season. Now please, Chloe. Please." Jack extended his hands to her. "Let's keep our wits about us."

She took his hand, stood quietly. As he prayed for protection and wisdom and grace, she prayed that God would get her through the next couple of hours. And the next fifty years.

Monday, 10:18 a.m.

Balancing a cardboard tray with corn muffins and two chamomile teas, Destiny carded open the door. Her room at the Hilton was four-star standard with a cream duvet and fluffy pillows on the bed, a rich peacock print carpet, maple writing table, Queen Anne chair. A door opened to the adjoining room.

"Hello?" Destiny set down the food, peered into Julia's room. She was asleep on her side, hand stretched out toward her iPad. Destiny tiptoed in, stared at the image on the screen.

A boy, asleep on a sofa.

Her vampire brother, the body-snatcher who couldn't survive without a piece of her or Chloe's liver. His skin had a yellow cast; otherwise he looked like any young teen with a wannabe mustache, gawky arms, and bony knees. A game controller and cell phone rested on his chest.

Thirteen years old and chronically ill—of course the kid wanted to stay in touch with his friends. Supposedly he made movies. Luke could teach those daredevil friends of his a few stunts, not risky enough to break any bones. Just rich enough to garner respect and a little awe. He was so good with kids.

If Luke were here, he'd say *go for it.* Have the blood test. Trouble was—would that be Luke's common sense? Or some desire to satisfy Jesus? Luke had already given her up. What more could his God ask of him?

Destiny's cell phone vibrated. Chloe. She stepped back into her room, pressed Talk. "Hey."

"Hi. We texted and called, still haven't heard back from Mrs. Whittaker."

"Julia. Call her Julia, for Pete's sake. She's your mother."

"That's kind of TBD over here. They're ready to meet with you guys."

"Am I invited?"

"I insisted, said you were part of the package."

Destiny smiled. "She's sleeping. What time?"

"In an hour? I'm sorry—"

"I know it's not your fault. You're just doing what they're tel—what they're advising."

"Yeah. I guess. This is all so . . ."

"So fantabulously freaky? Tell me about it. She's not a bad sort. Can you ask him to go easy on her?"

"He's not a bad sort either. He's just . . . concerned."

"Okay. We'll see you in a few."

Destiny shut the phone, yelped when Julia stepped into the room, her face looking all night-of-the-living-dead.

"Sorry, I didn't mean to interrupt."

"That was Chloe. They're ready for us."

Julia pressed her injured hand to her stomach. "I slept wrong. And I can't—with this on my hand—I can't do my hair—"

Destiny pointed at the vanity. "Sit. I'll make you presentable."

"You don't have to."

"Oh yes, I really do."

"Okay. I've got my makeup case and curling iron in my room."

"I'd prefer to use my stuff." No way was Destiny going in there. What if Dillon woke up and called for his mom? She didn't want to see him. Chloe was okay, didn't come with any obligations of the flesh. Dillon was a gaping wound, and she wasn't ready for that.

Maybe she'd never be ready for that. And how would she tell Julia *thanks for the ride but no liver for you*?

Destiny dampened a facecloth and wiped Julia's face of foundation and two days of travel crud. Julia grasped Destiny's wrist. "They're going to hate me."

"If they do, it won't be because of your hair or face. Now hold still."

"Do you hate me?"

"Not at the moment." Destiny shook off her hand. "Will you hate *me* if I say no?"

"Don't ask that."

"You asked, I answered. Now it's your turn."

"How could I?" Julia stared at the mirror, gaze locked on Destiny. "And how could I not?"

Monday, 10:38 a.m.

After changing and freshening up, Chloe went into her office and locked the door. Jack was in his office, sorting through another of the various reports on the Whittakers. This kind of instant information gathering had to be costing tens of thousands of dollars. Her husband might drink coffee from a warehouse store, but he wasn't shy about resources when it came to protecting his turf.

Why shouldn't she just leave? She could dash across the park and keep running until she got to the Hilton. She could fly back to California with Destiny, get to know her. Or maybe New England. She would rent a house and not tell Mother or Jack or Julia Whittaker where she was.

She'd stare at the icy waves pounding over the rocks and wonder why God felt as deep and cold as the ocean.

If Jack wouldn't listen, she knew someone who might.

HANDS _ ON: Hey there. Thought I'd try for a quick hello. Working?
WAVERUNNER: Not on deck for a few minutes. You OK?
HANDS _ ON: Life is weird, that's all.
WAVERUNNER: Anything I can do?
HANDS _ ON: Tell me what you see, right now.
WAVERUNNER: Ha. A mess on my table.
HANDS _ ON: You can't see the water?
WAVERUNNER: Not sitting down. Wait.

Chloe imagined him getting up, going to the porthole. They had both agreed not to share photos. Their intimacy came from knowing the person within—or beyond—the shell. They knew the basics: age, the region where each other lived, their vocations. *And so much more.* Like how he liked mustard on his fries and rain on his face; how she abhorred snakes and loved spiders; how fixing things made them both feel closer to the driving mechanism of the world.

Jack thought she was silly for screaming at dead snakes and fixing toasters when she should be studying. Every time her husband told her she was meant for more, it somehow made her feel less.

WAVERUNNER: Okay. Still there?

HANDS _ ON: Absolutely. What's happening out there?

WAVERUNNER: The sky is gray, water is calm. Storm coming, they say. We're probably heading to anchor.

HANDS _ ON: I hate being anchored.

WAVERUNNER: Sometimes what's going on around us dictates what we have to do.

HANDS _ ON: Will you be caught in the storm? Is it bad?

WAVERUNNER: Remember that movie *The Perfect Storm*? It won't be that, but we'll have to take care about that front forming near Nova Scotia. And what about where you are?

HANDS _ ON: Cold front.

WAVERUNNER: I could change that for you. For real. It's just a short flight. If you'd ever consider . . .

HANDS _ ON: I'd like to—

A hard knock on the door startled her. She shut her laptop. "Come on in."

Jack stuck his head in the door. "Henry's back and your mother is here."

He meant Mother and not Julia because Julia was an outlier, a reminder that Chloe was more than Middlebrooks and Deschene and that something unknown had burst into the spreadsheet of their lives.

"I'm coming," she said, remembering to send her chat to the trash, empty it, and blank out her browsing history.

And wasn't that what happened to her? Julia Whittaker emptied her life of her second daughter, and Mother and Father and now Jack were doing a splendid job of blanking out the history.

Chloe took a deep breath and walked out to embrace the variables.

Monday, 10:59 a.m.

What do you say to a group of people when you know *what* you say—no matter how you say it—will make them hate you?

Chloe's husband, Jack. Sitting as judge.

Twenty-two-years old, he took his responsibility as head of the household seriously. He had replaced his rimless glasses with darker frames, a futile act of gravitas for one so fair-haired. He had changed his shirt from this morning's button-down blue to a muted gray with subtle pinstripes.

Did he iron his own slacks like Matt did because no one could make a better crease? They would get along wonderfully, both financial whizzes, according to what Destiny had gleaned. Matt would tell Jack to lighten up because *this is the day, man* and *we should rejoice in it.*

And what joy they could have in this moment! Her two daughters in the same room, so lovely in such different ways.

Still in ripped jeans and motorcycle boots, Destiny had changed to a knit wrap, knotted to show a minimum of cleavage. The orange-spice print that would be garish on pale skin blended well with her black hair and shadowed eyes.

Chloe had changed into a green plaid jumper over an ivory turtleneck sweater. The expensive outfit teetered between L.L.Bean and prep-school uniform. This was a style that Matt loved; he often bemoaned that their brides were either too gaudy or exposed too much skin.

Were Dillon a part of the gathering, Julia's delight would be complete.

Instead, her son's—their brother's—shadow loomed over them with a chill of mortality.

Susan Middlebrooks hadn't stopped staring at Julia since

she and Destiny were escorted to their chairs. They had shaken hands briefly; the woman's hand had been cold and she'd quickly withdrawn it after a crisp hello. She was dressed impeccably in a houndstooth suit of soothing gray tones, likely Armani or Donna Karan. Her eggplant pumps and purse were exquisitely expensive and so old school that they were almost fashion forward. She was a lovely woman with soft skin and faded brown eyes—almost elderly. She had to have been fifty when she and her husband, John, adopted Chloe.

Perhaps that explained why Chloe was apparently content to be managed rather than partnered in her marriage. She clung to Jack's hand as he made introductions. Her glances at Julia had been hurried, her handshake a wisp.

Chloe retreated to a sofa and locked her gaze on Destiny with a shy smile that held a flicker of amusement. Perhaps this would be the blessing—bringing sisters together.

If only they would consider meeting their brother.

Destiny. Chloe. Dillon. Three fathers, three lifetimes. Three heartbreaks, Tom and Andy of her own stupid doing but, *Why Dillon, dear Lord? Why afflict him for all my mistakes?*

Julia sank into the armchair Jack had indicated. She had no status here except as a supplicant. How would—or could—she ever say what needed to be said? *I loved you enough to give you life. Now please, forgive me enough to share some of that life with my son.*

Jack stopped his small talk midsentence. "Excuse me?"

Julia leaned to Destiny and whispered, "Did I say that out loud?"

"For the whole world to hear."

"I didn't quite catch that." Jack stood up. "Could I ask you to repeat what you said?"

"Hey," Destiny said. "Let's chill. Get to know each other."

"Mrs. Whittaker." Jack's eyes narrowed. "What did you say?"

"Jack. Please." Chloe took his arm, tried to move him back to his chair.

Cold inched up Julia's throat.

Patience.

Matt's voice, because lately that was the only way she could hear God's voice. *Prayers in a dark closet, on the mountain top, in Matt's car, in his arms, prayers in Jerusalem because, Lord, Your Son was born there and You let Him die so my son wouldn't have to, so please hear me hear me hear me hear m—*

"Come on," Destiny said. "A little patience here."

Jack kneeled next to Julia and took her hand. His was surprisingly large and warm. "I'm sorry, Mrs. Whittaker. We're all a bit on edge. It's such an . . . unexpected situation. May I get you a cup of tea?"

Suddenly Chloe was on her other side, slender fingers grasping Julia's shoulder. "I'll make you some coffee. Destiny says that's what you like. Would that be okay? Or I could get you some orange juice or water."

"Thank you," Julia said. "I would like coffee."

"I'll help," Destiny said and the two girls were off.

Jack sat back in his chair, making small talk with his lawyer with enough nods and glances at Julia to make sure she understood she could be part of the conversation if she cared to be.

She could barely breathe, let alone speak. She studied the room, tried to glean something of Chloe's personality from the décor. Judging by the contemporary styling, either the girl was a professional designer—or a guest in her own home.

Susan Middlebrooks nodded at her. "I'm sorry, Mrs. Whittaker. You've been here ten minutes and I still haven't thanked you." Her voice was rich and confident, despite the tremble of her hands. "It must have been a difficult thing to do, to give my daughter up."

Her daughter? Julia deserved that—she was the intruder here. These people must think that she was either a tramp or a fool to have gotten pregnant twice outside marriage and to have surrendered two children.

"I'm grateful," Julia said. "For all you've done for Chloe."

"Coffee's ready." Destiny stood in the doorway holding a tray of coffee mugs, sugar, and creamer. Chloe followed her into the room, coffee pot in hand. Jack and Mr. Metzler took cups, Mrs. Middlebrooks abstained. Chloe went back into the kitchen, returned with a glass of water for her mother.

Destiny poured for Julia, added three heaping teaspoons of sugar.

"No, thank you," Julia said.

"Take it. You're in full zombie mode," she whispered. "So shut up, take it, and sharpen up."

They drank in silence for a couple of minutes. Susan Middlebrooks took Chloe's hand, lacing her fingers through her daughter's.

Destiny tapped her fingers on the arm of the chair. When her foot joined the rhythm, she put her mug on the coffee table and said, "Okay, people. I've got a flight to catch, a sweet private jet with leather seats and Wi-Fi. So maybe we could get the discussion going?"

That's Tom coming through. Julia reminded herself that she was not the only one in the equation.

"Don't everyone speak at once." Destiny dinged her mug with a spoon. "What do you need to know about Julia that your cyber-colonoscopy hasn't told you?"

Jack shot her a dirty look. "We needed to make sure this is a fruitful meeting and not some sort of trap."

"I understand," Julia said. "Believe me—I understand."

"This is counterproductive," Chloe said. "It seems like it would be better for me to sit down with Julia by myself." Without making eye contact, Jack shushed her with a touch of his hand.

Henry Metzler leaned back in his chair, crossed one leg over the other. "Mrs. Whittaker, I apologize for what must look like a united front. Please understand, we have been approached more than once by people—claiming a family tie—who wanted to profit from the circumstances of Mrs. Deschene's parents and her husband."

Chloe swiveled to face her husband. "We have? Why didn't you tell me? I would have wanted to know."

Jack shrugged. "There was nothing for you *to* know. They were all scam artists. Criminals. Why would we expose you to any of that?"

"Because I'm your wife, Jack."

He stared at her for a long moment before turning to Julia. "Mrs. Whittaker, we're taking up time that should be devoted to you. What would help us get to know you better before you explain why you've made this trip?"

Julia fumbled in her bag for her iPad. "You've all had the pleasure of meeting Chloe's sister. I've known Destiny for two days now—the day of her birth and yesterday. And I've been blessed."

Destiny gave her a quick smile that faded as quickly as it had come. She knew *why* Julia was here and had studiously avoided the subject as they flew cross-country. Her silence on the matter was ominous.

"Chloe, you also have a brother. Dillon."

"Your son with your husband," Mrs. Middlebrooks said.

"Yes." Julia handed her the iPad. "That's Dillon—Chloe's and Destiny's half-brother—taken last month."

Chloe peered over her mother's shoulder, then glanced at Destiny. "He's got our eyes."

Destiny smirked. "Genetic manifest destiny, forgive the pun."

"He looks like a nice boy," Mrs. Middlebrooks said.

Julia launched into the spiel that felt more like a college essay than a mother preparing to plead for her son's life. How creative Dillon was. The volunteer work at the hospital. The left-handedness and big feet that made him a constant visitor to the emergency room, stitches on his forehead, a broken wrist, and battered knees. And too many other visits to the clinics and ERs and *how do I find mercy from all these people who assembled to guard Chloe from me?*

Henry Metzler took the iPad. "What is the point of this, Mrs. Whittaker? What kind of help does Dillon need?"

"We're all people of faith—"

Destiny folded her arms and whispered. "Do not speak globally on that."

Something's there, Julia realized. Something that needed tending, but Julia could only focus on one child at a time. The legitimate child—what a cruel term. Destiny and Chloe being born out of wedlock didn't make them any less of God's children, or her own.

And yet, the two girls had lifetimes ahead of them. Dillon—*How long how long? Dear God, please make the sun stand still and make "not long" enough time.*

"Dillon has had liver disease since he was born—"

Jack shot from his chair. "No."

"—and he desperately needs a liver transplant—"

He crossed the room in a flash. "Get out."

Chloe jumped up after him, pulled at his sleeve. "Jack, don't."

"Don't you understand what she wants from you?"

"What is she saying?" Susan Middlebrooks looked at Henry Metzler, who gave Julia a stern look.

"Mrs. Whittaker," he said. "This is extremely inappropriate."

"—and we can't find a compatible donor, and please understand, time is so short—"

Jack stood over Julia, fists clenched. "I said, get out."

Destiny got between them. "And *this* is why I'm not a fan of you Christians. Because you're all gooey-lovey when it looks good but when someone asks you to dig deep—"

"Dig deep? She wants my wife to donate part of her liver. Why not you, Destiny? You're one of her bastards. Let her harvest you."

"Jack! Stop it." Chloe pushed into the mix and it all became a blur. Jack trying to get to Julia, Destiny pushing back at him, Chloe holding on to both, Mr. Metzler standing to the side as if ready to catch someone if they tumbled.

"Please." Julia wanted to stand but she was blocked by the tangle. "Let me explain, please someone just let me explain."

"Stop it." Mrs. Middlebrooks stood, a dainty woman with a suddenly large voice. "All of you, sit down!"

Destiny backed away, hands up.

Jack glared at Julia. "Get—"

"Jackson Isaac Deschene, I won't ask you again." Mrs. Middlebrooks pointed to the sofa as if he were a child.

He is a child. All three of them were and she was asking them to do something that would be impossible for anyone—to honor blood ties that she had severed when she surrendered them to the Connors and to the Middlebrooks.

Chloe gave her a pained look and sat on the arm of Destiny's chair. Jack seemed stranded in the middle of the room.

"I'm so sorry," Julia said. "I wouldn't be here if it weren't such . . ." Her throat closed. The pain of going back to Dillon and Matt with no hope was impossible to bear.

"Tell me," Chloe said. "Tell me and my sister what this means."

"No," Jack said. "We're not listening to this."

"You're right. You are not listening to this." Chloe stood. "I am. We're going out. Destiny and Julia and I. And no one is coming with us."

She gave Jack such a dark stare. Something's there. Something that needed tending but first—

First, Dillon.

Monday, 11:13 a.m.

Chloe hadn't splashed in a puddle in twelve years.

She used to jump with both feet, howl with laughter when she made the water fly. That made Father chuckle. Mother would wrinkle her brow and tell her to come inside and change those wet pants before she caught a devil of a cold.

When Chloe heard in church that the devil prowled like a hungry lion, she clung to her father and swore she'd never get her pants wet again.

It took him fifteen minutes to figure out what the fuss was about, another five to explain that a *devil of a whatever* was merely an unfortunate expression. He bought Chloe fisherman boots and a red rain slicker that was more watertight than a submarine. She had grown out of the boots years ago but she had kept them, cherished them as deeply as Mother cherished Father's wedding ring.

This was a devil of a mess and a devil of a decision.

Chloe sat at a table in the park with Destiny and Julia, shivering under her ski jacket. She knew her own psychology, understood that she had been as protected as an orchid in the Arctic, and she had submitted willingly. The thing with *WaveRunner* was a diversion, just a form of entertainment. A place where she could go and pretend to be herself—whoever that was.

The appearance of Julia Whittaker had made her dual realities totter. And now her birth mother asked her to go into a dark unknown where there would be no pretending.

"So how much do they take?" Destiny said.

"A lobe." Julia's voice wavered. "Maybe a third of your liver."

"It'll grow back," Chloe said. "The liver is one of the few organs that regenerates."

Destiny poked her arm. "So you're making her case for her?"

"I'm just giving the facts. What is the mortality rate, Mrs. Whittaker?"

"Please. Just call me Julia. This is hard enough."

"So you're the victim here?" Destiny said. "That's a *ha*-and-a-half."

"This is hard enough on all of us," Chloe said. "Let's just get the facts out and then we can discuss."

"Do either of you know your blood type?" Julia said. "If you're not type O, the discussion is irrelevant."

"So we're only relevant if we've got the right blood?" Destiny said.

"Stop it. She's only trying to make it easier on us," Chloe said.

"That's her history. Get knocked up, pop out the kid, and sayonara until she needs a body part." Destiny turned to Chloe. "How old were you when they told you that you were adopted?"

"Four or so," Chloe said. Father had taken her for ice cream after church, told her so matter-of-factly that it rolled off her like rain. "Someone had adopted a little girl from China and my parents explained . . . the usual spiel. We chose you because you were special, la-di-dah and all that."

Destiny leaned across the table, stare locked on Julia. "I was eleven because my mother didn't have the guts to tell me before then. Or maybe she didn't think I was special enough."

"You're making this harder than it needs to be," Chloe said.

"I just want her to know that she's not the only one who paid a price. We did too."

Was that really true? Chloe wondered. She recognized the

profound privilege the Middlebrooks name and money conferred on her, and she valued the deep love that her parents had showed her. Yet there was a void in not understanding why her birth mother had asked for a closed adoption—as if Chloe were something she needed to put behind her like she never happened.

Julia wrapped her hand over Chloe's. "I'm sorry. This is so sudden. So bizarre."

"If you say you're sorry one more time," Destiny said, "I'm taking Chloe and we're leaving."

"Don't speak globally on that," Chloe said, drawing a laugh from her sister. "I don't know my blood type, Mrs. Whi—Julia. I've never had surgery. And I'm ashamed to say I never seem to have time to donate blood."

"And you're going to have time to donate part of your liver?" Destiny said. "How long will we miss work if we do this? And remember—this is not a discussion about donating. This is merely us considering whether we'll even have a blood test. Right, Chloe?"

"We're still in the discovery phase." Chloe wrapped her fingers around her sister's arm. So strange, so wonderful to have a sister. Especially one who said what she thought, even when it's contrary.

It was the silence at home that drove her to seek friends elsewhere. She had been taught to be always polite and forward-looking. Didn't Jack ever feel compelled to move beyond the boundaries? That was what marriage should be—a growing out of yourselves, two halves becoming a new and wonderful whole.

Too often it felt like Jack had adopted Chloe rather than married her.

"I gave blood once," Destiny said. "A friend was in a terrible accident on the 405. He was in surgery forever. A crew of us went down to the Red Cross because we didn't know anything else we could do. I was so freaked, it never occurred to me to ask what my type was. We thought that giving our blood would somehow shift fate into his favor."

"What happened?" Julia said.

"What do you think? The whole blood thing was stupid. He died."

"So what is the mortality rate?" Chloe asked.

Julia dropped her gaze. "It's zero point five percent."

"And that means . . . ?" Destiny said.

Chloe did the math. "Five people out of a thousand die."

"The odds are much better when the donor is younger," Julia said. "And you would be given a comprehensive checkup before."

"And what about after," Destiny said. "How long will we be out of work? Or in Einstein's case here, school?"

"One to two months. Matt and I understand it would be a hardship for any donor. Legally, we can't compensate for donation, but we can provide living expenses."

"It's not about the money," Destiny said. "I have a career. Missing a couple months . . . people will slide into my place and I might not get back in the stack."

Two months. That might as well be two lifetimes in terms of Jack's plan. If Chloe missed the next semester, she could kiss her scheduled start of medical school good-bye.

And would that be a bad thing? Perhaps she would give a portion of her liver just to get some breathing space. What a ghastly thought. How could Jack or Mother—or God—forgive such persistent ingratitude?

"Two months of your life," Julia said. "Two months gives Dillon a chance to go to college. He's bright, Chloe, like you. Two months gives Dillon a chance to have a career. Someday, Destiny, someday the two of you could make films together. He's like you. So creative, so full of life. Two months gives your brother a lifetime."

Destiny cursed, shot to her feet, and stomped away. The bushes in the park were barren, the grass a hazy brown. The white Christmas lights that had seemed so cheerful a few hours ago now seemed futile.

Without their help, Dillon Whittaker could be dead before the dogwood trees bloomed in the spring. If he was as sick as Julia described, he must be high on the transplant list. Maybe today would be the day that someone with type-O blood died.

Maybe that death, that sacrifice, would spare Destiny and Chloe from having to make a decision. This was an impossible situation. Even the most merciful heart would balk at this request.

Destiny circled back to the table. "If we say no . . . we're the worst kind of sludge."

"If you would just consider being tested today," Julia said. "We can see if any of the pain of taking the next step is even necessary."

"And no one you know has qualified?" Chloe said. "How is that possible?"

"You think I'm not asking that question?" Julia slapped her hand on the table. "You think I'm not shouting at God that this is just so totally wrong and cruel? Neither Matt nor I have type-O blood, and our friends and family members who volunteered and do have type O have unusual complications—too many tattoos, a history of cancer, a surprise pregnancy."

"Ah, the fateful surprise pregnancy," Destiny said.

Mother would say she'd pray about it and then say no. Henry Metzler would say it was too high a risk. Jack would say no and think—too kind to say it—that this was proof Chloe was a helpless lamb in need of his shepherding.

Father would say *find Christ in the question before you demand the answer.*

How? Even Jesus felt like a straitjacket, not letting Chloe take a single breath without wondering if she would disappoint the people who loved her.

"Oh, God." She buried her head under her arms. "God, help."

She felt her sister's arm around her waist, guiding her away from the table. "I have an idea," Destiny whispered. "And it's pretty cool."

As she explained her idea, Chloe had to agree it was pretty out-of-the-box. The thought of taking off with her sister, finding an unplanned adventure—no matter where it led—was irresistible. And there was no way Jack could say no. Not to this.

This was her birthright.

She took a deep breath, felt something tear away inside and thought, *This decision hurts and feels good at the same time.* Like a boat being torn from its mooring and drifting toward a boundless horizon.

"She owes us *knowing*," Destiny said. "Before we can decide about her son, she owes us this much."

"Okay," Chloe said. "Let's tell her."

They walked back arm-in-arm, just the right size for each other.

"I was afraid you wouldn't come back," Julia said when they sat down.

"If we agree to be tested and one or both of us is compatible, will that put us under any obligation?" Chloe asked.

The eagerness in Julia's eyes bordered on tragic. "No, of course not."

"Okay. Just one thing."

"Anything, just tell me."

Chloe cleared her throat. "Just say it," Destiny said.

"We will agree to the blood test. After you take us to meet our fathers."

Monday, 12:18 p.m.

The jet was on stand-by for Boston—and Tom Bryant—after all these years.

"You never told me the name of Hope's father," Matt said. The lines in his face had deepened in the two days she'd been gone. "You said it needed to remain confidential."

"It did." Julia burrowed into the blanket like a child, iPad close to her face. The girls had gone back to Chloe's apartment to pack for the trip. It would be a miracle if Chloe actually returned with Destiny—and they so needed a miracle now.

There was an eerie gallows humor in his FaceTiming from inside the pantry, discussing matters of life, death, and potential scandal while he was surrounded by boxes of oatmeal. They took their phone calls from Dr. Annie and other medical professionals here—it had the best Wi-Fi reception and was farthest from the family room where Dillon was curled up on the sofa.

"I respected your privacy," he said. "Respected the work that God had done in your life."

"Oh, Mattie," she said, trying to choke her tears with the blanket. "I love you so much."

She wanted to climb through the screen and into his arms, to feel his stubble on her cheeks and mingle her breath with his because they had been blessed with such life. *Oh, God, such a perilous life because whatever you have created us to be must include Dillon, so please, please save him and please let Andy forgive what I'm about to do.*

"And I love you so much, and even more," he said. "But this . . . this going to see the men. They had no right to ask you this."

"I'm asking them to do something outrageous," Julia said. "They get to ask me for something outrageous in return."

"No. We've disrupted Destiny's life and the Deschene-Middlebrookses' universe. Now you're going to dig deeper into the past, bring more families into this? I'm not sure we have the right to go that far."

"Dillon. He gives us the right. He's their blood too. And if I'm asking them to consider that, then they have the right to ask me to give them the full story."

Matt glanced away, stone-faced. "What if they want something from you?"

"Who?"

"Thomas Bryant. And the one you still haven't named."

"For goodness' sake, Matt. It's been over twenty years."

"Do you blame me for being . . . concerned?"

"Of course not. I do blame you for letting some petty jealousy keep me from getting Dillon the help he needs."

He stared into the screen, an iciness in his eyes that she rarely saw. "Back then, what you shared with each of them. That wasn't petty for you. You would have chosen either one in a heartbeat. What if . . . seeing them brings up that old stuff?"

"I'm a different woman. You said that you respected the work God had done in my life. The work you helped walk me through."

"That doesn't mean I'm happy about you digging into that old mess."

"Mess? Is that what you think I was before *you* saved me?"

"I didn't save you, Julia. I never said I did."

"But you take pride in being the stable one."

"This is not the time, Julia."

"You made it the time."

"I'm just bringing up a concern about two more families you and those girls will disrupt."

"Those girls? Those *girls* are a part of me."

"You think I don't know that? When I had the investigator doing all that work, tracking through documents and your mother's journals and talking to people at the churches. It took six months, Julia. Six months of digging into your past love—"

"Stop it, Matt."

"—tracking down the flesh-and-blood reminders that you had two lovers who consumed you so much that—"

"Now stop it right there, Matthew Whittaker. You were not a virgin when we met."

She tried to curl her right hand into a fist. Agony shot through her broken fingers. There was a reason the surgeon wrapped her hand in a heavy cast—to protect her from herself.

There were reasons to let the past stay shrouded. And yet, sometimes wounds need to be opened to heal properly.

Matt closed his eyes, shook his head. "It wasn't the same."

"Why?"

"I was a loose kid . . . doing what loose kids do."

"And that's better?"

"They were easier . . . ," he said, blinking back tears.

"To walk away from?"

He nodded. "Shameful. But that's over. I repented, remedied the best I could, and let Jesus walk me forward."

"I'm sorry, Matt. I don't mean to hurt you. They're the past."

"Then why won't you tell me who Chloe's father is?"

Julia burst into tears.

"Oh, Julia."

"There's shame still on me for this one."

"Julia. It's okay. Whoever he is, we'll work through it."

She swiped at her tears, did her best to look her husband in the eyes. "Hope's father—Chloe Deschene's biological father—is Andrew Hamlin."

"Andrew . . ." Matt squinted. "You mean . . . *the* Andrew Hamlin?"

"Yes, I'm afraid I do."

Monday, 12:19 p.m.

Why did Destiny let Chloe go back home by herself? The power trio probably barricaded her in the bathroom. She could see them plying her with honey and castor oil, trying to drive out the devil that was her birthright.

Destiny's phone binged. Luke, texting yet again. For the two years they were together, she had loved his persistence. Depended on it. Now it only annoyed her.

LA: I know where u r.

Don't answer, she told herself but her fingers had already done the work.

DC: Not unless u r stalking me.
LA: I spoke to Melanie.

Destiny laughed. He was faking and knew full well she wouldn't fall for it. Melanie Connors would be on the front lines if she knew about this, fighting shoulder-to-shoulder with Chloe's mother and the other two. Like the Soup Nazi on *Seinfeld*: "No liver for you!"

The irony was that Luke would tell her to have the surgery. Yes, he could knock back beers or race in the desert or swan dive off cliffs. But when things got real, he listened carefully and found ways to help. His pockets were perpetually empty from tossing cash to anyone who had a good story and sad eyes.

Empty pockets, full heart, he used to say.

Destiny closed out the text, dialed his number. "Hey."

"Hey." His voice was deep and warm.

"What did Mom tell you?"

"That your birth mother showed up after all these years. Are you okay?"

"Why wouldn't I be?"

"Dez. Come on. It's like . . . a life event."

"Only if I let it be."

"So where are you?"

"Why, Luke? Why do you want to know?"

"I love you and want to make sure you're okay. Is that a sin?"

She laughed, her voice like brittle sugar. "You said it was."

"You need to let me explain. When do you get back from . . . ?"

"Nice try, man."

"Destiny." He *whuffed* into the phone. A patient man, blowing out air through his beard was usually the limit of his exasperation. "I don't want you to be alone . . . in whatever you're going through. I want to be there with you."

There is getting a little crowded. "I'll call you, Luke. I'll call you if I need you."

"What if I need you, babe?"

"You don't need me. You've got Jesus to keep you warm at night."

"Destiny, don't—"

Destiny pressed the power button on her phone. She needed a minute alone. No Luke playing I-want-you-but-I-can't-have-you games. No Chloe calling to say Mummy and Jackie wouldn't let her go out to play. No Julia crying that she was sorry, so sorry.

No anyone wanting to know if she was all right.

Destiny Connors was all right. She made sure of that and she didn't need her family or lover or God in heaven to make sure of that for her.

Monday, 12:42 p.m.

Mother sniffled. Jack ranted. Mr. Metzler calmly protested. It ran off Chloe like rain.

". . . a restraining order . . ." Jack waved his arms as if pulling her strings. A female Pinocchio was all she was. Crafted, not born as a Middlebrooks, adopted without flesh-and-blood as a Deschene.

My name is really Hope McCord, she wanted to say. I don't know my father, but my birth mother promises I will, and that's enough for me.

Nothing could be heard amid the tears and fear of those who claimed to love her. And clearly they did love her—as long as she was Chloe Middlebrooks Deschene and not some college student who had never been anywhere without a passport, a first-aid kid, and three pairs of clean underpants.

"Chloe, you're getting caught up in the moment," Jack said. "You need to dial it back. So you can think."

"I'm sick of thinking." The sound of her own voice startled her. Chloe didn't recognize herself with the volume turned up.

"Jack is correct, dear." Mother dabbed her eyes with a lace handkerchief. Monogrammed with her family's initials, it was a relic of ages long past. She and Father had lived under glass, public personas in a climate-controlled biosphere. Always generous, always careful. "You could be walking into human trafficking for all we know."

"Mr. Metzler spoke with the company that hires out the private jet. Tell them," Chloe said. "You know Julia is for real, that she has carte blanche for traveling wherever she wants."

The lawyer pulled at his bottom lip, remained silent.

"Tell them!"

"Yes," he said. "I don't think there's any physical danger to Chloe in this trip. I confirmed that the plane was reliable, the pilot trustworthy."

"See." Chloe stared at her mother, then turned to Jack. "See?"

"However . . ." Henry Metzler held up his hand. ". . . emotionally or otherwise, Mrs. Deschene, I must strongly urge caution."

"That's me." Chloe zippered her suitcase. "One strongly urged caution."

"Chloe, I beg you." Jack grasped her hands. His felt dry—as if she had wrung something out of him. "Don't do this."

"I told you I needed a vacation. You should have listened."

"I'm listening now." Tears puddled in his eyes. "Please. Tell me what's wrong?"

"What's wrong? Look around you, Jack. It's three against one here. It's never just you and me."

"How can you say that? We got married so it would be us."

"Us." Chloe pressed her hand against his chest so he couldn't embrace her. "There is no *us*. There is only you—and what you decide we should do."

"Chloe, my dear," her mother said.

"Don't you see? I went from you to him—with no *me* in between?"

"Tell me," Jack said. "Tell me what you need to be you."

"I shouldn't have to," Chloe said. "You should know."

Chloe grabbed her suitcase, wheeled it down the hall with the three of them following.

"Chloe." Jack followed her into his office. "Whatever you think you need, you won't find it . . . doing this."

The sharp edge to his tone made her stop, stare at him. "Doing what, Jack? What do you think I'm about to do?"

He stared back, his jaw tight. "Wherever you go or whatever you do, remember that I love you."

She grabbed the laptop and the power cord and shoved them into her bag. She pushed past him without another glance.

Destiny's father worked in Boston. They'd be there well before nightfall.

A storm was coming to the Northeast, *WaveRunner* had said.

One might never know what—or who—would wash ashore.

six

Boston

Monday, 7:04 p.m.

Livin' the life.

Chloe's mother—the one with the Middlebrooks bucks—had reserved rooms for them at the Westin in Copley Plaza. Not just rooms. A suite. As Destiny washed her face in a marble bathroom, she thought Luke would laugh and say that she was living like a star.

The joke was on Julia. Mummy had booked her in an elegant but single room on a different floor. Julia hadn't wanted to take Middlebrooks largesse. Chloe also balked, until Destiny reminded them they all looked like garbage and maybe they should rest up before tracking down Thomas Nathan Bryant, Esq.

Julia was a bundle of nerves and Chloe was wide-eyed and tight-lipped. It was bizarro world and Destiny had set them on this course. No way, she would not back down now, even if her stomach was churning. She had every right to face the man who had spermed and spurned her.

If he freaked, good. That was the real measure of a man. Once she stared him down, she could check him off, check Julia off, and no more questions.

Except Chloe. So straight, such a yawn. Somehow, though—somehow Chloe was hers in a way Mom and Dad couldn't be, and certainly in a way Julia McCord and Thomas Bryant would never be. Destiny had a day to get to know her because she didn't put long odds on Chloe actually going through with meeting *her* sperm donor.

And she put very short odds on Jackie-boy making his way north and dragging his wife home. What was wrong with that man?

"Hey," Destiny yelled as she blotted her face with a plush, white towel. "Mrs. D!"

Chloe gave no indication of hearing her. She had had her face in that laptop since three seconds after they checked in. Destiny shook her hair out of its clip, reapplied her eyeliner and lip color, and went to find her sister.

Sister.

Sophie had inhabited that word for the last fourteen years. Destiny had been ten when her mother got pregnant, an event that seemed to take both her and Dad by massive surprise. She remembered feeling relief because when the baby came, Mom's always-hefty attention was divided. Sophie had Dad's eyes and Mom's dimples and didn't look—or act—like Destiny.

She never used the adoption card against Sophie, not like she did against her parents. When she was a teen, it was a mighty weapon, especially in those times when Dad hadn't made it home for a couple weeks, or months. The longer her father's absence, the more Destiny aggravated and manipulated her mother.

Mom and Dad would love Chloe—the ready-for-prime-time version. There was something there, though. Something that drew Destiny to her and scared the spit out of Mr. Jack Deschene and Mrs. Susan Middlebrooks.

Something real. *Real* wasn't too much to ask, was it? That's what she had had with Luke. They knew where they stood at all times. No stunts from him, no sleight-of-hands from her. Both out there on that cliché of a limb and still loving each other.

Why did he go looking elsewhere?

If he had wanted a woman, there were thousands around. She could have forgiven him that because he was a man's man and his shaggy strength drew people to him. But she had given up trying to contend with almighty God years ago. She could not be the upstanding citizen Dad was or the holy warrior Mom was or the sweet-tempered good girl that Sophie was.

She couldn't be the virgin-in-Christ that Luke wanted.

Maybe she had more in common with her birth mother than she dared admit. A better brand of birth control, for sure. But that wild streak had to have run through Julia. How else would she have rushed into bed with not one but *two* guys who were so wrong?

Being impetuous was a good thing. Beauty erupted in the sudden and unexpected.

Being stupid was an entirely other matter. And wasn't that what was so hard to forgive in Julia, that she had borne Destiny to a guy who couldn't stick?

Hi, Tom. I'm the kid you couldn't even look at. You just signed the papers, dumped me off, and went on to do whatever you pleased. Oh, and have a nice day.

Jerk.

At least Luke tried, despite being totally off the cliff with his faith thing. Destiny had to believe he'd come to his senses. What would he think of this crazy trip to Boston? What would he say about Thomas N. Bryant, attorney-at-law?

Julia's eyes sparked when she spoke about him. A lot of that was anger. That was clear from the clenching of her left hand. But not all, though. Julia would rub her hand against that horrible cast and her wedding ring would slide up and down.

Something else. And Destiny would know tomorrow when she met her biological father face-to-face. She'd know if Julia had really gotten him out of her system for good—when she got his daughter out of her body and out of her life.

"Chloe!"

Still no answer. Destiny would give her five more minutes and then she'd rip that laptop away. Before she realized it, she had grabbed her phone and speed-dialed.

Luke answered with what sounded like a smile. "Hey, Dez."

"I suppose I should tell you where I am."

"Tell me first how you are."

How do you think? she wanted to snap. That would not be cool. How could he know if she refused to tell him?

"I'm running a little freaky right now," she said.

"The birth mother thing?"

"Yeah. That, and more."

"Dez, please don't make me pull teeth. Tell me."

"She showed up out of the blue, just as you . . ."

"Was that her? The tall one with the broken hand?"

"Yeah."

"And?"

"It's complicated. This is all I can tell you right now. We went to North Carolina to pick up my half-sister and now we're in Boston—"

"Wait. What? You have a half-sister?"

"She's also illegitimate."

"Dez, don't. Whatever the circumstances of your birth—and hers—God had some plan."

She squealed through her teeth. "This was a mistake, calling you."

"No, babe. Don't. Don't go. Just tell me what's in Boston."

"My birth father."

"Whoa. That is weighty stuff. Are you all right?"

"Why wouldn't I be?"

"Cross-country with all these strangers? Are you sure everyone is who they say they are?"

"I'm sure, Luke. I know who they are. I just don't know *who* they are. Get it?"

"Got it. Maybe . . . I could fly out there, hang if you need me?"

Destiny pressed her lips to the phone. How could the way Luke loved her and the way she loved him be anything but a gift?

God, You're not seeing this right. Not if You think what Luke and I have is wrong.

"Dez?"

"Thank you, babe. I mean it. Thank you. This is something I've got to sort out by myself."

She heard his steady breathing, imagined his strong chest moving slowly up and down. For such a physical guy, he pondered things long and deep.

"You still there, Luke?"

"Always."

"Yeah, okay. I gotta go, see what bio-sis is up to."

"Will you call me tomorrow?"

"Maybe."

"Please, Dez."

"I called you tonight, didn't I? Just leave it at that, okay?"

"Okay."

She waited for a long breath—waiting for *I love you, Dez*—and when she waited a heartbeat longer than she could stand, she clicked off the call.

Monday, 7:26 p.m.

Chloe got up and shut the door. She didn't need Destiny hearing this. Knowing her sister—for a whopping nine hours now—the girl would rip the phone out of her hand and threaten to flush it.

"Is this why Mother booked us a nice suite?" Chloe whispered into the phone. "So you would know where to find me?"

"Are you telling me you don't want me to know where you are?"

"What I want is for you to let me have these couple days to myself, Jack. Please."

"I want you to! It's just that . . . Julia Whittaker reeks with desperation." *As does Jack's voice.* "What if she does something horrible?"

"Stolen kidneys are urban myth, Jack."

"Really? What if she uses, like . . . the date rape drug or something and somehow coerces you into donating."

"First of all, Rohypnol is not even sold in this country, and where it is prescribed in Europe, it's now colored with a dye. The drug of choice for sexual coercion is Gamma-hydroxybutyrate. GHB. Or Ambien, I think."

"Listen to yourself. You're the scientist. I'm the numbers guy. We are who we are, Chloe. Running off on some wild-goose chase won't change that. And there's nothing wrong with us that needs to be fixed."

"Really?"

"Don't keep saying that. Is that woman putting ideas into your head?"

"That woman's name is Julia."

"Julia, Destiny. We don't know either of these women, Chloe."

"And that's the point, Jack. I want to know them."

"At what cost?"

"What's that supposed to mean?"

"You're on the ground now. So okay. But what about the next leg of the flight? What if it heads to Guatemala or someplace where you have no support, no help, and what if—"

Chloe laughed. "Imagination? From you, Jack? It's kind of sexy."

"You didn't answer my question."

"Henry Metzler spoke to her son's doctor. She's reputable, published many articles, received accolades. You know that."

"Then tell me this. Did *you* speak to her?"

"Dr. Rosado? No. Why would I?"

"You shouldn't. There's already too much pressure on you. I don't need some medical professional explaining the glories of LDLT to you."

"Oh wow. Someone's been working the search engines." Chloe waited for his *don't take that tone with me*. Not that he ever had—but the deep breath he took seemed to warn of the marital equivalent.

"And you haven't researched living donor liver transplantation?" Jack said.

"No."

Of course she *had*, the instant Destiny dragged her away from the picnic table and launched her idea about meeting their fathers. Chloe did a quick search on her phone, scanned all the triumphant stories.

"Bleeding. Infection. Scarring. Blood clots. Does that sound like fun, Chloe?"

The poor outcomes were way down the list. She'd look at those later, though *later* pressed on her with an urgency that ached. Julia couldn't wait too long for a decision on being tested. Despite Destiny's protests, once the blood was taken, the die was cast.

Fathers. Blood tests. Surgery. What an odd road they were heading down.

"Letting my own brother die, when I could save him. Does *that* sound like fun, Jack?"

"Let Destiny do it. She's got a more . . . flexible lifestyle."

If it came to that, Destiny wouldn't do it. She was a runner—had run away from college, and now had run away from this Luke guy. But Chloe had to admit, the girl wasn't all about running away. She had run to a good career in her chosen field, had run to North Carolina to meet a sister.

Maybe running away meant running to something else. How could she know, when she was barely allowed to walk anywhere, let alone *run*.

"When, Chloe? When are you going to think about what you've done?"

"I haven't *done* anything yet, Jack."

"Please. Just let me come up there. I'll . . . I'll book a room across the city somewhere. So if you need me, I'll be close by. Hands off, darling."

Hands off . . . if he only knew. Chloe stared at her computer. She had just logged on to talkatnight.com when Jack called. How easy it would be to flick the keyboard and exit the site. Sometimes the connections at sea were spotty and it took awhile to connect. She needed someone to talk to, someone who wouldn't lecture. Just listen.

"I'm twenty-two years old, Jack."

"You're my wife." His voice cracked. "Isn't this the type of thing we signed on to do together?"

That wasn't his fault; that was all on her. She had told him on their second date—if a prep-school study session could be called a date—that she had been adopted. The Middlebrooks name carried a lot of weight in North Carolina and she needed him to know that she hadn't been born into it. That she, despite whatever assurances Father had given, believed she must earn it.

Jack was the same way. He bore the Deschene fortune like a Sisyphean burden.

That they received the best education possible and lived in a very expensive home was something both families had pressed on them. She had agreed to living sparely at Jack's urging. No vacations. Wearing clothing that was well-made but out of date.

His personal choices were to be lean and thus, in God's eyes, clean.

"I love you," Jack said. "You know that, right?"

Her finger hovered over the keyboard. "I know that. With all my heart, I know that. It's just . . . you know how you stop by my lab and your eyes just glaze over?"

"I try, Chloe. The work you're involved with is a benefit to so many."

Classic Jack—attach a moral component to everything. "But it's not your thing. That's what this is. Not your thing."

"Of course it's not *my* thing. So why can't it be our thing? I'd like it to be."

Her laptop *plunked. WaveRunner* coming online. Chloe felt suspended over shifting realities. "I have to go."

"I love you. Tell me you know that."

"I just said I did."

"Do you—"

"Stop it, Jack. Casting about for assurances of devotion is . . ." She settled on one of his favorites. ". . . unbecoming."

Her laptop plunked again. The sailboat icon had come to life on her screen. Right-click the talkatnight icon, choose *close window*, and be done with that.

Left-click the sailboat and . . . who knew. It could be a night of physics or mechanical engineering or flirtation.

She clicked off the call, tossed the phone on the bed, and turned her attention to the laptop. This was all a game, right? Role-playing. A way to shrug off stress and certainly, if anyone had stress, it was Chloe.

She left-clicked and the text window came alive.

Monday, 8:02 p.m.

"You did it right." Julia scanned the photos of Jeanne's daughters. So lovely and confident. So happy. So healthy. "Three beautiful girls."

"Jules, it wasn't about doing anything right. Patrick and I have been blessed . . ." Jeanne twisted her hair with her left hand, an old habit. Her right hand usually held a paintbrush or her prayer beads.

Jeanne Potts should have been a mystic. Instead, she had married Patrick Donegan, become a middle-school art teacher, raised three daughters, grew a garden, and had remained steadfast in friendship and faith.

Her life stacked against Julia's was like a rose in a briar.

Having hungry sex and pretending it was passionate love. Two daughters born out of wedlock, surrendered to strangers. What had Julia's sins brought on her girls, one with an aversion to depending on anyone and the other with an affinity to depending on almost everyone?

And then there was Dillon.

If she had been washed clean in the blood of the Lamb, as that Spirit who entwined around her soul promised, why wouldn't God wash Dillon's blood clean?

A new liver would fix everything. But with that new liver came the antirejection drugs to prevent a body from going to war against what it considered to be a dangerous invader. Though Julia had been transplanted with the heart of Christ, guilt and doubt battled like gladiators to reject that gift.

Jeanne had volunteered for testing. She had type-O blood and would have donated in a second but she was excluded because of lingering Epstein-Barr.

"I'm glad Matt called to tell me you were coming." Jeanne tapped the back of Julia's cast. "You should have called me."

"Pottsie, it's been insane. I didn't even know until lunchtime. This whole trip is pure desperation. It's nice . . . nice to just sit." Julia slumped into the chair, lulled by the fire. This shop on Newbury Street specialized in ambience and ten-dollar coffee, a sanctuary for the well-to-do shopper that they used to mock in college.

"So what are they like?" Jeanne asked.

Julia dug her iPad out of her bag. She had taken a photo—over Destiny's protests—on the plane. "Can you tell which girl is Tom's?"

"Wow. I can tell they're both yours. The eyes, and this one," she said, pointing at Destiny, "has some of your facial features. The other one has your hair, though much lighter. She's dressed so Brooks Brothers that I'm tempted to say she's from the Bryant line. But the one with your cheekbones, she's got a give-me-your-best-shot posture. So I'm guessing she belongs to Tom."

Julia laughed. "That's Destiny. And yes, she's got a big portion of his bravado."

"Destiny and Hope. What are their adoptive names?"

"Destiny's parents kept her name. Her father is the chief of staff for Senator Dave Dawson. And Mom is Melanie Connors."

"Melanie . . . that name's familiar."

"She runs the Lord's Heritage ministry."

"No kidding? Melanie Connors is on the front line of the pro-life fight, among many other worthy battles. She takes a lot of flak from the pro-*do-whatever-you-want* groups."

"I expect raising Destiny prepared her for it."

Jeanne smiled. "I take it she was brought up in the church?"

"Brought up, for sure. Happy about it? Not so much. She doesn't seem fond of the concept of being God's kid."

"She's young."

"And thinks she knows everything," Julia said.

"Tom's kid, all right. And Hope?"

"Her name is Chloe now."

"She looks more like an Ann or maybe a Sarah." Jeanne munched on an anisette biscuit. "What are you going to do when it's time to visit her father?"

Jeanne was the only person alive—apart from Matt now—who knew Andrew Hamlin's identity. She had been a mainstay throughout that pregnancy. Jeanne had bought a sofa bed for her tiny apartment so Julia wouldn't have to go home to Oklahoma for those long months of pregnancy. She had harassed Julia into returning to school, had been there for Hope's delivery, and had held Julia tight when it was time to hand the baby off to the lawyer who had arranged the adoption.

When Jeanne and Patrick decided to elope because they couldn't afford a wedding, Julia planned one for them on a shoestring budget. She was astounded when a guest asked for her help in planning her daughter's wedding. And thus, Myrrh slowly came into being, one rose petal at a time.

"I can't think about Andy," Julia said. "I have to get through Tom Bryant first."

"I haven't seen him in years. I expect he's grown up."

"Do people really change, Pottsie?"

"Did you?"

Julia sipped at her hot chocolate, the sugar rushing to her brain. "Yes. Of course."

Her friends, employees, and church family considered her a rock. The bridal industry and her clients called her a visionary. Matt promised she was the best wife God could give a guy. Dillon knew her as the mom who nagged and pleaded and disciplined and held him tight when he hurt.

She didn't realize she was crying until Jeanne squeezed into the booth next to her. "Jules. It's okay." She dabbed at Julia's face with a linen napkin. "Hush now, it's okay."

"I'm so scared," she said, clutching Jeanne's sleeve. "I'm so scared that God is punishing Dillon for what I did."

"You know that is not true."

"How can I believe that? There should have been a liver available by now. We had so many people volunteer, so why was every single one with type O disqualified? Statistically, that shouldn't have happened. And where is God's plan for Dillon, when even his parents are incompatible?"

"It's crazy. But maybe . . . I don't know. What if you needed to meet these girls?"

"How is that a blessing? Chloe's family is utterly freaked out and Destiny snarls most of the time. And, Pottsie, think of Matt having to deal with me going to the men I slept with. Think of the families whose lives I'm disrupting. Think about the regard people have for Andy—I could ruin everything he's worked for."

"Sex takes two people. It's not like you raped him."

"No," Julia said. "But in my desire for affirmation and—*forgive me, Lord*—for a warm body against my skin, I played my part in the seduction. A very big part."

"It's over." Jeanne hugged her. "Give it up. It's in the past."

"Really? I have two adult daughters I did *give up* and now they're the present. And here's what I'm really afraid of—that if I persuade one or both to be tested and they decide they would be willing to help and what if after all of that—they're as incompatible as I am? Or what if this trip is for nothing and I've lost these days with Dillon?"

Jeanne wrapped strong arms around her. "I'm taking your jet tonight to Dallas. If you can't be with Dillon, I will be."

Julia jammed her fists into her eyes, trying to stop the tears. "Thank you."

"It's the least I can do for my godchild. The jet will be back tomorrow night so you and the girls can head to wherever Andrew is these days."

"Promise me one thing," Julia said.

"Anything."

"I need you to tell me if it's time to come home. Matt will hope against hope and if the girls still haven't decided . . . I need you to tell me to come say good-bye."

"Jules, in a second. But we're praying it doesn't come to that."

Julia leaned her head on her friend's shoulder. Weariness seeped through her bones. "My hands are slipping, Pottsie."

"Mine won't, Jules. I promise you—mine won't."

seven

Boston

Tuesday, 6:46 p.m.

Destiny finally abandoned her attempts at sibling bonding over a bottle of Chardonnay and decided to take a long bath. As soon as she heard the water running, Chloe logged onto talkatnight.com.

She double-clicked and the text window came alive.

WAVERUNNER: So have you thought about taking a quick trip?

HANDS _ ON: I already did.

WAVERUNNER: Where are you?

HANDS _ ON: Boston.

WAVERUNNER: Wow. This is meant to be.

HANDS _ ON: What?

WAVERUNNER: Us. Sitting down with a glass of wine. Watching the water. Talking. Really getting to know each other.

Chloe held her breath. Her hands were stiff, as if she couldn't find the will to type another word. She could hear the faint hum of traffic, the flutter of her pulse.

WAVERUNNER: It would be nice to sit across a table from you. Or to huddle against the wind and watch the roar of the ocean.

HANDS _ ON: Why did you say it was meant to be?

WAVERUNNER: Because I'm in Gloucester. Practically on your doorstep. We're off-loading what little cargo we have and then we're anchoring to ride out the storm.

The storm. Strange that Jack hadn't jumped on that as an excuse to haul her back to North Carolina. Probably because it was supposed to rain in Boston, dump snow in New Hampshire and Maine. Destiny could meet Thomas Bryant, and they could either go on to Colorado or Chloe could jump a flight home before weather became an issue.

HANDS _ ON: How far is that from Boston?

WAVERUNNER: What's going on?

HANDS _ ON: Long story.

WAVERUNNER: You want to tell it to me?

HANDS _ ON: Maybe.

WAVERUNNER: How long are you here?

HANDS _ ON: For a day or so.

WAVERUNNER: It's a forty-five minute drive, tops. I'll come there.

HANDS _ ON: No. Not here.

Not anywhere, Chloe told herself. She couldn't. She double-clicked the icon, ending the chat. The sailboat came alive again on her screen.

Sitting there, a cartoonish icon that seemed more real, more vital than the beautiful hotel suite in which she sat. She cracked her knuckles, then crossed her arms and stuck her hands under her armpits to keep from touching the keyboard.

The straitjacket pose wasn't lost on Chloe. Was she keeping herself in trust or keeping herself from abundant life? She flung her arms outward and shook them like a crazy woman.

One simple mouse click. Either say hello or shut down. Deep breath. *Oh, God, dear God, I don't want to know what You think, not in this moment, because I need to believe You never intended us to live like robots—well-mannered, good-intentioned automatons.*

Chloe left-clicked and the icon blinked to life.

WAVERUNNER: I guess we got cut off.

She waited. Tossing in cyber waves.

WAVERUNNER: I'd like to hear your voice.
HANDS _ ON: Isn't it better this way? Keeping an arm's length?
WAVERUNNER: Is that what you think?

How pathetic was she, not *knowing* what she thought. She loved Jack and he loved her. She adored Mother and Mother adored her. She respected God. Feared God. But that was all one life. One cloistered, cushioned pathetic life—lived under the red slicker.

What if she splashed in a puddle, just this one time? Just to talk. How could it hurt anything if she had coffee with some guy, talked engineering, watched the rain come down.

HANDS _ ON: Is there some place—

Just this one time.

HANDS _ ON: —where maybe we could have coffee?
WAVERUNNER: Sure.

This was insane, immoral, horrible.

Stop the drama. It was only coffee. Julia and Destiny would be busy today with Thomas Bryant. Chloe could rent a car, take a ride, have a coffee, be back tonight before anyone realized she was missing.

And why should any of that matter? She was an adult.

Oh, God, I am a married adult. With responsibilities and duties. But surely You see how things are. How I am. Trapped.

WAVERUNNER: Two Brothers café. Late afternoon? I still have to literally batten down the hatches.

HANDS _ ON: Sure.

He gave his number and she scribbled it on the Westin's notepad.

HANDS _ ON: See you then.

WAVERUNNER: Wait. Shouldn't I know your name?

HANDS _ ON: You first.

WAVERUNNER: Rob. Rob Jones. You?

She could be anyone. Why not be the person she first was?

HANDS _ ON: Hope. Hope McCord.

WAVERUNNER: Can't wait to hear your voice, Hope.

HANDS _ ON: Me too.

WAVERUNNER: And see your face.

HANDS _ ON: Nothing special.

WAVERUNNER: What you are on the inside will shine through.

And that was the problem—Chloe didn't know *what* she was inside. Maybe this was the only way she'd find out.

Tuesday, 9:16 a.m.

"Woman, you are a horror show," Destiny said.

Julia shrugged. "What does it matter?"

"You reflect poorly on my skills. We are not leaving this hotel until we redo your face and hair."

Destiny had made Julia up over an hour ago. Now her eyes were deeply shadowed, her face blotchy. She'd been crying again.

Julia turned to Chloe. "Do I look that bad?"

She shrugged. "Not my field of expertise. Sorry."

"We should just go."

Julia clicked her fingernails against the cast until Destiny grabbed her hand and said, "Stop or I'll tie it to the table. I swear I will. Now sit."

"Did someone treat you like that?" Julia asked.

Destiny yanked a comb through her hair. "Are you hoping my parents are abusive so you can rescue me?"

"No. Of course not."

"That's harsh," Chloe said.

"I'm kidding, guys. Just kidding. This one"—she touched the top of Julia's head with the brush, playing fairy godmother—"this one needs to chill. Now sit still, Julia. You're not even fit for a garage sale."

"Aren't you nervous, Dez?" Chloe seemed nervous as well. She wasn't as sold on this meet-the-daddies thing.

"Why should I be?" She should have known a consequence of this trip would be extended navel-gazing. Not that they had the right—and yet, wasn't that the point of this? To know who you could have been. Destiny would take that head-on. No tears like Julia, no hiding in the laptop like Chloe.

What ifs never scared her. That was her vocation, her gift.

What if an asteroid was about to explode on earth? What if aliens had an insatiable appetite for human brains? What if angels were plotting a second rebellion?

What if Tom Bryant had stayed?

"A big-time lawyer. He's probably . . . running the world, or something," Chloe said.

Destiny pointed the brush at her. "Your husband would be thrilled if you came from the same kind of intelligent, ambitious gene pool."

Julia grabbed her hand. "Destiny. Don't."

"Tell her who her father is."

"I will, as soon as I get back from this Tom thing."

"Chloe!" Destiny glanced at her sister. "Can you close that stupid laptop?"

"I'm sorry. What do you need?"

"You to stop apologizing, for one thing."

"I'm sorry for being sorry."

"We could use some support."

"I thought you didn't want me to go with you today."

"Not that. With bio-mom."

"She thinks I'm uncooperative," Julia said.

"You have no vision. The point is," Destiny said, "what do you want *him* to think?"

"I don't understand."

"You'll have a split second to make a first impression before the memories rush in. Hair and makeup tell a story. How you tie that scarf tells a story. Even how you walk, your posture. So what do you want it all to say?

"Do you want him to think that you are just as successful as he is? Or"—Destiny winked at Chloe—"do you want him to see you and think, *Wow, she's sexier than ever and I am the biggest fool to have ever let her walk*?"

"First of all," Julia said, "I didn't walk. He did. So perhaps we could drop the sassy and smart and just go for dignified?"

"Ah. So you want him to see you as mature and serene—despite the fact that he had his way with you and then tossed you like a snotty tissue?"

"That's cruel," Chloe said.

"The truth often is," Destiny said. "Crueler not to see it."

Julia shifted in the chair so she could see Chloe. "What do you think?"

"Me? I don't have a basis for an opinion."

"So why can't I be *me*?" Julia said.

"And who are you?" Destiny said.

"Mother. Wife. Friend. Employer."

"And Christian," Chloe said.

"My faith is intrinsic in everything I am. At least, I hope it is."

"You're lying," Destiny said, curling iron in hand.

Julia squinted up at her. "Apparently *you* do have a basis for every opinion."

"It doesn't come naturally," Destiny said. "If it did, they wouldn't have to drill it into you. 'God. Family. Church.' And then, if you're a member of the Connors clan, you add 'country,' cue the trumpets, and salute the flag."

"I'm sure someone has mentioned to you at some point," Chloe said, "that you might be a tad cynical?"

"Yeah, that might have come up once or twice."

"I could have used a healthy dose of cynicism at your age," Julia said.

"Or a healthy dose of spermicide," Destiny said.

"Are you nervous, Dez?" Chloe asked. "Is that why you're being such a brat?"

So nervous her skin curdled. Not that she would admit that. "No." Destiny tossed her head as if to punctuate her statement.

"You're lying."

"Who's cynical now?"

"What about you, Julia? Are you nervous?"

"Can I answer honestly?"

"Will you?" Destiny said. "Answer honestly, that is."

"Shut up and let her," Chloe said.

Julia swiveled on the stool and stared up at Destiny. "The truth is that I'm angry. Angry with Tom for leaving me to sort out . . . *us*. I am angry that I need to be away from Dillon. I am angry that I had to come to both of you as a supplicant and not as a woman who loved you so very much. I'm angry because I can't expect you to believe that, not when I am so desperate to have your grace. And . . . I am furious that I have such severe spiritual astigmatism that God is like an out-of-focus photo."

"Do you forgive him?" Chloe said.

"God?" Julia said.

"Tom," Destiny said, suddenly desperate for an answer to a question that should be irrelevant to her. "Do you forgive him for not being what you needed?"

"I haven't tried to, not for a long time," Julia said. "So I don't really know."

Tuesday, 10:06 a.m.

They rode the elevator to the thirty-second floor. It was no surprise that Tom had reached this height, a steel and glass building where he'd be able to look down over Boston Harbor.

Julia had resisted googling him since the search engine made its debut in the mid '90s. She had wanted to, as if gathering details on his life could supply the end to part of the story. Her loyalty to her family had kept her from typing in his name.

She searched him online last night because now it was appropriate, or as appropriate as it could be when one is about to blast through another's privacy fence.

Matt had known for two years—or maybe longer—that Tom had become a leading attorney in media law and a name in First Amendment cases. Had he looked for some evidence of Tom having married and fathered children, like she had? Or did Matt take in the information and spreadsheet it to be sorted when they needed it?

Julia knew the answer to that. That Tom Bryant existed ate away at Matt. That Andrew had risen to such prominence in evangelical circles meant any jealousy her husband harbored would be multiplied tenfold.

"Stop fidgeting," Destiny said, though she was the one who danced from foot to foot, dragging her fingers through her hair hard enough to pull out long strands. She had dressed with enough care to show she didn't care. Skinny jeans, faded with tattered thighs. Ankle boots with turquoise socks peeking out, and despite the cold, a form-fitting black leather jacket. Underneath, a T-shirt that simply said RIDE. And with all the fuss she had made over Julia, the only makeup Destiny wore was eyeliner.

Tom would have to see how like him she was and thus forgive Julia for opening up this old story. As much as she hated him for taking the easy way out, she also knew it would have hurt him some small bit. Perhaps as a failure in planning or execution, or perhaps as a lapse in judgment—he would carry some regret forward.

Then again, if he had had any regrets about letting Julia go, he could have easily found her. She had finished school in Boston, though it hadn't been easy. For most of that time, she was within a mile of him—or closer.

The elevator stopped, doors opened to let a silver-haired woman in. She carried a laptop like a school book, worked a phone with her free fingers.

"What are you going to say to him?" Destiny whispered.

"I won't have to say anything," Julia said. "He'll see me, he'll see you, and he'll know."

His photo on the law firm's website showed very little change. A little gray at the temples, of course, but the same wide smile and unforgettable blue-gray eyes.

"And then what?"

"I don't know, honey. How could I possibly know?"

The door closed, the elevator resumed its upward crawl. Julia was tempted to push the emergency stop button until she could figure out what she might say to Tom that would persuade him to persuade Destiny to save Dillon's life.

The elevator stopped again at the twenty-sixth floor. The woman got out.

"What do you want from him?" Julia asked.

"Nothing," Destiny said. "I'm just nosy."

"You wouldn't have crossed this country if you didn't want something."

She glared at Julia. "Acknowledgment, all right? Just a simple *I know you exist and that mattered to me.* If that's all right with you, *Mother.* You're the one who kept him from me with the closed adoption."

Julia opened her mouth to answer and couldn't because the elevator opened onto the thirty-second floor and Tom was right there, waiting to get on.

"Oh," Destiny said and followed Julia out of the elevator.

He moved toward them, almost onto the car, when he glanced at them. He narrowed his eyes, perhaps sensing a cosmic shift, and then opened his eyes wide, said, "Jules," and opened his arms.

She wrapped her arms around his waist and let him hold her while she breathed his expensive cologne and that little tang of his skin when he worked hard. She felt his strong body—of course he'd be a workout fiend—and she could almost taste the coffee he had just drunk under the hint of bubblegum because, after all these years, he was still the kid from Southie.

She could almost feel his lips on hers, even though he planted them kindly on her forehead. She had feared all along that she would never be free of him, and she could feel him now, sneaking under her skin.

Julia loosened her grip. Tom kept one arm around her waist and stepped to the side so he could extend the other arm to Destiny.

"I know who you are," he said, "but I don't know your name."

Destiny pulled her arm back and, in a blur, punched Tom Bryant in the stomach. "That's my name," she said. "And don't you forget it."

Tuesday, 10:07 a.m.

Chloe wasn't much for makeup. A little lipstick, the occasional eye shadow, and she was done. No need for mascara, not with the long lashes she had inherited from Julia. Jack liked the natural look, and Chloe couldn't be bothered to try something new.

Until now—when she was poised on the precipice of everything new and different. She fingered the items in Destiny's makeup case. So much to choose from.

You'll have a split second, Destiny had told Julia, *to make a first impression.*

Chloe was good with her hands. If she wanted, she could create a new look for herself. All the tools were spread out before her.

What do you want it to say?

Was she the girl who was about to make a devil of a mistake? Or the woman who was about to choose something for herself?

Someone knocked on the door. Hard.

Chloe pressed her hand to her throat. So silly to be startled. Leave it to Destiny to forget her keycard and have to come back for it.

"Stupid," Chloe said as she opened the door.

"I beg your pardon?"

"What—" She stepped back, her heart thundering.

"Sorry," Jack said. "I didn't mean to startle you."

"What are you doing here?"

"I missed you." He took her arm and led her to the sofa. "Are you okay?"

She nodded. He wore gray slacks, a white shirt open at the collar, and a navy-blue V-neck sweater. The cowlick in his blond hair was gelled into submission. He found the closet, stowed away his raincoat and umbrella, and sat down next to her.

"I told you not to come." The shiver in her voice was embarrassing.

Jack took her hands. "I really scared you."

"No. Not at all. My head was somewhere else. I was just . . . thinking about calling Dr. Monroe and asking him to run a new assay for me."

He leaned over and kissed the back of her hand. "What assay?"

Panic bubbled under her ribs. Jack never asked for details. When people asked him about his wife's research, he simply said she was working on a disease model for some cancer pathways.

Tiny steps, painstaking work. That's how they unravel the

groaning of creation. One strand of DNA at a time. My wife has the patience of a saint.

Chloe launched into a genuine explanation of nucleotide excision repair and a bogus protocol to map a synthetic XPJ prokaryotic pathway. Jack leaned closer, his lips moving as if memorizing the key words so he could look them up later.

His sudden interest warmed her—until she realized his query was to distract her from asking why he had shown up uninvited in Boston.

"I told you not to come," she said.

"And I told you I didn't want you to go through this alone."

Chloe got up, went to the window. The weather was damp. She had wanted her first view of Boston to be sunny and hopeful. People in the street shrank into their scarves and gloves. Chicago was supposed to be the windy city, not Boston. Narrow streets, cold ocean, just enough tall buildings to create tunnels for cold air.

According to Google, Gloucester was an old seaport with cozy shops and restaurants, fishing boats and scenic piers. The thought of sipping hot chocolate in a snug café, listening to the rain and the waves—having a genuine conversation—how could she give that up?

"What time is the rain supposed to start?" Jack said.

"I don't know." Chloe would stop at a mall on her way north and buy an umbrella and rain boots. A big enough storm to bring Rob Jones's boat into harbor could drench her.

How ironic—how typical—that Jack showed up here already prepared for stormy weather.

"They said it would be snowy up north. We need to keep an eye on that."

Maybe she'd pick up some stormy-weather clothing—lined coats for herself and Destiny. All three of them were unaccustomed to icy rain. Boots, even gloves. Julia would need a good cape, of course. Hopefully this weather front wasn't making her broken fingers ache.

Chloe fixed her gaze on the mist hanging over the buildings. Jack had come up behind her. He radiated heat. She could feel him on the side of her face.

"Why did you come when I asked you not to?"

He slipped his arms around her waist and pressed his face to the back of her hair. "I don't want you here alone."

"I'm not alone."

He gently pulled back her hair and kissed her ear. "I was."

Chloe felt a stirring in her throat. Just one tender kiss was all it took to make her lean back against him and hope for more. She hated that she yielded so easily.

Was marriage intended to fulfill her primal longings or protect her from herself? If God had designed His children for both, why couldn't she find a balance?

Destiny—playing shrink—might say that Chloe projected neediness so she could be cared for. Coddled by Mother, managed by husband, lauded by professors, guarded on all sides by lawyers and trusts.

Just call me Velcro.

"Chloe. What are we doing here?" Jack's breath was hot on her cheek. He was safe, his steadfastness as securely buttoned-down as his collar.

"Your seminar is this evening," she said. "If you catch a flight by noon, you could make it."

"I don't want you here alone. Or wherever you're going. Mrs. Whittaker didn't tell you who your father was, did she? That should be a watch-out for you."

"He's . . . someone we'll recognize, she told me. So she wanted to talk it through with me after she gets through with Destiny's meeting. As for myself, I still haven't decided if I even want to meet him."

"Julia is playing you. Can't you see that? She's desperate and you're so easy to manipulate that—"

Chloe pulled away from him. "So I'm *her* tool too?"

"What're you talking about?"

"You're smothering me, Jack. How you can smother me and keep me at arm's length at the same time—I don't know. But that's what you do."

"I don't know what you're talking about. You're not yourself."

"That's for sure."

"This little . . . journey won't tell you who you are. These women are strangers. A blood tie that was severed the instant you left Julia's arms. Whatever you're looking for—it's not with them."

She stiffened. "What am I looking for?"

"I honestly wish I knew." Jack dragged his fingers through his hair, making his cowlick stand up. "Please. Just come home."

"Ah, there's the truth, Jack. First you say you want to do this with me. But it doesn't take long to get to your bottom line. Be a good girl, Chloe. Come home, Chloe. As if Hope McCord never existed."

Jack stretched out his hands. "You were only that girl for a day. One day, and then you were a Middlebrooks, and then a Deschene. We love you so much." His voice cracked. "I'll give you . . . space, is that it? Is that what you need? I'll give you whatever is missing. Just come home."

Tears burned her cheeks. "All I'm asking for is a couple of days. Can't you just give me that?"

"Okay, yes. If that's what you need. I'll book a room somewhere else. The Ritz is across the Boston Common. I'll head that way and when you're ready . . ."

"No. Absolutely not. Go home. Go back to your classes. Let me be . . . me."

"That is such a cliché."

"Fine. Let me be a cliché. But let me *be*. If you love me—just let me be."

Jack closed his eyes, pressed his hand to his heart. "I promised your mother I would bring you home. She's worried."

"She'll be okay."

"You said it yourself yesterday morning, remember? She's brittle."

"Don't, Jack. Don't use her as a crowbar to get me to come home."

"Think of what you're doing. Jetting around the country with people you don't know, about to ruin some man's life—"

"Ruin? RUIN! How can you say that?"

"The history is clear by his absence. He hasn't posted on any of those birth-parent or adopted-child sites. Twenty-two years of silence, for both him and Julia. Now that she needs something she has absolutely no right to ask you for, she decides she wants a relationship."

"You're afraid I'll say yes to the donation."

His face tightened.

She poked his arm. "Answer me."

"I don't know what you'll do. And that . . . worries me."

"Do you understand, Jackson Deschene, how absolutely insulting that is?" Chloe dug her fingers into his arms, on the verge of shaking him. This was what she was running from. Not boredom or obligation but a tightly held anger that all her choices had been made for her: prep school, university, career, family. Even her God was chosen for her.

"Leave. Please," she said.

"Fine. Have your little . . ." He shook his head. "I'll text you when I check in somewhere."

"Durham. Go back to the condo, back to your seminars."

"Didn't you hear what I said—"

"Now. Or I swear, Jack. I swear I will not come home. Not ever."

Color drained from his face. "Are you giving me an ultimatum?"

Chloe smiled. Surprising how good an ultimatum could feel. "Yes, I am. Now go. I'll call you and let you know when I'll be back."

"Soon. Please."

"When I'm ready, Jack. Now go."

Tuesday, 10:12 a.m.

Tom hustled them into a conference room with floor-to-ceiling glass that looked down on Boston Harbor. The ocean was a musky green, the sky a steel gray. "*A storm coming in,*" the weatherman had said on the morning news. Then he furrowed his brow to show his deep concern.

Destiny smiled to think that the storm was here and Thomas Bryant was totally unprepared. He stared at her with gray eyes, a muscle jumping in his cheek. She stared back at him, strangely calm because she knew his story and he didn't have a clue about hers.

Julia stood to the side, breathing through her mouth and almost REM-blinking. This is something she thought she'd never see, Destiny realized.

"So," Tom said. "I don't know if I should hug you or have you arrested for assault."

"The latter would be the safer option."

"Are you going to tell me what's going on here? To say this is a surprise . . ."

"For me too," Destiny said. "Two days ago I was in Los Angeles, minding my own business, when she showed up in my driveway."

"I don't even know your name." Tom held up his hands. "And this time the words will suffice."

"Destiny Connors. I am twenty-four-years old—"

"Wow, Jules—are we really that old?"

"Hey," Destiny said sharply. "This is my time. Unless you're billing us by the quarter hour."

"No. Of course not," Tom said. "I'm just trying to slow the room from spinning. What can I do for you, Destiny? Do you . . . need some help with something?"

"No."

"Then I'm not really sure what's going on here."

Stupid, Destiny thought. After all these years, it had been stupid to think her birth father would dance a jig if they ever were reunited.

Julia took his hand. "I need help."

They stared at each other. She could feel the heat coming off Julia's face, see Tom's hand tighten on hers.

"What do you need?"

"My son." Her voice cracked. "My son is dying."

Tom pulled her in to him. She cried silently into his suit jacket. "Shush, it's okay."

"She wants my liver." Destiny hated the juvenile tone of her own voice. "Her son needs a liver transplant, and she's gone looking for a donor from one of her daughters."

"Daughters?" He put his hands on Julia's shoulders so he could look her in the face. "How many daughters did you . . ."

"There're two of us," Destiny said. "She got caught twice before she began choosing more wisely."

Tom turned to her, eyes tight on her face as if he finally realized he and Julia weren't the only ones in the room. "And where do I come in?"

"Are you thick, dude? I said I'd think about it but I wanted to meet you first."

"It's urgent," Julia said.

Tom grasped her elbow and said, "I'm going to lawyer up on you here. This isn't the kind of thing you just jump into. And if you expect me to help you with this decision . . . how could I? It just speaks of impulse, and that's no way to face something like major surgery."

"Is that what you think?" Destiny said. "That for twenty-four years I didn't give you a thought and now I'm playing *Where's Waldo* with you?"

"Fine. So you caught me. What do you need to know?"

"Why."

"What?"

Julia stepped to Destiny's side. Another shift that she could feel, a scent on the sweeter side of sweaty. "She wants to know why you left us."

"*She* wants to know, Julia? Or you want to know?"

"I want to know that we made the right decision, Tom."

"We can't rehash it, not all over again." He stepped back. "Not after all these years."

Destiny grabbed his arm. "It's not *after all these years.* Not for me."

His lips tightened. *This is his game face, the one he wears in boardrooms and court.* He exudes goodwill and friendliness, is ridiculously good-looking but behind that was something hard. Maybe not a bad hard—she had the same spine, the will to stand for herself.

"Okay." Tom stretched out his hands in a conciliatory gesture. His eyes were icy gray. "I should be asking for some proof of paternity here."

"We don't have time," Julia said.

"I can see she's yours. But how do I know she's mine?"

Destiny swore, then said, "She wouldn't pull a stunt on you. And how can you . . ." Destiny chewed the side of her tongue to stop the words from coming out.

How can you not know me?

Tuesday, 11:12 a.m.

"We've got to stop meeting like this," Julia said.

"You don't like my home office?" Matt said. "Macaroni and tuna fish are chic these days."

Dillon must see through these trips to the kitchen, iPad in hand. A bridal emergency, they had said, to explain why she had to fly out directly after surgery. Their son knew he had half-sisters, had never really shown interest. Or maybe he had deliberately withheld his interest.

"How're the numbers?" Julia asked.

"I'll tell you if there's something you need to know."

"I need to know if . . ." She couldn't say *time was short.* She could, however, say, "If Dillon needs me."

"We always need you. He hates my cooking, so we're doing lots of takeout. Hopefully Aunt Pottsie will help with that when she arrives. Otherwise . . ." Matt smiled, the lines on his forehead so pronounced that she knew he was forcing it. "We'll see Dr. Annie tomorrow. Just for a checkup."

"Have you asked her where he is on the list?"

"Would it change anything, sweets?"

"I should be there."

"You need to be there. So what did Destiny think of her bio-dad?"

Julia cringed. "After she punched him in the gut?"

Matt laughed. "She's your girl, all right. So . . . did he have her arrested? Or threaten to sue?"

"He invited her to lunch in Cambridge. With him and his family."

"Interesting. And Chloe? What did she think?"

"She didn't come." He won't ask, so she'd have to say it. "It was strange, seeing him."

Matt waited, a warm smile on his face. His eyes betrayed him, that flicker of doubt he rarely displayed because generally, the world added up for him. He knew how deeply she had loved Tom Bryant, and that was okay because he was a variable long solved. And now Julia was less than an hour removed from having been in Tom's arms again.

"I forgave him," she said.

"You forgave him years ago."

"I forgave what he did. This morning I hugged him, Matt. Hugged him hard, for a long time. I whispered that I forgave him. And—after we yelled at each other for twenty minutes because there were still things to be said—he forgave me for popping out of nowhere with Destiny. And then we . . . let each other go."

"Good."

"Mattie," she said, caressing the screen. "After Destiny took possession of Tom, I stepped back and smiled because . . . , Matt?"

"I'm here. You stepped back because . . . ?"

"Because I heard God's voice."

"Saying?"

"Saying I chose wrong. But He chose right. He chose you for me."

"I know," he said, blinking back tears.

"And I'm so thankful that God saw fit to give me something—someone—far better than I chose for myself. Better than I deserved. I am so lucky to have you."

"I'm the lucky one, Julia. I'm the lucky one."

Tuesday, 11:12 a.m.

"You forgive awfully fast," Destiny said.

"It's not like you threw a wicked punch." Tom Bryant swerved his car into the left lane, invoking a horn blast from the driver he had just cut off.

"And you drive like you're from LA."

He laughed. "We were here first. So if there's any *taking after* to do, it's you on the left coast taking after us."

"She told me that, you know."

"What, that Boston drivers rule?"

"That I take after you."

"Did Julia think that was a bad thing or a good thing?"

Destiny shrugged. "Just its own thing."

"Do you think you take after me?"

"How would I know? We just met."

Tom swerved into the right lane, passed a line of cars waiting at the stoplight. Destiny had been invited to lunch at his home and—of all crazy things—to meet his wife and their two daughters. Crazier still, she accepted.

The sky was ashen, though it wasn't even noon. Rain coming, the news had said. Los Angeles was sunny and brisk today. This trip with Julia had been an impulse—in a strange way, a *creative* choice.

Creating something new? Or just marking time, waiting for Luke to come to his senses?

"We're about to cross the Mass. Ave. bridge, over the Charles," he said. "Across the river, on your right, is MIT. Keep going straight and you eventually end up in Harvard Yard."

"I didn't agree to have lunch with you so I could have a geography lesson," Destiny said.

"I know. It's just . . . so weird after all these years." He glanced at her. "Weird in a good way."

"You never expected to see me, did you?"

"Not in a million years."

"Did you think about me?"

"Of course. Every Thanksgiving. I would think . . . *the baby is about to turn two, I wonder if she's a terror like Mum said I was.* And then a couple more years would pass, and I'd think *Devon must be in kindergarten.*"

"Devon?"

"That's the name I knew you by. Julia always said she wanted that name for her eldest daughter. And it stuck in my head."

"She named me Destiny."

He slammed on the brakes because the car ahead of him suddenly stopped. "Where Jules came up with Destiny, I have no clue."

"When did you know?"

"That Julia was pregnant?"

"That you were going to walk."

"You really don't pull any punches."

"Blame yourself, dear Father."

Tom hunched over the steering wheel. "About the time Julia was seven months along and I had started working. I've always worked, been good with my hands and fast with the mouth. But being a first-year in a law firm, it's like serfdom. And you've got to be on your toes all day long because otherwise someone was going to climb up your back. Days stretched into nights and I'd still be there when the sun came up. On those days, it was like . . . nothing outside the walls of my cubicle existed. I'd finally catch a few hours of sleep, see Julia and she was so beautiful. Like ripe fruit, those eyes—like yours—and red cheeks because it was getting chilly. And I'd realize I couldn't see how this could happen.

"And then your grandmother called me."

"Grandmother. You mean, Julia's mother?"

"Yeah. I'm sure you've heard the song-and-dance about this being the best thing for the baby."

"Did Julia know that?"

"No. I became more absent. Because Mrs. McCord's wisdom had become gospel truth—that we couldn't take care of ourselves, so how would we ever manage a baby?"

"People do."

"Not well. And it's the child who suffers. The statistics are not good, and for a couple weeks I thought, *I can beat those statistics.* And now I'm further down the road—now that I've seen things in our practice—families torn apart because people just won't listen."

Destiny pressed her forehead against the window. The glass was cold, hard. She needed that. "When did you put it all behind you?"

"Never. December third is burned into my brain. I counted the years as they passed. And time seemed to fly because I was suddenly thinking, *the girl is a teenager and heaven help her parents if she's more like me than Julia.*"

She studied him now, his dark hair so like hers, the silver at his temples. "And now you know?"

Tom shrugged. "It's probably just ego speaking, but I'm guessing you ran a little wild."

"I take umbrage at the *little* part, but yeah."

"Are you okay?" he said. "Now?"

"Define *okay.*" Destiny's voice cracked. "Besides, wild isn't necessarily synonymous with bad."

He laughed. "I hope not. I suppose you know that this is where I should ask you if you want to talk about it?"

"And I suppose you know I don't. What about you? Are you okay?"

"The jerk who walked out on the beautiful and sweet Julia McCord? Define *okay.*"

"I mean now."

"But it's all the logical extension from then until now because I busted away from Julia so fast, I must have created a vacuum. And she didn't deserve that."

"Since we're going there—maybe it's just ego talking—did I deserve that?"

"When you have your own kids, you'll understand we did the right thing for you."

"What if I don't have kids?"

He grinned, flashing dimples. "Someone's got to make me a grandpa."

"What are your daughters' names?"

"Natalie. She's eight and Olivia is six."

"So what if someone treated Natalie like you treated Julia?"

His hands gripped the steering wheel. "I deserve that. And you deserve the right to tell me how miserable your life has been. So have at it, Destiny."

"That's not why I'm here."

"Really. It pretty much sounds like that."

She laughed. "Okay, let's make the groveling a given."

"Done and thank you," he said. "So we're heading for west Cambridge."

"Which means nothing to me."

"And what does?"

"Seriously?" Destiny said.

"Seriously. I would like to know. What's important to you?"

"My parents. Melanie is a pseudo-public person who's afraid of her own shadow. And Will—my *real* dad—"

"Ouch," Tom said.

"—Will Connors is always doing important business in Washington. My parents and I have been like tectonic plates. As much as we grind, they're my rock. Though I don't tell them that."

"Of course not." He smiled. "Parents know. What else? Clearly you're not a homebody."

"My craft means a lot to me. I started putting lip gloss on extras when I was eighteen, moved into conceptual art. Now I'm almost in demand. And it's not always monsters. I can transform Anthony Hopkins into Alfred Hitchcock and you would believe it within seconds of the first scene."

"Do you believe in transformation?"

"What I need," Destiny said, "is for you to believe in transformation. And you—and millions of others—do. Which means I am very good at my job. And that means a lot to me."

Tom tapped the steering wheel. "And the love life?"

"Ah, the love life."

"I know you've got one, Destiny."

"Luke. We've been together for two years. He gets me, even though I'm not easy to get. And now he's taking this faith journey that I don't get. He was just fine where we were. I kicked him out because it's the only way he'll see that he needs me."

They stopped at a red light. Destiny glanced at the high, brick walls on the far side of the sidewalk, realized this must be Harvard Square.

"That's a high-risk move," Tom said. "Letting him walk and hoping he'll come full circle back to you."

"Isn't that what Julia did with you? Let you walk and hoped you'd come back?"

Tom slammed the gas pedal, roared forward through the intersection. She resisted the urge to grab the dashboard. They rode a full minute in silence before he said, "Your birthday was last week."

"Another year gone by."

"Another year that I didn't forget."

"Thank you."

"No." He looked at her and smiled. "Thank you."

eight

Gloucester

Tuesday, 11:45 a.m.

Forty minutes from Boston to Gloucester.

Most of that time was spent trying to get out of Boston in the rush hour that never seemed to end. Chloe kept to the middle lane because that's what Mother had taught her to do when she was sixteen.

Strange to think that she had already been in love with Jack then. There had never been anyone else, not even a crush. Just the fair-haired, clear-eyed Jack.

What would Father have taught her if he had still been alive? Though he was a gentle man, he was not a pushover, and not a middle-lane type of guy. That's what Chloe sensed, though God only knew because God decided to take him before she could really know him.

A saint's death, someone had whispered to Mother at the funeral. A cerebral aneurysm, no warning, just shut out the lights and—what a blessing—there was no suffering.

Except for those left behind.

No way to know you've got an aneurysm, a doctor friend had explained. *Unless it leaks. Then we might get some gleaning and see if we can fix it. Could have been there for years, silent until the weakened blood vessel couldn't hold anymore.*

Was that what she was? An emotional or psychological or even sexual aneurysm, about to explode?

Mother called it nurture and Jack called it love. *You've both wrapped the cashmere scarf too tightly around my neck. And now I'm choking.*

She had already squirreled into the narrow and confusing roads of Gloucester and nailed down the pub where she'd meet Rob later this evening. The cover story for Julia and Destiny was ready—*a chance to consult with someone at MIT and no, you guys would be bored out of your minds so stay at the hotel, don't know when I'll be back. These sessions can sometimes go all night.*

With the meeting place nailed down, it was much too early to go back to Boston. An attendant at a gas station directed her to Good Harbor beach. Chloe parked her car, the only soul foolish enough to be here on this cold, gray day. All that warm-weather gear she had bought at Copley Plaza would come in handy for their trip to Colorado. Julia still hadn't said exactly where they'd be going. She promised the whole story once they got through with Thomas Bryant. The woman had been jumpy at breakfast. Haunted, almost. And wouldn't she be? Facing what *could* have been?

If Chloe chickened out on Rob Jones tonight, would she be haunted forever by what could have been?

Or was it safer to just keep this as it is—a cyberfantasy, effective for relieving stress and not hurting anyone.

Jack wore responsibility like a crown of thorns. How had he gotten like this? Chloe had never gone there, just took his achievement and forging of the future as a given. She knew how he brushed his teeth and took his notes and drank his coffee. She knew his plan.

She didn't know his *why*. And without that, she really didn't know him.

Chloe walked the boardwalk over a salty marsh. The wind was brisk and icy cold. The smell of the sea was invigorating. The water melded into the overcast sky, so it was hard to tell where one ended and the other began.

She wrapped the scarf around her face and trudged across the sand. The waves were quiet here, not like the Outer Banks. And the sea was far more brown than green. No blue in sight. Just right for sitting and thinking. Maybe prayer.

Maybe not. God was just another stressor, another Master of the grand plan. If she couldn't bear up under her husband, how would she stand under the hand of the Almighty?

Chloe pulled up her hood and tightened it around her face. The wind off the water stung her eyes. She sat on the sand, nestling against the dune. Her phone rang. *Ignore it*, but with Mother's age, she had to at least look. Julia. How was that for irony? Chloe thumbed the Talk button. "Hi."

"I was going to take you to lunch."

"I'm not there."

Julia laughed. "I can see that."

"I wanted to get out. See some of the city."

"Tell me where you are. I'll grab a cab, we can meet somewhere."

The eagerness in Julia's voice was almost too much to bear. "I rented a car. I'm north now."

"New Hampshire?"

"Yeah." Chloe tried to remember the geography she'd seen on MapQuest. "Portsmouth."

"Oh. I could join you. I spent a lot of time up there years ago. Sketching, painting."

"No, no." Don't dig the hole deeper. "You should stay in the city. In case Destiny needs you."

"Shall we . . . plan for dinner?"

"I'll get back to you," Chloe said. "I know some people at MIT. I might see them."

"Oh."

That *oh* felt like a concrete block.

"Julia, I appreciate the offer. And I'll be ready to leave tomorrow morning. I know the time is important to you."

"Have you thought any . . ."

She left it hanging. *Nice, thanks. Pile it on.* "I'm still processing—"

"No, wait," Julia said. "I didn't mean to put that on you. I'm sorry."

"It's okay." Her phone *clunked*. Chloe looked at her screen and saw Destiny's name. "I have to go. Destiny's on the other line."

"Sure. Tell her . . . I hope it's all going okay."

"Sure. Bye." Chloe clicked off, now obligated to take Destiny's call. Even seven hundred miles from home she couldn't find a place for quiet. *WaveRunner*—Rob—had the whole ocean to dream. She couldn't even curl up inside her own head.

"Hey." Destiny was whispering. "I'm at his house. In the bathroom now."

"And . . . is it what you wanted? Or expected?"

"He's what I expected. And different at the same time. The grown-up Tom is still very handsome. And I'm so much more him than Julia."

And what does that make me? The daughter of a father whose story Julia has purposely left untold.

"What about the sisters?" Chloe said.

"Little kids. Cute. We're about to play dress up."

"Nice for you."

"Yeah. You okay?"

No. Yes. That was what she needed to figure out. "Fine."

"I just wanted you to know . . ." Destiny lowered her voice.

"What?" Chloe had to pull down her hood and jam the phone against her ear so she could hear.

"You, Chloe Middlebrooks Deschene, a.k.a. Hope McCord, will always be my number one half-sister."

She laughed. "What an honor."

"Gotta go. Thanks for . . . being there to share."

"You got it." Chloe hung up, wondering if she should have added a *love you*. She enjoyed what she knew of Destiny. She didn't know her well enough to love her—and maybe these couple of days would be it for the sisterhood. Yet didn't the genetic tie that they shared require love? Were that true, wouldn't she owe the same consideration to Dillon Whittaker?

She was sick to death of asking questions. Sick to death of having to figure everything out. Couldn't she just *feel* for once and leave the analysis out of it?

Just as she huddled back into the dune, her phone chimed again. Jack. If she didn't answer this, he'd be back on a plane north.

"Hi," she said. "Good flight?"

"Chloe, for Pete's sake. You sound like a polite stranger."

She winced. This hit closer than he knew. "Sorry."

"So do you know where you're going next and when?"

"I don't know, Jack. Destiny is spending the afternoon with her father. We'll reassess after that."

"If you left tonight, you could still make that interview at UNC."

"I already cancelled."

"You mean postponed, right?"

"Yeah," Chloe said. A lie but at this point, nothing as

earthshaking as the betrayal that could be ahead. Would he even notice if she had been in another man's arms?

"What is going on there? Is Julia pressuring you?"

"No, not one bit. I rented a car and drove north to see some of the coast."

"Alone?"

"I know how to drive, Jack."

"That's not what I mean. We could have done that together."

"No. We couldn't."

"I'm sorry if I was . . . overwhelming yesterday."

"And today. You came a long distance to get your *overwhelm* on this morning."

"I'm just so worried about this whole thing. I want to protect you."

"Jack Deschene, white knight, protector of the realm."

"What's that supposed to mean?"

"It means that sometimes, Jack, . . . sometimes I just need to handle things myself. Why can't you hear me when I say that?"

"Darling, I know how capable you are. How bright, how giving. I just want to share in that with you. Tell me if I'm doing something wrong."

"You're not." Chloe shivered under her jacket. "Sometimes, Jack, . . . just sometimes."

"Okay. I'll step back and let you have your *sometime*."

"Thank you." She bit the inside of her cheek to keep from saying any more. "I'll call you first thing tomorrow."

"Tonight. Please. I know I'm being a pest, but I just want to know you're okay."

"I'm fine. Nothing is going to change in the next twelve hours." And that was mostly the truth. She'd be talking with Rob Jones across a table instead of typing back and forth with him over Wi-Fi. "I'm going now."

"Wait. Just one last thing, Chloe." He cleared his throat. "Watch the weather before you drive or fly anywhere. There's a storm off the coast."

Yes, there is. And it's coming ashore tonight.

Boston
Tuesday, 12:37 p.m.

Short and pleasantly chubby, Jenny Bryant was the anti-Julia. Her hair was auburn with a hint of fiery red when the winter sunlight framed her. Her eyes were small and more green than brown and her freckles suited her.

Jenny was warm and comfortable, even with her husband's out-of-wedlock child sitting at her kitchen island. Tom insisted on firing up the gas grill and making steaks for lunch. The equivalent of the fatted calf, though Destiny would have been fine with peanut butter and toast.

She had spent thirty minutes playing with her sisters, surprised when she did not grow bored.

Natalie was a dark-haired beauty and, though she was the older of the two, she was less assertive. Not shy but reserved and deliberate. After Destiny explained the ins and outs of Hollywood makeup, Natalie thought about it, made a choice—the right choice—and went with it. Analytical, as Destiny imagined their father must be. The colors in Destiny's makeup kit fit Natalie's skin tone perfectly, and the princess dress was a simple velvet, some sort of prom dress Jenny had kept.

"In case I had daughters," she explained. Had Jenny ever imagined having a step-daughter who was fifteen years older than her own daughters?

Tom and she had joked all the way to his house, an easy banter that was smart, funny, and at arm's length. Just the way Destiny liked people. She had asked him to stop at a department store, where she bought a lovely perfume for Tom's wife as a peace offering and a full set of makeup because she knew the girls—her sisters—would love to play.

Olivia tried every color, declaring them all "amazing." She was Tom's kid in terms of personality, though she looked every bit like her mother. Redheaded, impetuous, outspoken—telling Destiny *she* was not her sister until Olivia decided she could be. Destiny laughed, fist-bumped her, and a sisterhood was sealed.

She had begun Sunday morning with one sister and found herself three days later with four sisters, only one of whom she had known longer than a day. And a brother. Couldn't forget the brother—though she tried. He came with strings attached. Destiny couldn't untangle those right now.

Jenny brought her a Diet Coke and a glass filled with ice. "Are you happy you came?"

"Yeah. Are you happy I came? This has to be weird for you."

Jenny toweled off a carrot and began to peel it. "I came into this marriage knowing every bit of Tom's history. So I—"

"Wait. Hold on, dude. How do you know it's *every* bit? No one can know someone all the way."

"Let me rephrase: I came into this relationship knowing how he had surrendered you for adoption. And how he had booked it out of his girlfriend's life and basically hid from her until she left Boston. So baby Destiny was never a surprise. Grown-up Destiny—well, you're a cool revelation."

Destiny laughed. "So you buy this package?"

"Let me rephrase again."

"I can tell you're married to a lawyer."

"Right on. Lots of rephrasing in this home. What I mean to say is it's really cool to finally meet you. Tom has carried a lot of regret about what happened twenty-five years ago."

"Really?" Destiny folded her arms across her chest. "Or have you just been witness-prepped to tell me this?"

Jenny grabbed a knife from a butcher block. "The truth, the whole truth, and nothing but. On December third of every year, he stops in at St. Paul's parish and lights a candle for you."

"A candle? Like that means anything."

"He didn't know how else to mark the day that was his great shame and what he said he hoped would be his baby girl's great beginning. He's not much for praying." Jenny grinned, chopped the carrot with the speed of an executive chef. "Not yet."

Tom came in, fork in hand. "I need more sauce. Everything okay?"

Destiny felt a strange weight lifting from her shoulders. "Yeah. Except I'm starved. I hope you know what you're doing out there, Pops."

He grinned. "Every once in a while, I get it right."

Boston / Nahant
Tuesday Afternoon

When Julia's fingers itched—when her *soul* itched—she knew what she needed to do. She walked three blocks to Newbury Street, to the art supply store that was too pricey when she and Jeanne were students, and bought some chalk.

And she kept walking.

First to the Public Gardens, the grass winter brown, flowers long dead. They'd come back in April, the same blazing ripples of tulips and daffodils as when Tom and she sat on the benches overlooking the Duck Pond and he made promises he didn't keep.

Not here.

She hiked back up Boylston Street and crossed behind the Westin to Huntington Avenue. How ironic that Susan Middlebrooks had booked a hotel so close to the Massachusetts College of Art.

A salty breeze stung her face. The wind coming off the water, misting the city. Nothing felt right. And yet, her fingers itched under the cast. The doctor would say the wounds were healing, and Julia could only pray that was so.

The leaden sky pressed down on her. *Thank You, Jesus,* because sometimes you need a storm to cleanse the shame. Julia stood on the sidewalk outside her old dorm, stared at the door as if willing her twenty-year-old self to walk out so she could tell herself *it's all going to be okay. Not easy. Not the way you planned. But there is no shame in doing the right thing for your beloved child. Shame off you, Julia McCord. Jesus died to take the shame off you, so let Him.*

She hiked back to the Westin Hotel, sweating under her shawl even as the wind picked up. She knew where she needed to go and it meant renting a car.

Though it was midday, traffic was heavy coming out of the city. Rain in Boston, the weather lady had said, and snow in New Hampshire and Maine. Maybe a lot of snow if the Arctic air mass danced with the warm air coming up from the Gulf.

A good, old-fashioned Nor'easter. Not that Julia missed those—not one bit.

Chloe probably didn't understand what can happen in New England when weather moves in from all sides. Julia wouldn't call and pressure her. Maybe she'd send a text, just reminding her to head back to the city before night came and the rain began.

The traffic jam broke a couple miles north of Boston. After fifteen minutes, Julia took the exit for Lynn. A few miles later she crossed the long causeway to Nahant. She took a left onto Ocean Boulevard, then found the right to Marginal Road, where the big homes overlooked the water. It was only a short half mile to the mansion they had restored. Julia parked, got out of the car, and stared down the driveway.

Surely the massive house had been renovated a couple times in the past two decades. And yet, she could see the barren branches of the roses she had reclaimed climbing the trellis on the front porch. They would bloom red in July. Tom would pick the biggest bloom and sprinkle petals on—

Long forgiven, child.

She felt God's touch—that flame in the haze—and she heard His voice, *dear God, thank You*. Nothing could erase what she and Tom had done, yet redeeming the past and the future—redeeming Destiny—was God's delight.

Julia got back in the car and unwound the Ace bandage that enclosed her cast. The half casts finally came loose but stuck to the surgical packing that was stiff with dried blood. She pulled the old gauze away from her skin, cried out when it stuck to the stitches in her fingers. This was insane, to think she could chalk with a broken hand.

This was faith, to believe—to *know*—that God specialized in using the broken.

All she had was her thumb and little finger. The middle three were crusty and swollen, so tremendously painful without the support of the packing and cast. She selected the blue and the red chalk, then got out of the car and crossed the front lawn.

She expected the homeowner to come out and challenge

her as she crossed the property. The massive door that she and Jeanne had stripped and refinished remained shut. The gardens had been put to bed properly for the winter with mulch and burlap.

Julia picked her way down the path, through the scrub pines. This craggy point of land had no beach, just the ocean crashing against the rocks in cold fury. In a few hours, this would be a maelstrom, but for now she could make her way to the flat rock where she and Tom had hidden from their friends and made love.

No, not love. *Make-believe.*

The tide was coming in. Julia had a half hour at the most to do this. She squatted down and clutched the blue chalk between her thumb and pinkie. The pain in her hand was terrible, shooting into her wrist and up her arm. She began to sketch, one swooping letter at a time.

Free Baby Doe.

She outlined it in red, melding with the blue to make that amethyst color, the color of sacrifice. The pain in her hand lessened as the cold seeped through her skin. The spray drenched her as she worked. The tide came closer now, but this had to be . . . not perfect because only God was perfect. Her job was to make it just right.

When Julia was done, she slipped her frozen hand under her shawl and thought about the blues and reds of frostbite. How if you let it go too long, the skin blackens and dies.

God had saved her, and in saving her, had spared Tom.

Please, God, save my baby.

Heavenly Father, please save all my babies.

A wave crashed over the rocks, flooding the flat rock. Julia watched as her words were swept out to sea.

Gloucester
Tuesday, 4:35 p.m.

Chloe sat at the bar in the Two Brothers Café. *Rob Jones will hate me.* She typed a good game but was useless out in the world. Twenty-two-years old and this was the first time she had actually sat in a bar and ordered a drink.

Ridiculous to have experienced so little of life. Was she supposed to tip the bartender when she paid for each drink? Not like she could call Jack and ask. She dug a twenty out of her backpack and hoped Rob would get there before she finished her wine.

On paper both Chloe and Jack looked like a Christian power-couple. They had worked in West Africa on mission trips, facing deprivation and disease. Their labor and money had been a nice contribution; however, though they were the most willing benefactors and hardest-working volunteers, they were well-fed and well-immunized. He regularly volunteered at local shelters, helping people regain life skills such as balancing checkbooks and interviewing for jobs. For her premed package, she volunteered in pediatric oncology, soothing children and assuring parents that the professionals would do every possible thing to save their babies.

Was it some kind of cosmic irony that she couldn't assure her birth mother the same thing about Dillon Whittaker? It was blasphemous to even consider fate might have a hand in their lives. She had to excuse God somehow because as reckless as Julia McCord had been, she had given up her first two children for their benefit. Why an almighty Father hadn't blessed her with a healthy child she could raise to adulthood was a calculation only prophets and pastors dare touch.

Chloe fidgeted as she stared at herself in the bar's mirror. She looked good. The saleswoman at the boutique had said so, and the mirror agreed. Would Rob Jones find her attractive? The whole eyes-of-the-soul thing she inherited from Julia made every look seem meaningful. The clothes she bought after Destiny's tutorial accentuated the slender body that Jack took for granted. The haircut she'd gotten at the ritzy salon stepped her up five notches from the home-clipped college student.

She paid cash because Jack had a program that informed him of every credit card purchase. *Good stewardship,* he'd said, *and a good hedge against fraud and identity theft.* Did he understand that it made her feel guilty every time she charged something at Starbucks or on Amazon?

He'd be humiliated if she told him that, a fact that bound her even tighter to his control. It wasn't his fault that she fell so quickly into beta mode behind anyone—male or female—who wore the mantle of alpha dog.

After Father died, Mother took the reins of the dos and don'ts. *Love the Lord your God* was always rule number one. On those lonely nights when she cried for the parent who wasn't there to comfort her, God's arms seemed too short to substitute. And Mother had her own tears to contend with.

Love your neighbor as yourself. Chloe wanted to do that. Becoming a pediatrician would be an act of sacrifice and commitment to others. She had done the volunteer work above and beyond, something that their wealth and faith decreed. And yet the concept of neighbor was vague. Church, school, and social obligations formed the community in which Chloe moved.

Among the residents of their exclusive condominium complex, they only knew Dr. Marj MacArthur well enough to invite for tea. Chloe could have bonded with her fellow premed students if she lived in the dorms or ratty apartment buildings. In class and labs, they climbed up another's back and stepped on faces to distinguish themselves as the best candidate for Harvard or Stanford or UNC.

Before *WaveRunner*, Joe Phinney was her only friend. An equipment repairman, he seemed perpetually in residence at the labs. Joe was ex-military, trained in making things work correctly without worrying about the theory. She was a lab assistant freshman year, relegated to washing glassware and mixing acids and bases, when she met him. The first time he removed a panel and she saw the guts of the machine—the circuits, micropumps, fluid lines—Chloe felt like she'd tumbled into a living mystery.

"What if I changed to a hands-on discipline?" she asked Jack that night at the library. "Some sort of engineering, like electronic or even . . . biomed?"

"You could," he said, his eyes telling a different story. "It would delay the wedding by a year."

At nineteen, the wedding was still a sacred pact—and a secret. When they were with family or at church, Jack would clutch his right hand over his left as a shared signal of betrothal. The plan was to tell Mother and his parents at the beginning of their sophomore year. Jack said they would freak at first. Eventually they would acknowledge a Deschene-Middlebrooks match was wonderful enough to have been made in heaven and thus should be cemented on earth.

"Why would a change to engineering mean changing the wedding?" Chloe had asked.

"So you could catch up in your studies."

She knocked him affectionately on the side of the head. "Duh—premed at Duke. You think I can't make it in the engineering school?"

"Of course you can. Except . . . Advanced Calc. Remember?"

Jack had aced it first semester. She had done so poorly she had to drop it before it ruined her GPA. Four years later she understood how her mind worked—she needed to touch things to grasp their essence.

Now in marriage, Chloe longed for the touch and not the plan. Jack's intention was pure, almost too pure. She wanted a luxury sex life; he preferred to dole out his touches like his stupid manufacturer coupons. Chloe didn't know whether he despised his own sexuality—or hers.

Her phone chimed. Julia, sending a text.

> Hope day is going well. Pls watch weather. Boston can be treacherous.

Should she respond with a quick *I'm with friends*? Best not to. Julia would know she had the phone on and she might call. If something developed of this evening—and the thought made Chloe's hands sweat—then she'd send a text.

She swiveled on her stool so she could look out the window. Outside, the harbor had gone dark except for the occasional security light on the piers. Cars passed by on the street, framing fog in their headlights. She had gotten to Two Brothers early, wanting to see Rob before he saw her.

How would she handle the greeting?

She'd have to remember that she was Hope McCord. Just for tonight while she sorted out this nature-or-nurture question. Which would win out? Nature—the young and foolish Julia McCord? Or nurture—Jack, Mother, Mr. Metzler, countless professors and mentors and advisers and youth leaders?

She imagined Rob Jones folding strong, calloused hands over hers. His face would be wind-burned, his eyes so alive. It doesn't matter, he would say. Let's just live this night and let the rest go.

Mother would say this whole adventure was sordid and unworthy of a Middlebrooks. She still had time to turn back.

A blast of cold caught Chloe on her neck. She turned and saw

Rob Jones framed in the door. So *not Jack* that she almost wept at the sight of him. Even as he stared at her with a shy smile, she wanted to text him and say this is a mistake.

And yet, like the ship on which Rob sailed, the turning radius was long, and she'd built up too much momentum to change course.

Tuesday, 4:45 p.m.

"I didn't kill him, if that's what you're thinking," Destiny said.

Julia stood in the hall outside the suite. "I'm glad."

Destiny fidgeted with the doorknob. "I'm sorry you guys didn't work out."

"God . . ." Julia paused, understood Destiny wasn't the biggest fan of the heavenly Father. ". . . God has a way of putting things together in ways we don't always choose."

"Whatever. So are you coming in or are you going to evangelize to the rest of the guests on this hallway?"

"Tempting." Julia grinned as she followed Destiny in. "Where's Chloe?"

"She's not with you?"

"No, I texted an hour ago, didn't hear back. I just texted again."

Destiny took out an iced tea for Julia from the mini-bar and popped a beer for herself. "I spoke to her before lunch. Called a couple times since, heard *nada*."

"Ouch." Julia's injured hand throbbed, tiny shocks like electricity in the knuckles.

"Something wrong with your hand?"

"Bad weather, I think."

Destiny took a long swallow of her beer. "Rain. They've been saying it all day. So what?"

Julia pressed her injured hand to her abdomen. "Not rain. Snow. I think it's going to be bad."

"Not in Boston."

"It's hard to get it right in the Northeast because of the ocean and all. They say rain, we get a foot of snow. We have to find Chloe right now. Because she won't know."

Destiny stared at her. "Know what?"

"Your sister won't know how bad it can get."

Tuesday, 5:18 p.m.

Melanie Connors would say to trust a mother's instinct. *It's a spiritual gift.* Julia was right, a worm of worry twisting in Destiny's belly.

"This was under the door when I got back." Destiny carefully opened the envelope marked with the Westin logo and Chloe's name. "It's from the concierge desk. A car rental receipt. Why would she rent a car if she was going to MIT? That's just across the river. A cab would be cheaper."

"Maybe she had an invitation to someone's home out of the city." Julia dragged her left hand through her hair. "And she's not answering the phone . . . either the battery died or there's no cell reception."

"You'd make a terrible cop. If she's in Boston, there'd have to be reception. And if she's outside, then she'd call us."

"Why do you think she'd call us?" Julia said.

"Scratch that. She'd call *me*."

Julia handed Destiny her phone. "Call Jack Deschene."

"Me? Are you crazy? If she's just having dinner out with some geekoids, she'd kill us if we set off the Deschene early warning system."

"What if she went back to North Carolina and didn't tell us?"

"No. Her laptop is on the desk. She wouldn't leave without that. She's fine. You're just being irrational."

Julia stared at her. "Really. Is that what you think?"

"I am not calling her husband. No way." Destiny grabbed the laptop, pushed the power button. The desktop came up with no password. Double-clicking on Internet Explorer brought up the most vanilla form of Google.

"Anything?" Julia said.

"Hold on." Destiny clicked the browser arrow. "Ah, MapQuest was her last . . . hold on."

"What? Tell me."

"I said, hold on. Good grief, woman, would you be so snippy if I was the one miss—"

"Yes." Julia stroked Destiny's hair. "If you were missing and bad weather was coming and you weren't used to it, I would be more than a little crazy."

"Where's Gloucester?"

"Gloucester?" Julia pronounced it *Glah-ster.* "Why would she be there?"

"She's got directions to 221 Front Street. Maybe she's meeting up with friends there. Though why wouldn't they come here to meet her? I never even heard of Gloucester so why woul—"

"Destiny. You're in the film business. Surely you've heard of Gloucester." Julia walked to the window, pressed her face to it. Her breath steamed the glass, making a hazy halo. "Gloucester, commercial fishing, George Clooney."

"Oh yeah, *The Perfect Storm*. Where the fishermen left from before they . . . you're not saying this is another perfect storm."

Julia handed Destiny her phone. The radar map showed a blotch of thick white swirl stretching from Maine to Rhode Island.

"This is Massachusetts weather. Unpredictable. And if the tides are right and the storm is coming from the Gulf of Maine . . ."

Destiny found the remote, clicked on the television. She flicked through channels until she found Channel 7 and the big banner: *Blizzard Warning.* "It was rain when we checked it this morning."

"She doesn't know," Julia said. "She doesn't know how quickly things can go bad around here."

On the Road to Gloucester
Tuesday, 6:07 p.m.

Julia insisted on driving, even with one hand in a cast. "You grew up in Nashville, live in Los Angeles," she said. "You won't know how to handle this."

"And you're the picture of sure-handedness. Right." No way Destiny would admit she was relieved to not be driving.

A blanket of snow coated the windshield, even with the wipers on. The headlights reflected on a wall of white, as if they were driving through cotton batting. The traffic was stalled coming north from Boston, commuters leaving too late to beat the storm. Destiny stared out the window, queasy as the snow built up on the roadways.

Julia had browbeat the concierge until he told her that Chloe was driving a subcompact. Nice in the city, useless in the face of a blizzard. Chloe could already be off the road somewhere.

Stop it, you fool. She's smart, brilliant. She'll figure this out. But will she, without Jack to do the thinking for her?

They had rented the only 4-wheel drive the rental company had on hand—a Mercedes SUV. A fun ride if Destiny weren't so convinced that their car would skid off a bridge and plunge into a river.

How ironic that Luke drove cars off bridges and cliffs for a living! All illusion, of course. Perfectly timed, safety harnesses everywhere, green-screened whenever possible. He said driving stunts were finely honed performance art. His mind divided time into split seconds: accelerate, jerk the wheel, slam the brakes—all in perfect timing.

The adrenaline rush came after, when they cut him out of the safety harnesses and proclaimed *we got the shot, man*.

"Call her again," Julia said.

Destiny scrolled to Chloe, pressed Talk. It went straight to voice mail. "Hey, sibling," she said. "Don't mean to play stalker, but the skies are dumping white hell on us, and Julia and I want to make sure you're warm and cozy somewhere. So please, call back."

Julia's phone rang. "Maybe that's her." She took her good hand off the steering wheel.

"No, drive," Destiny said. "I'll get it." The screen read *unknown caller*. Must be Chloe, calling from a different phone. "Hello."

"Is this Mrs. Whittaker?"

She recognized Luke's voice immediately. "What are you doing, calling this number? And how did you get it?"

"Not Chloe?" Julia's hand clutched the steering wheel.

"No," Destiny said. "Give me a minute."

"Melanie told me Mrs. Whittaker's name," Luke said. "And the name of her business. I called that number, got her husband and, after explaining who I was, he gave me this number."

"Why would you do such a creepy thing?"

"Because you're ignoring my calls."

"I'm keeping the line open."

"I saw something about a blizzard coming into New England. Did you fly out of there yet?"

Destiny could lie and be done with the interrogation. But she liked hearing his voice, even on someone else's phone. "No."

"Are you safe? They're talking power outages, record high tides, natural disaster."

"I'm cozy. You don't have to worry."

Julia glanced over at her. "Who is that?"

Destiny mouthed *Luke.* "I have to go. I didn't answer my phone because we're keeping both these lines open."

"Why? Is something wrong?"

You're not here. That's what's wrong in all of this. Steering through Tom and Julia and Chloe would have been so much easier with Luke along. Instead, he took off down a path without her.

"Dez. Tell me what's wrong."

"My new sister. Chloe. She's driving out in the storm somewhere, and we just want to know she's all right."

"You're inside somewhere."

"Yes," Destiny said. It was warm and comfortable in the Mercedes. As long as Julia could hold on to the road. One-handed. What kind of fools were they? "We just want to hear from her, make sure she's okay."

"Okay. I'll pray that she's safe and she'll call soon. Is that okay, Dez?"

"Go for it," she said.

"I love you. You know that, right?"

Destiny squeezed the phone as if she could strangle the truth out of it. "I have to go, dude."

"I'm praying, babe. I'm praying."

She clicked off the phone, stared into the snow.

"So, Luke," Julia said. "Do you want to talk about him?"

"No," Destiny said, but she did want to talk about him, so desperately that words came without her willing them. "He's a bear of a guy. Lovable and tough, almost a cliché except that everything about him is so real. You meet him one minute, next thing you know he's helping you change out your radiator because you can't afford to take your car to the garage. Or you've been dumped by some loser, and he's there with a six-pack and a Crock-Pot of stew, and he listens and makes you laugh, and by the time the sun is back up, a new day is there. Or you're sliding over the line on the blow because Los Angeles is supposed to be golden but it's turned to rust so you need a little something to get you going each morning and to reassure you when night comes that everything's going to be all right. You know that nothing's all right, you know you're killing yourself one high at a time, and so Luke is there and he's walking you through each moment while you sweat and curse, and he's got his arms around you and you know he amps you up better than the cocaine, and you put your arms around him and squeeze the demons out of him until somehow, you're both different people and you're going forward together, and life is crystal clear, and you're clean and this love is solid and works because Luke makes it work, and you're now in a place where you can make it work too."

Destiny stopped, couldn't breathe. She focused on the *ruff, ruff, ruff* sound of tires on beaten-down snow and the *whoosh, whoosh* of the windshield wipers.

"Is that what happened to you?" Julia's voice was soft.

"Maybe. Sure. We both sailed tough seas for a while and we walked out of some tough places together. Everything was going good—we were solid in our careers, we share tight friends. No fakes or wannabes, real people. We ride and hike and he sings and I sometimes draw pictures. We have some charity things that are important to us, especially projects that support wounded veterans. Even my parents, who have never gotten me, *got* Luke. We had a solid life. And then he walked away."

"To what?"

Destiny slapped the dashboard. "What do you think? He decides

I'm not enough—that *we* have become not enough—to answer the great *why* of life. He starts reading the Bible and talking to people and suddenly he's got this hunger, this light in his eyes, and I'm imagining him being taken down by the people I grew up among who frowned every time I wore a ring in my nose or my jeans were too tight or I got busted at school. And they would pray, as if I was so bad and so sinful that no one in this world could manage what I was, so some nosy fool or concerned youth pastor would make sure I was on a prayer list, and the list would get passed around, and more people would look at my piercings or my spiked hair and give me hugs and smiles and all the time pray, *God, she needs to change.*

"And Luke begins attending these rocking prayer services. And that was okay because we don't crowd each other. It was when he took quiet times without me. We used to do quiet time together. Suddenly, he's got to talk to God and I know he's praying, *God, she needs to change because I'm better now and she's not.* And now he can't even bear to touch me."

"Is that what he said?"

"Isn't that what you're telling your son? That making love outside marriage is dirty and evil and an abomination?"

"I'm telling my son to hold on," Julia said. "I don't have room for much else."

Destiny pressed her face against the glass. "Oh. I'm sorry."

"Did Luke say sex was evil in God's eyes?"

"We don't have sex. Not like you did." The glass fogged up with each word she spoke. "We make love."

"I know."

"No, you don't."

"I can tell by the way you talk about him," Julia said. "I know love when I hear it."

"So speaks the expert in popping out love children."

"You were blessings. You just had to be someone else's blessings because we weren't ready to be the kind of parents that you deserved. I've messed up enough to learn that God redeems our past when we trust Him with our future. And I had no other choice but to trust Him with your future as well."

"Nice words. Luke tried to clothe his removal from our bed with nice words about loving me so much he had to make sure he honored me by not loving me so much. It made no sense, so I told him to shut up. And when I couldn't bear him so close and yet a promised land away, I decided he needed to get out.

"If he loved me, he would have fought harder for me. Told me what an idiot I was, and how things really wouldn't change. You were there, eavesdropping on the whole thing. You saw how meekly he went away."

"Love sometimes means stepping back. And letting God work."

"That's how you people explain anything that goes bad. God is working. Well, I am sorry, *Mother*, but God just doesn't work for me."

Destiny's phone buzzed. She fumbled to answer it, adrenaline making her clumsy. "Chloe? Where are you?"

"And that's the question, isn't it?" the man on the phone said.

"Who is this?" Destiny said.

"This is Jack Deschene. Where is my wife?"

Gloucester
Tuesday, 6:10 p.m.

"We're easy together," Rob Jones said. His deep baritone made it impossible to stop smiling. "Are you glad you came, Hope?"

"To Gloucester in a snowstorm? Oh, for sure."

They'd been chatting for over an hour, talking about school

and Julia and what the latest forecast had been—*let it snow, let it snow.* Rob had made a beeline for her because, as he said it, his eyes found the most beautiful girl in the place. They'd fallen into an easy companionship, driven more by his good humor than her ability to make conversation while her tongue felt tied around her molars.

Rob slid his arm around her shoulders and whispered, "You want to get us thrown out of here?"

"Why?" She jerked back. "What did I do?"

"You said Glou-ches-ter, instead of Glahster. People will know you're not a townie because you talk wrong."

"You mean the whole Harvahd Yahd thing?"

"It goes deeper than that, baby. Way deeper. Hold on." Rob flipped open his phone, typed in WOBURN. "Say that."

"Woe-burn," Chloe said.

He laughed. "In this state, we say woo-bun. You can always tell a news anchor from somewhere else because they say the names of towns wrong. Try this one." He typed in LEOMINISTER.

"Leo-minister. I mean, Leo-ministah. Right?"

"Lem-ins-tah." Rob wore a green T-shirt, tight enough to show muscled arms and a hint of softness around the belly. His hair was chocolate brown with streaks of gray behind his ears. He was attractive in all the rugged ways she had imagined.

He had ordered Chloe a White Russian—contents unknown but so sweet and creamy she was already on her third. He had ordered himself a Blue Sapphire martini.

"Try this one." He typed BEDFORD. She leaned closer, felt the heat radiating off his chest.

"Based on the algorithm, I would say Bedfahd."

"That's where you're wrong. Because it's Bedford. You say it like you see it."

"So there're no rules."

"Absolutely no rules." Rob brushed her cheek with his fingers. "We like it that way."

A shiver worked up from Chloe's toes and into her arms. Was she really so hungry for touch that a wisp of tenderness turned her to syrup? "Give me another one."

"I'll give you whatever you want." Rob's eyes were a pale blue, fixed on her. "Just ask."

"Give me another one," she said. "I'll get it right this time."

Rob grinned, typed MEDFORD.

"Deductive reasoning implies it's Medford." She laughed, the alcohol going straight to her head. It felt good to laugh and not worry about anyone hushing her for being silly.

"Don't depend on deductive reasoning." Rob tucked a lock of her hair behind her ear, then trailed his thumb along her earlobe. "It's Mef-fahd."

"You're making that up."

"Absolutely not," he said. "Now lay some Carolina on me. See if I get it right."

Chloe took Rob's phone and pecked at the keys. "Try this one," she said.

KISSME.

Tuesday Night

Two hours later Rob Jones was still kissing Hope McCord—between buying her drinks and nachos and listening to the account of her birth mother and newly discovered sister. He had mumbled something like *is she as stunning as you* and Hope had mumbled something back like *one at a time, sailor* and they both bellowed with laughter.

At some point in the evening, the bartender flicked the lights on and off. A tribal signal, Chloe decided, like clinking glassware at a wedding reception.

"Hey, folks," he said. "Everyone's gone. I gotta close."

"I thought I'd have time for coffee or something," Chloe mumbled, panic inching around her haze. "I can't drive home like this."

"You can't drive home in that." Rob wiped the fog off the window. Chloe couldn't see anything except the lights on the pier, swinging in the wind.

"We're in a snow globe," Chloe said.

"You're not afraid, are you?"

Was she afraid of betraying the people she had left behind? Or afraid that Rob Jones with his strong hands and sunny laughter would find her as insufficient as her family did?

She pulled away from him and pressed her face to the window. The snowflakes looked like large moths. With each gust, the snow drove sideways.

"Chloe."

"What? What did you call me?"

"I said Hope. That's your name, isn't it?"

The *Chloe* must have been a product of her guilt. A click of the familiar shackles that bound her to virtues that had more in common with the mounds of freezing snow than the burning in her belly.

Such melodrama, Destiny might say. So what—sometimes it felt good to go with emotion.

"I'm sorry," she said. "Didn't mean to zone out."

"There's a motel around the corner," Rob said.

"I can't," she said even as the image of wrapping in a down quilt with him dampened her qualms. "Not tonight. I'm sorry if I led you—"

"Hey, I know, baby. And we won't. Not tonight. You can't possibly drive home in this. I'll get you a room."

"What about you?"

"I'll stay with a buddy. I got a couple within walking distance."

"You can't walk in this."

"Honey, I can dance on a boat tossing in thirty-foot swells. A little snow doesn't faze me. Come on, they need to close up."

Chloe squeezed her eyes shut and tried to stop the room from spinning as Rob helped her into her coat. *Jesus, calm this storm.*

"Stay warm," the bartender said. Rob opened the door and the frigid air hit Chloe like glass shattering across her face.

She slipped and fell. Rob helped her up and held her as she stumbled through the snow. She gasped and breathed in crystal air, then breathed it back to the storm as alcohol.

After a minute, she found herself in a dim motel lobby that smelled like burnt coffee, watching Rob Jones hand her credit card to a man hunched over a Sudoku book.

"Ms. Deschene, could you sign this?" The clerk waved his pen at her.

She wanted to say no but couldn't. Her tongue felt swollen. Her mind was slow in reminding her why she should object—especially as her body said *yes, certainly.*

"Chloe," Rob said. Clearly—but she couldn't figure out why that suddenly mattered. And why did he slip her credit card into his pocket?

Chloe tried to add one plus one, each time getting Jack and remembering that she had told her sister that Jack didn't *get* her. Back into a storm that swallowed her and spit her out onto a brown bedspread that smelled like old cigarettes and she heard a man who wasn't her lawful husband saying *I got you some orange juice.*

She was so thirsty that she gulped it down, and then she said *I'm hungry* and heard the man say *I hope so.*

And he leaned over her, his eyes suddenly as black as the night beyond the snow. *Let's dance, Chloe. Time for you to dance.*

Tuesday Night

Julia couldn't remember the last time she drove in weather like this. They had left the city in rain and now were in the middle of a near whiteout.

She clutched the steering wheel, thoughts torn between Chloe and *steer into a skid, not against it.* The jam outside Boston finally relented and they had made winding progress on Route 128. She stayed in the right lane, tried to follow the tracks of the few idiots still on the roads.

Two Brothers Café in Gloucester was still four miles away. Destiny had used the Reverse Phone Book to find the name that matched the address. By the time they called the place, no one answered. If only they had thought of that before they left the city.

The governor had already declared a statewide snow emergency, something Jack reported when he called. Destiny rolled out the phone-in-the-room story and said Chloe was off with her science friends, "thinking great thoughts."

"Maybe Gloucester means nothing," Destiny said.

"Then why did she search for the directions?"

"Why not? We're making too much of this. She probably just left her phone in her room. We should have ripped the place apart before we got in a car and headed into Snowmageddon."

"You talked to her. That's what you said."

"While Tom was making lunch. That was, like, a million years ago. And stop biting your lip," Destiny said. "You're leaving teeth marks. She's okay."

"Is that what you really think—that she's okay?"

"Wrong question," Destiny said. "What you should be asking is: do you have the right to nose into her business?"

"Hey," Julia said. "You came along for the ride. So you answer."

"I asked you first." Destiny poked her arm. "Mummy."

"You have more . . . *rights* isn't the correct word. You have more responsibility than I do because you've got the beginnings of a relationship. I really have none."

"Nice dodge, considering you're asking her for a piece of her liver."

"Asking isn't the same thing as requiring. I can't take it from her. I can't beg her or browbeat her or sweet-talk her." Julia leaned over the steering wheel, trying to see the guardrail. Her speed topped off at fifteen miles per hour. She flicked the headlights to low beams, cutting some of the reflection off the curtain of snow. The only sign that they were even on a road was from the car tracks, but those were filling in too rapidly. "I'm not asking either of you to do this for me. I'm asking you to do this for your half-brother."

"We don't know him. So we're taking your word that he's worth saving."

"None of us are worth saving. Which is what makes grace so spectacular."

"You do realize that words like that mean nothing. I've heard all this stuff before."

"From your parents, but not from Luke."

"Why don't you watch the road and keep your paws off my love life." Destiny opened her window an inch, slid her fingertips out.

"Luke *gets* you. That's what you said. If he's got something to say, maybe you owe it to him to listen."

Destiny opened her window halfway. A rush of cold air caught Julia in the back of the neck. Within seconds, the girl's head and shoulders were sprinkled with snow. "Pull over, pull over! There's the exit!"

Julia slammed the brakes. The car skidded sideways into the middle lane.

"Don't tap," Destiny yelled. "Antilock, press them. Don't tap, you idiot."

Drive into the skid. Matt's voice or God's? It must be divine because driving into the skid was so counterintuitive.

"Antilock, stop tapping!"

The car slid into the left lane, facing the wrong way. Destiny fought her for the steering wheel to turn against the skid.

"No no no, you're pushing wrong, let me let me!" Julia shoved her injured hand under the horn so she was fighting the car with her left hand and her right arm. *Into the skid, into the skid, my child* and her hands stopped shaking and Destiny stopped yelling.

The car did a complete 360 and then slid sideways along the middle lane, at least in the direction of traffic. There was no traffic. If they flew off the road, they would be buried in snow and not discovered for days.

I have always known you, Julia. Always known where you are.

"Oh, God," Destiny said and Julia prayed *yes, dear Father, remember my little girls* as the slide continued.

The car bashed into the guardrail on Destiny's side and the air bag blew.

And it was over.

Destiny coughed and pushed down the remains of the air bag. "I need a shower. There's, like, dust or something from the air bag."

Julia tentatively tried the gas, was surprised when the car actually moved forward. She turned the wheel very slowly to maneuver back into the lane. "Thank God that you don't need an ambulance. And I mean that literally, thank You, Jesus. And thank You that I paid extra for insurance on this thing."

"Yeah, yeah. Turn here. This is it."

The town roads were even worse, with a good four inches of snow and no snowplows around. The Mercedes handled like a trooper. Julia went slowly, driving in the middle of streets to avoid any cars.

"There it is," Destiny said, pointing down the block. "Two Brothers. The place looks closed. Coming here was stupid. She's probably back in Cambridge."

"I don't think so. I think she's here."

"Where would she be?"

"We've got to find her car. People caught in blizzards get stranded in their cars, run the engine to stay warm, the snow covers the exhaust and . . . carbon monoxide poisoning."

"If you get any more cheerful, I'll puke. So are you saying that is what's going to happen to us, given we're in a whiteout in a strange town with nothing open?"

"Let's worry about Chloe first. The concierge said she rented a silver Honda."

"You're kidding, right? Everything's white."

"Stay here." Julia put the car in park, undid her seat belt, and got out of the car. The wind punched her, making her stumble. The wool shawl she had bought this afternoon was no protection against the driving snow. She wore flats, never thinking to bring sneakers on this trip because all she could think of was Dillon.

And now Chloe.

Destiny stuck her head out of the window. "What are you doing?"

"Finding her car." Julia swept snow off the back window of the sedan that was parked nearest the pub. The wind made her face burn and then, too quickly, go numb. The bones in her feet shrieked with pain, even as her toes deadened. Brick-red, wrong car.

She tried the cars up and down the row. No Hondas. She trudged across the street in snow over her ankles. There it was, and the Westin rental sticker on the back windshield.

No sign of Chloe.

"Get in here," Destiny said. "You want to die from hypothermia?"

Julia slogged back to the car, slid onto the seat, and knocked her feet together, trying to dislodge the snow. She welcomed the heat on her face. Her hands and feet protested with pain, nerves waking up in the warmth of the car. She should have thought to bring a couple of blankets from the Westin. They would be warm as long as they had gas in the car.

Chloe . . . *dear Lord, Chloe.*

"No luck?"

"The car's here," Julia said. "I don't know where she could be."

"Look." Destiny held up her phone for Julia to see. "Right around the corner there's a motel. She's a smart girl. If she's not with friends, then she probably booked a room."

"So why hasn't she called us?"

"Let's go ask her that."

Tuesday Night

Chloe was a fool and Destiny would tell her that the moment she had a chance.

What a terrifying ride. That colossal spinout had nearly made her wet her pants. Raised in Nashville, and now a dyed-in-the-wool Angeleno, Destiny hadn't ever given a thought to blinding snow and howling wind. And now the Mercedes had punked out on them in the middle of the parking lot, spinning on ice and going nowhere.

Luke would love this. He'd suit up and dash into the heart of the storm so he could experience the crashing waves in the harbor, the gusts of wind, the driving snow.

She should be with him now in her canyon in the Hills, sitting on the deck and watching the stars blink on, one by one. *The heavens declare the glory of God,* he said last week. If he were here now, she would say the heavens declare a disaster, and God seems to have no willingness to stop it.

Julia had prayed before they came into the motel lobby, squeezing Destiny's hand and asking her to pray too. The only thing she could muster was *Luke*—and a debilitating dose of fear.

Chloe doesn't know how bad it can get, Julia had said. Destiny certainly couldn't have imagined this. She had had less than a day with her sister, most of it spent with Chloe poking at her laptop or muttering noncommittal things. The girl was her own high-pressure system, with her gnawed nails and compact movements, as if she didn't want to leave footprints in her own life.

The Perfect Storm thoughts. Framing the scene—Chloe hidden under turtleneck and tights, wrapped in scarves and lost in the storm, huddled over her phone for light. The screen flickers, then wind howls, and drifts cover her until all that remains is a pale light that is swallowed by the night.

"She's got to be with friends," Destiny said. "The simplest explanation is the most likely."

"She's here. I know it." Julia stomped off as much snow as she could, then went to the desk.

The registry was manned by a guy who looked like a stale raisin and smelled like black-market cigarettes. "Bad night to be out," he said with a bronchial wheeze.

"We'd like a nonsmoking room," Julia said. "And if you could, book us next to Mrs. Deschene."

A bluff. No clerk would reveal the name or room number of another guest. Not even in a motel with orange vinyl easy chairs and a coffee table made out of a sailing boat's wheel.

"I'm booked solid," he said. "People who couldn't make the commute home. Sorry. You're welcome to camp in the lobby. I won't charge."

"We'll stay with Mrs. Deschene then. If you could tell us her room number?"

The guy frowned, tapped at his computer. "I'll give her a call."

"Thank God." Julia turned to Destiny. "Thank God she's here."

He dialed, listened for a few moments, then hung up. "She's not in her room."

"She's got to be," Julia said. "No one would be out in this."

"When did she check in?" Destiny said.

He held his hands up. "All I'm saying is she's not answering."

Julia leaned across the counter. "What if she can't answer? What if she needs help?"

He snorted. "Lady, trust me, she's got all the help she needs. Now, I ain't saying anything else."

"I'd like you to give me her room number."

"Sorry. We don't do that."

Destiny pulled Julia aside and whispered, "Leave it. Clearly she's got business she doesn't want us to know. That's why she did something stupid like driving up here with a blizzard coming down our throats. We don't have any right to meddle in whatever she's got going on."

"Something's wrong. I know it." Julia's cheeks were stark white.

Destiny pressed her hands to Julia's face. "You're getting frost-bite. Let's get some warm paper towels or something."

"No."

"We can catch up with her when the snow stops. We should just camp out and get some sleep."

"No," Julia said. "I am telling you, something is wrong."

"And I'm telling you that you don't know her. You don't know me. And you have no right to meddle in our lives, even when we're being blinkin' idiots."

"Shut up and stop telling me what I have a right to." Julia stomped back to the counter. "And you—you tell me what room she's in."

"Don't make me ask you to leave," the clerk said.

"Now." She fumbled with her bag, came up with a fifty-dollar bill.

The man held up his hands. "We may not be five-star, but we don't mess with our guests."

"You listen to me." Julia leaned over the counter. She was so tall, she could get in the clerk's face. "You're going to give us Mrs. Deschene's room number or I am going to pound on every door in this flea-bitten hole until I find her. When I tell your guests that a mother is looking for her daughter that's been lost in the storm, you're going to get a lot of phone calls and I *ain't* the one they're going to be screaming mad about."

"Impressive," Destiny whispered.

"Lady, this is Massachusetts. You go bangin' on doors, you're gonna get stuffed headfirst into a snow bank."

"Really?" Julia was screeching now, her cheeks suddenly red. "How about I stuff you into a snow bank?"

"Come on. Let's give it a few minutes and then we'll have him call her again." Destiny tugged at her elbow. Julia yanked away from her and stormed to the clerk's side of the counter.

"You want me to call the police?"

"Be my guest." Julia towered over him, her left fist clenched.

"I can't tell you anything," he said. "I could get fired."

"Show her then," Destiny said, leaning over the counter and tapping on the monitor. "Show her."

The man reached over and tapped some keys.

"D.E.S.C.H.E.N.E," Julia said.

He made a sarcastic grunt as he typed, then stepped aside.

"Room 141. Now that wasn't so hard." Julia took a deep breath. "I apologize if I . . . was harsh."

"Where's my fifty?" the man said.

Destiny winced as Julia drew back her right arm. Maybe she should have asked Jack Deschene if her birth mother had any assault priors. Or maybe this was just maternal desperation in its raw form.

Julia grabbed it from her bag and threw it at him. It fluttered to the floor. He scrambled to pick it up and she shoved by him, into the office.

"What're you doing?" he said.

"We're taking these," she said, tossing his boots to Destiny.

"You want me to call the cops?" he yelled. "Stealing a man's boots in a blizzard is a hanging offense."

"Here," Julia said, throwing more bills on the counter. "We're renting them for the next ten minutes. No worries." She jammed her feet into the guy's boots, grabbed Destiny's arm, and said, "Come on."

Wow, Destiny thought as they headed out into the storm. Luke was a black-diamond skier and Destiny a pretty good snowboarder. They'd camped in the snow, snug and toasty in down sleeping bags and wool caps, Coleman lantern between them so they could see each other. Looking without touching was a sweet way of making love.

We have no fear because we control the details, he said about his stunt work. And suddenly, Luke decided he didn't control the details, that he needed God to step in and measure his every step.

Julia and Destiny linked arms so they could stay on their feet as they hiked to Chloe's room. She was booked all the way at the back of the complex. Fluorescent lights flickered and then held in the walkway. If they had to do this in darkness, they might walk off a pier.

Julia slipped, yelled as she fell.

"Get up, get up." Destiny put her hands under Julia's arms and lifted her. "Did you get hurt?"

"My hand." Julia pressed her hand to her abdomen, bent over it as if to comfort it. She wore the clerk's boots and her wool wrap. Otherwise, she was unprotected against blizzard conditions.

"We have to keep moving," Destiny said.

The outdoor lights went dark—*no, please, God*—and then came back up. Thankfully Chloe's room was on the ground floor. No way they'd make it up those stairs to the second level. It was an end unit, not the best of circumstances.

They passed room 131, Destiny's arms around Julia to try to protect her because at least she had thought to wear one of Chloe's ubiquitous turtlenecks and a Duke hooded sweatshirt. No gloves meant freezing hands. Julia's broken fingers must be in agony.

Room 135. They could see Chloe's window now at the end of the row, a strange glow peeking through the blackout curtains. Not the yellow lights in the other rooms, this was a diffused white light that Destiny knew well. Julia's son—the kid who was supposed to be her brother—would also recognize it.

"A camcorder," she said. "With lights."

Room 139. Almost there.

"What does she need a camcorder for?" Julia said.

Oh, God, Destiny thought, shocked that she meant it because whatever was going on behind those curtains was something beyond her or Julia or even Luke to fix. *Oh, God, let her be safe and I mean this, so don't let me down, please don't let her down.*

Julia raised her hand to knock and Destiny stopped her. "Stay. Stay right here." She pressed her ear to the window, heard the rumble of a man's voice. Nothing from Chloe, if she was indeed in there.

She has all the help she needs, the clerk had said.

"What?" Julia said.

Destiny turned the handle on the door. Locked. She pounded. No answer. She pounded again, deepened her voice the best she could and said, "Police! Open up."

The light went out.

"What do we do?" Julia said.

"Police. I said open up!"

Nothing.

"We have to go back to the desk," Julia said, "get him to open up."

"Not yet," Destiny said. "Stay here."

"No, I—"

"I'm just going around the back. I'm pretty sure these rooms have patios and sliders. Please, stay right here." Destiny trudged around the side of the building. Her feet no longer hurt, no longer felt anything.

She made it to the glass slider just in time for a man to fly out of the room. He shouldered her hard and knocked her into the snow. With the camcorder under his arm, Destiny could not allow him to get away. She grabbed his ankle. He turned and kicked her in the jaw.

It hurt so much but only for a heartbeat. She slipped into the snow and dreamed that she was in Luke's arms because everything was so soft and so warm.

nine

Tuesday, 10:23 p.m.

Twenty-five years.

Twenty-five years Julia had prayed for the safety of her children. First Destiny, and then Hope, and without ceasing for Dillon.

And this is how You repay my prayers? One child naked and drunk. One child kicked in the head and tossed in the snow. And one child still dying, after our prayers and the prayers of multitudes.

If this is love, Father, I would hate to see what abandonment looks like.

Oh, wait—she knew every sign of that as well. Daddy stretched out those business trips from three days to five when she was about eight or so. By the time she was a teenager, he was gone two weeks here, three weeks there—until one day he didn't come home again.

By the time her mother tracked him and his girlfriend and step-children to Idaho, reconciliation was a joke and child support a ten-year writ of desertion. Alicia McCord had clung to her God with iron hands. If she cursed God or Daddy, Julia never heard it. Maybe if Mom had shown some anger, Julia wouldn't have wallowed in her own.

Julia adored the God of creation. She didn't so much trust the everlasting God—until Matt proved to be as close to everlasting as flesh could be.

And so, heavenly Father . . . if You won't hear my prayers, please hear his.

Why had she been so surprised and devastated at losing Tom and then Andy? Julia bore more responsibility for those relationships. Maybe if she hadn't been so needy—*or forgive me, God, maybe if I hadn't felt such a desire to connect with a man*—but that notion made her angry too, because it diminished herself and it diminished God.

Anger drove her now, giving her the strength she needed to drag Destiny out of the snow and into the motel room. The girl struggled to stand. "Shush, just stay here," Julia said and propped her against a chair.

She slammed the slider shut, found the bathroom, and started the bath. Warm water, not hot. She ran back out to the main room and pulled the sheets over Chloe to cover her nakedness.

The stench of alcohol was overpowering; her dilated pupils spoke of something stronger. The girl stared up at her with blank eyes.

Julia knew advanced first aid: how to clear an airway, how to perform effective chest compressions, even how to start an IV. She and Matt had prepared for medical emergencies. What should she do with this?

She grabbed the phone, tried to dial 9-1-1, but there was no dial tone. Her cell, then. No, they had left their phones in the car. She dumped Chloe's bag, found her wallet and car keys. No cell.

Julia checked the bath, adjusted the temperature, went back out to Destiny. "Talk to me."

"I'll kill him," Destiny said through clenched teeth. A nasty bruise was forming along her jaw; otherwise, she seemed okay except for being soaked with snow.

The man had come face-to-face with Julia as he rounded the corner. She grabbed his coat and he shoved her. She held on tight and said, "Who are you?"

He laughed and flung her down. By the time she got up, he had disappeared. She had found Destiny in the snow, stunned.

"Not if I find him first. After we get you into the tub."

"Huh?"

"You're hypothermic. We have to warm you up." Julia helped her out of her clothes down to her underwear. "Can you stand?"

"My feet. I can't feel them."

"I know." Julia couldn't feel hers either. Her cheeks burned as if she had been slapped. Damaged skin coming alive in the heat of the room. "Come on, help me. Get up."

Destiny struggled to her feet and stared at Chloe. "Date rape?"

"We don't know that. Not yet. Come on, while you still have toes." Julia steered her into the bathroom, helped her into the bath. She kicked off her boots and took off her slacks and stepped into the warm water with her daughter. It felt like iron rods were being jammed through the bones of her feet.

She used a facecloth to warm Destiny's cheeks. The bruise grew angrier. "I'll find him and kill him," Destiny said, shivering so hard that Julia had to hold her shoulders. A good sign, the body coming back.

For the first few months after Destiny was born, Julia thought about simple tasks she had relinquished. Like bathing her baby. No time to dwell on the irony of this moment. Chloe needed her too.

"Don't try to get out without my help. I need to check on your sister."

"Don't call the cops unless she says it's okay."

"I have to."

"No, not unless she says so."

"Then what do I do?" Julia said.

"You're her mother. Figure it out."

I brought this on them. I brought this on my daughters, and I brought judgment on my son, and anything I do—

I search you and know you, Julia.

Not Matt's voice, not a voice at all, but a truth, the truth she had staked her life on, no matter how angry she got. Because unlike her father, and unlike Tom and unlike Andy, God had a way of staying with her.

And so she prayed. *Dear Father, show me what to do.*

You're their mother. Be their mother.

Tuesday, 10:32 p.m.

Close them, Chloe told herself.

Though the light scalded her eyes, she couldn't force her lids to drop and make all this go away. What *this* was, she wasn't quite sure. She only knew it was unforgivable, and if she could make the light go away, she could crawl into a ball and fade away.

Mother had promised that Father waited for them on the other side, two fathers if you believed the math. *I know my transgressions, and my sins are ever before me*, a burden too heavy for Chloe to consider, let alone lift to the throne room of heaven.

Washed whiter than snow didn't add up because that was what had made her stumble, the notion that snow would hide what she did today and that tomorrow she could go to see her birth father—*surely I was sinful at birth, sinful from the time my mother conceived me*—and no one would know.

Instead, her tracks led her other mother and only sister to her, and now her sin would be ever before them. And the *WaveRunner*, though it wasn't clear why she thought that. Perhaps if Julia would stop stroking her face, she could figure out the sum of all of this. Then she could tally her debt and slip into the black ocean where the uncountable and irrevocable could hide.

"Let me pray with you," Julia said. Chloe couldn't find those words because Rob had kissed away her prayers. Suddenly the sister had her arms around her, saying "You pray and I'll say the amen," and so Julia did.

Chloe clawed at the girl—who? Oh yes, Destiny, who was far stronger than she looked because she held her tight while their mother asked God to soothe His child and strengthen her and let her know—*KNOW*—she prayed. *Let her know the peace that transcends all understanding,* and Destiny said *yeah, that*, and then said she would go to the car and get their phones and Julia said *no, I will* and Destiny said *no, she needs a mother now and you're the only one who qualifies for that* and Chloe clutched Julia's hands because the wind howled and the light flickered and died.

And she was suddenly so very terrified of the dark.

Tuesday, 11:14 p.m.

Destiny trudged through the storm, bundled in Chloe's down jacket, a cotton blanket wrapped around her head and shoulders. She had to browbeat Julia into giving her the keys to the Mercedes so she could retrieve their phones.

What Julia didn't know was that she had also taken the keys to Chloe's rental.

As insane as it was to hike that extra block, Destiny was not going to let the kick to her head, or whatever had been done to Chloe, pass without a fight. The wind whipped at her, and she had to bend over to fight it. When she straightened up, she realized the motel windows were lit with a spooky red glow from the emergency lights. No electricity and the snow was up to her calves, some drifts shoulder high.

Destiny had packed towels inside the top of her boots. Luke would be proud of her forethought. She would never do to him what Chloe had just done to her husband.

How bitter to hope her sister had been date-raped rather than to discover she had indulged in the most sordid type of sex. And Julia—what was Destiny to make of her? How humiliating to have a near-stranger strip and bathe you to save you from hypothermia. It was a kind and wise thing to do—but *still*.

Destiny clicked the key to unlock the Mercedes, then had to dig through snow to get to the door handle. She grabbed Julia's wallet, iPad, and phone and shoved them into her own backpack. The glove box yielded up a flashlight. The spare-tire compartment in the back provided another flashlight and a couple road flares that might be useful if a snowplow came along. Luke would be proud of her clear thinking.

Survival was easy to sort out. It was matters of the heart and body that remained complicated.

With the backpack over her shoulders and blanket over her head, she headed for the street where Chloe's car was parked. She should have dried her hair before she came out. The strands stiffened in the frigid wind. She could be wrapped in a down blanket right now if they had thought ahead before racing out of the Westin.

Turn back. That would be the smart thing to do.

No way. If she could hitchhike from Illinois to California, she could trudge one block in a blizzard. She'd run Chloe's car for a little while and dry her hair over the heater.

She turned left at the main road, then spun around. Which

way had they come to get from Two Brothers Cafe to the motel? She couldn't see a thing, could barely keep her eyes open against the wind. Somewhere nearby was the harbor. She had seen it on MapQuest.

Take a long walk off a short cliff could easily translate into take a snowy walk off a short pier into the angry Atlantic.

Destiny sheltered in the doorway of a shuttered shop, took off one mitten, and dug a phone out of the backpack. Julia's phone—but she didn't have the luxury of searching for hers under all the other stuff in there, not with her fingers numbing rapidly.

She thumbed it on, trying to find the navigation feature.

It rang. *Home*, the screen said. No way, Destiny was not going to talk to Julia's husband.

The street map came up quickly. Yes, she should have turned right. More good news—she was only a couple hundred feet from the bar, and Chloe's car was on this side of the street. She'd get warmed up while she searched for any scrap of paper that would indicate who that guy was.

The phone rang again. More *Home*.

None of my business, she told herself. Then again, Julia had been good to her. It would be twenty minutes before she got back to the hotel and who knew what kind of crazy was going on there, with the Chloe situation.

Destiny owed it to Julia's husband to tell him that his wife was okay. She clicked on the icon, was startled when the screen came live with the face of a teenager.

"Hey," he said. "Who are you?"

Do You see, God, why I have no patience with You and Your tricks?

"I'm Destiny," she said. "And I'm guessing you're Julia's son."

"Yeah, something like that. Where's my mother?"

"She's in a motel room."

"So why do you have Mom's phone?"

"She left it in the car. I volunteered to get it for her."

He peered into the screen, his hair matted and his face puffy. "So who are you?"

"I'm traveling with your mother. Helping her with some things."

"You look like the Virgin Mary with that thing on your head."

She laughed. "Hey, dude, I gotta run. In case you haven't heard, we're in the middle of a blizzard."

"Wait, don't go yet. Can you show me the storm?"

"You want to see the snow?"

"My mother says I'm a curious pest." His mischievous grin was almost a smirk. Exactly like Destiny's. Luke had run film on her so she could see what she looked like when she wheedled for something.

She had to end this call before she found herself donating her liver, kidney, eyes, and heart to this kid.

"Please?" Dillon said.

"I suppose." Destiny stepped out onto the sidewalk and aimed the phone at the store so the snow would contrast against the faint light from the window. She moved back into the doorway. "Did you see it?"

"That is one radical storm," he said. "So my mom's okay, right? My dad's trying to book a flight to New York and hire a truck or something to come rescue her."

"No one needs rescuing. We're at this motel in some town north of the city. We got caught out and took a room."

"What are you doing now? You have the phone, so why are you still outside?"

"You are one nosy cashew," Destiny said.

The kid laughed. "Yeah, everyone says that."

"I'm going to the car to get some stuff."

"I thought you said you already went to the car."

"This is a different car. Now can I go?"

"Wait," he said. "Why do you have a blanket on your head?"

"I came from Los Angeles, wasn't exactly prepared for the Snowpocalypse."

"Los Angeles, whoa. Do you work in film?"

"Pal, it's not like I have time for an extended conversation." Destiny was about to end the call, but the look on his face—a cross between fascination and awe—stopped her. "Yeah, I do conceptual art. Which means—"

"You make monsters and aliens and all the cool stuff. So what's your name? I study the credits and follow some of the artists. I might know you."

"Destiny Connors. Do you need my social security number too? Come on, man, I gotta go."

"Before you hang up, could you turn to your left? Please."

She sighed, did what he asked before realizing the kid had maneuvered her into the faint light from the shop's security light.

"Oh my goodness," he said. "You're my sister."

Oh, God, if You love me like Luke says, please don't make me do this. Please, Chloe is enough pain for me to swallow.

"Why would you say that?"

"Because you have the cow eyes," he said. "No offense, I have them too. I trim my eyelashes, you know. Because they're so girly."

Destiny laughed. "I got teased when I was a kid, so I used to squint to try to make them smaller. Gave myself a headache for a full year in seventh grade."

"Want to know how else I know you're my sister? And by the way, thank you for not denying it."

She gave him an exaggerated squint, making him laugh. "Tell me quick because I'm freezing my tush off here."

"Mom told me about her two babies when I was, like, in fifth grade. And I just knew, even then, that at least one of you would be in Hollywood. Because that's what I want to do, and it's such an itch in my blood that I knew you or the other girl would have the same thing. Because . . . see, I love my parents but they don't *get* me. And I just imagined somewhere one of my sisters would be like me. Because I didn't want to be, like . . . out on this island of weird by myself."

"You're not, Dillon." Destiny pressed her hand against the window, let the cold glass freeze any notion of tears. "You're not alone."

"Are you going to come to Dallas?"

"Sure, someday. That would be cool."

"Promise?"

"Sure, man." Destiny would promise anything to get off this phone call.

He blinked hard. "Can you come soon? I mean, like, real soon."

"Let me get through this blizzard first, okay? I gotta run, pal. Tell your dad Julia will call as soon as I get this phone to her."

"See you soon."

"For sure," Destiny said, then ended the call before she promised anything more.

After sliding her mitten back on and rewrapping the blanket, she headed for Chloe's rental. The snow had filled in the back windshields of the cars Julia had swiped less than an hour ago. The wind shrieked, rattling the phone wires overhead.

The gusts were so fierce, she could imagine a telephone pole snapping in half, wires snapping like a whip and slashing through her skull.

Destiny couldn't help herself—she had to frame the scene. The next morning, blizzard past, sky razor-blue. Snow blazing in the winter sun. People poking out of their stores and homes like frightened mice. Drifts high enough to swallow any man. Parked and abandoned cars, only the occasional sideview mirror or car antenna poking through the mounded snow. A teenage boy, shovel in hand, is the first to brave the sidewalk. Clearing the snow in front of his father's butcher shop, he works quickly to stay warm.

The shovel hits something hard. He prods, sees something like a ruby under the snow. He digs eagerly as if for buried treasure or just to alleviate a burdensome task—until he realizes that he's uncovered a frozen river of red. He wants to back away, hide his eyes, but his curiosity won't let him and so he scoops and sweeps until he sees a woman's head, crushed on—

"Stop it," Destiny yelled. "You make yourself crazy."

The wind howled back as if to laugh. *Sister, you're two blocks past crazy.*

She held the flashlight with one hand and swept the snow off the back of the car she thought might be Chloe's. No Westin sticker. Should she go back a car or keep moving in the same direction? A ten-second silent debate was all it took for the snow to whiten where she had just cleared.

Use your head. Destiny fumbled in the pocket of Chloe's jacket, found her keys, and pushed the unlock button. She heard the *beep, beep* but couldn't see a thing in the snow. She couldn't even tell which way the sound came from.

Don't panic. Panic button. She stabbed at the key, thrilled when a horn sounded. *That way*—she turned and saw red lights flashing through the snow.

Three cars down, an absolutely chilling hike. Destiny brushed the snow off the door handle, opened the door, and got in. The

Honda was considerably smaller than the Mercedes Julia had rented and warmed up quickly.

The radio was set to an all-news station. Destiny sneered at the reports of the Nor'easter, state emergency, power losses. Unnaturally high tides perked her interest. How far was the motel from the water? What she knew about ocean tides could fit in a tube of eyeliner. The heat felt so good, her eyelids suddenly felt like high tide coming in . . .

. . . everything sliding away . . .

. . . snow-shrouded sleep, so warm . . .

. . . and what really did happen to Chloe . . .

. . . and why should she really care . . .

And then a crack of thunder, glass shattering as something crashed in on Destiny. She didn't care, just wanted to sleep but cold air poured in, fresh air that somehow she knew to drink in until she was strong enough to open her eyes.

A sign had crashed through the passenger side window, missing her by inches.

Her head throbbed. She opened the door to the storm because she had to throw up. She gagged and splattered what was left of Tom Bryant's lunch into the night.

Stupid, stupid, stupid.

Julia had warned about carbon monoxide poisoning in the snow. Words that hadn't registered as Destiny ran the car, taking in the heat and the comfort while snow piled up all around, blocking the tail pipe.

She struggled to get her backpack on, dug the flashlight out of the mess of safety glass and splintered sign. There were shopping bags in the backseat. Chloe had bought stuff for the Colorado snow, enough to go around. She shouldered the bags, wrapped the blanket back around her head, and headed back into the storm.

Wednesday, 12:13 a.m.

"Thank God," Julia said as Destiny tumbled through the door, arms laden with bags.

"Sure," she said through blue lips. "Now stop staring and shut the door."

"I was worried sick." She had been pacing between the bed where Chloe dozed and the window. Ten minutes passed and then twenty. Julia was about to wrap in a bedspread and search the blizzard for Destiny.

Julia led her into the bathroom, helped her with her boots and socks, then—over her protests—made her take off her jeans. She used the flashlight Destiny had brought back to check for frostbite. Her legs were stark white, cold to the touch. Julia soaked a towel with warm water and wrapped her feet and legs.

"I'd tell you that you're an idiot," Destiny said, "but I can't feel my tongue."

The bathroom had cooled considerably. If the power didn't come back soon, they'd be left with wet towels and blankets and no heat.

After a minute or so, Julia hung the wet towel over the shower and rubbed her daughter's legs with her hands.

"Chloe bought us coats and stuff," Destiny said through chattering teeth. "In the bags."

"Don't move," Julia said.

"Like I can?"

Julia went back into the bedroom, checked Chloe. Her breathing seemed fine and the stench of alcohol had somewhat worn off. She should have called for an ambulance when she had the chance and not let Destiny browbeat her. What could she say now? *This woman who is really not much more than a girl got drunk and maybe got drugged and maybe got raped—dear God, please no—and I know we're in the middle of a blizzard but I haven't been her mother long enough to know what to do.*

Julia grabbed the bags Destiny had brought in, shook off the snow into the tub. She pulled off her slacks and put on the snow pants. They were beyond cold because they'd been sitting in Chloe's car.

"Real nice," Destiny said. "I sit here half naked and you—"

"Can't you shut up, just for once?"

The girl laughed. "Finally, a family resemblance asserts itself."

"Here, put these on." Julia helped Destiny into the slacks she'd just taken off and a dry pair of boots.

"Can I have the jacket too?"

"Not yet." Julia went back into the main room and stuffed the winter clothing Chloe had bought along the length of the baseboard. The pipes were still hot, though with the way the wind howled and the temperature plunged, they wouldn't be for long.

Julia went back into the bathroom and used a hand towel to dry Destiny's hair. "Why did you go all the way to Chloe's car?"

"I thought there might be some clue as to who that jerk was. At least I found all this snow gear. And Chloe's phone. Why do you think she left it in the car?"

"I don't know. Denial, maybe?" Julia jogged in place, trying to warm up. The cloak was a nice, soft wool, a blessing despite the hideous fire-engine red and olive-green plaid. That she took any time to buy snow gear for all of them was lovely, especially since the early forecast had been for all rain in Boston.

"This is your fault," Destiny said. "I had my life, Chloe had hers—that's what you said you gave us up to. Good lives and all that blah-blah. And then you literally drop out of the sky and now she's been messed with and I'm . . . I don't even know what I am.

Obligated to her, I suppose, even though I didn't know she existed three days ago. And I feel guilty as sin because you need a chunk of my body for your son, and to get it, you put a claim on me as your daughter and you tied me to you by my sister and it's all sick. You realize that, don't you? I was sick to go with you; Chloe was sick to come with us. And something sick led her to this place and made us follow her."

"You're looking for something," Julia said. "Or you wouldn't have come with me from Los Angeles. You're the one who jump-started this third leg of the trip so you could meet Tom."

"Big whoop. Like any five-dollar shrink couldn't tell you what I was looking for? You see what love gets you, right? Luke gets the heart, you get the liver, and Chloe gets my frostbitten toes and nose and—"

"—and nothing, young lady. Enough now." Julia didn't know whether to shake her or hug her.

"Oh, Big Mama talk. I'm scared." Destiny mocked a tremor, then got caught in a convulsion of genuine shivers.

Julia wrapped her cloak around the girl's shoulders, fastened the buttons under her chin. "You've blamed me your whole life," Julia said. "Haven't you?"

"You told me to shut up. So you don't get to psychoanalyze me."

Julia went back into the bedroom, flashed the light on Chloe before retrieving the pants she had shoved under the baseboard. Back in the bathroom, she knelt on the hard tile, pulled off Destiny's boots, and worked the snow pants up her legs. The sturdy fleece and wadded down made it tough with only one hand.

Destiny made a motion as if to help but her arm fell back. "You warmed them up for me?"

"Least I could do, considering I've ruined your life forever."

"You were an easy target. Because I didn't know you, I could blame anything on you. Can't sit still in class—must be something genetic because my parents and sister are perfect. Can't buy that old-time religion? Must be because bio-mom was a slut. Won't go to college and meet a nice Christian boy? Must be because bio-dad's wild blood is having its way."

"Is that what your parents said?"

"Of course not. They're perfect, remember? They took great pains to hide their displeasure. This one time I heard them praying. I must have been eight or so, and it was Palm Sunday and our Sunday school teacher told us to draw a card for our parents to surprise them with for Easter. And I drew a picture of Jesus on the cross and I drew Him as a baby because it didn't seem such a far stretch from Christmas to Easter and because my sister had been born a few weeks earlier—a miracle birth, my mother said to anyone who asked. They hadn't bothered to tell me I was adopted yet, so I figured I had to have been the opposite of a miracle."

"Oh no," Julia said.

"Shut up and let me finish. So I gave them the card on Easter morning, and I could see it in my mother's eyes even though she tried to hide her horror. She thought I had drawn my baby sister, Sophie, on the cross. And, like you, I could draw so beautifully, even then, so the baby Jesus *did* look a lot like her. Only because she was the only baby I had as a model.

"They sent me to my room without a word because my mother couldn't even look at me. They went into their room and I heard my mother crying. I snuck out to ask them to ask God to forgive me, and that's when I heard them pray that God would wash away any darkness in me.

"And I felt something being ripped away, right then and there. As if a clawed hand tore something out of me because this is the truth, Julia—that Jesus had showed me that picture of Himself and so I *had* to draw it. I thought that my parents would help me understand what Jesus wanted me to know, but instead, they wanted Him out of me—and they wanted you and Tom out of me—because they feared it was all part of something very wrong and bad."

Julia slipped her arms under Destiny's and helped her stand so she could get the pants up all the way. "We think we can create those we love in our own image. When we realize we can't, we get scared. They didn't know that you had been given a gift."

"They didn't see it like that."

"They do now. Don't they?"

"How could you say that? You don't know them."

"No," Julia said. "But this time we've been together, you have never once run down your parents to me. You say they're perfect, and that's as derogatory as you get. You could have ripped them to shreds and maybe found a willing cheerleader in me. You haven't done that. So tell me how they *do* know you."

Destiny clutched Julia's shoulders. She hadn't sat back down, and she wouldn't come into the hug that Julia so desperately wanted to give her. Face-to-face was enough, for now.

"Tell me, Destiny. Please."

"They invited Luke into their home, treated him like a son, though it made them crazy that we lived together. They knew he was good for me because he never reacted in the moment. *Wisdom to wait*, my father called it. They knew I was good for Luke because he's laid back and sunny California and, for all my bucking the system, they knew I was ambitious and would push him."

"What about when you were younger," Julia said. "When you left college?"

"I ended up in Los Angeles with literally nothing. The first month I slept in a booth in the restaurant where I worked in exchange for giving the manager half my tips. I hustled and finally earned enough to rent a room. My parents bought me a bed and a dresser so I wouldn't have to sleep on the floor or keep my clothes in a box.

"When I was in high school, they renovated the garage so I'd have a studio to work in. They got me art lessons and supplies and encouraged me to work at my craft, even though my art confused and sometimes offended them.

"There was this guy . . . as off-beat and quirky as I was. I couldn't resist him, couldn't keep my wits about me. So when I was fifteen, I had a pregnancy scare. Mom caught me digging through her files for abortion providers within a bus ride of Nashville. She didn't yell—though she couldn't be more pro-life if she were the pope. She reminded me"—Destiny leaned into Julia—"that every day she and Dad gave thanks that there was a woman out there somewhere who had loved me enough not to abort me. That this woman had blessed them beyond measure and if need be, I could do the same.

"If I had been pregnant, I knew she'd stand by me and wouldn't try to hide me away or make excuses. She and my father would just . . . give me room to do the right thing. So what does that all mean?"

"They knew you well enough to free you," Julia said.

They freed Baby Doe.

Wednesday, 1:05 a.m.

"You're a genius," Julia said a little while later. Destiny had stopped at the motel office on her way back to the room to return the clerk's boots and to bribe him to unlock his snack cabinet. Julia and Destiny sat on the bathroom floor, munching Twinkies and potato chips and drinking Coke. The sugar rush made Julia light-headed and brought some heat back into her legs and feet.

"Nicest thing you've called me today." Destiny's cheeks had

flushed to a healthy pink in the glow of the flashlight. No sign of frostbite. "Why are we still in the bathroom?"

"We're avoiding the obvious."

"We are not calling the cops."

"It's too late for that anyway," Julia said. While Destiny had been gone, she'd been on her knees. Praying for an answer, understanding she didn't even know the question.

"We don't even know if this was involuntary."

"*This* what? That's the question, isn't it?"

"You ever work with any celebrity brides?" Destiny said.

"What does that have to do with Chloe?"

"Just answer the question, woman."

"Matt screens our clients very carefully. It's the best marketing ploy ever—because not everyone can book Myrrh, everyone seems to want us. Why do you ask?"

"Because Paris Hilton and Kim Kardashian both made sex tapes and became famous. The Kardashians converted her so-called shame into an industry worth hundreds of millions of dollars."

"Chloe doesn't seem the type."

Destiny poked her with her foot. "You know an idealized version of her. The perfect baby you handed off to adoption. And I will admit, the instant I realized I had a sister, I created this idealized image in my head of who I decided she should be. And when she was almost the opposite, I re-created her in my mind to be a Pygmalion I could reshape."

"What about her husband? Surely he knows her."

"Maybe he does," Destiny said. "And maybe that's why he keeps her on such a short leash."

"That's harsh."

"And this isn't?"

"So you think that man shot a video of her?"

"The question is—did he get the money shot?"

"I don't know." Chloe stood in the doorway, wrapped in a blanket. "I don't remember what he did or saw."

"Oh, sweetheart." Julia struggled to stand.

She tried to wrap her arms around Chloe, but Destiny got in between them. "No. Chloe is getting dressed and then she's going to 'fess up whatever she does remember so we can figure out what we need to do."

"Julia—" Chloe tried to escape Destiny's grasp.

Julia folded her arms. "Your sister is right. Get some clothes on and then we'll sit down and see what we need to do."

"Now," Destiny said. "We put your clothes under the blankets to try to keep them warm. Get dressed, we'll give you some food, and then we'll talk."

"I don't want to talk," Chloe said. "I just want to go home."

"Sweetheart, we're not going anywhere for a long time," Julia said.

Wednesday, 1:34 a.m.

Chloe sat on the bed and tried to snap her bra. Her hands shook from shame more than cold. Destiny rolled her eyes and did it for her. "I'm sorry," Chloe said.

"What for?" Julia's voice was thin, tinged with a kindness Chloe didn't deserve.

"*What for* is the question," Destiny said. "We didn't call the cops when we still could have because we didn't know what you had done."

"Terrible things," Chloe said.

"Stop it," Julia said in a stronger tone. "Let's put aside the adjectives and get to the facts so we can know how to help you."

Chloe took a deep breath. "My marriage is not the happiest. Please don't take that to mean I blame Jack for any of this."

"I don't mind doing that," Destiny said. Julia gave her a stern look. She curled up on the bed so she practically surrounded Chloe.

"Jack has his ways and they're good ways."

Destiny opened her mouth to speak. Chloe pressed her hand to her sister's mouth. "He measures everything we do in terms of what can best bring Christ to a needful world. And how could I say I needed anything for myself when my husband has plotted out every move in his life to bring glory to God?"

"I don't get how this type-A thing he's got going brings any glory to anyone but him," Destiny said.

"You don't know him. The success that he's working so hard for and is pushing me to work hard for is part of a plan to serve Christ. He wants to go to Washington and intern for the Federal Reserve. Because he's got this grand vision of work being good for the soul."

"Maybe my husband could understand the link between the Fed and the soul," Julia said. "I'm not getting it."

"Jack could step into one of our family's companies and be a great success. We could lead a normal life with the house, kids, church. Like our parents had. He had this other idea, what he sees as his calling. Starting in ninth grade, he studied the global economy extensively because he knew himself even then. He got into currency in his first class at Duke."

"Money is the root," Destiny said. "You know that, right?"

"The *love* of money is the root of all evil," Chloe said. "Everyone gets that wrong. Not Jack. He sees so much manipulation in currencies, especially in third-world nations. In America, if interest rates rise or fall, our 401(k)s feel the hit, the stock market quavers, some companies go under. In poorer nations, people starve. And that's what Jack grasped when he was still a teenager—that one way to ensure justice was through a stable and honest money supply. His vision is so far-reaching and so pure that it's awe-inspiring."

"Terrifying is more like it," Destiny said.

"Maybe. Is it bad out there?" Chloe said.

"Horrible," Destiny and Julia said together, then laughed.

"Dez, what happened to your face?"

"I slipped and hit it on the car door. Enough about my stupid black eye. Talk."

"I got . . . the worst way to say it is that I got bored," Chloe said. "It's one thing to point to the glory of God twenty-five years down the road, but it's another to try to live each day as if that was all you could see. We ate on schedule, studied on schedule, prayed on schedule. And we even . . ." Chloe covered her face.

Julia sat next to her. "You made love on schedule?"

She nodded. "It was like Jack used his passion on everything else. He was kind and loving and careful and . . . always holding back, as if he was afraid. I didn't know how to talk to him about it. It was all knotted up in my mind. Was it because he was afraid of giving up control in the one place you should be able to lose yourself? Or was I tainted in some way?"

"You were a virgin when you married him," Destiny said. "How could he see any baggage in you when you hadn't traveled enough to get any?"

"This is the man," Chloe said, "who is able to project complex economies for the next five or ten years. When he became so . . . hesitant . . . I began to think that he'd seen some trend in me and projected it out to a bad place. It got so I was afraid to show my pleasure because I thought—feared—that somehow it scared Jack. And he's pretty fearless. The only thing he admits to being frightened by is disappointing God. So I guess, in my mind I saw wanting a more vibrant sex life as the equivalent of disappointing God."

"Stick to bored," Destiny said. "That's what really happened, right? He wasn't giving you what you needed."

"Honey, it can be so much more complicated than that," Julia said.

"Not if you keep it between man and woman. Once God gets in the mix . . ." Destiny curled tighter around Chloe. ". . . everything blows up."

Julia sat on the bed next to Chloe. "So what happened?"

"One night—a Saturday night, of course—we made love the usual way. Jack cradled me and fell asleep. Like you'd see in the movies. And I was left wanting—so much so that I had to get up and do something. I figured I'd work on my research. I turned on the computer and went to download my latest data. The condo was dead quiet. And I felt alone. Just so alone. I typed something like *alone at midnight* into my search engine. The first few pages connected to a song by some group. Deeper into the search, I found some sites claiming to be a place where you can talk to someone. Most of them were filthy, and I backed out as quickly as I clicked in. But I found this one called talkatnight.com where people actually do discuss things and not talk dirty. I went looking for people who were engineers—"

"Engineers?" Destiny said. "You're a med student."

"And I'm good at it. Because I'm supposed to be. It's just that when I see how things work, I get really jazzed."

"So you trusted some guy you met on the Internet," Destiny said. "You've never heard of Catfishing?"

"What?"

"Creating an online persona to punk someone. Like that poor football star, a couple years back."

"I thought we were compatible," Chloe said. "I just needed someone to talk to and he always seemed to fit whatever . . . mood I was in."

"So why aren't you in the engineering program?" Julia said. "Duke must have a great one."

"Jack," Destiny said.

"He thinks premed is more useful," Chloe said.

"That's no excuse for you taking the Jack way out." Her sister's words stung.

"She's right," Julia said. "That's no excuse."

Destiny tugged gently on her hair. "Told you."

"I know," Chloe said. "I should have fought for what I wanted. But I wanted Jack so much. I thought being the good girl was the way to hold on to him. But he was such a good boy that I was afraid . . . that being . . . you know . . ."

"Oh, for grief's sake," Destiny said. "Do you ever talk openly to him, or is it all about Jackie boy all the time?"

"Not on this. I don't know how. I have been afraid if I admitted my desire—my sexual need—that he would see me as something foul. So I began to wonder how it was for other people."

"Did you have sex with this man?" Julia said gently.

"No." Chloe closed her eyes, tried to corral the slippery images that danced in the back of her head. Rob giving her juice, telling her to take off her clothes and get into bed. *"I'll tuck you in,"* she remembered him saying and she sat there waiting—untouched and getting goose bumps, her head spinning—while he did something with a white light. Then he took her hand and said, *"Dance for me,"* and she thought she was dreaming, so she danced and danced until she heard someone yelling *"POLICE!"* Then Rob exploded in curses and suddenly the cold air came over her, and the howling of the wind, and maybe Destiny's voice. And she just sprawled back and lay there so the frigid air would sweep away his filthy kisses.

"How do you know you didn't have sex?" Destiny said. "You were drugged."

"I may be stupid but not so ignorant that I can't tell whether or not I had sex."

Julia wrapped her good hand around Chloe's. "What do you want now?"

Chloe wanted the safe Jack. The considerate and determined and really good Jack. She couldn't tell him what she'd done, and she couldn't not tell him. Either way, he would hate her. He wouldn't divorce her because that would be unmerciful. Instead, he'd hedge her in tighter—and hedge himself on the far side so he could never be touched by all that was wrong in her.

There was only one path for redemption. "I want to go to Dallas. And see about donating."

"No," Destiny said, peering over Chloe's shoulder. "You can't let her, Julia. Not like this."

Chloe ignored her. "As soon as the weather clears, we'll go to Dallas. I'll get tested, meet with Dillon's doctor, and we'll get this done."

"No." Julia cradled Chloe's face with her hands. "I can't allow that."

"I didn't have sex with him," she said. "I should still be . . . physically clean."

"Oh, my dear child. As desperate as I am to help my son—to save my son—I'm not going to let you go into this out of guilt."

"I screwed up. Screwed up terribly. I need to redeem that some way."

"You need to start with Jack."

"No! How can I ever even face him again?"

"Oh, man," Destiny said. "And they accuse me of melodrama. Listen, guys, can we push pause on this *Chloe stinks and Julia's gonna fix her* show?" She climbed out of bed and went to the closet. "Has anyone noticed how cold it is in here?"

Not cold enough. Not cold enough to stop the stink of alcohol and the stench of her foolishness. Maybe if she threw open the door and just lost herself in the snow. The harbor was nearby . . .

. . . but Julia was gently pushing her into bed and climbing in beside her while Destiny piled blankets on them and pulled the knitted hats Chloe had bought onto their heads.

Destiny climbed in on the other side of Chloe, snuggled close, and said, "Okay, Mother dearest. Isn't it about time that we heard the story of you and Chloe's father?"

Julia snuggled in from the other side. "Chloe, you might not feel so end-of-the-worldish once you hear how I screwed up. A big part of that has to do with the man who is your father. So I'll start, if that's okay with you."

"Please." Chloe found Julia's hand and held it tight.

ten

Albany, New York

23 Years Earlier, May

Julia McCord had come to Albany to make peace with herself.

Peace with Thomas Bryant would never be possible. That much was clear.

She had taken to loitering in the lobby of Tom's law firm, hoping to catch him on the way to lunch or court. She called him so many times that he changed his phone number. She banged on his apartment door, only to have it opened by a sleepy-eyed guy in his forties who worked third shift and growled that "the other guy had to move because some chick was climbing down his throat."

Julia prayed that Tom would run to her and say *it was a mistake* and *the court will reverse our surrender* and *we will be the family I promised.*

She took to chalking again, abstract pictures of a baby with big eyes and open arms. She used the walkways of Tom's life to display her dream. The sidewalk in front of the courthouse. His assigned parking space in his firm's building. On the side of his mother's apartment building.

She welcomed rain because the pictures would wash away, and

she despised the sun because the compulsion to draw her baby—her Destiny—would itch in the tips of her fingers.

As the months passed, Julia imagined her daughter with her first tooth, and then three more, jawing on toys. Maybe starting to crawl and clinging to her adoptive mother so she wouldn't tumble.

When Tom threatened her with a restraining order, Jeanne intervened with tough love and a sleeve of cookie dough. She had to spoon it into Julia's mouth, alternating cookie dough with fudge sauce and some stern words.

"You've become a stalker," Jeanne Potts said. "You need to move on, Jules, before you get arrested. And I know just the place. IronWorks Ministries is looking for someone who can paint."

Julia's brain buzzed with sugar. "Walls or pictures?"

"Both. My cousin said they need a jack-of-all, someone who can help renovate their activity space and teach some enrichment classes for the kids. They offer minimum wage and room and board. It's better than jail, Jules. Because that is where you're heading."

"I want to go back to Nahant," Julia said.

Jeanne wrapped her arms around her. "Go to Albany for the summer, see what you can do to help." The day after finals Jeanne borrowed her father's SUV and drove Julia the length of the Mass Turnpike, across Vermont, and into Albany.

IronWorks was a consortium of churches that ministered to children in gang neighborhoods. The director, Reverend Paul Woodward, hired college students to help renovate the granite mansion the city had given them, to make lunches and scrub pans, to teach a variety of skills from dance to math to art. The consortium wanted to do it all. Day care. Tutoring. Sports teams. Living and enrichment skills. Counseling, and more counseling, and emergency shelter. So many needs to be met.

Julia prayed her own needs would flake away like dead skin.

Dark clouds rolled over the city, thunder rattling to the west. Spring storms, something Julia knew well from the plains of Oklahoma. She had a full class for Young Adult Art. A misnomer, to be sure, because no one older than eighteen was allowed in the IronWorks house before 6:00 p.m. In the evenings, they shuffled the young ones home for supper, cleaned up the day's mess, and reopened the doors at night for older teens to hang.

Julia's strategy was to present narrative art as the key to making it in video games or graphic novels. The boys had endless visions of blasting heads or impaling hearts. Liz Sierra, a grad psych student, assured her that as long as the dead bodies didn't resemble any of the living under the IronWorks roof, they'd go with it.

Better to get it out on the page than on the street.

The girls preferred to make fashion sketches, with enough enthusiasm that she lobbied Reverend Paul to add pattern making and sewing to their programs. In her third week at IronWorks, Julia observed thirteen-year-old Sasha designing maternity clothes. "These are for me," the girl said. "In six months."

Julia held her tears until the kids had put away their supplies and gone out to the main room for pizza. Then she went into the supply room and cried. *Children having children.* That's what her mother tagged her with, as if she were little more than a girl playing with a doll.

For the first time, Julia considered that her mother may have been right.

"Hey there."

Someone had come in behind her, and in a moment of insanity, and maybe unreleased anger, she swirled around and shoved the intruder. He staggered out into the art room and fell on his backside.

"I'm sorry," she said.

He held up his palms. "Is it safe to get up?"

"Of cour—" *Stop staring*, she told herself. A ridiculous command, because who could turn away from eyes so winter blue? His hair was blond and his face angelic, despite being built like a Cowboys linebacker.

He stood, brushed off the back of his jeans. "I'm Andy. Andy Hamlin."

Julia took his outstretched hand. "Julia McCord. I'm the art teacher and whatever else Reverend Paul needs me to do. Are you a volunteer?"

"Paid staff, just in. Onboard to do some pastoring."

"You're a pastor?"

"Someday. I'm a divinity school grad. With my social work undergrad, Reverend Paul thought I could help in bridging with parents. The whole Stephen Ministry thing, linked to what y'all do here at the Works."

"We," Julia said.

"Huh?"

"What *we* do at IronWorks. You're part of that now."

He grinned. "Well, I guess I am. Thanks for the welcome."

"Anytime you need a good shove," she said, "I'm happy to oblige."

23 Years Earlier, June

Rain pelted the roof in sharp bursts. The power had gone out and with it, the air-conditioning. The attic room Julia shared with four other girls was steamy and thick. Her friends were stone-cold asleep, even in this heat. Julia lay awake, listening to the storm, anticipating each burst of lightning.

Surrounded by kids and staff, she filled her days with physical labor and mental gymnastics. At night, she might cry silently—only for a minute—until collapsing into exhausted slumber.

Not tonight. Tonight her skin ached with loneliness.

Jesus, take this, Julia prayed, even as she traced Andy Hamlin's face in her mind and then with her finger on the sheet. Trying to quiet her mind long enough to fall asleep wasn't in the realm of possibilities. She pulled on a pair of shorts and crept down to the foyer. A safety bulb burned red in the stairway; otherwise the house was in darkness. When her skin ached like this, the only mercy was the chalk.

If only it weren't raining. The pavement of the basketball court had been poured last week and presented a literal blank canvas. What if she chalked in the storm? The colors would run and make something she hadn't intended. That could be the best art of all.

With her luck, she'd be struck by lightning.

Thunder erupted, rattling the windows before the night settled back into driving rain.

Focus. Focus on what God has given you. Maybe she could draw something on the dry-erase board. Swirling colors, night shades in deep purple with slashes of yellow. The challenge of making something unique and subtle with markers appealed to her. She'd have to mix, of course, difficult by flashlight—if she could actually find one. And then she'd have to wait for the light of day to reveal what was crafted by night.

Now there's a rotten spiritual metaphor for you.

Four steps to her left, into the room that held multiple services: Art. Study. Dance. Even yoga. Who was in here last? She had no desire to maim herself tripping over a chair. Wait for the lightning—see what it revealed.

Open space, chairs and tables folded against the wall. Thunder followed, and darkness. Reverend Paul had trained them for every kind of situation, including needle sticks, drive-bys, and hostage taking. How had he forgotten the simplest of preparation?

Where did he keep the flashlights? The kitchen was the likeliest place. She could cross the front room and then inch her way around the table in the dining room. Or she could go back to bed like a sane person would do.

"The nature of love is to create," Madeleine L'Engle wrote.

Is it still love if it has no recipient? Is it still love if the one created in love is then ripped away? Was expressing what God could create through her enough to qualify as love?

Like Reverend Paul, it seemed God had forgotten to supply Julia a light for the darkness.

She charged forward, crossing the room in quick strides. Into the dining room, hand brushing the backs of chairs. Through the swinging door, into the kitchen and—

—into someone.

She screamed and he wrapped his arm around her waist and put his hand over her mouth to stop her shriek and said, "Hush. It's just me. Andy."

As he took his hand off her face, she smelled cinnamon. "You okay?" he said.

"Are *you* okay? Good grief, I screamed loud enough to wake the dead." She leaned against him because he showed no inclination to let her go, and she thought, *The dead in me is waking up, and it's a fearsome thing.*

"I am so sorry," Andy said. "I was just hungry. You?"

Starving. "I was looking for a flashlight."

"Spooked by the storm?"

"No. I wanted to . . . it's silly."

He slipped his arm away. "Tell me."

"I wanted to . . . draw something on the white board. It's what soothes me."

"What can I do to help?"

"Find me a flashlight."

"Seems to me you can't draw and hold the flashlight at the same time."

"Probably not."

"So let me hold the light," Andy said.

23 Years Earlier, July

The nights stretched into days and the days into nights. The whiteboard art became a game for the kids and the staff and sometimes inspired them in class. Julia would slip downstairs in the middle of the night and Andy would be waiting for her with the flashlight.

Always the flashlight. Somehow it made the art more mysterious and less in the artist's control. Julia would swirl the colors, let them speak for themselves. She drew what the kids knew. The snarling cat that the hoops kids wore on their team shirts. The oak tree that shaded story time. Comical pictures of lawn gnomes standing on the front porch, looking at statues of kids on the lawn.

Anything was possible those nights because somehow Andy made it so. When the work was done, they'd sit in the kitchen for fifteen minutes, drinking orange juice and eating toast. They would say good night without a single touch because even on the calmest, starriest nights, they felt the lightning under their skin and knew—without a single word—that they had pledged to let Jesus calm the storm.

Julia told him how she grew up in Oklahoma. Mom was a school teacher. Dad owned a parts store for farming equipment until he decided he wanted a jazzy sports car and a girl to hang on his arm and disappeared into the Northeast. She explained her course of study at Mass Art and her two summers at Nahant that made her skilled in painting, plastering, wood refinishing, hanging crown molding.

Andy was from Georgia, the son of a pastor of a large church and since *I'm the only child, I had a lot of spotlight time*. His mother was nice, he said. Active at church and the local YMCA where she fought to keep the Christian in the mission without being pew-jumping, Bible-thumping obnoxious. He did undergrad at Kansas State, played football, thought NFL was his future until he wrecked his knee and then the NFL didn't think much of him. Seminary was a fallback, something to do while he got over his football dreams.

Falling in love with Jesus was a shock and a delight.

"And IronWorks?" Julia asked. "Why so far north?"

"I had to get out of the establishment, try something new."

Something in the tightening of his tone made her say, "And what else?"

"I have some personal things I needed to get away from," he said.

So do I, she thought but she couldn't tell him. Not about her shame, or her loss. She gave him the noncommittal *anything I can do?*

"I'm married," he said.

"What?" Her stomach went into free fall.

"Married isn't the correct designation. Not now."

"Are you saying . . . she died?"

"I'm saying she and I died. My wife is divorcing me. I signed everything she asked me to. Now it's just a matter of waiting for her to get the paperwork done. It's a terrible thing. My parents are crushed and hers are not happy, but they see how this is wearing her away."

"Oh. I'm sorry," she said. "I'm really sorry."

"Julia McCord. Do you always apologize for nothing?"

"It's rarely for nothing. Is repentance bad?"

"Forgiveness is better. That's what I'm learning here at IronWorks."

"So who needs to be forgiven, you or your wife?" The word seemed to bounce on the walls and echo back—*wife wife wife.*

"We all expect the world to be one way and, when it's not, we get confused, then angry, and then resentful. It started early with me, the preacher's kid who was supposed to hit hard in football and turn the other cheek the rest of the time. Katie and I looked great on the surface. So clean-cut, scrubbed in the blood of our parents' faith. We wanted purity and wanted the other stuff too. We realized we could only enjoy the other stuff . . ." He shrugged. ". . . if we got married."

"You can say the word, Andy. I won't melt if you say *sex*."

"Pathetic, huh?"

"So why Albany?"

"The failure of my marriage felt like a failure of my father's ministry. He swore it wasn't but we are—I should say, *he* is—all about families riding out the hard times. And Katie and I just couldn't manage. She knew coming into the marriage that I wanted a ministry someplace like IronWorks. It doesn't pay, of course, but I said we were young and we'd have time for that later. She wanted to be a traditional pastor's wife, and my dad's church had an opening she wanted me to jump on. I didn't want to have to follow in every step my dad made. I want to follow wherever God is leading me.

"I thought she was clear on that. Suddenly I was this terrible disappointment to her. She starting nipping at me. E-mailing me job postings. Telling me about church opportunities where we could have a parsonage and a car allowance. *Play missionary on the weekends,* she said.

"And I started nipping back. *Where's your vision for God's hand in our lives?* I would ask. And that would wound her because she didn't see what I did. It was like night"—Andy grabbed the flashlight and pressed it against his chest so the light formed an eerie circlet over his heart—"without any safety light or flashlight or even one flickering candle.

"The louder she got, the more silent I was."

"Women hate that," Julia said.

"I know that. *Now.* It was intolerable for both of us, so she kicked me out. I went to my parents and they sent me back to her. She said I was wasting her time. She couldn't in good conscience be the one to keep *Saint Andrew*—that hurt the worst—from where God was calling him. I slept on a mat in the kitchen until I found this opportunity."

"Are you communicating at all?"

"It's a lost cause. Sometimes we make stupid mistakes and God gives us enough grace to manage to live with them. Other times I guess God is merciful enough to let us move on."

"So what happens next for you?"

Andy reached out, took her hands in his. So big, so warm in the summer night. "I want to redeem my mistake by being with someone who shares my vision. I want to know real love. Do you understand, Julia?"

"Yes," she said and let her lips brush his.

23 Years Earlier, August

Stolen kisses. That's what Julia thought their midnight forays were.

Not stolen from God because they were doing God's work. These moments where their lips pressed together and she felt his heart beat against hers and knew how close they were to being one—these moments felt like a little sliver of heaven.

How many times did he tell her that she understood him like Katie could not? How many times did he tell her that she was the angel of his healing, the inspiration for him to move forward in ministry and deeper into the Father's heart?

How many times had he kissed her and made her feel completely loved without making love? Tom had mixed sex into their equation so quickly that Julia had never had the opportunity to sort out emotions and decisions. This summer was different than the last two.

This summer was right.

In the middle of August, Reverend Paul found a sponsor to send all five basketball teams to New York City for a Friday night street tournament. This required emptying the house of staff to act as chaperones and gatekeepers. Julia and Andy volunteered to stay behind for any emergency needs in the neighborhood.

Reverend Paul called an hour later to say they left the soccer nets set up and *could you bring them down and also spray for yellow jackets in the fencing on the east side of the court?*

"Which one of us is doing yellow-jacket duty?" Andy said.

Julia laughed. "I did a ton of it during our renovation work. I'll do it."

"I'll hold the ladder."

"You're quite the holder, Andrew Hamlin. Hold the flashlight. Hold the ladder."

The stars were out by the time they finished killing hornets, cleaning up soccer equipment, fishing Nerf balls and Frisbees out of the trees. A warm breeze had picked up, rustling the leaves and cooling their sweat-soaked clothes. Sheltered from the street by the granite mansion and the sweeping front lawn, the back play areas were quiet.

Andy had turned off the spotlights on the basketball court so

Julia could spray the various wasps nests without rousing them from slumber. Creatures with nothing but instinct, they would not move from their poison-soaked environment and would be dead by sun-up. The only light came from a distant bulb on the back porch.

"Another good deed in the service of IronWorks," Andy said.

Julia used the hose to wash her hands, gave him a quick spray. "Yeah, I do good work."

"Hey, look what I've got." He dug into his back pocket, handed her two pieces of chalk.

"Oh, so you're the artist now."

"You've been itching to do something on the court. Now's your chance."

"I don't know. I don't even have an idea."

Andy lay down on the court, a gray shape in the darkness. "Draw me," he said, spreading his arms as if he were about to make a snow angel.

"This is crazy," she said.

"Crazy is often the place to start."

She bent down and drew an outline of his arm. Amazed at how he had such a strong body—a football player's body—and such a sweet temperament.

She traced carefully, moving up his forearm, using blue chalk that fit the color of his eyes. She shifted, groaned. "The pavement is biting into my knees. Maybe I should go change into long pants."

"No. Wait. Just . . . sit on me," Andy said. "I can take it."

Julia knew she should go inside, grab a towel or maybe find an old stack of newspapers to kneel on. But she swung her leg across his body and settled herself on his abdomen. She leaned forward so she could trace his neck, then the side of his face.

Leaning all the way so she could reach the top of his head.

Blanketed by stars and night breezes, she stayed there, feeling his chest rise and fall beneath her, her self-control evaporating like chalk dust in the rain.

23 Years Earlier, August

All those stolen nights, when IronWorks lay in darkness, perhaps Jesus slept too.

Three weeks later Julia took a pregnancy test.

She slipped to her knees in the bathroom, test strip still in hand, and bowed her head to the cold tile, praying, *I know it's not perfect but please bless this child, bless us. Please, God, hear my prayer.*

She hadn't meant for this to happen, of course. When Andy asked about protection on that first night, she said she had just finished her period and all would be fine. That's what she believed, or at least, decided to believe.

After that, he carried a condom in his pocket, blushing because he had to hide them from the guys he shared the bunkroom with. Too late, Julia now knew.

Each time they had been together, Andy said he wanted this forever. When Julia prodded for a definition of *forever*, he said that the divorce paperwork was moving through the system and they needed to be patient.

She knew immediately how she would tell him. The staff would be gone again this coming weekend. She'd sneak out to the basketball court and chalk a tiny corner, just for him. A simple picture—her hand, his hand, and between them, a dark-haired, blue-eyed baby. The Midnight Chalker would come full-circle, and Baby Doe would live on in Andy's son.

The grief redeemed, the promise reborn.

But for now, Julia had kids coming soon and easels to set up.

Today was the day they'd have their first full-sized blank canvas. She washed her hands, brushed her hair, and came downstairs with that queasy flutter in her stomach and a bounce in her step. The doorbell barely registered when it rang.

When she heard a woman's voice, she thought, *One of the kids' moms.* They always rang first as if this were still the mansion it once was. When she heard Andy's voice, she felt a pang, trouble at home for someone.

Julia eased her way into the foyer, saw Andy embracing a young woman with sun-streaked hair, holding her as if a single breath would tear her away. Someone's mother—so young, but they often were. Someone's mother in deep distress. Until she realized the woman was laughing and crying at the same time, and Andy with her.

"Excuse me," Julia said, stepping back.

They turned and stared at her, Andy's face flushing to the roots of his blond hair. The woman pawed away her tears, then extended her hand and said, "Hi, I'm Kathleen Hamlin. Andy's wife."

"Oh," Julia said, fighting for composure. Fighting for breath. "Visiting from Georgia?"

Katie tipped her head to the side. "I've been in Uganda. Volunteering for Village2Village. I wasn't due back for another few weeks but . . ."

Andy stood behind Katie now, pleading eyes. Giving Julia a little shake of the head.

". . . the government pulled my visa. No reason given, but they do that sometimes. So I thought I'd surprise Andy." Katie smiled. "We agreed to do separate missions this summer. I didn't know how much I'd miss him."

A strong cramp seized Julia's stomach, a fist around her uterus, and she thought she would miscarry on the spot. *Take him, Jesus, because all I can give this child is disappointment and shame.*

The pain passed and she mustered the breath to say, "Welcome home" and "Please excuse me because I've got kids coming any minute." She backed into the art room and stood among all the blank canvases, her hands itching for chalk. When the kids came, she took them outside and told them to fill the court with whatever they wanted and so they did—with fanciful and adventurous and sometimes bloody images.

These would draw a reprimand from Reverend Paul and a deep hosing because it was one thing to draw your pain on something small enough to show Dr. Liz and talk about it. It was another to announce on the pavement that dreams always died in bloody and awful ways. So Julia commandeered her piece of the pavement, the outline of her and Andy's love long gone but the image of that night tattooed in her knees and hands. She drew Baby Doe for the last time and then folded him into a closed flower and prayed that God really would engrave him on the palm of His hand.

She found Reverend Paul, told him she had a family emergency and was so sorry that she had to leave. She accepted his offer of a ride to the bus station. Andy caught her as she was packing.

"Let me explain," he said.

"There was no divorce," Julia said. "And I was a fool."

"I cared for you," Andy said. "I've been trying to figure out what to do about Katie."

"Let me make that decision for you. Good-bye."

While waiting for the bus to Boston, Julia called Jeanne. "Please, can you help me?"

Jeanne said *of course* with no questions asked.

Julia rode the four hours in silence, with one thought. *It is not Andy's son. It is my daughter, and I will name her Hope because God will surely give her what I cannot.*

eleven

Boston

Thursday, Midday

Yesterday should have been the stuff that movies were made of. Julia had huddled under the covers with the two daughters she had given up at birth, eating junk food and talking about silly things. Every hour or so, one of them would jump out of bed, run in place for five or ten minutes, and then bring their body heat back under the covers to share.

A grace day with her daughters. A lost day for Dillon, another twenty-four hours whittled out of *not long* with no hope in sight. Julia sneaked into the bathroom to phone him several times, not wanting him to know that she was with his sisters. A bright kid, he'd put two and two together and come up with liver—the correct result but only if one of the girls was compatible and would donate. She kept the conversations light for his sake.

Matt had to tell her to stop calling because Dillon needed to rest.

So she climbed back under the covers with the girls and talked about everything except the two elephants in the room. Julia longed to tell Destiny and Chloe about their brother. How he laughed.

How he was close friends with the quarterback of the football team, the head cheerleader, and the autistic girl he made sure to sit with sometimes at lunch.

The other topic that had been forbidden was the camcorder. Once Chloe was clear of the drugs—though horribly hungover—Destiny nagged and Julia gently prodded. Chloe had nothing more to say on the subject and screamed at them to *let it be.*

The roar of the snowplow came on Wednesday night like a trumpet blast from heaven. They bought the last shovel at the hardware store around the corner and dug out the Mercedes. Julia cringed at the damage from the highway spin-out until she saw Chloe's rental.

A renegade road sign had smashed through the windshield, something that Destiny had somehow forgotten to tell them. Chloe's phone was filled with messages from Jack and her mother, even though Destiny had texted them both to explain where they were and that they were safe. Chloe made arrangements for the rental to be towed and then drove back to Boston in the battered Mercedes with Julia and Destiny.

Covered in fresh snow, the city was like a dream. Christmas lights glittered everywhere. Shoppers crowded the sidewalks, volunteers rang the Salvation Army bells with good cheer. Snow banks were higher than Julia's head. Boston's rainstorm had yielded almost two feet of snow.

Julia heard a report about some poor soul who had been killed by a tree limb, and she trembled to think that could have been Destiny. Then she hated herself for wondering if the victim had a donor card and type-O blood.

Sally had brought the plane back from Dallas after the airports reopened. She called a half hour ago to say the flight plan was filed and they could be in Colorado by dinnertime.

Chloe refused to say anything more about Rob Jones. *Maybe it's for the best,* Destiny said. Sleeping dogs, and all that.

Julia FaceTimed with Matt, asking his advice on what she should do to help Chloe.

"Nothing," he said.

"I have to do something."

"She's twenty-two-years old. This was her mistake—her emotional adultery. You can't fix it for her."

"She's like a wounded puppy," Julia said. "She doesn't know whether to turn left or right."

"It sounds like that act is playing well with you, Julia. Did you stop to think that this is simply clever manipulation?"

"Don't say that, Matt. You don't know her."

"Neither do you."

"And that's my sin."

"Drop it, Julia. Your part in this is long over. Long ago addressed and forgiven."

Oh, God, give me the words, she prayed. "Not completely. There's the matter of Andy Hamlin ahead of us."

"I thought . . ." Matt rubbed his head. ". . . this was just like the Tom situation."

"I let you assume that." Julia wanted to turn away so he couldn't see the shame flush through her face. She forced herself to look him in the eye. "All these years I let you assume it was over and done and my repentance and reconciliation was complete."

"Say it, Julia." Matt's voice hardened. "Just tell me."

"I never told Andy about the pregnancy."

"What? What! He doesn't know he's got a kid?"

"I was so humiliated when I realized I was just a summer fling, I couldn't bear to look at him—or his wife—a moment longer than it took me to get out of that place. I came back to Boston and had the baby. Andy did not legally surrender Chloe because he didn't know she existed.

"I knew I'd lose custody. The second kid in less than two years, no income, no stability, no sense of what was right. I felt like filth and I hated Andy and his pretty, sparkling wife for making me feel like that.

"For a day, maybe a couple of insane days, I thought about going to Tom and telling him he owed me this—to help me go to court and make sure Andy and his wife couldn't take her from me. So I went to his office. I could see him through the glass, and he looked so tired and yet so happy at the same time that I thought . . . I thought I had to let him go, and let baby Destiny go. And I had to let the child under my skin grow and then let him or her go too.

"Mattie, I don't mind if Andy and his wife hate me when I tell them he has a daughter. But I can't bear the thought of them hating her."

"Then don't put them through this," Matt said.

"What do you mean?"

"I mean—these girls initiated a joyride through your past and look at the mess it is already. Why drag two more people into this? I want you to come home."

"I can't. I promised I'd bring them to their fathers, and they promised to get tested. I can't stop now. And Chloe's in such a mess—"

"Chloe?" Matt jutted out his jaw. "The rich girl with a perfectly healthy liver has a mess of her own making to clean up. Boo-hoo. You're not there to play social worker, Julia. Come home before you do any more damage."

"Before I do damage? Is that how you see me—like a one-woman wrecking crew?"

He drew a long breath. "I see you as a loving, *desperate* mother. We took a risk, having you meet the daughters. It's not panning out. God must have something else planned . . ." He squeezed his eyes shut.

"Tom had a choice to parent or surrender. I never gave Andy that choice. I carried his daughter and then I carried this secret until right now. It's nearly unforgiveable. And Dillon. Our son's illness, our inability to find him a liver . . . all of it is on me.

"Maybe," Julia said. "Maybe if I lay my sin out to Andy, give him his due after all these years, maybe God will redeem this for Chloe, redeem something for Dillon."

"I don't think it's a good idea."

"The decision isn't yours or mine anymore. It's Chloe's. And if she says Colorado, we are going to Colorado."

"But, Julia—"

"I'll call you from Colorado," Julia said and ended the call.

Thursday, Midday

"A video camera? That sounds kind of dodgy," Luke said.

"Tell me about it," Destiny whispered, hoping her voice wouldn't reverberate on the marble walls of the bathroom.

"So, no cops?"

"We don't know if a crime was committed. She claims there was no sex, and without all that forensic stuff and blood work, we can't even prove she was drugged. This guy would probably say she was fantabulously drunk."

"I guess you sail with it awhile, then."

"I guess."

Luke, I talked to my brother. Words she should say were caught in her throat. *I met my brother and he needs part of my liver and I'm so scared.*

"Dez, talk to me."

"How . . . ," she began and then tried to stop, but the words had their way. ". . . how do you recognize a miracle?"

"Why do you ask?"

"I just want to know."

"All we've seen, baby. The ocean and coastline, the desert blazing into sunset, the Cascade mountains ripping into the sky, the coyotes screeching at night, and the birds proclaiming the dawn. Open your eyes and you're looking at a miracle."

"I'm looking at a toilet right now, Luke. I'm talking theologically. How do you recognize a miracle?"

"Ah, I'm no expert. Maybe ask your mother?"

Destiny laughed. "I've got two of them, remember? And I don't think I'll get a straight answer from either one."

She heard the fake clearing of his throat and the *huff, huff* of air through his fist as he tried not to laugh.

"Okay," he finally said. "Dictionary definition: 'an event attributed to a supernatural cause or as a manifestation of a work of God.' "

"What if it's a negative thing? Something kept from happening because God somehow intervened."

"I can't read your mind, Dez."

"Actually, you can," she said with a smile. "But here's the theoretical—let's say an old lady is sitting in a rocking chair in her living room and she has this sudden urge to get up to get a glass of water. A split second later a car crashes through her house. It would have killed her if she hadn't gotten up. Is that a miracle?"

"Not for whoever is driving the car. Did something happen to you?"

Destiny stared at herself in the mirror. For their differences in style and personality, she and Chloe looked like sisters. But when she looked at herself, it was Dillon she saw.

If she had been killed by carbon monoxide and Julia had found her soon enough, her liver would probably still have been usable. She was dying from carbon monoxide poisoning when out of the storm, a road sign slams through the window and brings the breath of life. A foot or two closer and that would have killed her as well. Head injury—perfect scenario for an organ donation.

The one thing that could have killed Destiny saved her from what *was* killing her. And she never knew. So why did she survive? Was that some curse on Dillon? Or some mind-bending trick of God to get her attention when even Luke couldn't?

"Dez, did something happen?"

"Of course not," she said. "We were stranded in that room for over a day. We had some whacked-out conversations. I just wondered what you thought."

"I think you're a miracle," he said.

"Luke."

"I want you to know that—"

"Destiny!" Chloe pounded on the door. "Destiny!"

"I have to go, Luke. The errant sibling demands my presence."

"Let's talk again, Dez. Soon. Promise?"

"Promise. I gotta run."

And she had been running her whole life. Maybe the miracle was that she finally understood that.

Thursday, Midday

What a fool she had been. An absolute fool.

Chloe didn't know which hurt worse—her head or her heart. If she hadn't danced. If she hadn't drunk the orange juice. If she hadn't gone to the motel. If she hadn't had all those drinks. If she hadn't gone to Gloucester, if she hadn't met Rob Jones, if she hadn't gone looking for something that wasn't her right to have.

If she hadn't thought she needed more than Jack could give.

And now he called and called, despite her texts from the motel, and now from the Westin, to reassure him. Chloe couldn't speak to him—he'd hear it in her voice. Instead, she had texted him an hour ago.

JD: Call me.
CMD: Can't. I'm in a hurry to pack.
JD: Can't we talk?
CMD: Nothing to say. I'm fine, will call when there's something.
JD: Come home.

I can't. Not until something washes away the filth on me.

CMD: No. I need to meet my father.
JD: Why? You had a father. One you loved. One you respected.
CMD: I need to go.
JD: Where to?
CMD: Mother has already told you, I'm sure.
JD: Where in the Springs?
CMD: Don't know exactly. I have to go.

Andrew Hamlin's ministry was based in Colorado Springs, but he might be at his home, address unknown, or at some conference. Julia said they'd have to get through his security staff before they got to him.

JD: Chloe, ple—

She closed the window before he could finish his plea.

Now Destiny knocked at her bedroom door. When Chloe opened it, her sister shoved her phone at her.

"Your husband is calling me. Why is he calling me?"

Chloe smothered the phone with her hand. "Answer it and tell him I'm fine."

"You're about three light-years from being fine. Talk to him. You'll have to deal with him sometime."

"Not now." *And not ever.* Julia had found a way to keep Andrew Hamlin's paternity secret for all these years. Maybe the *WaveRunner* episode would be just something dirty in the bottom of her spiritual hamper that would eventually get pressed down and long forgotten.

"Please, Dez. Not now."

Destiny gave her a dirty look, then answered the phone. "Whassup, birth-bro?"

She listened, rolled her eyes, and said, "Yeah, we're packing to get out of here. Not answering her phone? Maybe because she doesn't want—"

Chloe pressed her hand to her sister's mouth. "No."

"She doesn't want to delay us any further. She's downstairs, buying . . . ah . . . what was it she said? Shampoo."

Chloe watched with dark fascination as Destiny spun out a bizarre story.

"Yes, Jack. I suppose she brought some with her, but who knows where it went. Maybe the maid took it. Yes, the Westin provides shampoo in its suites . . ." She shook her fist at Chloe. "She said something about taking those to a food pantry Julia told her about, a couple blocks over." More glaring. "Yes, this is in a beautiful part of the city. I don't know, you moron. I'm sure she'd love to tell you."

Destiny pushed the phone at Chloe. She waved her hands *no no no.* She wouldn't stand up under another round of Jack's questions. Time and distance were needed to pave this over.

Her sister gave her another eye roll—ridiculously exaggerated—and then put the phone back to her ear. "I'm sorry. I didn't mean to be rude. I'll tell her you called and I'm sure she'll call back if she has time before we leave, and if not, when we arrive."

Destiny knocked on the bathroom door. "Oh, I have to run. Someone's knocking. No, not Chloe. It's Julia. Hold on."

Destiny put the phone against her chest and said in a theatrical voice, "Is Chloe back yet?" She paused, then said, "Oh, Jack's been calling," and then said into the phone, "Julia says she's already downstairs. We've got to run. Hey, Jack? I just wanted you to know"—Destiny stared at Chloe—"that we'll take good care of her. Bye now."

She clicked off the call and handed the phone to Chloe.

"Thank you."

"Don't make me do your dirty work again."

"Destiny . . ." Chloe grabbed her arm.

Her sister shook her off. "Grow up," she said and stormed out of the room.

twelve

Colorado Springs

Thursday, 3:35 p.m.

Julia couldn't stand it any longer. Despite the warnings to leave the cast in place, she unwrapped the packing and washed her broken hand. She hated the dried blood and faded iodine on the surgical sites. She hated the tight, black stitches and the puffy knuckles.

She hated that she had brought this on herself.

And maybe just for this moment, she wanted to take another swing at God because they were five days into this journey, five days closer to losing Dillon, and still Chloe and Destiny had not agreed to be tested.

Everyone she knew, including Matt, had read Andy's mega-selling book *When God Is Not Easy.* Their church had done the full-year program with videos and workbooks. Julia had used her frequent travel as an excuse not to participate. Andy's ministry had brought comfort to so many. If she had told him about the pregnancy twenty-two years ago and let him take Hope, Julia would have blown up the marriage—freeing Andy for herself?

The water softened the scabs and Julia picked at them, drawing blood on her ring finger. Which was worse—an open wound or crust on your soul?

Someone knocked on the door. That must be one of the girls, ready for dinner. Julia wrapped her right hand in a towel and then opened the door.

Matt.

Julia was in his arms without a single heartbeat passing. He held her, gently walked her into the room, and closed the door behind them. She sobbed and laughed and still wouldn't part her body from his because—for all her stupidity, for all her sins—God had still given her this man. He knew the worst now and he came to her and claimed her love, and poured his into her in a simple embrace.

Let the sun stand still, she prayed, because she couldn't bear to leave the heat of his body and the strength of his arms.

Thursday, 4:45 p.m.

Hamlin Ministries was headquartered in a two-story building two miles from the Air Force Academy. Julia and Matt waited in the reception area, pretending to drink water that a bright-eyed volunteer had poured for them.

"Are you sure Dillon is all right?" she said.

"Julia, you've asked me that five times. At least. Dr. Annie checked him yesterday, Jeanne is with him today. He's tired, cranky, and he's . . ."

". . . he's sliding away." Julia clutched his hand. *Not long* was a steady drumbeat. Matt heard it too. She could tell by the new worry line to the side of his left eye. "Maybe if I make this thing right with Andy, maybe God . . ."

"Shush. You know it doesn't work like that."

"I have to believe it does, Matt. Because I have to believe there's some way to make God relent and heal him."

"The girls."

"I've ruined Chloe's life."

"Ah, I see Destiny has given you a lesson in melodrama."

Julia shook her head. "If I hadn't dropped in out of the blue—complete with fun sister and a private jet—Chloe would be in class or at a med school interview and none the wiser. Instead, I gave her the opportunity to leave her husband and the means to seek out this other guy."

Matt brought her hand to his lips. "She would have found a way. Maybe not with this guy but with someone, somewhere. Imagine if this was ten years down the road and she had children or a busy medical practice, and she felt the pressure on every side with no way out? This thing could be a tremendous opportunity for redemption."

"I don't see how. Jack Deschene is . . . *hard* is not the right word. *Upright*."

Matt smiled. "Up*tight*, I expect you mean. Like the poor bean counter whose heart you stole."

"No, sir. He's not like you. He's like the young ruler in the gospel and Chloe is like his wealth. I don't think he can bear a blow to his worldview."

"Mr. and Mrs. Whittaker?" An older man with wispy straw hair and watery hazel eyes stared down at them.

Matt stood, offered his hand. "I'm Matt Whittaker. And this is my wife, Julia."

"I'm Pastor Hamlin's public liaison, Rick Stanley." He shook Matt's hand, reached for Julia's. She held up the cast, gave him a weak smile. "I understand you requested some time with the pastor."

Julia couldn't catch her breath to respond.

"It's a personal matter," Matt said. "Between my wife and Mr. Hamlin."

"I see." Stanley didn't even blink.

"If we could speak in private," Matt said.

"Please," Julia whispered. "It's really a situation of life and death."

"If you need someone to pray with you, we're always happy to do that."

"No." Julia grabbed his arm. "I need to see Andy."

"He's not available right now. He travels—"

"Tell me where, then. I'll go to him."

"He's not available to the public at this moment. Much of what the pastor and his wife do requires quiet time, apart from the ministry. I'm sure you understand that, and why I can't give you that information. Can you help me understand what you need?" Stanley said. "I'll do what I can to help."

"Julia, give me your license," Matt said.

She raised her eyebrows at her husband, did what he asked. He handed it to Rick Stanley. "Take this and show it to Mr. Hamlin or scan it and e-mail it or text it, or whatever it takes for him to lay eyes on my wife's photo in the next five minutes. As soon as he sees her, trust me—he is going to want to meet with us."

Stanley stared at them for a long moment. Julia's pulse raced and her knees wobbled. Finally, the man took her license and said, "Yours too, Mr. Whittaker."

"Why?" Julia asked. "Why his?"

Matt handed his over. "It's okay, Julia."

"No, it's not. This is between me and Andy."

Rick Stanley touched her forearm. "Mrs. Whittaker, please understand. Someone in Pastor Hamlin's position is subject to all sorts of scams and scurrilous claims. Sometimes people come here and they're horribly unbalanced. We had a man here a couple weeks ago who came with a gun. He'd never met either of the Hamlins, just got it into his head that they were tools of Satan. Before I arrange to let the pastor know that you're requesting to meet with him, I need to confirm you are who you say. If you'll agree."

"It's okay. Give us whatever we need to sign," Matt told Stanley. "I'll give you some people to call who can vouch for who we are. But please, quickly. This is urgent."

They gave Stanley their cell phone numbers, hotel information, and a list of references to call.

God told Abraham that he would make his descendants as numerous as sand. Julia felt time—and Dillon—slipping away like that same sand. As she and Matt returned to the rental car, she stared at the line of mountains that bordered Colorado Springs to the west. *I lift up my eyes to the hills*, then slammed her left hand on the hood of the car.

"Too long," she said. "It's all taking too long."

Matt took her hand and pressed her palm to his mouth. "Be patient," he said. "We'll keep praying. And no more punching."

"No." Julia tore her hand away. "What if we've already gotten the answer? What if God is saying no? What if this journey with Destiny and Chloe, this hunting down the men I slept with, what if it's all chasing after the wind?"

"You can't call reconnecting with two biological children 'wind.' You've now laid eyes on the two girls who emerged from your own body . . . given them a glimpse into their own history. That's a priceless gift, Julia. You think you're doing this all to ask them for something, but you've also given them something very precious in the process. You've given them *you*."

"Yeah, and I bet they're wondering where to go to return damaged goods."

"You're *not* damaged goods, Julia. You're a beautiful broken vessel."

She forced a laugh. "More like a crackpot chasing old ghosts."

"No, I mean a broken vessel—the only kind God can use. The Lord *is* using you, Julia . . . in their lives . . . in Dillon's life . . . in my life. I can't imagine my world without you." He held her close, moving his fingertips up and down her spine to relax her frazzled nerves. "No matter how all of this turns out, we've still got each other."

"But will we still have Dillon? I can't bear that answer if it's no."

"We have him *today.* As long as he's still breathing, there's room for God to move. And He's done bigger miracles than this. This is small potatoes for Him."

Julia clung to him, feeling the rise of his chest, praying that her heart would still to his. "But such an immovable mountain for us."

"Hold on, Julia. Just hold on."

Thursday, 5:01 p.m.

Mother had booked them in the Broadmoor, a lavish hotel at the foot of the Rockies. Her act of kindness provided another suite for her and Destiny. Was it anger or fear that led her to reserve a separate room for Julia?

Susan Middlebrooks was a caring, giving woman, yet this trip had to be eating at her. And now she was calling to check up on her. Chloe tried to keep her end of the conversation short so she wouldn't give anything away.

"Jack is concerned," Mother said. "Please call him. He feels shut out."

"He wants to know what is going on every minute. It's tiresome."

"If he were there with you, he wouldn't be such a pest."

Chloe laughed. "Really?"

"He wants to make sure Mrs. Whittaker isn't pressuring you. She's not, is she?"

Images crept through her mind. Julia in the cold motel room, asking over and over—*What happened? What did you do? Why did you do it? What can I do to help?*

The only pressure Julia exerted was the same Chloe put on herself, and it had nothing to do with a liver for her son.

What—why—help. Please, God, help me.

"No. She's doing what she promised. Destiny met her birth father and liked him. Now it's my turn."

"Can you tell me about him?"

"Not yet, Mother. I promised not to reveal his identity unless he agrees to meet with me. Julia and her husband are there now."

"I envision some drug addict or someone reckless. Please tell me he's not been in prison."

Chloe laughed. "No. Quite the opposite. If this all comes about, I'll make sure you know everything. Until then . . ."

"Can't you tell me *anything*?"

"He's a man you would know. Someone with a good reputation that you would respect."

"Not likely," Mother said. Chloe could hear the discomfort in her voice. It had always been Mother, Father, Chloe—with a place at the figurative family table for someone like Jack.

"People change, Mother. People grow up."

"Yes. I suppose they do." And in the tiny catch in Mother's voice between *they* and *do*, Chloe heard fear. Fear that Chloe, too, might change. Father's unexpected death had stunned both of them. Mother had her charities and vigorous volunteer work, and she projected a serene and gracious public image, even in her grief. At home, she held so tightly to her daughter that Chloe dreaded ever disappointing her.

Jack had become Father's surrogate—the man who could be trusted and admired. Perhaps that was as weighty a burden for Jack as it had been for Chloe.

"I've got to go, Mother. Try to keep Jack in North Carolina. Please."

"Wait. Can you please tell me *why* you've gone off like this? Is there something your father or I didn't provide? Maybe there's something Jack needs to do."

Make love to me like he means it—like it's the spiritual experience it should be and not another task on the list.

"No, Mother. Please."

"What will meeting this man accomplish?"

"I have no idea. Probably nothing."

"Then just come home. We want you home. And you're endangering your medical-school admission by delaying these interviews."

"Mother, I didn't go looking for this. You know that. But sometimes God drops things in your lap and you've got to go with it. I don't know where this is heading or if it means anything—I just need to let it play out."

"Don't agree to anything in regard to this liver thing until you discuss it with either me or Jack. Preferably with both of us."

"Of course not." Donating part of her liver was the least of her worries.

Rob Jones. How incredibly stupid she had been to think that they'd had an intellectual and emotional connection. Any reminder of that sordid evening made her want to rip her skin off.

Jack made everything orderly. She, on the other hand, had demonstrated a talent for making everything insurmountable. Like those mountains outside her window.

"Sweetheart, may I pray for you?"

"Please, Mother."

"Heavenly Father, we praise Your name. I thank You for giving me this lovely child, for raising her up to be a lovely woman, a blessing to all who know her. Please shine Your light on Chloe's path so she will be led into Your will, for Your glory."

Her mother left a few moments of silence. Chloe could find nothing to add—*I flirted, I drank, I danced, dear God, can You ever forgive me?*—so she said, "I love you, Mother."

"I love you, darling. Call Jack," Mother said and ended the call.

What a comfort it would be to slip back into those little-girl rain boots and let Mother hold her tightly.

What a relief it would be to not have met *WaveRunner*. Hopefully that foolishness was over and that Hope McCord was buried for good in the blizzard. In the haze that alcohol-soaked evening had been, she must have only imagined him calling her Chloe. The product of a guilty conscience, for sure.

Imagine what it would be like to have no more guilty conscience?

No more lofty expectations. No more of Jack's blueprints for her life. No birth mothers popping out of nowhere on a Monday morning with a private jet and a desperate request. No sister to make her feel like a puppet on everyone else's strings.

No deviation from the norm.

If only she could erase these three days and go back to Costco coffee and Duke University degrees and her husband's plan to shape her so she could help him save the world.

And she saw it in a flash—Jack's miscalculation of how she could best serve. Excitement made her pulse race. She grabbed her phone, dialed him. "Hey there."

"Chloe. Hi!"

"Hi."

"Are you all right?"

Deep breath. No, she wasn't all right, but she soon would be. "I'm fine. It's just a tiring trip. Emotionally and everything else."

"Don't let them wear you down. Don't agree to anything without us discussing it."

"That's why I called you."

"You're not thinking of going through with this donation, are you?"

"Jack, I'm not thinking about that at all."

"You sure?"

"I'm thinking about us—and how we've been talking for years about what we can do to provide help to a suffering world," she said.

"Glory to God."

"Of course. And this whole thing about rooting out corruption so private aid and industry will come to poor nations. Jack, I know you're right. It's a wanting area in Christian mission work."

"The concepts are difficult to grasp," he said, "and they sound worldly."

Chloe felt excitement building, thought maybe—despite all the terrible things she'd done—maybe God still had a calling for her. "Here's what I've been thinking about. If you've got time . . ."

"Of course I have time." Jack's tone was eager.

"So third-world countries need medical services. There's never enough to go around."

"Why do you think I was so rattled about you missing the UNC interview? That's one of the best med schools in the nation."

"Just listen for a minute. Part of any emerging economy—especially one that's been through a natural disaster—has to include solid infrastructure. Roads and electric grids and clean water."

"That's a given. Hard to do, with grants slipping into black holes, contractors providing shoddy materials and shoddier work."

Chloe smiled. Maybe this would be easier than she anticipated.

"We thought I could best serve as a physician . . . but, honey, wouldn't it be even better if I served at your side?"

"I would love that. You don't like economics, finance, any of that."

She laughed and it felt good. "Love you, hate that stuff. Here's the thing, Jack—I love building things. And I'm really good at fixing things. Think about us working directly together, you helping guide battle-torn or disaster-ravaged areas through the financial morass, and I would work with civil engineers on actually building infrastructure. Isn't that where corruption is most likely to be rampant? The two need to be a pair. Think about drought-stricken places like West Africa or Kenya. Deep wells would help irrigate crops. And think about Haiti after the earthquake and the desperate need for road rebuilding."

"Why all this now, Chloe?"

"Because I need to be using the gifts God gave me."

"You are. You're a sure thing for getting into med school. The science is all so easy for you."

"I don't want to be a physician, Jack. I want to do hands-on engineering."

"You put that to rest freshman year, didn't you? Remember how you struggled with Advance Calc? Engineers have to whiz through those types of courses."

Chloe swallowed her sigh. *He* had put it to rest, not her. No use slapping him with that now. "I'm four years older. A lot more experienced in handling difficult classes."

"You'd make such a good physician," Jack said. "To walk away from that? I don't see it."

"Think how many medical missionaries there are, and how few structural engineers."

"Those are skills that you're four years behind in learning."

"Yes, I've got ground to make up. If you stay at Duke or go on to Wharton or Sloane for grad school, I can find a good engineering college nearby. I don't need an MIT degree to make a difference. Just a solid program, maybe a dual civil/mechanical engineering degree."

"You agreed we were on a good track. Remember?" He sounded as breathless as she felt. "You did agree."

"I was eighteen years old. I agreed as an excuse for not stepping out in faith to do what God had created me for."

"So it's a spiritual argument now? Who is putting these weird ideas in your head?"

"Is that what you think of me, Jack? That I am as malleable as chewing gum?"

"No, darling, no. We want to be clay for the Potter."

"Just call me Play-Doh and leave it at that. I've got to go."

"Wait, don't. I'm sorry—I miss you, that's all. Why don't I come out there and we can discuss it further? I'll get on a red-eye out of DC. We can talk about this then, consider our options. Give me a few hours to think this through."

"Good night, Jack. And don't even think for one instant about coming here."

"If we're going to build anything," he said, his voice cracking, "it needs to be us."

Chloe clicked off the call. He dialed back immediately. She let it go to voice mail.

She had allowed Jack to manage the currency of her well-being and purpose instead of personally accepting Jesus's gift of *debt paid, now go and serve as I call you.*

It is always easier to let someone else manage the spiritual checking account. If Jack didn't know her—the essential Chloe, not the constructed one—it was her fault because it was more convenient and painless to go with the holographic image than to let the Savior smash her to bits and rebuild her in His image.

Lovingly. And hands-on.

Chloe fidgeted with her phone. Could you love someone as fervently as Jack claimed to love her and not know them?

Perhaps. Sure. She loved Jesus and yet so often found Him beyond understanding. Did the unknowing make her love any less genuine?

What an excellent question to ask Andrew Hamlin. Assuming he agreed to meet her. Why would he? She'd only bring trouble to his carefully constructed ministry.

Her birth father was a national figure, a respected lecturer and author, a leader in the contemporary evangelical movement. Surely he could help Chloe understand what God required, help her navigate Jack's objections, and help her forget that a cyber-creep who called himself Rob Jones ever existed.

Good plan. Even Jack would agree.

And then her phone rang and her good plan went up in a blaze.

Thursday, 5:24 p.m.

Destiny's phone wouldn't stop binging and buzzing and chiming.

Her sister Sophie texted her:

SC: Is it tru U have 3 new sibs?

DC: Tr. No worries, sis. UR the fav.

SC: Swear?

DC: On a stack of pancakes.

SC: :)

Her phone rang. "Hey." She recognized Tom's voice in a split second.

"Hey back-at-cha."

"Did you make it through the blizzard okay?"

Kicked in the head. Almost poisoned by carbon monoxide. Hypothermia. A foot closer and she might have been decapitated by that sign that crashed through the windshield.

"Just peachy," she said. "And you?"

"The girls went nuts in the snow. Building forts and sliding down the hill at the side of our house. So I guess it was worth losing power for a few days."

"Bummer. I missed all the fun," Destiny said.

"Maybe not. The girls are bugging me to take them to Disneyland in February. Would it be the worst thing in the world if we took you out to eat one night while we're in LA? We don't want to impose. Though Natalie wants me to tell you if you happen to know Justin Bieber . . ."

Destiny laughed. "Is Jenny coming?"

"Would that be okay?"

"Absolutely. Do you do roller coasters?"

"What do you think?" Tom said.

"Hah. I guess I know. Bet my stomach can outlast yours."

"It's on, child. It is so on."

She and Tom chatted for a couple more minutes. Jenny came on, spoke with her for a while, and that was that. It was easy to see how this was going to work out. See each other occasionally, otherwise let three thousand miles keep them out of each other's business.

While she was on the line with Tom, an e-mail from her father—the real one—came in from Washington, DC.

> Mom says you are on quite the adventure. Can we talk this weekend? Love, Dad

Talk about a three-thousand-mile relationship. Then again, she and her father had communicated more easily once she'd left the household. She blamed him for always being in DC. He didn't blame her for anything except making her mother crazy. She had, and apologized to both after Luke finally called her out on it.

Luke. No call or text today. Not that she had any right to know where he was every second. They used to sync their calendars so neither would have to bug the other. They worked odd hours, different projects, and varied locales. It was convenient—and yes, nice—to at least know where the other one was.

Her calendar was empty since Saturday's wrap. He was scouting locations for one of those gritty cop dramas.

The phone rang. *Whittaker.* Not Julia's number. Her husband, perhaps? He had arrived unexpectedly in Colorado to face Saint Andy with her. Maybe he needed something.

"Yes?"

"Hey, Destiny." A scratchy, adolescent voice.

No. Good grief, don't make me do this.

"Destiny. You there?"

"Yeah. How did you get this number?"

"My father left a cheat sheet for Pottsie."

"Pottsie who?"

"My godmother. Weird name, right? She's hanging with me while Dad is up there with you guys. Did you meet him?"

"No, not yet."

"Don't let the bald head fool you. He's pretty cool. Anyway, he wanted to make sure Auntie P. knew who to call in case of the zombie apocalypse."

"Considerate of him. Shouldn't you be in bed or something equally responsible?"

The long pause made her want to bite her tongue. He probably *was* in bed, day and night.

"Nah," he said. "I'm cool."

"So, what's up? You prowling for another blizzard?"

He laughed. "I know how to use weather.com. It's thirty degrees and dry in Colorado Springs."

"So what's up?"

Dillon cleared his throat. "Nothing."

"Just like the sound of my voice, huh?"

He laughed. "Better than talking to myself. My voice sounds like a wet cat."

"You'll grow into it. Give it a couple ye—"

Dear God, do You hear this? He doesn't have a couple of years. He may not even have a couple of weeks.

Destiny wanted to slap herself. For someone who threw Luke—and God—out of her house and out of her life, she sure was praying a lot.

"So here's why I called. When I'm in film school"—he cleared his throat—"would you be willing to take me on as an intern?"

Oh God oh God oh God, don't do this to me!

"I know it's a lot to ask," he said.

"No, it sounds like a great idea. Maybe, like, when you're feeling better, you can come out here for a week and do a school project. I'll help you make a couple creatures. Maybe get us into a green room so we can do some computer stuff. You're taking art?"

"I'm not taking much of anything right now."

"I'm sorry, man. That stinks."

"Yeah. Hey, don't you think it's cool?"

"What? What's cool?" Destiny bit the inside of her cheek. She could not let him hear her cry. She could not let him *make* her cry.

"I never wanted to go into the wedding business. Come on, a guy doing the bride thing? My dad's like a martyr, doing that stuff. My parents have their gig and I have mine. I figure it's got to be a God thing."

"What does?"

"Us. You and me. You're doing what I want to do. Now I have someone in the family, someone I can trust to help me learn. So thanks."

"Anytime, pal. Anytime."

They ended the call. Destiny went to her bathroom and splashed cold water on her face. *Tick tock*. Time is running out. She would either have to cut out of this caravan or get tested. And if she got tested, and was a match, she would have to do it.

She liked Dillon too much not to.

Thursday, 5:55 p.m.

This is the longest walk of my life.

Matt held her hand as they followed Rick Stanley down the hall. The steps from the reception area to the conference room where Andy waited seemed endless.

She thought about the long walk in Boston, searching for a place to put Tom, and that past, to rest. Finally driving to Nahant, the long hike to the rocks. The waves washing away the chalk.

Jesus. Cleansing. Redeeming.

Tom would never replace Destiny's father but he would add to her life, and she would add to his life and his family's. Boston was good, but this dark hall and the march to face her past could only lead to pain.

Julia had left Andy and Katie in the dark all these years.

Clinging to baby Hope as her treasure—her secret—and not giving him the chance to claim her.

Not giving Katie the chance to forgive her husband. Did she even know? Surely Andy told her, given they'd gone on to the kind of speaking ministry they enjoyed. They had expanded Andy's first book, *When God Is Not Easy*, to a variety of life circumstances.

They passed one office after another, windows showing dark night outside. Rick Stanley opened a door and motioned for Julia and Matt to go in.

She saw Kathleen Hamlin first, though Andy's physical presence seemed to fill the room. Both were composed, body language loose and inviting. How many people did they receive in a day, listening to stories, counseling with grace, the personal touch of a man and his wife who had a vibrant—and very public—ministry.

She and Matt could leave right now, leave these people with the life that they had built. Send Chloe home to North Carolina, tell her to put that awful thing with Rob Jones behind her and just live the life that God had set before her.

If Julia chickened out, Destiny would freak, neither girl would get tested, and Dillon would lose the best hope they had for his recovery.

Julia shook Katie's hand and then Andy's—his palm sweaty—as Matt introduced himself and her.

"Of course! I remember you," Andy said. "We worked together at IronWorks. Reverend Paul and his people are still going strong up there, praise the Lord."

"You're the gal whose place I took," Katie said. "You had some emergency and had to leave. I was a poor substitute for you but I did my best."

Oh, dear Father, Julia prayed. *Does she really have no idea about what I'm about to say?*

"What can I do for you?" Andy said.

"We were hoping to see you alone," Matt said. "Perhaps if you would excuse us, Mrs. Hamlin . . . ?"

Katie stared at Matt, then turned to her husband. "What is this about?"

A tremor passed between Julia's shoulder blades, as if her very center could not hold. "Please, if I could just speak to Andy for a couple of minutes. That's all I'm asking."

"I'm sorry," Andy said. "We never do that. I'm sure you understand why."

"You might consider making an exception," Matt said.

"If that isn't acceptable to you," Katie said, "we'll wish you well and send you on your way."

"You don't understand," Julia said, catching Andy's eye. He hadn't told her. All these years and Katie never knew.

"Sweetheart . . ." Andy put his hand on his wife's shoulder, tried to turn her toward the door.

She shook him off. "No. If some . . . accusation . . . is going to be made, I need to be here."

"Could we sit down?" Matt said. "It might be better that way."

Julia could see the guilt in Andy's eyes now, coming to the surface as if wrenched free from a deep mooring. Perhaps he had persuaded himself that it had never happened. Time could do that. Or perhaps—Destiny might say—the man was a serial scumbag and thought he'd never be caught.

"You're from Dallas," Katie said, forcing a smile. "One of our favorite places to visit."

"Andy, tell her," Julia said.

"Pardon me?" Katie turned in her seat, looked at her husband. "Tell me what?"

Andy stood and simply said, "Why now?"

Julia couldn't take her gaze off Katie. These were the last few seconds before they blew that poor woman's world apart. *God, forgive me—have mercy on her.*

"Because our son is dying," Matt said. "That is *why now.*"

"I'm sorry," Andy said. "That's terrible. I'm not sure I follow what that has to do with us?"

Matt tightened his arm around her shoulder. "Julia. This is your story."

She could still get up and walk away, knowing Matt would not tell the Hamlins because it was *her* hidden shame, her past to hold on to or to let go of. *Shame off you, Julia* and she knew that was true, just as she knew that the consequences remained.

"Please," Julia said. "Please, don't make me say it."

Katie turned her gaze on Julia. "What is going on here?"

"That summer," Andy said. "Before you came home from Uganda, I was missing you, and that missing became loneliness . . ."

His wife jerked back, her chair scraping the floor. "What are you saying?"

"I'm sorry, Katie. I have been faithful since . . ."

"Since you slept with her? Is that what you're saying?"

"We were young. And you were gone and I . . . I forgot who I was. Who you and I were. When I realized how selfish I was, the sin I was wallowing in—"

"Now wait just one minute," Matt said, rising to his feet. "You didn't *wallow* in my wife. You seduced her."

Katie leaned forward as if she needed the table to catch her. A flush rose up her throat. "Is that true, Mrs. Whittaker?"

Julia resisted the urge to jump to her feet and run from the room. What a terrible revelation for Andy's wife. "He told me you were finishing up a divorce—"

"He said that? Andrew, how could you?"

Andy hung his head, tears falling into his lap. "I am so sorry."

"Why now?" Katie clutched her throat. "Why come in here and vomit this up *now*? Do you want money? That's it, isn't it? You want money."

"Mrs. Hamlin, that's not what we want," Matt said. "Nor do we want to hurt you. We know this is hard for you."

"Hard? HARD!" Katie pressed her hands to her ears. "Do you think *hard* describes what it's like to have your heart ripped out of you?"

"Why do this now?" Andy said through clenched teeth.

"There are circumstances. Things that need to be addressed." Matt squeezed Julia's hand, whispered, "Tell them."

"Andy, I am so sorry," Julia said. "We have a daughter."

Katie gasped.

Andy sat down, hard. "And you never told me, Julia?"

"I thought it was for the best just to deal with it by myself. That I should remove myself—and the child—from the situation so you could move forward with your wife."

He glanced at Matt. "You raised my child?"

"No," Matt said. "Julia gave her up for adoption."

"Hold on here. Just stop for a minute. Please, everyone, just shut up for one moment." Katie dug her fingers into her hair as if to keep her head together. "Let me understand this. Andrew had an affair with you, Julia. You got pregnant and never told him."

"Yes."

"Sleeping with a married man is bad enough. But you surrendered Andrew's child," Katie said, "without him having any say in it. That's unfathomable. How could you be so cold?"

Andy covered his face, his shoulders lifting as if trying to bring in air. Julia's chest constricted. *Dear Father, if I am having a heart attack, take me instead of Dillon.*

"Breathe," Matt whispered, and as if she heard him, Katie took a deep breath. Andy was white-faced, his big hands trembling. Julia remembered Tom's embrace and how everything was forgiven in an instant. If she embraced Andy in this moment, he would kill her.

"Tell me," he said.

Matt gave him the facts of Hope's birth and now Chloe's life, stopping short of Dillon because the Hamlins seemed on the brink of collapse. Katie shrank into herself, arms tight around her chest.

"I'm so sorry," Julia said.

Andy glanced up at her. "You had no right."

"I did what I thought was best for the baby. And for you and Katie."

"And yourself," Katie said. "You did what was best for yourself."

"I did what I could bear," Julia said.

"*This* is unbearable," Andy said. "After all these years."

"Chloe was raised in a Christian home," Julia said. "You would be proud."

Katie began to sob, heavy gasps punctuated with a keening cry. Andy reached for her and she shoved him away.

"We'll step outside for a couple of minutes," Matt said. "Give you a little space to process this."

"No! No one is going anywhere." Katie pointed at Julia. "Let her witness my grief."

Matt glanced at Julia. She closed her eyes and nodded.

Andy tried again to hold his wife. She held up her hand to keep him away. "You too, Andrew. This is on you too."

Julia and Matt watched while Kathleen Hamlin grieved so deeply that her soul seemed to turn inside out.

Andy Hamlin paced the room, turning frequently toward the window. As he stared out into the black night, he stroked his jaw hard as if trying to smooth away what had been revealed.

Katie finally allowed Andy to put his trembling hand on her shoulder. He started to say something but she shushed him. "No, Andrew. I'm not ready to hear anything from you right now."

She turned to Matt and Julia and said, "Now. What's this about a dying son?"

Thursday, 5:55 p.m.

The walk across the sitting room to Destiny's bedroom was the longest of Chloe's life. Destiny stood at the window, staring out at the mountains.

Chloe shoved the phone at her. "Help me."

"No." Her sister waved her away. "I'm not talking to Jack. Not again."

"Please. Read the text."

Destiny squinted as if trying to rearrange the letters on the screen. Impossible. Chloe had been trying to do the same thing since the text came in. She squeezed her eyes shut and still she saw the words as if they had been burned into her eyelids.

> Chloe—call this # by 9 P or my next call will be 2 Jack.
> XXOOXX Rob J

"He knows who you are? That's bad."

"I don't know how. I don't know . . . I feel faint . . ."

"Shush." Destiny shoved her into a chair, pushed her head to her knees. "Breathe."

"I can't call him. How can I call him?"

"You can, and you'd better."

"Julia will be back before then. She'll know what to do."

Destiny kneeled down next to her. "Look at me."

Chloe stared at her. Same eyes, same flesh and blood, but Destiny would never have been this stupid.

"He doesn't know we're in Colorado," Destiny said. "Right?"

"Unless I let it slip . . . I don't know what I did. *Oh, God, forgive me.*"

"Yeah, okay. The point is that he's on Eastern time. Which means you've got to call him in the next hour or so."

"I can't. How can I?"

"Fine." Destiny stood up, made a show of brushing her away. "Let Jack handle it. That's your modus operandi, isn't it? Let Jack tell you where to go, what to wear. Whom to love."

Jack is my infrastructure. And Chloe was the corruption, about to make both of them collapse.

"You do it for me."

"No." Destiny handed her the phone. "I'll be right here. Go on, you can do it."

Chloe took the phone, punched in the numbers, and held her breath. Rob Jones answered, his voice silky. "Hey! What's up, Chloe?"

"My name is Hope."

Destiny rolled her eyes.

"I know who you are, Chloe Middlebrooks Deschene," he said.

"What did you do to me?"

"Only what you wanted me to do. We had such a fun evening together. So much fun, I had to run some film."

"That's . . ." Chloe rubbed her chest to stop her heart from pounding. "That's illegal."

"You agreed to it. It's right on the film."

Her knees wobbled. She sunk into the chair.

"I wouldn't have agreed to anything like that," she said. "You did something to me."

"Can you prove that?"

Chloe couldn't prove anything except that she drank so much, anything that happened after that—including some version of a date-rape drug—was a sink hole, about to drag her all the way down.

"Ask him what he wants," Destiny whispered.

"What do you want?"

"Some media outlet might pay good money for this movie we made. But I thought you should have first shot at it. Being you're the star and all. Open-market price should be about a hundred K. For a girl with feet in the Middlebrooks and Deschene money, I figure five hundred K would be a good figure."

"I don't have that kind of money."

"Sweet cheeks, I've known who you are from the second time we met online. And I sure as blazes know your net worth."

"How did you know who I was?"

"I make it my business to know. Usually my 'dates' are worth a couple thousand. But you . . . hmm, baby. Nice of you to fall into my lap like you did."

"The ship. The fishing thing . . . ?"

He laughed. "Talk about an easy hook to bait. I worked you like a psychic works her marks. Ask a broad question, hone in on any positive responses. Easier even because I could google as we chatted, learn enough terms to nail you. Most of the time I was just reframing your responses and spitting them back at you. Keeping you online long enough to get everything I needed to know about you."

Destiny wrapped her hand over the phone. "What does he want?"

"Money," Chloe said, tears running down her cheeks. "Half a million."

"Tell him he can go—you know. Tell him that."

"Chloe? The longer you wait, the hotter the film," Rob said.

"Hold on. Give me a minute." She handed the phone to Destiny, ran into the bathroom and gagged, wanting the filth gone, wanting herself gone. Destiny wrapped her arms around her, dabbing her face with a washcloth. "Come on. Finish up the call and we'll figure it out together. Come on, girl."

Chloe took the phone. "Rob."

"Sexy name, eh, baby? Fun to play fantasyland."

"I . . ." Deep breath. "I need to see what I'm buying. And then we'll talk terms."

"Exactly what I'd planned. Hang up, take a look. And let's reconvene in ten minutes."

"No. No one keeps that much money in liquid assets. I need . . . a day or so to see what I've got."

"Can't promise I'll hold it that long. The tabloids and smut shows are always looking for blockbuster news. And that rich husband of yours probably carries that much in pocket change. Maybe I'll focus-group a minute or so on YouTube while I'm waiting for you to tell me when and where to pick up my money."

"This has got to be illegal. Extortion or blackmail or something."

"No, baby. It's a brand-new world, and this is just a sale to the highest bidder."

"Send it and I'll get back to you."

"No, you won't. I'll get back to you. Sweet dreams, baby."

He clicked off. Chloe leaned over the sink, washed her mouth with water. The taste of his kisses lingered like a decaying animal. She smeared Destiny's toothpaste over her teeth, gargled, and spit.

"What now?" Destiny asked.

The phone pinged.

"Do you want me to leave while you view it?"

"No. You know . . . you've seen the worst of me. Too late now to pretend anything else." Chloe linked her arm through her sister's, held tight, and tapped the link.

The first few seconds was a scan of the motel room, catching one item of clothing at a time. Boots, coat, slacks, and sweater. Black bra. Chloe gasped and Destiny held her tighter. Underpants. She had worn the black lacy ones that Jack thought were frivolous.

"He knows how to set a scene," Destiny said. The camera scanned the bed. Hand, arm, hair flung over a pillow.

"Chloe." Rob's voice was off-screen.

"Hmm," the video-Chloe said, slowly opening her eyes.

"You want to dance, right?"

"I dunno. No one lets me."

Music came on—something almost like a salsa—and the camera caught Chloe's naked back as she sat up.

"Show me," Rob Jones said.

Chloe staggered to her feet and then turned full-frontal to the camera.

"God forgive me," Chloe whispered.

"Amen," Destiny said.

The video showed ten minutes of her drunken, drugged dancing. Whatever Rob suggested she do, Chloe had done. Finally, there was a banging off-screen.

"That's me," Destiny said. "Knocking."

The video went black.

"Well?" Chloe said. "What do you think of me now?"

"I think you've got some really good moves," Destiny said.

Chloe laughed and then sobbed because no one—especially Jack—could forgive this. She'd have to find some way to bury that video forever.

But first. First, she had to remember how to breathe.

Thursday, 6:17 p.m.

"You wanted to punish me," Andy said. "That's why you didn't tell me."

"What would it have gained me?" Julia said. "Except maybe a custody battle—and I couldn't bear that."

Andy tried to take Katie's hand. She slapped his away. "I can't even bear to look at you, Andrew. The only reason I'm still in this room is because of your daughter. And the Whittakers' son."

"That summer," he said, "was the only time in our twenty-five years. I swear, Katie. I saw a situation and took advantage. I thought . . ." He rubbed his face hard enough to leave streaks in his fair skin. "I thought no one would know, that she and I would never see each other again."

"Not me," Julia said. "I thought we were going to get married."

"Did I ever say that?"

"A guy doesn't have to say it," Matt said, "for a woman to believe that. To count on that."

"He didn't ask you, Mr. Whittaker," Katie said.

"Don't talk to my husband like that," Julia said.

"After what *you* did to my husband? I don't think you have any right to tell me what I can or cannot do."

Andy made a fist, pounded it into his hand. "I didn't know how vulnerable you were. You didn't tell me about your first pregnancy. I thought you were just a college student, looking to do good and willing to . . . do what we did."

"Have sex. Are you afraid to say it?" Julia said. "I thought we were making love, but for you, it was just a little summer fun."

"And you were just a spectator?" Katie said.

Matt slapped the table. "I'll ask you not to talk to my wife that way."

Andy covered Matt's hand with his own. "Maybe we should take a moment to ask for God's guidance here."

Slowly—so slowly—Katie extended her hand across the table to Julia. Julia took it. *How cold. The poor woman.*

Matt cradled Julia's broken hand in his lap.

"God, have mercy," Andy said. He prayed in a soft tone, invoking the Lord's promises of peace and wisdom and asking that whatever was going on in this room be to God's glory.

Only You can make that so, Julia prayed.

"Thank you," Matt said after the final *amen*.

"What do you need?" Andy asked.

"What does Hope need?" Katie said, covering his hand with hers.

"She wants to meet her birth father," Julia said. "And she's scared. She's used to a well-ordered life. This is as messy for her as it is for us."

"This doesn't sound like something we should rush into," Katie said.

"They need Chloe to decide on the donation," Andy said. "So it's got to be quick."

"You're asking a lot from people you don't know," Katie said.

"What choice do I have when God has made finding a liver for my son so blindingly difficult?"

"Hold on. Just hold on." Matt wrapped his arm around her neck and drew her close. "I want to assure you that no one has any desire to make this public. Mr. Hamlin—"

"Oh, for Pete's sake, call me Andrew. We're almost in-laws or something like that. Assuming paternity is proved."

"If we need to," Matt said, "we'll post a bond or something to prove our word. A DNA test—I'm sorry, but that would take too long."

"I need to see her," Katie said. "You have a photo?"

Julia fumbled with her phone. Matt took it from her, scrolled until he found the photo she had taken when they arrived in Boston. "The dark-haired one is the eldest daughter. Chloe is the one with blond highlights and no piercings."

Andy and Katie leaned over the photo together. They studied it for a long time. "She's got your eyes," Katie said, glancing up at Julia. "Otherwise, she looks like her brothers."

"You have kids?"

"We don't talk about them in the ministry. We have three sons," Andy said. "They've got the same hair, same jaw line. I can't believe this."

"They have a sister . . . ," Katie said. "Whatever will they think?"

"This doesn't need to go beyond this room," Julia said. "If it weren't for Dillon, I would have kept this to myself."

Andy stared at her. "And compound the loss?"

"I'm so sorry."

"Okay, the apologies are getting tiresome," Katie said. "Let's ask God to show us the next step, shall we?"

They prayed for a long time, some aloud, much in silence. *Letting mercy rain and wash away everything but God's grace.*

Thursday, 7:30 p.m.

Destiny tried everything to calm Chloe's hysteria. A long hug, rubbing her back. Stern words. Tender words. Walking her outside in the brisk air. Back in the suite, making her drink a nip of brandy from the mini-bar.

Rob Jones had titled his little production *Heiress Unplugged* and set it to a suggestive song that had been a popular hit a couple years ago. The creep should have titled it *Heiress Unhinged*. Because that's what Chloe was now.

If this had happened to a Hollywood starlet, the press would be all over her. She'd end up on David Letterman, leaking some tears and making some jokes, and she'd become a pathetic victim. It would probably boost her career.

A rich girl—and a Christian—was another story. The press would have a feeding frenzy, going after her family and her faith. Any opportunity to show evangelicals as hypocrites was like crack cocaine to the media. It would actually be to Rob Jones's benefit for that to happen. He'd probably get a six-figure book deal out of it.

Chloe lay facedown on the bed, shoulders heaving. The girl remained inconsolable.

She has a point. What a massive mess this was. Not that Destiny hadn't seen something like this coming. No one brings a camcorder into a cheap motel room with a drunk—and probably drugged—girl without something nasty in mind.

It probably would have been better if Chloe had actually made a sex tape with this creep. Then they'd at least have Rob's face on camera.

"Get up," Destiny said, shaking Chloe's shoulder.

She burrowed deeper into the down comforter. Destiny grabbed her sister's shoulders and twisted her around until Chloe had no choice but to sit up.

"I can't," she said.

"I haven't asked you to do anything," Destiny said. "Just . . . stick with me. Okay?"

Chloe nodded. Her face was an unholy mess. Destiny grabbed her brush. She sat on the bed behind Chloe and slowly drew the brush through her hair.

"What are you doing?" Chloe said.

"Shush. Just shush." Out of options, Destiny reverted to the tactic her mother had used to calm her. She brushed and brushed, and wished Luke were here because he would know in an instant what would take her an hour to reason through.

After a long minute, Chloe stopped those horrible noises in her chest and throat. She still breathed raggedly and swiped away tears.

"Funny how your hair feels like mine—the texture and thickness. You have the same curls at the nape of your neck."

"I suppose."

"You got our very dark eyes. These blond streaks are natural, aren't they?"

"I suppo—yeah."

"Andrew Hamlin is fair-haired. I googled him."

"Oh," Chloe said and collapsed into another string of sobs. "If this gets out, I'll ruin his life too."

Destiny lightly tapped her with the hairbrush. "Enough. Surely you've learned by now you gain nothing by freaking out."

Chloe pulled away from her. "And surely you've learned by now you gain nothing by running away."

"I gained a second father."

"And you gave up on Luke."

"Shut up," Destiny said. "You have no right to lecture me about Luke."

They stared at each other for a moment. And then Chloe burst out with a single snort that sounded like a laugh. "I guess we just had our first fight."

Destiny smiled. "And we survived. So let's figure out what we're going to do."

"How did you do it?" Chloe said. "Get out on your own. How did you have the . . . guts . . . to walk away from college and go all the way to California?"

"It wasn't guts," Destiny said. "It was pretty much foolishness. And it wasn't all good. I got a job quickly, for sure. But I got in with some bad people, did some nasty drugs, and was on the edge when I met Luke. He was coming off the edge—onto the good side—and he kind of walked me through it. Even when I was being an A-1 jerk."

"Don't give up on him, then."

"He gave up on me. Wanted more, found God. *Amen* and *the end*."

"No. Let it be a beginning."

"You're giving me advice?" Destiny rested her chin on the top of Chloe's head. So alike, yet so different.

"I could just disappear. Like you did."

"I didn't disappear. I felt like it, but my parents—somehow—always knew where I was. And when I needed something, they made sure it was available. Including rehab."

"I can't bear the thought of Mother knowing what I've done." Chloe pressed her hands to her temples.

Destiny pulled her hands away and said, "I have an idea."

Thursday, 8:05 p.m.

"I wish I could stay," Matt said as Julia drove him to the airport.

"And I'm glad you're going back to Dillon."

"Are you going to be okay?"

She parked a little way from the drop-off area. "Not until I know you're home. You?"

"I'll be okay when you've worked this through with Chloe. And then they'll get tested?"

"Both girls promised. If I can get them to agree to fly to Dallas and have it done there, I will. But I'm not expecting that."

"Why?" Matt said.

Julia twisted in her seat so she could touch his cheek with her good hand. "Because they must know that if they meet Dillon, they won't be able to say no."

Matt leaned to her, his lips almost brushing hers. "This can't go on forever. We need you home."

"I know that, Mattie. You think I don't know that every second of every one of these days? Each breath I take, I think, *Is this Dillon's last breath?*"

"He's stable," Matt said. "That's a miracle in itself. But . . ."

"We need a bigger miracle. I know."

"Is either one of those girls inclined to be that miracle?"

Julia pressed her lips to his ear. "I don't know. If only they knew him."

"They know you, Julia. So we keep on hoping. Promise me you'll hold on to hope."

"What if it's a no from God?"

"We'll get our boy through it, even if it means we're . . ." Matt pressed his face to her cheeks to wipe away his tears. ". . . if it means we're preparing him to go home. But we aren't there yet. So we hold on to hope."

Julia wrapped both arms around his neck. "You hold on to hope, Matt. And I'll hold on to you."

Thursday, 8:15 p.m.

Destiny scrolled through numbers on her phone until she found the one she wanted. Two-hour difference between Colorado Springs and Boston. Too bad.

After eight rings, the phone went to voice mail. She hung up and dialed again. This time Tom answered. "Destiny?"

"I need your help."

"Are you all right? Julia's son—what?"

Destiny heard Jenny's voice in the background and Tom telling her he'd be back in a minute.

"Okay, I'm awake," he said. "What's up?"

"Some guy is blackmailing Chloe. Julia's other daughter."

"What did she do?"

"Nothing illegal. Something incredibly stupid." Destiny looked at Chloe, mouthed, *Can I tell him?*

She shook her head violently. Destiny put her palm against her sister's cheek, made her stop before the girl rattled her brains away. "Let me tell him."

Chloe gave the smallest nod. Destiny launched into the story as she understood it.

"I wasn't bored," Chloe said as the only correction she made to Destiny's account. "I was selfish."

"Whatever," Destiny said. "Tom. What do we do?"

"Put me on speaker," he said.

Destiny did and set the phone between them.

"Chloe," he said. "I'm sorry we didn't get a chance to meet in Boston."

"Me too," Chloe said. "Maybe I wouldn't have messed up like this if we had."

"Welcome to the human race," he said.

"I didn't know how stupid I could be."

"Tell that to Adam and Eve," Destiny said. "Now let the man talk."

"So you know nothing about this guy?" Tom said.

"I thought I knew everything."

"Real name? Where he lives, what he does for a living?"

"He must live up north of Boston because he knew where to set up our meeting and that the motel was just a block away."

"He could have figured that out from MapQuest," Destiny said.

"But given the blizzard conditions, he couldn't have gone back to wherever he came from," Chloe said. "So maybe him having a buddy near the motel was true."

"So you ask around up there?" Destiny said.

"Honey," Tom said, "do you really think he told the truth?"

"He sounded like he knew what he was talking about," Chloe said. "When he talked about the boat and all that."

"To create this persona, he only had to watch *Deadly Catch* or *Wicked Tuna* and know enough about engineering to keep a conversation going. He's probably more predator hacker than sailor."

"Will that help?"

Tom laughed. "You know that saying *more fish in the sea*? Substitute 'computer nerds' and 'Massachusetts,' and you see the issue. You said you didn't have a photo, Chloe?"

Chloe shook her head. Destiny poked her, pointed at the phone. "No," she said.

"What about a car? Did you see his car?"

"No, he walked me to the motel."

"Why didn't he drive?" Destiny said. "Your rental was right out front."

"Chloe may be right on that," Tom said. "Maybe he is familiar enough with Gloucester to walk around and know where he's going. Some of those streets are narrow and you have to fight for parking. Maybe he does live there. Though, if he's a serial predator, he's not likely to do his dirty work in his own neighborhood.

"I have to tell you some hard truth here," Tom said. "The best way to beat blackmail is this: he can't extort you if you have nothing to hide."

"I have everything to hide."

"From whom?"

"My husband, my mother—all her friends and her charities.

Our church family, some of the missions we support. My horrible behavior and my humiliation would all reflect on them."

"'He was despised and rejected by men . . . ,'" Destiny said.

"Are you kidding me?" Chloe raised her eyebrows. "You're quoting Isaiah?"

"Hey, I never said I didn't know the Bible. Just said it trips me up a lot. So take the hit. If these really are your people, they'll help you get through it."

"Your sister is right," Tom said. "You can't undo this. You can't give into it. You go through it, trust the people who know you, and find something good out of it."

"They don't know me," Chloe said. "They know the person I try to be."

"Stop putting it on them," Destiny said. "You play *poor me* as if you had nothing to do with who you are, or what you've done, or what you could be doing. It's easier to be their dress-up doll and then whine about it. Well, those clothes are off now, so isn't it about time to be owning up to the bad? And the good?"

"You have a lot of nerve."

"I do. And I'm a pain in the backside, but at least no one weeds me like a garden and mulches me to make me grow. You like the attention, like not having to take responsibility."

"And you like to complain," Chloe said, her voice rising.

Destiny laughed. "Yes, there is that."

"Ladies," Tom said, "back to the subject at hand."

"Mr. Bryant, can't we have him arrested?"

"We need grounds. Did you get a drug test so we can claim a dating assault?"

"No. The blizzard . . ."

Destiny groaned. Julia had begged for an ambulance, and she had said no. "That's on me. I wish we had."

"So what you've got is an embarrassing tape that he's going to claim was consensual. And if you say he's blackmailing you, he'll deny it and just find some magazine or television outlet to air it."

"God, help me." Chloe rocked back and forth. "God, help me."

Please, I know I'm a pain but please, show Yourself here, God. She tried to pull Chloe into a hug, but her sister resisted, catching her on the side of her head.

"Ouch." The pain shot through Destiny's jaw and down her neck. "Watch it."

"Are you okay?" Tom said. "What's going on?"

"I'm sorry," Chloe said.

"Shut up with the apologies. You sound like Julia," Destiny said. "Nothing, Tom. She caught me where . . ."

And then, out of nowhere, or perhaps out of the divine, she realized what they could do.

"Tom, we can't have him arrested for what he did to Chloe if we can't prove she was drugged or that she didn't consent to the filming. But what if he committed another crime?"

"I don't understand."

"We have to Skype this." Destiny ended the call, clicked onto Skype. She waited, smiled when Tom answered and she could see his face. His hair was a mess and he needed a shave, and the worry in his eyes was unmistakable.

"What am I looking at?" he said.

"This." Destiny pulled back her hair and showed the dark bruise under her ear that stretched along her jaw. "That jerk kicked me in the head. He also knocked Julia down. Unfortunately, she doesn't have the bruises to show for it."

"Whoa. Are you all right?"

"I'm in love with a stuntman. I know how to take a punch."

Tom smiled. "Turn the phone so I can see Chloe."

Destiny did and brushed back Chloe's hair so Tom could see her face. "Hi," she said weakly.

"Honey," he said, "we've got him on assault. Make sure you get a picture of Destiny looking like that."

Chloe's eyes widened. "Thank you."

"But let me tell you something. I waited a year before I told my wife about Julia and the child we had given up. It was the second-worst year of my life."

"Second?"

"The first was walking away from Julia and Destiny. A lot of that was me being selfish and I knew it. I also knew we would be terrible parents and end up divorced with Destiny caught in the mess. Then I met Jenny at a blood drive. She wasn't flashy or hard-driven. She was just so genuine. Not a pushover either. Smart and kind and I didn't want to lose her, so I sat on my past and trust me, Chloe, it was like being eaten by a tapeworm. I finally told her, we worked through it, and we're in a good place. Not perfect because I am so not perfect. It's good.

"If you sit on this, regardless of the outcome, it will eat *you* alive. Tell your husband, let him help you figure out how to get through this."

"I can't," Chloe said. "I just can't do that."

"You've got two lovely ladies there to stand alongside you. I'll help you, Chloe, but the very best advice I can give you is to tell your husband."

She sat, silent. Not crumpled anymore but with her back a little straighter. That's something. Destiny took the phone and smiled at Tom. "Thanks."

"Anything," he said.

"So how do we get this guy on assault?"

"First, get some really good pictures taken of that bruise. And go to a doctor so it's not just them saying it's Hollywood makeup. On the topic of pictures, if I had one, I could hire an investigator to go around the area and see if we can get his real name. Good thing you're an artist."

"Oh, Tom." Destiny glanced at Chloe, cringed at the hopeful spark in her eyes. "I am not a good portrait artist. It's the hardest thing to do."

"Julia," he said. "She is good at it. And she saw him, right?"

"Better than I did. Face-to-face. And Chloe can help."

"Then it's settled. We find this guy and get him for assaulting my firstborn daughter."

"Thank you," Chloe said. "Thank you."

And thank You, God, Destiny thought. *Thank You for finally showing up.*

Thursday, 9:32 p.m.

Julia returned to an urgent message from Destiny. "The INSTANT you get this," she said on voice mail, "you have to come see us. We don't care what time it is. We need you NOW."

She couldn't think straight NOW, so she put on a pot of coffee and kneeled next to her bed. If only Matt were here. If only she didn't have so much to be sorry about. If only she could remember how much she had to be grateful for.

If only Dillon had been born whole.

If only any of them had been born whole.

If only Katie Hamlin had punched her in the nose and exacted retribution. Maybe then her forgiveness would be easier to bear.

If only Matt were here to talk her through these exhausted notions, to hold her in the dark hours of the night.

She went to her suitcase, found her Bible, and opened up the Psalms. *God is our refuge and strength, an ever-present help in trouble. Therefore we will not fear, though the earth give way . . .* and my will and my courage and my baby boy . . . *and the mountains fall into the heart of the sea.*

She read on, struggling to keep her eyes open. *Be still, and know that I am God.*

Julia let stillness take her—for how long, she didn't know. Too soon, someone grabbed her shoulders and she screamed and swung her cast around and heard someone say, "Ouch."

Destiny. Glaring down at her, security guard at her side. "Are you okay, ma'am?" he said.

"I'm . . ." Her heart lurched, making the room spin. "Dillon."

"No," Destiny said. "Your problem child, Chloe. Didn't you get my message?"

"I'm sorry. I fell asleep."

"If you're all right, ma'am . . ." The security guard extended his hand and she tried to stand. She couldn't feel her legs below her knees. Destiny looped her arm around her waist, helped her sit on the bed.

"She's all right, thank you," she said and pressed a ten-dollar bill into the guard's hand. He shrugged, then left.

"I fell asleep on my knees." Julia rubbed her eyes, trying to orient herself. The clock on the bedside table read 1:45 a.m. "Is Chloe okay?"

"No, dude. She's not. But you're going to make her okay. Can you walk or do you need like a cold shower or something?"

Julia stomped her feet. "I can't feel them."

"Wait." Destiny kneeled down, took off her shoes, and rubbed her legs vigorously.

"Yow, that hurts," Julia said.

"Aha, an improvement."

"Pain—it makes a good spiritual metaphor."

"I'd call it pins-and-needles," Destiny said. "Let's go. We need your help."

Friday, 1:55 a.m.

Chloe was screaming and pacing the room. "Don't let her see the video," she cried.

"I don't need to, sweetheart." Julia tried to swallow her rising anger. What did this girl think would happen if she made a date with some guy she knew from the Internet?

God, forgive me. Everyone made terrible mistakes, and this one was a doozy. "What did Tom say?"

"He said we should threaten to bring an assault charge."

"Against whom? Is Rob Jones his real name?"

Chloe buried her face in her hands. Destiny pried apart her fingers. "No ground-hogging on us. You promised."

"Yes. I did promise." Chloe shook like a dog tossing off water, then sat up straight. "Tom thinks his investigator might be able to track down who Rob Jones really is if they have a picture to show around."

"Do you have a photo?" Julia asked.

"No," Destiny said. "That's why we need you to draw one. You got a good look at him in the lights when he pushed you down. That's what you said. I only saw the side of his boot."

Julia sank into the closest armchair and held up the cast on her hand. "Did you forget?"

"Oh . . ." Destiny sighed. "I did."

"You're an artist. You do it."

"I'm not good with people. That's why I do monsters."

Chloe burst out laughing. Destiny gave her a quick look and then laughed with her. Smiling, Julia began to unravel her Ace bandage. "We'll do it together. Do you have some paper?"

"I got some from the business center," Chloe said. "They gave me some pencils too."

"Ugh, Julia," Destiny said. "Your fingers look like they have spiders growing out of them."

"I like spiders," Chloe said. "Rob Jones knows that."

"And that is relevant—how?"

"Rob knows that. Jack doesn't."

"Tell him," Destiny said. "Just tell your husband whatever it is that you want him to know."

"He won't listen."

"Why should he, if all he hears is silence?" Julia said.

Chloe shrugged.

"So, Julia," Destiny said, "you got fungus or something growing out of the top of your fingers?"

"Those are the stitches," Julia said.

"How did you hurt your hand?" Chloe asked.

Strange. That had been one of Destiny's first questions, and yet the intellectual sister didn't think to ask until she saw the mess under the bandages. Was it from politeness—or from being too insular?

"She punched a wall because she couldn't punch God," Destiny said.

"That's harsh," Chloe said. "Do you still feel like that?"

"After meeting with your birth father and his wife, I now want to punch myself silly."

"But they beat you to it," Destiny said with a smirk.

"No. Quite the opposite. Once we all survived the first two

hours, they were quite gracious. Chloe, they are anxious to meet with you."

Chloe scooted back on the bed until she was jammed against the headboard. "No, I can't do that. Not now. Half of America thinks those two are saints."

"Oh, for goodness' sake," Destiny said. *"I can't do this, I can't do that, I'm such a loser.* Look at Julia—she just told two nice people how she pretty much screwed them out of a child and she did it face-to-face. For your sake, you idiot."

"Don't forget what's at stake here. She did it for her son," Chloe said. "We're just tourists in her journey."

Julia laughed. "Well, well, look who's got a sharp tongue."

"She got it from me," Destiny said, joining her laughter.

"Dude," Chloe said, with a giggle.

"Coffee," Julia said. "And then let's figure out how to get this picture drawn."

Two cups of caffeine later, Julia still hadn't been able to make her hand cooperate. There was no way she could bend those three swollen fingers. Her grip of the pencil with her thumb and small finger was tenuous at best, clumsy most of the time.

"Destiny, you have to do it," Julia said.

"I can't do it. I don't have that kind of talent."

"Help her," Chloe said.

"I just said I don't know how."

"Steady my hand," Julia said. "Lay your hand over mine. We'll hold the pencil with my thumb and your index finger."

"Gross," Destiny said. "I have to touch that mess?"

"Honey, that's often what it takes to get things done."

Destiny sat next to Julia. "I'm left-handed. My right hand has no clue."

"Then you hold the pencil and I'll guide you with my left hand."

Julia climbed on the bed, positioned herself behind her daughter, and laid her left hand over the girl's.

They sketched for almost an hour, with many erasures and as much input from Chloe as she could be coaxed to give. They finally produced a drawing that they agreed resembled Rob Jones. The thick, wavy hair that curled on his collar. The sleepy eyes. The long, thin nose.

"That's him," Chloe said. "Now take it away. I can't bear looking at him."

"I'll call Tom, fax it to him," Destiny said. "But first, you call Jack."

"No, I can't tell him about this. He's going to hate me."

"He's part of this, Chloe. Call him or I'll rip up this picture."

"Julia, tell her to give me that picture."

Julia shook her head. "She's right. Call him and ask him to come out here to meet Andy and Katie with you. And then you can decide what to do about this Rob Jones. Honey, you've got to start somewhere."

"I can't."

"Good grief." Destiny grabbed her phone, speed-dialed Chloe's landline number, put it on speaker.

"Destiny?" Jack asked.

She pressed the phone to Chloe's face.

"It's me," she said in a halting voice.

"Are you okay, darling?"

"Could you fly out this morning? I'm going to . . . meet my birth father later today and I'd like you with me."

"Of course," he said. The eagerness in his voice was touching. Chloe made a circle around the sitting room, giving Jack specifics on the resort and transportation.

Julia kissed Destiny's cheek. "Good work. Get some sleep after you fax that."

"Gonna get messy once he gets here."

"We can handle it," Julia said. "Sweet dreams, my baby girl."

"Back-at-cha," Destiny said.

Julia smiled. Should she tell her that *back-at-cha* was one of Tom's favorite sayings? No. She'd leave Destiny the joy of discovering that.

Chloe came back in the room. "He's coming as soon as he can get on a plane. Now what?"

"He loves you," Julia said. "You need to tell him."

"I can't." Chloe shivered. "It would destroy him."

Destiny squeezed her shoulder. "You heard what Tom said. That year of being eaten alive before he told Jenny he had a child? Hiding who you are is more destructive than being truthful about it."

Chloe stared at Julia. "After I was born—how did you get through it? How were you able to move on with your life?"

"It was a very difficult time," Julia said. "A dark time, full of blessings in disguise."

thirteen

Fort Worth, Texas

19 Years Earlier, September

They say you're the best," Matthew Whittaker said. "At making something out of nothing."

Julia tried not to roll her eyes at the young man who sat across the table. Her desk and phone were in the closet off this room. She met prospective clients—usually engaged couples—in an office she had decorated to look like a sitting room. The palette of the room was sparse and neutral—with off-white walls, a neutral-suede sofa she had reupholstered herself, an oak table she had refinished in natural tones.

After extensively interviewing a client by phone, she would prepare the room with pops of color and decorative items, based on what she gleaned of her prospective client's taste. Even table linens and water glasses or tea service were interchangeable. Her friend Patricia Howland supplied fresh flowers for every business meeting in exchange for referrals to her sister's florist shop.

The pillows, table linens, and artwork were all her originals—thank you, Massachusetts College of Art. Her office was like the seasons, changing not by the calendar but by Julia's gut instinct as to whom she might need to impress. She could go from gray silks to tie-dyed burnt orange and scalding red in less than an hour.

Today's meeting required simplicity and efficiency. She wore black slacks, a silk shell in the palest of grays, and a copper necklace she had hammered and burnished herself. She was always happiest when she worked hands-on in any medium.

Seeing, building, revealing—if only life were so uncomplicated.

Julia had stripped down her office for this meeting, a rare opportunity to design a business function instead of a wedding or shower. Modern art with sharp edges and chrome colors hung on the walls. She painted or inked her own artwork, sometimes the night before a meeting if she didn't have something in her mother's garage that fit the meeting's color scheme.

The painting and sketching helped. Working almost all the time helped. Trying to pray—*really* pray—helped. Her mother, bless her overbearing heart, helped. The passing of time—first days, then months, and now years—helped.

A nugget remained, that pinhole of pain that could burst at odd times. Some moments were predictable, like when Jeanne and Patrick had their first daughter two years ago. Funds were tight, so Julia drove from Texas to Massachusetts, raising money for gas and lodging by sketching ten-minute portraits in the parking lots of highway rest areas. She held the baby as the priest baptized her, and Julia prayed that her own joy for her friends would hide the twisting ache in her belly.

Guard as she might, pain could cyclone without warning.

Setting up her booth at the Dallas Arts Festival and watching a teenage girl rent a double-square of pavement that she filled with chalk art.

Taking a meeting with a young woman who begged Julia to put together a wedding in a week because she was pregnant and wanted to wear a traditional gown.

Hearing a newborn wail in church.

Dating nice guys. Zach. Aaron. Daniel. Wanting to enjoy them but not trusting herself to not jump into bed with them as a way to try to fill the gaping hole in her soul.

"So, can you do it?" the man behind the tortoise-shell frames said. "Make me look like a million dollars on a thousand-dollar budget?"

Julia smiled. "I specialize in optimizing resources."

"What?" He squinted at her, mild blue eyes magnified by thick glasses. He couldn't be much older than her but his sandy hair was already thinning and inexpertly combed in an attempt to hide his losses.

"Can you give me a minute?" she asked.

"Ah . . . sure, I guess." Matthew Whittaker sipped the coffee she had provided in a heavy white mug. She'd made a rich roast because the designer blends didn't feel appropriate. She hadn't bothered with table linen, not for this client. An accountant trying to grow into Financial Services, he impressed Julia as someone who quickly saw through artifice. From what she understood of his business, he wanted his clients to see that he could *see*—that he could measure trends and possibilities and make solid choices.

Julia took her sketchpad and pencil from her briefcase. She used different bags for different clients and borrowed this black leather case specifically for corporate events. She sketched rapidly, capturing the shape of his head and the line of his jaw. "Take off your glasses," she said.

"And this has *what* to do with my event?"

"Trust me," she said, thinking this was the one area in her life where she could be trusted, where her instincts were infallible. She finished the sketch in four minutes and told him to put on his glasses so he could see what she'd done.

"Where's my hair?" he said.

"Exactly."

"I don't understand."

"You look like an accountant. Shave your head, get contact lenses or better yet—Lasik—and you'll optimize your resources and look like the man who is fearless enough to steer clients through rough waters."

He smiled and she felt a strange flutter. "Does appearance matter that much?"

"If you didn't believe that, you wouldn't be here," Julia said. "Why hire an event designer when you could throw some Ritz crackers and squeeze cheese on the table and hope for the best?"

"That's a shallow way to approach building business relationships."

"I agree, if it's a false appearance. Mr. Whittaker—"

"Matt."

"I'm not interested in creating illusions, Matt. I want to reveal character."

"Nice sentiment. What if I don't want my character revealed?"

Julia leaned across the table, clutched his hand hard enough to make him cringe. "Then I don't want your business."

He laughed. "For a beautiful woman, you're tough."

"And you're lying."

"My eyes may not be good, but I know what I see."

"You're lying because you don't talk like that. Throwing empty compliments into a business negotiation. You can do better."

He blushed. "You're right, I don't. I apologize if I offended you. I just . . . couldn't help myself."

Julia grinned. "And now you're telling the truth. So, you have a thousand dollars to spend on a holiday party for clients you want to impress?"

Matt tapped the top of his thumbs together. She could imagine him poring over the stock market reports or whatever other magic runes these financial guys studied, tapping his thumbs until he got an answer that made sense.

"Total." His voice was low but he kept eye contact.

"Which is less than what my fee would be."

"I understand that. Can you give me a minute?"

"Are you going to sketch my picture?" she said, smiling.

"I already did." He dug a bound document out of his briefcase. He slid it across the table. "This is for you."

She paged through it, admiring the paper stock and quality binding but otherwise, thoroughly confused. "What is this?"

"If you waive your fee for my event," he said, "I'll give you the business plan I devised for you. Unless you already have one?"

"I don't even know what that is."

"I figured as much." Matt grinned. *A touch of elf,* she thought and she desperately wanted to redo his sketch because in capturing his precision, she had missed the humor. "You're the one-woman shop that every girl in Dallas-Fort Worth wants to hire to design their wedding. I bet you don't make a cent by the time you figure in time and expenses."

"True." Julia shrugged. "I'll figure it out."

"Or you'll never really get off the ground. I know promise when I see it—even through these thick glasses, Ms. McCord."

"Julia."

"I'm not interested in building illusions, Julia. I want to invest my time in the real thing."

"So we're bartering?"

"That makes the most sense for both of us," he said. "You help make me a success and I'll help make you a success. Deal?"

"Will you shave your head?"

"Would you turn me down if I didn't?"

"No. But I'd make you wear a hat."

As she said it, she *saw* it. Fedoras. She'd have to scour the flea markets and thrift shops for them, put out word to all her college friends. She'd need at least thirty, based on his list of invitees. She'd clean up the hats and personalize them for each attendee. It would eat a tremendous amount of her time and she'd lose money, but she could see it so clearly that she had to do it.

"Right now," she said.

"Right now what?"

"Let me shave your head right now. If you hate it, you'll have your hair back long before Christmas."

"That's rather . . . unconventional."

"And that's why you came to me instead of buying white paper plates, lunch-meat trays, and two-liter bottles of generic soda from Safeway. Right?"

He rubbed his head, barely causing a ripple in what little sandy hair he had. "Maybe I'll try it at home."

Julia was possessed now, her imagination filled with the image of him with a smooth head and jaunty camel fedora, greeting guests with a new confidence that said *I'm going places, wanna come?* And it would be no lie because he already knew she was a terrible businesswoman and had arrived prepared to share his gifts in exchange for hers.

"Now or never," she said.

"Okay," he said, laughing. "If you have an unused razor in this office, then I'm in. But I'm betting you do not."

Julia went into the bathroom—also perfectly decorated for any occasion—and returned with a disposable razor still in its wrapping. "I win," she said. "You in?"

Matt grinned. "Be gentle."

Julia set up a chair for him in the outer office. She spread out tissue paper on the floor and his shoulders, then used a dampened towel to moisten his head.

"I can't believe we're doing this," he said.

"Still time to back out."

"Not in a million."

"Then hush up and sit still." She lathered up a decorative soap that was lightly scented with lemon and scrubbed the lather into his head. "Last *last* chance," she said, razor in hand.

"Not a chance."

"Okay. Sorry."

Matt grabbed her hand as she went to put down the razor. "Not a chance—that I'm backing out."

"Do you want to watch in a mirror so you can see the transformation?"

"Sure."

She set up a makeup mirror. The whole time she worked, he watched her instead.

"This is insane," she said, blushing. "I might owe you a wig."

"Do you always do that?"

"Do what?"

"Second-guess."

Julia wrapped the damp towel around his head. "My judgment is not as . . . let's say *reliable* . . . as it should be."

"We all make mistakes." He turned in the chair so he could see her directly. "Surely you believe in redemption."

She rubbed the soap off his head, deliberately covering his face with the towel so he couldn't see hers. "I try," she whispered.

Praying night and day, day and night. Painting and working and praying all over again, and still Destiny's birthday and Hope's birthday would come once again and there would be no way to staunch her grief except to pray, paint, work, and pray all over again.

She took away the towel and held her breath.

"Wow," Matt said.

"Is that a good *wow* or a bad *wow*?"

"That's a *wow*, I didn't know that guy was there under that sorry hair."

"I did," Julia said, relief a flood now because his head was perfectly formed and, without the distractions of his wispy hair, the strength of his jaw and spark of his gaze were clear. "You need a little tan to even out the color but otherwise—"

"Hush now," he said, "and let me enjoy the moment."

Julia enjoyed the many moments of getting to know Matthew Whittaker. Planning the first gathering that became a combination seminar on how faith and finance intersect. Digging into a business plan that elevated her from an inexpensive freelancer to a sought-after event artist. Teaching him the difference between superficial and classic—between artifice and essence.

Attending the same church service on Sunday. Finding each other at potlucks and small groups so they wouldn't have to enter as strays.

Keeping her pain between them like a shield so there was no chance of being hurt, or hurting each other.

Until eight months later—on Hope's fourth birthday—Matthew Whittaker ruined everything by asking Julia out on a date.

18 Years Earlier, June

Matt Whittaker asked Julia out every Tuesday for two months.

Telling him *no, thank you* had become a chore. He was always kind and cheerful; she was drawn to him fiercely and feared that intensity. Why ruin what they had together by turning friendship into infatuation?

"Why not?" he asked.

"You think you know me. You don't."

"So tell me."

"I value our friendship too much."

"Oh." He squinted, eyes suddenly distant. "That old line, huh? *It's not you, it's me, but I still want us to be friends*. Is that what you're saying?"

"In our case—or I should say, my case—it's true, Matt. I'm damaged goods."

He laughed, put his hands on her shoulders. "We should all be so damaged."

Julia broke away from him. "That's not cute."

"You think I don't see the pain you carry? Most people wear it like a martyr's cloak so they can be fussed over. You've veneered yours."

"You don't know what you're talking about."

"So tell me."

"I count on you, Matt. I count on your experience and your wisdom and the way you calm my waters. I know you count on me to keep you away from striped polo shirts and mini wieners in biscuit dough, and to make your seminars something that draws people to your authenticity, your experience." She forced a smile. "We're good, just like this."

He wasn't buying it. "I'm waiting, Julia. Tell me why we couldn't be even better."

"Don't," she said. "You don't want to get caught up in the trail of my tears—"

"Oh, baloney." He slapped his hand on the table. "You can't hide behind that forever. *Life is tough. I've screwed up. Poor me, don't get too close because it'll be poor you*. What a load of manure. If you don't like me, just say so."

Julia wanted to, wanted desperately to dismiss him. The truth was that she did like him. He was fun. Smart. Good company. And sexy—not just his looks or the way he carried himself—but because of the kind of guy he was. That made him dangerous to a girl like her.

"I messed up in the worst way," she said. "And there's no getting around that."

Matt picked at his thumbnail. "Did you murder someone?"

"No."

"Did you rob a bank?"

"Stop it, Matt. Not everyone is like you."

"Really? You think you know me, Julia."

She smiled. "You're easy to know. Easy to like."

"Know this, then. I broke my grandfather's jaw," Matt said. "I was a strong teenager and he was eighty years old, and I outright assaulted the man."

"You're exaggerating."

"No, ma'am, I am not. My dad was stationed in Kuwait and I was running a little wild. Whoopin' it up with some booze and weed. Out all hours, even on school nights. My mom couldn't cope with my pa away, so Gramps took my car keys. I hotwired his truck and took that out for the weekend—sixteen years old—and when I came back, he tried to tan my backside. So I swung and broke his jaw. He had to have surgery. His jaw was wired shut for almost two months."

"Did you . . . go to jail?"

"I could have," Matt said. "If he was of a mind to bring charges. He didn't."

"Because he loved you."

"Unconditional love is sometimes penalty enough."

"Do tell," Julia said.

"It took me three days before I went to the hospital to see him. The side of his face looked like a shredded tire, all dark and battered. You could see the wire in his mouth, see him having to breathe around crusted blood. I wanted to beg for his forgiveness, but the tears and the regret were jammed up behind my brainstem. He motioned me to him and showed me this little white erase board he had by his bed. He had already written on it before I had even come to see him.

"*I forgive you, Matthew.*

"When I tried to apologize or find a way to, like . . . maybe pay his hospital bill, he'd write *debt paid*. I'd heard those words all my life in church and didn't understand until I saw Gramps get the stomach flu and then almost choke on his own vomit. He had to keep wire cutters with him at all times just in case something like that happened. One morning he almost didn't get the wire cut in time. He threw up, this strange whine in the back of his throat because the pain was so bad. I tried to wipe his face, but that caused him even more pain.

"'I'm sorry, sorry, sorry,' I said, crying. And he looked up at me and mouthed the words *debt paid*. And then he had to have more surgery to reset the bone and get wired up again, and the only thing he would write to me was *I forgive you, Matthew*. And when he finally got set free of that, he came to school and had me waived out of class. He took me in his arms—there was not much to him at this point—and he said in this scratchy voice so I'd know he really meant it, *I forgive you, son*.

"He died about three months after that. Caught the flu and was just so weak, he couldn't shake it."

"I'm sorry," Julia said. "That must have been devastating."

"It was pretty terrible. And I blamed myself, made myself sick for days with shame. And then in the middle of the night I got on my knees and prayed—no, begged—God to forgive that stupid, prideful moment when my fist connected with his eighty-year-old jaw. I felt the Holy Spirit"—Matt laughed as he wiped tears from his eyes—"whack me across the back of the head, and in a pretty much audible voice that sounded like my grandfather's deep Texas twang, that Spirit said, *You know better, son. Shame off you. Jesus died to take the shame off you, so let Him.*"

Matt took both of Julia's hands. "So when are you going to let Him take the shame off you, Julia McCord?"

"You don't know what I did."

"Then trust me enough to tell me," he said.

Julia told him everything. The raging hunger that was Tom Bryant, the searing pain of a daughter ripping from her body and then ripping from her heart. The sweet summer that was Andy Hamlin—who remained unnamed because she couldn't bear to even think of him—and the dull ache of growing a second child in her body and knowing from almost the beginning that she would have to watch her leave too.

Graduation and planning Jeanne's wedding numbed some of the pain. When Jeanne and Patrick paddled away in their kayak, the pain came roaring back like the icy Maine ocean. After all the guests had left, Julia remained to clean up the last flutters of napkins and paper plates. She stuffed everything in a trash bag and then stared at the water.

The sun beat down on her shoulders, a high-noon heat in July. She closed her eyes and imagined Hope somewhere in a covered stroller, three months old and smiling. Destiny would be walking—probably running because she was born to run—under a sprinkler maybe, her dark eyes squinting against the water.

That ache in Julia's womb grew until it swallowed her and she could see nothing but pain and shame, scorching her skin so that she knew—with certainty—that she was like soot, something burned and black that you tried to wash away with a hose and forget.

The ocean stretched before her, cold and endless.

She could walk from this pebbled beach into its icy waves. Three steps in, her feet would be numb. By the time the water reached her neck, she would feel nothing but the shame that reverberated inside her head. She could duck under the water and let the current take her out to sea. Her daughters—her precious baby girls—would never know that she had existed.

She stepped into the waves. Even in midsummer, the ocean off Maine was bone-chilling. She welcomed the numbness as it spread from her feet up her legs.

Ashes to ashes. Death was a gray veil that she could pull around her like a shroud because what else could blot out her shame?

And then her fingers itched.

Julia dipped her hands in the water, desperate to deaden this urge because her urges—her desire—could not be trusted.

But I can be trusted, daughter.

You don't know me, Father.

I do. I know you and I love you.

She backed out of the water, wanting to silence what she could not believe. She fell to her knees, tried to crawl into the water but her hands pulled backward, across the pebbles and sand, to the fire that she had doused after the guests had left.

Julia reached into the stew of ash and water and found a blackened stick of wood. She had no canvas except her own bare legs, so she let her fingers have their way, sketching and writing what they would while she looked longingly at the ocean.

When her hand dropped the charred stick, she knew it was time to see what she had done.

My grace frees you, Julia.

She washed the words away—not with the cold ocean—but with her own tears.

fourteen

Colorado Springs

Friday, 8:05 a.m.

Destiny woke up with the sun in her eyes and a jackhammer in her head. Concussion—or too much drama? Normally she liked drama, except when she was in the middle of it. Had she overstepped her bounds by calling Tom and by insisting Chloe tell Jack to come to Colorado Springs?

She called Luke to ask what he thought. It went directly to voice mail. "Hey, babe. Where are you? It's gotten a bit over-the-top here—*here* being Colorado Springs. Can you give me a call, do a sanity check? I need someone outside the madness to talk to."

She got up, washed her face, and then peered across the sitting room. Chloe's door was still shut. The girl needed her rest, with the very odd and ugly day that lay ahead.

Destiny dialed the number of the one person she knew would be awake and looking for company.

"Hey," she said.

"Hey," Dillon said. "Whassup?"

Everything. "Not much. Your old man make it home all right?"

"Yeah. Got bags under the eyes and was pretty ripe, but after he jumped in the shower he was the same old, same old. Did you get to meet him?"

"No, man. Sorry. He was in and out."

Dillon went silent. Destiny waited a beat, two more, and then said, "I feel like I know him. Your mom told us how they met. Pretty cool stuff."

"What does she say about me? Other than I'm dying."

Knife in the heart, God. Thanks a bunch.

"You like to put it out there, huh?" she said.

"Don't you?"

"Yeah, bro. We're pretty much peas in a pod, you and me."

"Except that I'm dying."

"You're repeating yourself."

"Because you're the only person I can say that to." His voice wavered. "Am I creeping you out?"

"Hang up," she said. "Let me call you back."

"You are creeped out."

"Hang up." He did, and Destiny redialed so she could Skype him. He answered, a broad grin on his face.

"See it and believe it," he said. His skin had brightened from the deathly pallor to a more injured yellow. Bad news, Destiny knew, and so did he.

"Why aren't you . . . ripping apart the furniture or something? I know I would be."

He shrugged. "Because I feel worse than I look. So if I wanted to, like, tear the head off something, I couldn't. And what would it get me except a mess that my father would have to clean up?"

"I'm sorry, Dillon. I really am."

"That's okay. I've kind of made peace with it."

"How the heck does anyone make peace with that?"

He laughed. "Okay, the first thing you need to know is that I'm no saint. My parents like to think I am because I'm sick. That's the worst part of it, I swear. They smile and pat my head and everyone puts me on this stupid sick-kid pedestal. Their friends, people at church, my friends' parents. You can see it in their faces. *Poor kid, big burden to bear, what a special kid he is.* Makes me want to puke.

"They had to explain the illness to me pretty young. Because of the frequent tests and all that. Needles are not my friend. Mom would say to pray and I'd get mad because what kind of God is this, letting little kids get poked with needles and enduring exams where they push your belly really hard?

"Then they started explaining about transplants and I thought, *What kind of God is this that He can't get it right the first time?* Like you have to go to the human-parts version of the junkyard to try to salvage something? That is so not cool. I freaked out about it for months, thinking about some dead person's liver—or worse, some little kid's liver—being cut out of them and shoved into me. Know what the worst part is?"

Destiny shook her head. "Not a clue."

"The worst part is that the dead guy's liver would work better than mine, even though I was alive and the donor was dead."

"Really stinks, man." Destiny pressed her thumbnail into her palm to block her tears. "So how come you're still smiling?"

"You sure you got time for this?"

"I called you, remember?"

"Okay, back when I was in fifth grade, they had these special activities after school. Volleyball and gym hockey and stuff like that—cool things I wasn't allowed to do. My mother especially worries about a blow to the liver, even though it's my bile ducts that don't work. Am I wigging you out yet?"

"No, your mother explained the whole thing. And I googled it to learn more."

"Hey, I googled you. You're all over imdb.com."

Destiny laughed. "Yeah, mistress of the monsters. So what happened with these special activities?"

"I took this candy-making course. They taught us a bunch of stuff, but I really loved doing the sugar stained glass. I made all these different colored sugar sheets and carefully broke them into pretty large pieces. I even scored them with a box cutter, trying to get good shapes. And then I polyurethaned them to make them stronger. I cut some light-weight balsam wood to hold them—you know, grooves and glue?"

"Your parents trust you with a table saw?"

Dillon laughed. "They ain't happy about it. But, yeah, they kind of have to because, like . . . what else do I have? I put it together so it looked like a palace. Then I shot some stills of it so I could storyboard a film. And the candy caught the light from the flash in the coolest way so that all the walls looked like they were . . . alive, I guess. And some of the candy with uneven thickness broke the light up, like a prism. The colors were spectacular.

"And I thought, *Where can I see this kind of light with my own eyes?*

"I got this strong feeling. *Heaven.* And I realized I don't want to die, and I went through the whole progression again—*not fair, everything to live for, I'll be good*, and all that bargaining stuff. And the image of the light and the sound of the word—*heaven*—kinda seeped into my bones and I thought, *Okay, this is my imagination.*"

Dillon lowered his voice. "Because my imagination has been known to work overtime."

"Been there," Destiny said. "Not sure if something really is true or you just want it to be true so badly that you created it into existence."

"I let it rest there for a few more months. My candy fort was dusty by this time, but I was afraid to even touch it to brush off the dust, with the sugar being brittle and all. And then I got to thinking, maybe the dust would make an even cooler picture, so I photographed it. It was, like, intriguing—but I didn't like the flash as much as before, so I gently took the thing out in the yard and put it in direct sunlight."

"Sounds like it was pretty fragile," Destiny said.

"Yeah, it was. But I thought, *You've got to risk breaking what you love to get something better.* So I laid it on this rise in our backyard, where it caught the sunlight.

"And it was insane, how awesome the light was. I lay there in the grass with my sugar palace, watching the light from all different angles. My dad finally came out and asked what I was doing and I told him about the light. Not the heaven thing because I didn't want to freak him out and make them give me some brain MRI or something.

"He lay in the grass with me and stared at the different lights. An hour or so later Mom got home from some florist meeting or something and stretched out with us.

"'What are you looking at?' she asked.

"I didn't say a thing—I couldn't, honestly—so Dad finally said, 'Revelation 21. Son, make sure you take a peek at that.'

"And I thought, *Whoa*. They told me to steer clear of Revelation because I made a movie about the seven bowls of wrath and they were so freaked out about it. Now here Dad is saying I should read part of it. Have you ever read it?"

"Long time ago," Destiny said. "It was pretty much incomprehensible."

"Isn't that the fun of it?"

"I suppose."

"Anyway, I read the chapter about the New Jerusalem that shines like precious jewels. That's when I knew—*heaven*. And I thought—no, I *knew*—that when the time came, I'd know the way there. That simple."

"I wish," Destiny said.

"Ah, you grown-ups make it too hard."

"I guess we do, Dil."

"Dad's coming to take my blood pressure. Thanks for listening, man."

"Thank you," Destiny said.

"Hey, if you don't make it to Dallas, no prob. I'll see you on the other side."

He clicked off the call and left her staring at a blank screen.

Friday, 11:32 a.m.

Getting the test done was easier than Destiny expected. She went to the urgent care clinic at the Colorado Springs hospital, under the pretense of having the doctor check her jaw. They took photos, promising that her record would be available to her—or her attorney.

I'm here. I might as well get it done.

Destiny explained everything to a sympathetic doctor. They drew her blood and asked her to wait for an hour while they processed it with the next batch to be run. "You're lucky," the doctor said. "We've got a full suite of surgeries going today and lots of requests for type-and-matches."

The clinic waiting room was small and clean. Two mothers waited with her, both with runny-nosed children. *I need to stay away from them. I have to stay healthy for the surgery.*

The receptionist called her back in and asked her to sit outside a procedure room. The doctor finally appeared, lab slip in his hand. "Ms. Connors," he said. "You're type AB, Rh-negative."

"Is that good?"

"It's great for you. You can receive blood or tissue from any blood type."

"What about donation? Who can I donate to?"

"You're pretty limited. What type did you say your half-brother was?"

"Type O," Destiny said.

He shook his head. "I'm sorry. Type O needs a type-O donor. Is there anything else I can help you with?"

She shook her head and thanked him for his time. And then she called the Broadmoor shuttle and rode back to the hotel to tell Julia that Chloe was Dillon's last hope.

Wounded, quivering, needy—and pretty much useless—Chloe Deschene.

Friday, 12:21 p.m.

Chloe met Jack in the lobby, made small talk as she led him to her suite. Once inside, she motioned him into the bedroom and locked the door.

"What have you been doing?" He studied her. "You look so worn."

She took off his glasses and caressed his face. She needed him close so he couldn't look into her eyes.

"Hey, hey," he said. "It's all right. I'm here now."

The familiar comforted her—his button-down shirt and navy blazer, the scent of his shampoo, his everlasting mint, the tight muscles in his back, the silk of his hair. She pulled him tighter.

Jack took her shoulders and carefully held her at arm's length. "What's going on?"

Rob Jones can't extort you if you have nothing to hide, Tom had said. The words were hot on her lips—*I've been stupid and cruel and I cheated on you*—but somehow they came out, "My biological father cheated on his wife with Julia."

"I guess we knew it would be something like that, since she withheld the name. Can you finally tell me who he is?"

"Andrew Hamlin."

"What? *The* Andrew Hamlin?"

"Julia worked with him one summer. His wife was on a mission trip in Africa and he . . . fell into a relationship with her."

"No one just *falls* into a relationship."

"Maybe not." Chloe gave him a weak smile. "Anyway, here I am."

"How many of his books do we have? And I went to that men's conference he led. I was so impressed and now this?"

Chloe went to the window, stared out at the snow-covered mountains. "People make mistakes."

Jack took her in his arms and buried his face in her neck. She tipped his head back and kissed him. Tom Bryant was wrong. Some things are best left hidden. The merciful thing to do was to bury this thing with Rob Jones so deep that it rotted away to nothing.

"You still want to meet your father?" Jack whispered. "Now that you know who he is?"

"Yes. Of course," Chloe said. "And I want you with me."

"That's the only place I've ever wanted to be." Jack kissed her and, though she was ashamed of how she had let Rob Jones kiss her, Chloe wouldn't let Jack stop.

She held him tight and prayed that God would freeze them in this moment—nothing before, nothing after—just locked in an embrace with her husband. So close that he couldn't possibly see the shame in her eyes.

The pulse in his neck quickened and his skin flushed. She couldn't let him make love to her, not until he knew.

"Jack, I have something to tell you. Something I'm not proud of."

"I know," he whispered. "I know."

"What do you know?"

"With all the money I shift around for our trusts and the foundations, I have to be careful with our online protections. One of the guardian programs spit out talkatnight.com. I thought it was an intrusion, so I set a feedback program. That caught the activity from your ISP account."

"Did you monitor all of it?"

"No. I saw the first one and then . . . I let it go."

"You should have stopped me."

"I wanted you to have the space to work through whatever you needed. I hoped—with every ounce of my being—that in the end, you would choose *us*." Jack gently disengaged her from his arms so he could see her face. She couldn't bear his eyes on her, tried to turn away, but he held her by the shoulders.

"I didn't want you to come back to me merely because you got caught. It was the most painful thing I've ever done—giving you enough space to either run away or come back to me. I knew I couldn't be your Holy Spirit. I've tried that, and clearly that pushed you away. I am so sorry for that."

Chloe's chest tightened.

Jack pushed back her hair. "Breathe. Just breathe. We'll work through this."

"How did you bear it?"

"Horribly. I wanted to throw away the computers, lock you in the house. After you sent me home from Boston, I realized smothering you was not going to help either of us. I decided to trust the God inside of you. I prayed so hard that you'd develop a keen sensitivity to your spiritual radar. And that I would develop a keen sensitivity to what you need. To who you really are. It's not that we don't trust you. We—your mother and I—hold you so tightly because we love you so deeply."

"That can't be true, not anymore. You must despise me."

"I couldn't," he said. "Ever."

"You will when you know how horrible this is."

He pressed his forehead to hers, so close that her lashes brushed his cheek. "Tell me. Tell me, Chloe, and I will tell you it doesn't matter. Regardless of what you tell me, I'm not going anywhere."

"Oh, Jack, you have no idea."

Friday, 12:30 p.m.

Julia's phone buzzed, waking her from a deep sleep. Fuzzy-tongued and bleary-eyed, she answered it.

"Hi, Jules." Thomas Bryant. "I thought I'd better check in with the adult, see how things are settling."

"Thank you," she said, heading for the bathroom. "For what you're doing to help Chloe."

"I didn't know about the second child until Destiny told me."

"You didn't need to know. Why would I tell you I was pregnant again?"

"No reason," Tom said. "You couldn't trust me, for sure. And I want you to know that I am so, so sorry for what went down between us. For how I bolted."

Julia dampened a washcloth, dabbed her eyes. "I'm sorry for being such a lunatic stalker."

"You were just being a . . . mother. I can't say enough how sorry I am for what you went through."

"Tom, I forgave you long ago. For years I prayed that you would find a good woman, have a lovely family. And just . . . go on."

"And I did, Jules. I did."

Silence settled between them. Not a bad or frantic silence. Comfortable.

After a few moments, Tom cleared his throat. "So. This thing with Chloe."

"A mess. Is there anything we can be doing?"

"I got a guy on the North Shore showing that picture around. If we can get a positive ID, we can strong-arm him with the assault charge. I don't have a lot of hope for that, though. That he got through the Deschene online protection so easily speaks to a high level of technical sophistication. I can arrange for a trace when he calls back tomorrow, but I'd expect him to use a burner phone."

"A what?"

"Disposable. Use it once, toss it. And his blackmail may be aimed at her husband."

"Clearly," Julia said.

"That's not what I mean. Distract Mr. Deschene on this matter, draw out repeated contacts and meanwhile, this Rob Jones character is probing for ways to get into the charitable foundation and drain some funds."

"That's disturbing."

"No matter what, the best course is for Chloe to tell her family, take away his leverage. Can you persuade her to do that?"

"I don't know, Tom. It's not like I have real standing with her."

"She's your flesh and blood, Jules. There's got to be something of you in her. There's plenty of you in Destiny."

Julia laughed. "There's a lot more of you."

"We did good, huh? We did bad and still—we did good."

"God did good, Tom."

"So let Him do some good here. Destiny can rattle some sense into the girl, but you're the one who can settle her."

"I want to help. Unfortunately, my attention is divided."

"That's the other thing. I got tested yesterday."

"You? Tom, why?"

"We're family, right? Destiny said you needed a type O. My mom had that blood type—you know she died from leukemia, right?"

"Pottsie told me, a couple years back. I was sad to hear it."

"I would donate. I swear, I would. But I'm type B."

"Tom, just the fact that you got tested—thank you, thank you so much." Her phone buzzed. Jeanne. "I have to go. May God bless you and your family."

"Back-at-cha, Jules."

Julia clicked to the incoming call. "Why are you calling?" she said, though she already knew.

"Dillon's blood pressure went sky-high. They're admitting him."

"The list . . ." *Tell me someone died so my boy can live.*

"Dr. Rosado said that he'll be near or at the top. But nothing yet. Matt will call you as soon as he gets through admitting."

"I'm coming home. As soon as we can get the plane in the air."

"He's stable for now. But I wouldn't drag my feet getting here."

Julia ended the call. Her knees wobbled and she slid to the floor. Facedown now, smelling the carpet shampoo, feeling the wool on her cheeks. Head spinning, she rolled onto her back and texted Sally to prepare the plane.

She speed dialed her son, delighted that Dillon picked up.

"Mom. You're gonna get me arrested."

"What for?"

"They have all these signs in the ER about not using cell phones. I'm probably setting off five cardiac monitors as we speak." His voice wavered. "I think they're gonna put me on one."

"Auntie Pottsie told me your pressure spiked."

"That's the bad news. The good news is that my MELD score is nice and high."

Julia blinked to hold back tears. No kid should have to know his own MELD—the Model for End-Stage Liver Disease that played a key part in moving a patient up the transplant list that UNOS maintained nationally.

"Dil, how are you feeling?"

He waited a beat, then said, "Like a turnip truck ran over me."

"Turnip? Why turnip?"

"To avoid the cliché about dump trucks. And because I hate turnips. Are you coming home?"

"Yes. As soon as we can get the flight plan scheduled."

"Is Destiny coming with you?"

"You know about Destiny?" This was unexpected. Staggering.

"Yeah. We're kinda buddies now. Been talking a bit."

"How did that happen?"

"During the blizzard. Didn't she tell you?"

"It must have gone right over my head, pal." Let Dillon believe that he had been a topic of conversation. Julia was quite aware of why Destiny hadn't mentioned they had spoken.

"Ask her to come. She's cool. And bring the other sister. We can party like it's the end of the world."

"Dillon, Dillon . . ."

"Sorry, Mom, they're coming at me with more stuff. Love you. And tell Destiny that—if she doesn't think that's too weird."

"Honey, I love you," Julia said. "I'll be home soon."

"And so will I, Mom. So will I."

Friday, 12:34 p.m.

"You actually *met* this guy?" Jack said. "How could you do something so risky?"

"Because," Chloe said, "I was frustrated. Bored. Feeling trapped."

"Did you sleep with him?"

"No."

"Did you . . . want to?"

"I just wanted someone to talk to, that's all."

"We talk, Chloe. All the time, we talk."

"You talk, I listen."

"Am I that controlling? Oh, God, forgive me—am I some sort of monster?"

"Don't beat yourself up. I let myself be . . . *managed* is too harsh a term. I let myself be guided because that was the calmer way. The easier way. The lazier way."

Jack kneaded the knuckles of his right hand into the palm of his left hand. "So what did you do with him?"

"I drank too much. And it snowed too much so . . . I had to go to that motel."

"I thought you went there with Julia and Destiny."

"They found me there, Jack. They searched for me in a blizzard and they found me. I don't know what would have happened if they hadn't."

"What do you mean?"

"You'd better sit down."

He sank onto the bed, the color draining from his face. *He knows what's coming.* How could he not put two and two together and come up with betrayal?

Chloe took his hand, then scrolled to the video on her phone.

If only Destiny could be here with her. Her sister would give her courage. No—Chloe needed to stand up on her own.

"I am so ashamed and I am so sorry. You don't deserve this."

"For Pete's sake, Chloe. Just show me."

She tapped the Play button and the video began. When he saw her nakedness, he made a guttural noise.

"I'll stop it now," Chloe said. "You get the idea."

"No." He grabbed the phone from her. "I need to see all of it."

Jack watched to the end, his hand tugging on his cheeks as if forcing his eyes to stay open. Chloe breathed slowly, beating back any cries or groans because this was his time to grieve and she had no right to take it from him.

When the video finished, Jack threw the phone against the wall.

"Don't," Chloe said. "We might need that for . . . evidence."

"Evidence of what?" Jack jumped to his feet. "Did he rape you because, I swear, I will kill—"

"No. Jack. No."

"So you were a willing participant in this?"

"Destiny thinks that he gave me something . . . to loosen my inhibitions."

"Do you hear yourself? Are you telling me this girl in the video is who you really are?"

She put her hands to his cheeks. "I don't want to be a facsimile of a wife, not anymore. I want to be the wife you can trust."

"So what was the point of this encounter?"

"For me—pushing the boundaries. And that's really all on me. I see that now." Chloe had to keep talking, not let herself dissolve. "And his? To extort money. For all your sophistication in our computer stuff, he learned pretty quickly who I really was. And it only took a few lines of conversation to see the gaping need in my life."

"Need! What could you possibly need? We are so privileged, Chloe."

"I need to be who God is calling me to be. Serve with the gifts He gives and not slip into a role you assign because that's easier."

"Oh, I'm a tyrant? Is that how we're going to play this?"

"No. It's just . . . you're so self-assured, confident—"

"So it's my fault because I know who I am and what is expected of me?"

Chloe clutched at his shirt. "I told myself that so I could just keep trailing in your wake."

"How much does he want?"

"Half a million."

Jack snorted. "Give it to him."

"No."

"If this goes public, it would kill your mother."

"We have a plan."

"Who is *we*?"

"Destiny, Julia, and Tom Bryant. Destiny's father. He's a lawyer."

Jack yanked away from her. "You told *them* before you told me?"

"They kind of saved me from . . . I don't know . . . maybe he *would* have raped me. Destiny and Julia tracked me down at the motel and Destiny tried to batter her way through the slider. I remember that hideous music and some sort of banging. He grabbed his stuff and pushed his way out of there, shoving Destiny into the snow. She held on to his ankle, so he kicked her in the face."

"Really? I may need to assess my opinion of her."

"Don't be assessing or reassessing anything. Take the time to get to know her."

"What happened with Julia?"

"He threw Julia down but she got a good look at his face. So—between the three of us—we put together a sketch."

"I want to see it."

She went to the dresser, pulled out a photocopy of the drawing. "We're going to use an assault charge to get the video. Tom's got an investigator—"

"Wait a minute! How many people know about this?"

"You can't save me from everything."

He sat down hard on the bed, head in hands. "Apparently I can't save you from anything."

"Don't you see, Jack? That was never your job." Chloe pulled him into her arms and held him until both of them had run their tears dry.

Friday, 1:44 p.m.

Destiny studied the lab slip, willing it to speak a different truth. She had always wanted to be unique—but not like this. Julia's type A and Tom's type B combined to AB negative—the rarest kind of blood group.

As if all she was could be captured on a single piece of paper.

Would Julia be done with her now? Would she put her on a plane for Los Angeles and focus all her attention on Chloe? Not that Destiny wanted anyone's attention. She already had two parents and a sister. Could she blame Julia for another twenty-four years of silence, now that Destiny had come up short?

Maybe she'd wait to tell her after Chloe got tested. If her sister were type O, Destiny could introduce her to Dillon. He and Chloe weren't much of a match, but they were as close genetically as Destiny and he were.

Did genetics even matter? Would she have been less of a pain-in-the-gut to her parents if she had real Connors blood running in her veins? None of that mattered at this point. She was an adult, had made adult choices—not always good ones—and her life was on her.

An easy choice. Involve a parent or friend or lover—or God—and then choices got harder. Then again, deciding she would donate to Dillon hadn't been hard at all, once she knew him. If he had the stick-up-the-spine attitude of a Jack Deschene, she might not have been inclined to consider the donation. Was that right—basing an act of self-sacrifice on the personality of the recipient? If her parents had been like that, she might be in a prison or on the street.

They had stuck with her. And so she would too. If Julia was crushed because her firstborn was incompatible, so be it. Destiny would stick with her, stick with Chloe, and see what she could do to help.

Did I get it right, God?

She closed her eyes and listened. She heard nothing. Colors swam through her mind like vibrant jewels and she thought, *Yes—Dillon's heaven.*

Her phone buzzed. *God doesn't use cell phones,* but glanced at it anyway. A text from Julia.

I'm in the hall. Please let me in.

Destiny shoved the lab slip into her jeans, grabbed her phone, and walked to the door.

Friday, 1:47 p.m.

Julia rushed into the suite's sitting area and pulled Destiny into a hug. The girl melted into her as if they had been doing this for a lifetime.

"I have to leave," she said. "Dillon's back in the hospital. He needs me."

Destiny pulled away, tears streaming down her cheeks. "I'm sorry."

"No, I'm sorry. I never should have asked you to do something so . . . extreme. And then leave you in Colorado. I'll make sure you have a flight home."

"Just shut up for once." Her daughter pulled a piece of paper from her back pocket. "This is what I'm sorry for."

Julia smoothed it out, squinting to understand what she was looking at. "Oh, God," she cried and the anger swept through her, and she drew back her arm and was about to punch a wall—

—when Destiny caught her arm and held her. She pulled her into a hug now, holding Julia as they both sobbed. Chloe watched from her bedroom door.

"Thank you," Julia said between gasps.

"I'm not good enough," Destiny said.

"You're everything you need to be. That's all that matters."

"I wanted to be Dillon's sister. Now that I know him."

"That doesn't change." Julia used her sleeve to soak up Destiny's tears. Destiny did the same for her and they both laughed.

Chloe wrapped her arms around both of them. "What's wrong?"

Jack appeared—out of nowhere, it seemed—with a box of tissues. Chloe wiped their faces while he went to the mini-bar and brought them each a bottle of water.

Julia handed Chloe the lab slip. Her eyes widened. "You got tested, Dez?"

Destiny nodded, wiped away more tears. "I'm not compatible."

"Where did you get tested? I'll go," Chloe said.

Julia held her breath, waiting for Jack to forbid it. Instead, he said, "I'll take her before we meet with Pastor Hamlin."

"What?" Destiny said. "You're in on this now?"

"She wants to," Jack said. "So I'll support her in that."

"Who gave you happy juice?"

He laughed.

Chloe would never make it through the psychological screening. Julia couldn't tell her that, could only pray that Chloe would be compatible and would be smart enough to fake her way through the screenings.

Julia gently disengaged from Destiny and hugged Jack. "Thank you."

"We'll be okay," he whispered. "I promise."

"I told him about the video," Chloe said.

Destiny doubled over, sinking to her knees with her phone in hand. "Oh, God help me, please don't do this."

Everyone turned to look at Destiny. Jack helped her up while Chloe took the phone from her. She read a text, hand to her mouth, and then handed the phone to Julia.

> Luke in ICU, coma from head injury. Cedars-Sinai. Come NOW. Not good.

"This is my fault," Destiny said. "My fault."

"Not your fault," Julia said, pulling her close.

"I'll book a flight to Los Angeles," Jack said. "We can go with her. I understand you've got to head home."

"I've got the jet," Julia said, cradling Destiny. "Sally can get us there right away."

"Dillon," Chloe said. "You need to get to Dallas."

"And I will. After I get Destiny settled. You two have some work to do here. Correct?"

Jack put his arm around Chloe. "Yes, we do."

Chloe leaned into him and Julia thought, *You are the God who sees. You are the Father who knows. Now please be the God who makes whole.*

On the Plane to Los Angeles
Friday, 2:30 p.m.

Julia tried to take Destiny's hand.

"Don't touch me," she said. "I hate you." Hate felt good. It was the only thing Destiny had left as fear spun in her stomach like a razor-edged propeller.

"I get you're angry."

"You think?"

They were scheduled to land in Burbank in two hours. Just in time for Los Angeles rush hour. They had to make it in time—*please, God.*

No. Look what dabbling in God got Luke. And what good had faith ever done for Julia? "This is your fault."

"Please. Tell me how," Julia said.

"If you had stayed in Dallas, Chloe would still be an oblivious college student and Stepford wife. And if you had stayed in Dallas and minded your own business, Luke would be okay."

"I don't follow."

"I wouldn't have left him."

"May I remind you—you were in the process of throwing him out when I turned the corner. I heard you shouting with the car windows up."

"I was trying to make a point. Because you Christians love to talk talk talk but when it comes time to listen, you just spout and then spout some more."

"Your break-up had nothing to do with me. Unless you want to blame me for how you push people away. Because you have a right to do that, correct? That's what you've told yourself your whole life. You were abandoned by your birth mother. So you had the right to put people at arm's length in case they wanted to abandon you."

Destiny got up, walked the ten paces to the back of the plane, back to the front. Trapped in a tin can with her fury and this woman who had disrupted everything less than a week ago. "That's a load of crappy psychobabble. You don't like that I can stand on my own two feet—unlike your other daughter who can't make it a day without some man in her life."

"You don't stand on your own two feet. You stand on your manufactured anger and your sharp tongue."

"And you stand on your old-time religion. So who's deceiving themselves? Huh? You're as ticked as I am. You admitted it—you want to take a swing at God, but He's not exactly showing His face, is He?"

"Do you think my anger or yours is powerful enough to keep Him away?"

Destiny spread her arms wide. "Do you see Him here? Do you?"

"I see you in a private jet, rushing to be with the man you love. What if I just left you to go to Los Angeles on your own? Would you rather wait in a ticketing line, then security, and then wait in a boarding line, only to have to make a connection somewhere? Look all around you and see His provision."

"That *what if* game doesn't work with me. Never has. Not going to start now."

"So you haven't played *what if* from the time your parents told you that you were adopted?" Julia smiled, pointed her cast at Destiny. "You have, haven't you?"

"Every child plays that game. What if I were a princess or a professional baseball player or rock star? What if my daddy had a zillion bucks and I could have a pony? It's fantasy. But Luke, he was—he *is*—reality."

"And what is Luke's reality?"

"He's confused."

"Do you really think that, Destiny?" Julia stood, blocked her path so Destiny was trapped between the cockpit door and the first row of seats. "And if Luke were here, he'd be asking you, '*What if* God is real, Destiny? And what if He is right? What if the biggest leap of faith one can make is to assume that there is a God?'"

"You don't even know Luke, so don't try to put words in his mouth. Nor do you know me, so save your sermon for someone who buys your bull. I'm done with it, done with it all."

Colorado Springs
Friday, 4:30 p.m.

Chloe stared at her birth father and his wife. *What kind of insanity is this?*

Jack made polite and intelligent small talk with Andrew Hamlin while she sat like a lump, embarrassment backing up her throat so that she could barely breathe.

Kathleen Hamlin alternated between glaring at her husband and studiously avoiding Chloe.

This had been a terrible twenty-four hours for the Hamlins. The revelation of what Andrew had tried to bury forever. Now to be face-to-face with the product of his affair had to be devastating. Why they even agreed to see her was a mystery. And what was she supposed to get out of this? With Destiny and Julia on their way to Los Angeles—and two lives on the edge—what did any of this matter?

"Do you hate me, Mrs. Hamlin?" Chloe said, interrupting the stream of conversation.

"Right about now I pretty much hate my husband. But this isn't your fault." Katie glanced her way, tried to force a smile.

"I'm the face of what your husband did. How can you even look at me?"

Jack squeezed her hand, remained silent.

"You are the face of the redemption of what Julia and I did," Andy said.

Chloe looked at Katie. "Do you believe that?"

"I have to. I have no choice. There's no other way to make sense of what they did. You go into marriage with expectations. And when those expectations are dashed to bits—you just let God make sense of it when you can't possibly. Not that I'm particularly fond of God right now . . . but we'll be okay."

"I was wrong in so many ways," Andy said. "I let Julia walk out of IronWorks and I never called to make sure she was all right. The pregnancy never occurred to me, not once. I was consumed with guilt and trying to hide that guilt from Katie. For years, the affair ate at me. And then it got to the point where the callous was hard enough that I could persuade myself it didn't really happen. But God knows the heart, and not telling Katie was like a cancer growing deep under the skin.

"When Julia and Matt arrived here yesterday, my first thought was to make them go away. I don't think the Whittakers would have forced the encounter. Katie saw something in my face, said we had to meet with them. So after twenty-four years, I had to confess what I had done. What I should have confessed to her when she came to Albany all those years ago."

"Mrs. Hamlin, you're being so calm about it," Jack said.

She laughed. "Oh, honey, I had a stormy night. And it's not over, not by a long shot. Andrew and I—we're going to need rain gear, trust me."

"How will you do it?" Chloe clutched Jack's hand. "Tell me how you go on when you've betrayed the one you love."

Andy glanced at Jack. "You acknowledge the anger and the hurt. I have to give Katie the space to do that for as long as it takes. Take however much of her pain that I can, that she's willing to allow me to bear. And then you accept forgiveness. That's really the harder part."

"What if it's too . . . ugly?" Chloe said. "The betrayal."

Katie shook her head. "You can't go there. When any of us fall into that trap, we're saying the blood of our Savior is insufficient to cleanse us. That we need something more. And, Chloe, there is nothing more because there needs to be nothing more. God does not despise us for stumbling in the wrong direction. Contentment and hope don't come from perfect living—it's a gift, Chloe. We have to surrender our emotional and spiritual pride to accept that gift. We can't be worthy of it. I've been proud of the ministry that Andrew and I built. Do you hear me—even now, I'm saying *we* built all this. My pride needs to take a big hit."

"I'm a proud guy," Jack said. "Really good at making plans for everyone else. Especially when I think I know what's good for them."

Chloe linked her arm through his and said, "I did something pretty bad."

Andy and Katie listened as she told the story, and in the end—she realized *they heard the worst, and they stayed.* And Jack would stay too. It was a good thing.

A gift.

Los Angeles
Friday, 6:05 p.m.

Destiny clutched Julia's arm because her legs wouldn't hold her.

"They found him in a ravine off Mulholland," Sean Gagnon said. He was Luke's fellow stuntman and closest friend. "He was riding up there alone. As close as the cops can figure, it was dark and his bike hit a For Sale sign that had blown off someone's property. It was lying in the road. It was a hefty one, supposed to be nailed to fencing but we had some high winds that night. When Public Works was called to haul it away, they saw the skid marks. One of them went halfway down the ravine and saw Luke's bike. Deeper down . . . they found Luke."

"Oh, God," Destiny said.

"Hold on," Julia said, sliding her arm around her waist.

"He went off the road, down the slope, and he was out there since Lord only knows what time yesterday."

Destiny couldn't beat back the scene in her head. Luke, sprawled in the darkness, lying on sand and brush. A terrible head wound. So dizzy and hurt that all he could do was open his eyes and stare up at the stars. And look for Jesus.

And where were You, Jesus, when Luke needed You?

"The cold . . . ," she said.

"It was cold, especially in those deep canyons. He was suffering from hypothermia when they brought him in. His body temperature was a bit over ninety-four. The neurologist said that might have saved his life by slowing everything down."

"Praise God," Julia whispered.

"Shut up," Destiny said. "Just shut up."

"They're trying to reach his parents up in Alaska. Apparently they're out ice fishing somewhere. So right now, you're next of kin. You're the person named in his Advance Directive."

"Don't say that." Destiny pressed her hands over her ears. "I'm not doing that. They can't make me."

Julia gently pried her hands down. "What, honey? What aren't you doing?"

"I am not pulling the plug."

"No one's talking about that," Sean said. "It's all about getting the swelling down in his brain and then seeing if he needs surgery for a blood clot."

"When can I see him?"

"They're doing a procedure now. No, no—don't freak, Dez. Just some normal stuff. The nurse said she'd come let me know when he can have a visitor. I've been trading off with some of the crew. But he'll want you there."

"Thank you," Julia said.

"There's a group in the coffee shop," Sean said. "Maybe you could walk down there with me . . . they want to meet you."

"Who?" She looked at Julia for her cue. Her brain was so numb, her heart pounding so hard, that she felt suspended in the moment.

Destiny was simply unable to consider that Luke might die. *Luke is Your guy. So if You hate me for being hateful, have at it. But Luke . . . please God . . . Luke.*

"Let's go meet Luke's friends," Julia said.

They followed Sean out of the ICU waiting room, down the hall, took a couple turns, and came into the hospital's coffee shop. It was jammed with people. The friends she knew hugged her. So many faces she didn't know.

"Who are these others?" she whispered to Sean.

"They're from our church."

Destiny let her eyes wander the crowd. Those who noticed her looking at them gave her a nod or solemn smile. They were all just people—men in flannel shirts and baseball caps, women in flowing skirts or tattered jeans. No halos, just concerned eyes and clasped hands.

"They all came to pray," Sean whispered. "They're here for you too."

Destiny gave them a weak wave and then nodded toward the hall. "He needs me."

"Yes, he does," Julia said. "We'll go and wait."

"You need to go to Dillon."

"Shortly. First . . . we see to Luke."

They walked back to the ICU, two turns and down a long hall. "He . . . needs you. You shouldn't be wasting time here."

"Dillon knows where I am. Check your phone. He said he left you a message."

Destiny pulled her phone from her pocket, listened to her voice mail.

"Hey, fellow freak." Dillon's voice sounded weak, and yet *so* him. "I hear my man Luke had an accident. I guess he's really your man, but I know when we meet, he's gonna be my man too. Anyway, I wanted you to know I'm talking to God and telling Him this isn't cool—not one bit. But Jesus is my Man, so maybe He can put in a good word. I know you're busy, so don't call back or anything. Just wanted you to know . . ." His voice faded. *Don't go. Not yet.* She heard him cough. As he resumed the message, there was a rattle in his throat. "Just wanted you to know that I've got this one covered. See you soon."

She clicked off the phone and was in Julia's arms because anywhere else in the world didn't make sense.

Friday, 9:46 p.m.

Destiny couldn't bear to look at Luke—his golden beard clipped, part of his head shaved. Wires and tubes everywhere. His eyes would not open, no matter how much she pleaded with him.

He had other injuries that seemed insignificant in comparison to his fractured skull. A broken forearm, a horrible cut in his thigh that could have killed him, the nurse told her. It missed the femoral artery by a whisper. A unit of blood flowed into his IV. She was stunned that Julia hadn't even looked at the bag because Luke's blood type was there for anyone to see.

The label read type A. A small mercy because Destiny couldn't bear the thought of Luke leaving her with only his organs to continue a life so fervently lived.

"You better go," Destiny said. "Dillon needs you."

"Soon," Julia said.

"He's got the greater claim."

"Mothers never use that measurement."

We're so helpless. So confident that nothing could get to us and then a freak accident and Luke is now hanging in some balance. If it's in God's hand, she hoped the Almighty measured by Luke and not her.

"What do I do about the anger?" Destiny said. "What do you do? You're the one who tried to punch through a door, getting at God."

"Anger is natural. It's nice to be able to blame stuff on God. So we acknowledge it. Not cast it like a bomb but open our hands and show it to God. Let Him deal with it."

"You make it sound easy."

"No, no way," Julia said. "Because anger is like any drug—you get used to needing it to move forward."

"Julia." Destiny grabbed her arm. "What if . . . you lose him?"

"I'll probably break my skull, battering it against the nearest thing I can find. Except . . . Matt, in his grief, would not let me. And we've got so many friends who would bear the anger and the grief with us. We'd get through. It would be horrible and I would be furious with God for a long time. Destiny, I have no other place to go. I can't see it now, but I have to trust that God's grace will be sufficient for me."

Destiny jerked upright. *My grace is sufficient for you.* She knew those words, had decided long ago that *she* would be sufficient. And yet, she needed Luke—and now Luke needed a miracle. *Make Your grace sufficient,* she prayed. *Because I've got nothing.*

And she suddenly glimpsed the nature of sacrifice. She almost succumbed to the hypothermia—as did Luke. She had been saved from carbon monoxide poisoning by a sign, and he had been felled by one. Luke would have offered to take all this because he loved her, and would have sacrificed to save her.

Destiny would do the same for him. Even in her anger with him or her parents or the universe or God—she would do the same for him.

And if she could understand that, maybe she could understand what all the prayer lists and Sunday school lessons and midweek services and loving care of her parents couldn't get through to her.

She slid out of her chair, kneeled on the floor, and put her face on Julia's arm. "Help me pray."

Julia smiled, then clasped her left hand over Destiny's. "Of course . . ." And then she looked up, eyes shadowed, before she said, "Here's the lady you need to pray with."

Destiny turned her head. "Mom," she said and was in Melanie Connors's arms before she took another breath. Her mother was smaller than Julia and yet felt so strong and substantial. "How did you know?"

"Julia called me. She had already arranged a flight for me. She knew I would want to be here with you and Luke. Dad's coming out from DC. He'll be here soon."

"All of you?"

"Of course." Melanie stroked her hair. "We're going to be here for as long as you need us."

"What about Sophie?"

"She's down in the coffee shop, getting a sandwich and listening to all the Luke stories."

Julia gathered up her bag.

"Wait," Destiny said and hugged her hard. "Thank you."

"Oh, my dear child. Thank *you*."

"I'll . . . be praying for Dillon. It'll be all right."

"Back-at-cha," Julia said and steered Destiny into her mother's arms.

fifteen

Dallas

Saturday, 9:15 a.m.

Julia had taken the text from Chloe on her way to the airport in Los Angeles.

Type A pos. I am so sorry.

She cried for a good two hours before finding the energy to text Chloe back.

Don't apologize. I love you. May God bless you and Jack.

She arrived in Dallas at dawn, took a cab straight to Cedar Springs Medical Center. Matt hugged her, said he's on the top of the list. And yet—still no liver. UNOS showed two type O's available overnight. One was in Seattle and the other in Georgia. Both jumped Dillon on the list because of geography.

She didn't ask *how is he?* because her husband's face told her everything. He texted Pottsie and she came up from the chapel where she was keeping vigil. She prayed with Julia and Matt, kissed them both, and went back to batter heaven with her love.

Dr. Annie hugged her and said, "We're not out of time yet."

Julia would not ask *how long?* and glared at Matt so the words would not even enter his mind. She went into Dillon's room, kicked off her shoes, and got into the bed with her son. His skin was dry, his belly swollen, his breath acrid. He was only hours from being past the stage where he could accept a transplant.

He stirred when she wrapped her arms around his neck and pulled him to her. "Mom," he mumbled and went back to sleep. She fell into a deep sleep, tried to fight her way out. Instead, giving in to Matt telling her that she needed her sleep too.

You're resting in Me now. That wasn't her husband's voice—though it was his will—and she let it be her will too.

Keep my baby safe, she prayed from her dreams. *Show him wonder. He loves wonder.*

And then bright sunlight shone on her face and Matt shook her awake. "Julia, Chloe is here."

Julia forced her eyes open and saw Chloe staring at the boy who was her brother, tears streaming down her face. Jack's arms were tight on her waist, and somehow Julia knew that he was not holding her back—just holding her up.

"I got tested too," Jack said.

"What?" Julia squinted at him.

"I'm healthy as a horse, probably too stable psychologically, and"—he kissed Chloe's cheek and then turned back to Julia—"I am a perfectly fine and very qualified type-O donor."

sixteen

Los Angeles

Columbus Day Weekend

People make bargains when they're dying.

"We try to measure the cost of our lives," was how Dr. Annie explained it. *"Then we try to offer some pledge in payment, thinking we can buy them back."*

Dillon had made a ton of bargains. *If you save me, heavenly Father, think of what I'll do for You.*

I'll be good.

I'll do good.

I'll go on missions to leper hospitals.

I'll become a leper by dating the girl in school who smells like mothballs and looks like a hairball.

None of it was necessary because Dillon's life had already been paid for. When he was so sick it hurt to breathe, when the toxins overflowed into his blood, when his abdomen felt like it would explode, Jesus was the promise who—one way or another—would get him home.

When he could think straight again, when his skin was pink instead of yellow, and when the only pain in his gut was from the staples sealing in his new liver, he made one last deal.

I will live—not pretend, not hide, not doubt, not be scared—I will really live.

Unfortunately, his parents took a dim view of *really living* and refused to buy him a motorcycle. But coming to Los Angeles—all by himself—was a big step in their independence from hospitals and procedures and making their own bargains.

And how cool was Hollywood? Okay, the tourist stuff was tacky in a cheap T-shirt kind of way, but when Luke took him on a shoot—cool beyond cool. Dillon and Jack had recovered two months before Luke. All that rehab. Sometimes Luke would Skype with Dillon during his therapy. *Giving you material for your next movie,* Luke said.

Luke wanted company. Not that he or Dillon would admit it. With Destiny back at work, Luke found it easier to huff and puff and fall down and get up with someone else with him. Dillon knew what it was like to shuffle through sickness. Not cool, not one bit.

Destiny had made a bargain too. *Save Luke, and I'll give You a try,* she promised. He did, so she did, and Dillon went to church with them yesterday and rocked it out something wicked. That was Dez's term—a phrase she'd picked up from her Boston birth-father.

This family thing was good, but a little complicated.

Dillon had gone from being an only child to part of an extended family you needed frequent-flyer miles to keep up with. Two sisters. One brother-in-law, *blood brother* now because they shared a liver. A soon-to-be brother-in-law who had to be the coolest dude on the left side of the Mississippi. Three somewhat-brothers from Chloe's side, that she was working up her courage to meet. Three kind-of sisters from Destiny's side.

This was nothing any of them bargained for. Good thing everyone was cool with it.

A motorcycle would make his joy complete. *When you're eighteen,* Luke had said, *we'll ride up the coast.*

Over my dead body, Mom had said, then sputtered an apology when she realized she was talking to two guys who had come back from their own dead bodies. It was all pretty comical and pretty amazing when you thought about it.

It'd been a good couple of days. Making aliens with Destiny on Hollywood's next blockbuster was so amazing, Dillon was nearly breathless. Watching Luke do the motorcycle routine on his shoot made Dillon's knees weak. *What if he falls again?* Except that was the point of the stunt and Luke crashed, burned, and ate a hamburger and salad from the food truck like it was just another day at the office.

This afternoon was beach time. Dez and Luke had something planned because Dillon was supposed to bring his handheld camera and his laptop with satellite hookup. Now that he was healthy, his parents buying him expensive equipment would probably stop. In another year or so, he'd get a part-time job and buy his own editing software.

Or maybe a motorcycle.

So this trip to the beach—maybe Luke would give him a surfing lesson and maybe stream it to Dallas? That was probably it. Dez would love to see him flop for a good laugh. He'd show them and use it in his next film. *Samson in the Surf* had a nice ring to it.

Dillon set the laptop on a blanket about ten feet from the water. The surf was mild here, barely a curl. Probably Dad had scared Luke into taking it easy. Shouldn't he have a wet suit or something? It was October, after all. Seventy degrees, but Dillon was just starting to put on weight, so it was hard to keep warm.

Luke and Destiny stood ankle deep in the water. Arms around each other's waist, they stared silently over the Pacific.

"I'm set up," Dillon said.

Luke grinned, joined him on the sand. "Link us up to Dallas, Tennessee, and North Carolina. Use that link I e-mailed you this morning."

Dillon clicked, brought up icons for the three streams. "What's this about?" Dad asked once he was connected.

"No clue," Dillon said.

Chloe and Jack popped up. "Hey, bro," Jack said. Chloe looked completely relaxed, not the sister Dillon knew those first couple of weeks as Jack recovered from the transplant. She had done the unthinkable—backtracked in college to be what she called a *super-freshman* in Duke's engineering program. Only Dad could understand what Jack studied in grad school—they were tight and could chat for hours.

While Dillon was still in the hospital, Dad and Jack had a lot of hush-hush conversations. Mom said they hired a forensic computer investigator to track back to some dude who apparently stole something from Chloe. With Dad's help, Jack set an online trap and caught the thief red-handed as he tried to drain from a Deschene charity account. The arrest resulted in the seizure of the guy's equipment and files.

"*What did he take?*" Dillon had asked his mother.

"*Chloe will explain someday. Not today.*"

Usually Dillon hated answers like that. Something about Mom's face told him to let it go. If Chloe wanted to tell him someday, fine. Otherwise, things were cool just like they were.

Destiny's parents appeared on the third screen, with her sister Sophie. He had met Mrs. Connors once, when they had all visited Luke at Easter.

"Hey," Sophie said.

"Yeah," Dillon said, wishing his voice would get through the squeaking phase.

"Everybody up?" Luke said.

"Online," Dillon said.

Luke waved to someone down the beach. The pastor of their church? He was a cool enough guy but didn't seem like a surfer. He trotted toward them.

"Okay, Dil," Luke said. "You film us."

Dillon pressed all the right buttons and the camera went live on the stream. "Testing," he said, waiting for a wave from each location. "Go," he told Luke. "We're live."

He pointed the camera at Luke, the shot following him and the pastor into the water, and then thought, *What a dope I am. Should have seen this coming.*

The pastor pressed one hand to Luke's chest and one to his back, and even though Luke towered over him, the man easily laid him back into the water. Luke came up sputtering and smiling.

He turned to Destiny. She grinned as Luke guided her into the water and the pastor said those cool words about being baptized in the name of the Father, Son, and Holy Spirit.

She came up, dripping and whooping, arms above her head. Dillon heard applause and happy sounds from his laptop—the families who had stood witness.

The motorcycle can wait a few years.

This was really living.

Reading Group Guide

1. What stereotypes are generally assigned to a woman who gets pregnant out of wedlock—not once but *twice*? Seeing what kind of person Julia turned out to be in spite of her earlier choices, do you think that such stereotypes are accurate or fair?
2. What lessons can women learn from the account of Julia's young-adult years? What kinds of vulnerabilities can women experience when they are enamored with a man and the hope of having a future together?
3. What can we glean from how Julia grew into a mature, successful businesswoman with a strong marriage and family of her own? What does this reveal about God's nature?
4. Describe what character traits would be required in order to so valiantly face such a painful sexual past in hopes of saving your child's future? How do we develop such character traits?
5. Destiny was raised in a Christian home with conservative values, yet she felt rejected when her boyfriend Luke "discovered Jesus" and then chose not to have sex with her until marriage. Why do some people (women and men) assume sex should come along with a committed dating relationship? Is following God's plan for our sexuality a burden or a blessing (or both)?

6. When we first meet Chloe, she seems to be a submissive wife who lives to serve God, her husband, and her medical research. However, we learn that she's got one foot in the real world and another in a fantasy. How common do you think this is for women in particular? For men? What motivates a person to compartmentalize his or her sexual and emotional energies in such a way?
7. Chloe obviously paid a high price for her poor judgment with Rob Jones. Although this may be an extreme case, what other consequences may arise when we try to turn a fantasy into reality?
8. If you were her counselor, how would you suggest Chloe go about rebuilding her life and restoring Jack's trust? Do you think it's possible to rebuild spiritual and relational trust after such a fall? Why or why not?
9. How did you see God's sovereignty, mercy, and unconditional love unfold through the development of the characters?
10. Was there a particular character in the story that you identified with? If so, were you challenged or inspired by the character in some way?
11. What are the risks of letting ourselves be fully known to those who love us? What are the risks of knowing *them*? How could it impact a person's life and view of God to feel as if another human being knows them intimately, yet loves them completely?
12. What message do you hope other readers get from *To Know You*? What message was most valuable to you?
13. Does God holds our sexual sins against us more than other types of trespasses? (See Hebrews 4:15–16.)
14. When loved ones fall into inappropriate sexual or emotional

entanglements, how should we respond? How would it impact our relationships if we showed as much grace, mercy, and unconditional love to our friends and family members as God shows to us?

15. What might happen if we fully accepted God's gift of forgiveness and chose to be as patient, kind, and loving with ourselves as God is with us?

Acknowledgments

Shannon and Kathryn:

Special thanks to Lee Hough and Joel Kneedler of Alive Communications for introducing the two of us. It's been a match made in heaven! We also want to express our deep gratitude for the Thomas Nelson team of professionals who caught this vision, guided us ever so gently, and cheered us on fervently. Working with the editorial and marketing teams has been a privilege and a delight!

Shannon:

I'm incredibly thankful for my husband and all of my non-fiction readers who've asked for over a decade, "When will you ever write fiction?" You kept the storytelling dream alive in my heart long enough to see it come to fruition. Thanks to Robert McKee for teaching me just enough about fiction to know that I didn't know enough. And finally but most importantly, to Kathy Mackel, whose perseverance, patience, and passion for this story was relentless. Your masterful creativity is what turned my lump-of-coal idea into a brilliant diamond.

Kathryn:

I am so grateful to my writers' group for what feels like a lifetime of support and guidance, matched only by that of my husband's loving care. A warm hug is due to my church brethren in Dunstable who, when they see me holed up in some dusty corner of our old New England church, know enough to simply pray God is there with me and my laptop. And of course, thank you to Shannon Ethridge for a vibrant and necessary ministry to women—young and old—and the men who love them.

An Excerpt from *Veil of Secrets*

Pizza runs.

Melanie Connors knew all about pizza runs. That's why she had to fly to New Hampshire and find her daughter. She needed to make it clear to Sophie that there would be no more pizza runs.

She sat in stalled traffic on the Everett Turnpike, staring at a sea of brake lights. To her right, she could see the Merrimack River, laced with ice. The wind surged, rattling the windows of the rental car. Even with the heat blasting, frigid air snaked down Melanie's back.

November was New Hampshire's ugly secret. The brochures and agencies boasted about the state's sparkling lakes, flaming autumns, and serene snows. No one talked about trees ripped raw and skies tarnished to soot.

The flight from Nashville had been poorly heated and blankets nowhere to be found. The wait for the shuttle bus was endless. By the time Melanie took possession of the SUV in Boston, her icy fingers could barely wrestle the key into the ignition.

It never should have come to this. Why couldn't Will listen to reason?

She scrolled through her phone, clicked on Will's private number. Did New Hampshire have a law against talking on the cell while driving? That didn't matter, given that she'd moved ten feet in the last five minutes. The traffic was a monolith, staked to the highway like a dying beast, gasping in jerks and starts.

As chief of staff to Senator Dave Dawson, her husband carried two phones. His assistant carried at least two more. Will said his family was his priority, important enough to separate their calls from the staffers or the press.

Will answered on the first ring. "Hey, sweetheart. Can I call you back in a whi—"

"No."

"No? Are you all right?"

"I'm fine. Will..." *I'm here*, she should say. *I'm here and I can't wait to see you.* But she couldn't get Sophie out of her mind. "You told me she'd only be in New Hampshire for two weeks."

He sighed. "Babe. Not this again."

The traffic bucked forward. "A couple weeks, Will. You said she'd only be in New Hampshire for two weeks."

"What I said was 'a short time.' You put the two weeks tag on it. Honestly, Lanie. You're a bit irrational about this."

"What's so irrational about wanting my daughter home?"

"You've seen her blog, the articles. And now she's working with video. Her portfolio is going to wow any admissions officer. Sophie will have colleges begging. And the father-daughter time we get—priceless." His voice softened. "I wish you were here with us. That's my only regret of having Sophie here. That you're not with us."

Melanie tugged at her scarf, trying to release the sudden heat under her skin. Talk about irrational. Flying all the way from Nashville to wrest her daughter away from a loving father—who is deep in the weeds of a presidential campaign. "Is she going with you to the *Sixty Minutes* thing?"

"No, she's at the phone center."

"Doing what?"

"She's working on a training video. And then she'll sit with the kids and make some calls on Dave's behalf."

"Is that wise? Talking to strangers?"

"Like you did? How old were you when you started for your father—fourteen?"

"Sophie's not like me."

"She's doing exactly what you did at her age, and what I did. Think about it—our little girl is campaigning for the best presidential candidate this country has seen in years."

"Don't play the *patriotic* card on me. I cherish Dave as deeply as you do, Will. But that doesn't excuse you from not supervising Sophie. Is it wise to allow our daughter to go off on her own?"

Melanie rifled her fingernails on the steering wheel. When was this traffic going to move? She was so close to the exit for downtown Manchester—twenty cars at the most—and yet the distance might as well put her back in Tennessee.

"For Pete's sake, she is not on her own. And she's not a baby," Will said. "Let me tell you, Lanie, she is definitely making an adult-sized contribution to this campaign. She manages the literature better than the people we're paying to do it. If something in the office or on the bus needs doing, she anticipates it and gets it done. Whatever your problem is with this, we'll have to talk about later."

"Pizza runs."

He laughed. "What?"

"Sophie told me that she does pizza runs."

"Bless her, on occasion she does pizza runs for us."

"I don't like you letting her drive in a place she's not familiar with."

"She knows all the roads, Lanie. She's got an innate sense of direction."

"She's barely sixteen years old. She doesn't have an innate sense of anything. Except adolescent foolishness."

Melanie shivered at the thought of Sophie caught in this cold mass of steel and insane drivers. Her car running low on gas, a truck coming up behind her on the breakdown lane. She wouldn't see the truck because she was too inexperienced to check the side view mirror and she gets out of the car and—

"Lanie, please. She's a safe and very mature driver. You know that. And now I really need to go."

He clicked off before she could tell him she was less than a mile away. And that she was going to sweep Sophie up, get her out of this foolishness and on the red-eye back to Nashville.

—she doesn't see the truck and she gets out of the car—

"I will not get crazy," she said to the rearview mirror. "I've exhausted all my crazy for the day."

Inching now. Close enough to see the roof of the Radisson in the city center. Close enough to wrap her arms around Will and feel his heart beat and remind him about how tricky pizza runs can be.

You make four or five campaign stops in one day. You don't dare drink the wine someone thrusts in your hand because you're exhausted and might say something dangerous if you let down for a second. You can't eat because everyone wants to talk to you because they can't get to the candidate. You need to make them think you've promised them the world when you'd made no commitment whatsoever.

Even though your hunger makes you cranky and light-headed, you don't dare hide in a corner and shovel something down fast. Everyone has seen the YouTube video of the governor who choked on a Buffalo wing and coughed it out with a chaser of vomit. You can save the economy and soothe the soul of a nation, but throwing up on camera can dump a candidate faster than a boatload of mistresses.

So you get back to the hotel around midnight, ready to chew

the wallpaper. If you're on a grassroots candidacy, guys like Will are working the phones until the West Coast donors are in bed. So some lower-level functionary grabs whoever is least essential and sends you to get the pizza because up here they only deliver on weekends, and *don't forget the gum and breath mints and No-Doz.*

The run itself is a shared experience; exhausted laughter as you and a stray pal unravel the day and poke gentle fun at the chanting crowds or narrow-eyed reporters. You arrive back as a conquering hero, the bearer of half-cold pizza. The feast becomes a grand communal experience, cheese and crust the great equalizer of presidential hopeful and staffers and you, the kid who literally brought home the bacon. There's no big world pressing down, no victories to be won, only the four walls of a hotel room that smells like pizza and beer and the popcorn that someone made in the microwave.

And sometimes, when you're the one left cleaning up the mess, someone senior will stay and help. That intimate time of quick glances and spilled secrets fill the late-night vacuum of campaigns until the sun rises and caffeine bubbles and you're climbing in the hamster wheel all over again.

"Stop it," Melanie told herself. She scrolled her phone, found Will's itinerary. They should be launching into the CBS interview right now. The spin–Dave Dawson, *shoe-leather candidate.* Going house-to-house because the campaign didn't have Karl Rove or Dick Armey funding them.

Dave and Will were due in Concord in less than an hour for the next event. Before Melanie even got to the downtown exit, they would be heading north. They'd know to use the surface roads because that's what grassroots was all about—shaking hands, driving the dirt roads, making people believe things could be better.

When Melanie worked for her father, she knew every back road in New Hampshire, Iowa, and South Carolina. And she knew every 24-hour pizza joint.

Traffic had stopped again.

Melanie opened the passenger-side window and gave the driver next to her a pleading look. He shook his head and crept forward into the gap she coveted. Behind him, the UPS truck waved her into the lane. She nosed into the break-down lane, chiding herself because the ticket she was about to earn would cost a fortune and the rental car company would not be amused by their SUV getting towed.

Some things just had to take priority.

And primary on Melanie's list had always been her daughters. She loved Destiny with her whole heart. But her eldest daughter's wildness had taught Melanie to keep Sophie close.

She pulled onto the dirt shoulder and as close to the guard rail as she could. She grabbed the keys and her purse, retrieved her suitcase from the backseat, and started walking.

The story continues in *Veil of Secrets*
by Shannon Ethridge and Kathryn
Mackel, available July 2014

About the Authors

Photo by Rebecca Friedlander

Shannon Ethridge is a best-selling author, international speaker, and certified life coach with a master's degree in counseling/human relations from Liberty University. She has spoken to college students and adults since 1989 and is the author of twenty books, including the million-copy best-selling Every Woman's Battle series. She is a frequent guest on TV and radio programs, and she mentors aspiring writers and speakers through her online B.L.A.S.T Program (Building Leaders, Authors, Speakers & Teachers).

Photo by Angela Hunt

Kathy Mackel is the acclaimed author of *Can of Worms* and other novels for middle readers from Putnam, HarperCollins, and Dial. Her latest book, *Boost*, tackles the thorny issue of steroids and girls' sports. Writing as Kathryn Mackel, she is the author of the YA fantasy series *The Birthright Books* and of supernatural thrillers including the Christy finalist *The Hidden*. She was the credited screenwriter for Disney's *Can of Worms* and for *Hangman's Curse*, and has worked for Disney, Fox, and Showtime.